"the SM fiction of choice among

MW00769996

"The Marketplace series was like water to a thirsty woman. I drank them. I inhaled them. I think they will become, if they aren't already, basic texts — the ABC's of BDSM for fiction — much like Capote's In Cold Blood is the classic for that genre of crime novel."
-Claire Thompson (author, Sara's Surrender)

"If you haven't read the…Marketplace series, you have been missing out on some of the best S/M erotica around." "(Antoniou) gives her characters an incredible depth and provides them with unique individual voices. I believe in them. In fact, I expect to run into them on the street."
-Girlfriends Magazine

"some of the best S/M erotica around."
- Blowfish

"Queens-bornAntoniou is heiress presumptive to some of the erotic territory staked out by Pat Califia and John Preston…Antoniou's writing moves with assurance between genders and sexual orientations, relentlessly exploring the dark side of sexuality."
-Michael Rowe (Writing Below the Belt)

"If you like smut with a plot, engaging characters and snappy dialogue, this (series) is for you."
- The Servant's Quarters

"Reads like cool silk on whip reddened flanks. Gay, bi, or straight, master, novice, slave, switch, Daddy, boy, fetishist, hedonist, and submissive will all respond to these erotic pages. Compelling, and charged with electricity, pleasurable as leather rain."
-Kitty Tsui (author, Breathless)

"quite simply, the best SM novels in decades."
- Cuir Underground

"Laura Antoniou… elevates the genre of SM erotica…The tales ring true, the dialogue achingly real, and the sex is as hot as you'd ever hope for."
-Kate Bornstein (author, My Gender Workbook)

"engaging storylines, developed characters, and startlingly realistic descriptions of BDSM relationships." "some of the finest BDSM erotica today."
-Miss Abernathy (author, Miss Abernathy's Concise Slave Training Manual)

"Antoniou is an elegant stylist of erotica whose various pseudonyms are worth seeking out."
-Pat Califia

"excellent read!...a wonderfully diverse world of lesbian, gay, straight, bi and transgendered characters, all mixing in the melting pot of sadomasochism."
-Lambda Book Report

"This is domination and submission at its best — a very well-written work that holds from page to page..."
-Shiny International

Reviews of **The Academy, Tales of The Marketplace**

"Sophisticated plotting, dynamic character interaction, steamy sex, elegant and witty dialog, exquisite local color, titillating revelation scenes, and a mind-blowing conclusion...what more could a reader ask?"
- Sheela Ardrian, Sandmutopian Guardian

"soars both as a work of fiction and as a work of erotica...likewise a genre-bending accomplishment because of its breakdown of traditional literary form...a rich and varied erotic tapestry as well as a profound meditation on what it means to be a good slave—or a good master. Overall, The Academy, Tales From the Marketplace is a stunning accomplishment."
-Melusine, Consent Magazine

"Laura Antoniou's Marketplace series is one of a kind. The books depict a rich alternative reality with an honor-bound system of slave market hierarchies, but this is no fantasyland of perfect masters and unquestioning servants. Antoniou creates fully realized characters who struggle with loyalty, duty and service.In this volume, Antoniou, with a little help from her friends, creates a sort of Arabian Nights of the Marketplace, with individual stories woven into a larger tale full of political intrigue, difficult choices,and of course, searingly hot sex. There's nothing else like this is in the world of erotic writing."
-Lori Selke

The Slave

by Laura Antoniou

The Slave

by Laura Antoniou

Fairfield, Connecticut

Published by

Mystic Rose Books
P.O. Box 1036/SMS
Fairfield, CT 06432

ISBN 0-9645960-4-0

Second Edition, fourth printing 2004

ATTENTION COLLEGES AND UNIVERSITIES, BDSM/
FETISH ORGANIZATIONS AND SUPPORT GROUPS:
Quantity discounts are available on bulk purchases of this book
for educational purposes, fund raising or gift giving. For information contact: Mystic Rose Books, P.O. Box 1036/SMS, Fairfield, CT 06432

(203) 374-5057
FAX (203) 371-4843
WWW.Mysticrose.com

Dedication

For Mitch and Gerrie

Chapter One
New York City, Autumn

The traffic in the streets below the hotel echoed upward, pushing through the window which was cracked open for fresh air. The city was restless; the pulse of the weekend had reached its frenzy. The customized horn of a wedding limousine blared out the identity of the newlyweds that the dark haired woman had passed in the lobby. The sound made her want to jump, but she held herself still with practiced tension.

The man sitting in the high backed chair paid no attention to the tacky sound of the horn, or to her for that matter. His eyes were busy scanning the papers in front of him, turning them over in patient, careful movements which didn't betray the slightest interest in their contents.

The urge to speak, to cough, to shift her body into a more relaxed position, to pour a glass of water from the sweating pitcher on the room service tray, all hit Robin at once. She had been standing still since she handed the file to him; he didn't seem to notice. She pushed all the thoughts aside with an almost angry strength. I will be patient, she chanted inwardly. I am patience.

"Why don't you make yourself comfortable?" His voice was a rough tenor, a singer after a grueling concert, a student at 4AM. It was also loud; it broke the silence and Robin's efforts to be calm.

"Please," Robin said. Her own voice shook, almost imperceptibly. When the man looked up, she swallowed hard and continued, "I'm unsure of the proper courtesy to show you, sir."

He nodded. "Very nice. Why don't you sit down on the couch for now? It's already been a long night."

Robin nodded and sat down, smoothing her skirt neatly down her lap. Sitting made it easier to relax into a more proper attitude. She took a long, softly casual look at her inquisitor.

He was older than she, but had the kind of face that refused to betray its years. His short black hair was very thick, and showed a slight tendency to curl, but was trimmed back so severely that Robin knew he would get it cut again soon. A sparse mustache and the vaguest of five o'clock shadows gave him a scholarly look, or, as she remembered in the dim light of the bar last night, the look of a terrorist. He wore tinted glasses in heavy steel frames. Today, he was dressed in a crisply clean long sleeved shirt and a muted tie. His jacket was draped across the arm of the other chair in the sitting room.

There was no sign of the leather jacket he had been wearing last night.

He finished with the papers and stowed them neatly back into their folder. Then he sat in silence, until Robin began to imagine that she could hear the swishing sound of the second hand on her watch. The silence was as oppressive as any heavy hand she had ever felt. She wanted to bend to it. For a brief moment, to her horror, a flush of shame and thrill passed over her, as clear to her interviewer as the strident horns of the taxis below.

The corner of his mouth rose in a twitch of a smile.

"You're very good," he said, leaning over to retrieve his jacket. "Tell me what your instinct was telling you to do."

Robin's mouth went dry. She licked her lips and coughed a little to clear her throat. "I wanted to kneel," she whispered.

"I know that. But there's more." He pulled a cigarette box from one pocket and snapped it open.

"I wanted to make obeisance at your feet." Robin's voice was still at a whisper. Her blush fairly glowed.

"Show me how you were trained to do that," the man said, leaning back into his chair.

Robin rose, quickly but without any jerky movements. In two steps, she was in front of him, but still outside of arms reach. With grace, she knelt, lowering her body to the carpet, and then continued the movement seamlessly until her forehead brushed the fibers. She could smell the chemical scent of the cleaners. It struggled with the richer scent of the well worn polished leather boots now within her reach. She held perfectly still.

"You may," came the voice from above. The man sounded faint, his tones overrun by the pounding in Robin's ears. She raised her head a few inches and placed one careful, soft kiss on each boot, firm enough to let him feel her presence, light enough not to leave the faintest smudge of her lips. Then, she retreated back and lowered her head again.

"Very nice," the man repeated. "Please seat yourself again."

She rose up to her knees and looked at him, her eyes meeting his. "Thank you."

"Oh, you're quite welcome." As she sat down again, he lit a cigarette. "Do you smoke?"

"No, sir."

"That's good. You would have to quit, you know."

Robin leaned forward, her heart pounding. "Does that mean that you're accepting me?"

"Yes. Your records are acceptable, your spotter is well known to me, and your behavior is impeccable. I just wanted you to realize that when you enter the Marketplace, you are not permitted to retain any addictions." He smiled suddenly. "Except of course, for the obvious one."

She smiled back despite the echoes of panic which resounded in her. "The addiction to submission?"

"To being owned, yes. That's a prerequisite. We weren't formally introduced last night. I am Chris Parker."

"Thank you," Robin said politely. "I'm sure you know all about me now."

"What, this?" He waved his hand over the folder. "No, that doesn't tell me much about you. It tells me how you've experienced some minor forms of service, which is helpful, but it couldn't possibly tell me anything about how genuine your devotion is, or how serious you are about a potential commitment, or how profound your need for this kind of life is. Those things I can only learn from you. I will need to test you some more, and to train you in the specific areas of behavior and service that I require any client of mine to possess before I present them for sale."

Client! Robin swallowed hard. When they called me a slave, I wasn't, and now that I am, they don't call me one. She resisted the urge to giggle, but her shoulders relaxed just a little bit more.

"I would love to have the opportunity to show you my dedication." Robin's eyes danced. "These are things I've been thinking about for years. No, not only thinking about, but dreaming about. Trying to do, in some way or another. This is something I've wanted all my life."

"All your life? That's impressive. Tell me." Chris flicked ashes into the glass ashtray beside him.

"Everything? From the beginning?"

"That's the traditional place to start a story."

Robin frowned for a moment, considering. Where do I begin, she wondered. What is the real beginning here? When I was little? Those games we used to play? Or when I first realized what power the fantasies had? Or with Maria? Or Troy?

"I'm sorry," she said softly, suddenly aware of time moving around her. Parker hadn't moved an inch, except to bring the cigarette up and down again.

"I'm so excited…so, relieved, I guess. But scared, too. This is turning out to be harder then I thought."

"I won't tell you to relax," Chris said with a slight smile. "But you shouldn't be trying to impress me with your story. I'm much more interested in the things you remember as important."

"But I remember everything," Robin laughed. "And I'm not sure what's important. I mean…it all was. And…and…nothing was." She took a deep breath, trying to remain calm. "I'm sorry. Now that I have a real chance, suddenly I'm nervous."

"Naturally. It's all right to be nervous." Chris ground the stub of his cigarette into the glass, twisting it down until the last sliver of smoke vanished. "Tell me about your first sexual experience as an adult, if that makes it simpler."

Robin nodded gratefully. "That's easy. But you'll laugh." When Chris remained silent, she blushed again and lowered her head. Everything depends on this interview, she reminded herself. He's accepted me for now, but I can still mess things up. I have to be perfect.

"I was at college," she began.

"Greg? Do you have the…things?"

"Sure, baby, right in my pocket." Greg Carneson, basketball player, drummer and communications major, patted his hip pocket with a knowing chuckle. "I wasn't going to forget. I mean, how could I? With you writin' it down and everything. That was a nice letter, babe. No one ever wrote me nothin' like that before." He grinned and shifted his knapsack onto one shoulder. "I wish we had a nicer place to go, though."

Robin laughed nervously. People passing them saw raised their heads to follow the sound and saw a really cute couple. Greg was tall, with raggedly cut blonde hair and a tight t-shirt that displayed his team number. Robin always looked like she stepped out of a soap commercial, her face bright and slightly pointy, her burnt mahogany hair swinging free around her shoulders in soft curls. Neither one would ever be picked out as a beauty, but they were young and healthy and seemingly happy and that made up for all their minor imperfections. They complimented each other, tall and slight, massive and elfin, fair and dark. Even their eyes, Greg's an uncomplicated bright blue and Robin's a deep amber-brown, were as different as possible.

"We'll just have to make do," Robin replied, eyeing her boyfriend's pocket.

Oh no, was her real thought. I don't believe it. He just brought condoms, the idiot! What the hell did he think I was writing about?

4

As she followed him to the parking lot, she tried to remember everything she had written about in that oh-so-hard-to-write letter. *I was as clear as I could get,* she thought desperately. *What do I have to do, scream it out? Serves me right for going out with a jock.* She bit her lip, trying to figure out what to do. *Damn it! I shouldn't have to do all this! Doesn't he get it?*

They had been dating for about two months. They had met in the gym, where they had been eyeing the same karate class. In the end, he didn't have time to take it, but Robin was enrolled. And since she was in the gym so much anyway, she came to watch him shoot baskets and drill with the coach. Soon, they were going for lunch together, and then wham, they were dating.

And of course, everyone knows what eventually happens when you date someone. What Greg was absolutely oblivious to was the fact that Robin had never gotten to that "eventuality" before. Nor, apparently, after all of her careful hints and coaching, had he gotten around to understanding her more specific desires.

A terrible, nervous weight settled in her stomach. *Oh God, why am I doing this?* was the thought that rustled through her consciousness as she followed Greg silently to the car, smiled blankly when he sang along with a love song on the radio, and then nodded when he pulled into a parking space near the off campus frat house where his friend was going to let him borrow his bedroom.

In the end, all that Greg had brought was the condom in his pocket. No scarves, not to bind her or to blindfold her, or *anything*. And if he'd seen any of the movies she had suggested he rent and watch or bring with him, his style certainly didn't show it.

Because the minute he closed the door behind him, he was all over her. His big hands encircled her body in a rush, and he kissed her hard and long, the way they kissed after at least twenty minutes of warm-up stroking, nibbling and licking. As he slid his fingers up inside her sweater, his sole concession to romance was whispering "Oh, babe, I've wanted this forever." Followed immediately by, "But we gotta get outa here by eight."

Robin tried to think of what she was doing as submitting to his desires. She allowed him to lead her to the bed, passively standing and turning for him as he pulled her clothing open, up, down, off. She closed her eyes to his kisses, to his glee as he fingered and then gently kneaded her breasts, but it just didn't work. Her disappointment over his lack of attention to her careful hints was so overwhelming, and his eagerness was so clean-cut and so achingly stereotypical!

His own body was as handsome as his face, a strong chest and beautiful long legs. And her first sight of an erect male organ wasn't disappointing; it was about the size she had expected, and Greg was fresh from showering after practice. She reached out to touch it, and he fairly purred.

Her imagination switched on, and she heard his purr change to a growl. "Do you like it, baby? Tell me you like it, slut. Tell me how much you want to kiss it. Get down there and make me believe that you love this cock. 'Cause I'm gonna slam it right down your throat, baby, and you're gonna take it. You're gonna take this cock anyway I give it to you, aren't you?"

Instead, in cold reality, he quickly guided her backwards to the bed and practically fell on top of her. He shifted to find a good position, trying not to lean an elbow on her, kissing her when he could, trying to keep at least one hand on her tits. And then, he remembered the rubber in his pocket and had to go back to get it, leaving her laying on her back, staring up at the ceiling. She looked over to one side of the room, where the frat boy had pinned up about a dozen overlapping beer posters, all featuring big chested girls in skimpy bikinis, running around at the beach, their hands full of dark, sweaty bottles. She looked back down at her own body, with her small breasts and her short legs, and felt a sudden wave of inadequacy.

By the time Greg got back, fumbled around in his idea of foreplay for a little while longer and then heaved himself up to put the condom on, she found herself wishing that the experience would be as painful as some of her romance novels suggested it was; naturally, it felt a little like a lightning fast cramp.

She then tried to imagine that he was someone else. Her very distant and cold Italian teacher, for example. Or maybe, if she squeezed her eyes really tight, she could believe that he was a pirate, a dashing serial villain, holding her maiden's body in his rough, churlish hands, breathing the scent of rum into her face, growling curses and taunts.

Yes, that was it! Or, maybe, when Greg was done, he would leap off of her, pull a pair of handcuffs out of his knapsack, and snap them on her while she lay back in an exhausted swoon. Then, with a leer, he would tell her that the price for the room was her body…and that all the boys in the house would be by to sample her charms. And they would come, first to ogle, and then to paw at her, and then to finally thrust their way into her body, again and again…yes…yes…

But before she could work that fantasy into a proper orgasm, he was done, his body heavy and sweaty over hers, his breath as stale as any pirate's, a wet, limp bag of latex dripping across her thigh and onto the musty sheets.

And to make matters so much worse, he nuzzled her throat gently, whispered, "Oh, baby, baby, that was great! Was it good for you too?"

"And it took every ounce of strength I had not to laugh in his face," Robin remembered, her own face finally showing her amusement. "I went to bed that night thinking that if I couldn't get this all American jock to tie me up and spank me, then I wasn't going to get anywhere. It was such a let down!"

"It was better than what many people have," Chris commented. "You did choose him, and he did not harm you."

Robin blushed, but nodded. "I know. But I still feel like I really messed that up. I should have waited...I should have been clearer about what I needed. I mean, I wrote these little coy phrases in this love letter, about wanting to be swept away, and be made powerless...but I never really said, 'Hey, Greg, I want you to tie me up and pretend you're a pirate, OK?'" When Chris didn't respond right away, she leaned forward a little and continued. "If I had waited, I might have been able to give it to someone...maybe to Maria, or Troy. It should have been special. And I threw it away."

"Having mediocre sex is hardly something to mourn several years later," Chris said.

"It's just that now, with this chance to really live it, I feel like I made this incredible mistake. Wouldn't I be more...valuable if I were still a virgin?"

"Certainly not. An oddity, perhaps, but not especially valued. Experience is what counts, Robin, and you should know that. You're allowing your fear and anxiety to distract you. You're over-compensating. You don't have to do that with me."

"I'm sorry, sir." She looked genuinely ashamed. "I'm really very nervous. I talk a lot when I get nervous."

"I can see that. And you'll speak a lot more before we're through. Just keep in mind that I'm not interested in hearing excuses or explanations. By the end of our time together, I want to know all about your past experiences and dreams and how you felt about them."

"All of them? My entire history?"

Chris Parker nodded. "As much as is relevant. I'll let you know when you're telling me something I don't need to know."

Robin glanced up and looked out the window. The late evening darkness was cool, enveloping. I could still walk out now, she thought, catching the shadow of her reflection in the glass. I could just tell him that I must have been mistaken, insane, I have a job to do. I have to go to Italy in two months. I can leave this and just go on like I was. I was happy. I am happy. I can find someone new.

But if I leave, I'll never know. Never know if I was really ready for this. If I could have been...

Robin turned back to Chris and lowered her head. "I've always been strong," she said, her tone a sharp contrast to her words. "I did what I wanted to, and

7

never let someone run my life. And I can't remember a time when I didn't want to be a slave."

"Good," Chris said smoothly. He rose, and with a speed she could have never suspected, pulled her up off the couch by the front of her jacket. She gasped at his strength, and rose to her toes, her eyes just barely above his. His fist was tight against her throat, his body terrifyingly close.

"Maybe I can make you into one, girl," he said softly. "What do you have to say to that?"

Robin gasped in another breath. Oh God! Oh, I want this! What do I say? What does he want me to say?

"That was a question!" he barked. "When I ask you a question, I expect an immediate, honest reply!"

"Yes! I mean, thank you, sir, yes, I want you to make me a slave!" Robin gasped again, her heart pounding, and her throat pressing against Chris' knuckles.

He let her go, and she fell back onto her heels, but kept herself erect. She tried to control the urge to pant; her breath returned in short gasps.

"Strip."

Robin took her jacket off immediately and cursed her trembling fingers. She laid it on the couch and tried to be graceful as she unbuttoned the silk blouse. She was glad she had decided to wear the garter belt and stockings rig instead of pantyhose, but Chris wasn't even watching as she took her skirt off. He had gone into the adjoining bedroom without a word.

Robin looked down. He hadn't said strip to your lingerie. So she unclipped the expensive stockings and rolled them off, and then wiggled out of everything else. Almost as an afterthought, she unclipped the gold necklace and dropped it and her watch and earrings on top of her clothing.

Now she was as naked as the day she had entered this world. She drew herself up into a standing posture that seemed appropriate, with her hands behind her back, and then fretted about whether she should kneel. He didn't tell me to, she reminded herself.

He kept her waiting for what seemed to be a long time. She jumped a little when she heard his voice in the bedroom, but it was clear that he wasn't talking to her. She could hear pauses, and the sound of his light laughter. He had to be on the phone.

I wonder who he called. Maybe he's calling someone else to come and…look at me. Or maybe to try me out. Oh, get a grip, Robin, you should be over those fantasies! It's just a phone call. He'll be back in a minute. A slight chill built in her upper arms and spread across her shoulders, raising goosebumps. As the first shiver ran through her, a tightness settled around her nipples and drew them achingly up.

8

This is only a test, she thought, trying to calm herself. I am being good. I am being patient.

I am patience.

When Chris Parker returned, he paused to examine her. He had taken his tie off, and unfastened the top button of his shirt, but that was the only change. His eyes registered neither interest nor appreciation.

Well, of course not, Robin thought. Think of where you met him, girl. This is one man who is just not interested in the temptations of the female form. And besides, if what they say is true, he's seen hundreds of slaves. Amazingly beautiful ones, men and women. So there's not much to be impressed by here.

He walked around her slowly, not touching her. When his finger finally did land on her shoulder, she jerked a little more upright, and a faint shuddering ran down her arm. He didn't comment, but slowly ran that finger along her collarbone and down her spine.

She couldn't help it. She freed a slight moan, an exhalation of pleasure and tension.

"You're very sensitive," Chris said, drawing his hand away. "Turn to face me."

She did, and met his eyes. She instantly dropped her eyes down, but kept her shoulders back.

"That was careless. You should have kept your gaze up, or turned with your eyes already cast down." Casually, he pinched one nipple. The sudden sharpness stabbed into her and she gasped again, feeling a flush rise along the back of her neck, and a familiar thrumming between her legs.

"Do you have to return home tonight?"

The sudden return to real issues startled her, but she recovered quickly. "No, sir."

"Then you will stay here. Go and lock the door; put the do not disturb sign out."

He sat down again, and watched as Robin approached the door, hesitated, and then maneuvered her way around it so anyone standing in the hallway could have only gotten a glimpse of her bare arm and shoulder. She slipped the chain lock into place, fighting back the familiar fear that came every time she played with someone new. Of course, this time it was far stronger than it ever had been before.

Hundreds of questions resounded within her in an instant. Would Chris Parker demand new or unfamiliar service from her? Would he be as brutal as his appearance last night had suggested? Was he really worthy of the trust she was about to give him? Would he want to have sex?

Can I get out of it if it gets to be too much for me to handle?

"Now come back here," Chris pointed to a spot on the floor in front of him, "on your hands and knees. With grace."

"Yes, sir," she whispered, dropping to her knees. Concentrating on moving her limbs cleanly and guiding herself around the corner of the chair without awkwardness took over from the morass of concerns which had temporarily flooded her, and she relaxed in the performance of that simple task. She halted in front of him, and let his hands guide her to the precise position he desired.

His hands swept over her body in an examination. While she held herself still, her hands and knees pressed firmly in place against the carpet, he touched every part of her which could be reached. His hands circled her throat and then stroked it, trailed across her shoulders and down her arms, probing at the muscles in her upper arms, tapping the inside of her elbows. His fingers tickled her ribcage on the way to gently cupping her breasts, pressing them up against her body lightly, then letting them fall.

Robin moaned, and dipped her head low.

Ignoring her, Chris placed one firm palm on her lower back while the other hand stroked and probed her midsection and her belly. A tap from that hand and she pushed her knees further apart, and then still further, so that one hand could comfortably reach between her thighs to explore the tenderness of her pussy. She had shaved only that morning; it was a habit left from her time with Troy. But Chris gave no indication as to whether he approved or disapproved. He did cup her entire sexual delta in one hand and compress his fingers around it until she moaned again. And when one finger slipped along the edges of her lips, she gasped, and lifted her ass just a little bit more, her face flooding in shame.

"Ah, hungry little cunt…" Chris whispered. But he left off teasing her in that fashion and continued his examination, cupping her round buttocks, squeezing her thighs and running his fingers across the bottoms of her feet.

She felt his hands suddenly leave her, and the creaking of the chair as he leaned back into it. Her entire body felt primed for attention. Every inch ached for another touch; her skin felt like it was alive with electricity. And this just from being so lightly handled! She drew in one long breath and said, "Thank you, sir!"

"I was wondering where your manners had gone," Chris replied. "There are much harsher ways in which I could have conducted that examination."

Robin cringed. "Yes, sir. I'm sorry, sir."

"Just for comparison's sake, then. Up, girl!" He snapped his fingers, and Robin drew her body up, coming off of her arms. But before she could complete her turn to face him, he grasped a hand full of her hair and dragged her toward him, throwing her off balance, sending her crashing into his knee.

"Keep yourself up, you clumsy idiot," Chris snapped, pushing and pulling her into place. She winced and he jerked hard on the fistful of hair he still held. With his free hand, he cuffed her lightly across the mouth, and she gasped in the shock of impact. No one had ever done that to her before.

"And don't let me see such exaggerated reactions, either. I know what you can take, girl." He cupped her chin and forced her mouth open. "That's it, show me what your teeth look like!"

Humiliated to her core, Robin tried to allow her body to follow his manipulations, but it was hard, because he moved quickly this time, never allowing her to fully relax. He twisted her head one way and then the other, and then dropped the hand from her face and slapped her heavily across her left breast. Before she even had enough time to gasp, he slapped her right breast and grasped the nipple between his fingers, pressing tightly.

Robin bit her lip to keep from moaning, and the heat from the slaps seemed to rise through her chest and into her face. Her breaths came in short gasps, punctuated each time he compressed that captive nipple, and when she whimpered at the pain, he switched and took up the other one and did the same thing. His hand went back and forth between her nipples, twisting and pinching them, while he still maintained a tight grip on her hair, bending her backward.

"Do you like this?" he asked suddenly, pulling her head forward so she could look at him. ""I asked you a question, girl!"

"Yes! Yes, sir, I do!" Robin managed to get the words out all in a rush.

"Then you should be thanking me." He jerked her head back again and slapped her breasts, harder this time, and as he savagely twisted one nipple and pulled it up and away from her body, she wailed and threw her hands behind her body to keep them still. Dimly, through the haze of intoxicating pleasure and pain, she heard her own voice offering thanks, again and again, until Chris pulled her back forward and touched her lips with his fingers. She panted, her chest rising and falling heavily, her nipples burning and itching with pain.

"You'd do better if you simply remembered to offer your gratitude on a consistent basis, rather then waiting for commands or invitations," he said calmly. He released her hair, and she wavered a little, catching her balance, but managed to press her lips against his hand, lightly.

"Thank you, sir," she breathed. "For the lesson."

"It's not over yet." He pushed her back, and when she fell onto her arms, he nodded. "That's it. Now raise your hips. Present that hungry cunt to me, girl, lift it high. And don't you dare fall until I give permission."

Robin followed his instructions, so that she was still resting on her calves, her back curved like a bow. Her legs were still wide apart, and this position opened her pussy lips before Chris, giving him a perfect view of the wetness his treatment had drawn from her.

He leaned down and opened her, carefully, keeping his eyes on hers. When she looked away, unable to bear his gaze, he thrust two fingers inside of her, slipping through her folds like a hand sliding through thick layers of glossy silk. Robin opened for him easily, she was hot and soaked with her own excitement, and her entire body shook with hunger and ecstasy.

In the same quick motion, he withdrew the fingers and snapped a lightning fast slap against her swollen cunt lips, and then penetrated her again. He repeated the motions again and again, pushing into her and then slipping out to deliver another stinging blow.

Robin thought she would go insane with the pleasure and the agony! She lifted her hips in surrender and fell slightly back with each blow. Her nipples, still aching from their torment, felt as though they were still being crushed, so tight was their arousal. And with each invasion, her clit seemed to nearly explode with the pressure, only to feel the sharp sting of his fingers a moment later. Her hip movements began to get more exaggerated, rising to engulf his fingers, jerking back in reaction to their impact.

Her arms shuddered with the pain of the position, and she knew that she couldn't take much more of this without falling, but she bit her lip again and straightened them out, fighting for the strength to keep going. And when finally, she was trying to prepare the words that would let her tormentor know that she had reached her limit, he stopped, and slapped one thigh.

"Over! Hands and knees again!"

She turned, trembling. As her thighs met, she felt the amazing warmth and the flood of her own juices which had covered her sex and her upper thighs. When she knelt again, and Chris pulled her legs apart, she whimpered.

"Oh, I'm not finished with you yet," Chris said, reaching under her body. He seized her achingly sore and needy cunt in his right hand and let the left one rest against the curve of her ass. Without warning, he began to spank her, but not in the manner of her past lovers, who used this particular form of chastisement entirely for pleasure. No, Chris' hand was heavy and punishing, and each time it fell, his fingers under her body accepted her thrust forward and hurt her in some way. At first, he would strike, and then pinch her lips, tugging her backward again. Then, he began to flick his fingers harshly across her engorged clit. He would go back to pinching after a while, and then spread her lips wide and press one finger up against the hood, until she wriggled with explosive agony.

And meanwhile, his hand on her ass cheeks gave rise to first a flush of heat, and then an insistent stinging pain, and then the awful, jarring pain that brought up red marks and left a lasting warmth.

Robin fell forward, onto her elbows, whimpering, inarticulate sounds of endurance and reaction mixing with every stimulus. And when the rhythm of the actions built up to a peak from which she could not escape, her hips thrust back and forth, her fingers gripped the carpet, and she gulped in breaths which couldn't sustain her until the next shock. The wave was coming, it was building up like pressure in a sealed bottle, and each new strike, each new twist, each torment drew her closer and closer!

And then Chris stopped.

"Wait there," he said as he drew his hands from her body.

Robin gasped, and it took all her strength to keep from collapsing face forward onto the floor. As Chris rose from the chair and walked behind her, the slight breeze caused by his passing swept between her legs, chilling the skin that was so covered with moisture. She moved slightly, and scraped her nipples against the carpet, and bit back a moan. Carefully, she pushed herself back up onto her arms, and stayed there, her head low, and waited.

I don't believe he stopped, she thought, feeling tears in the corners of her eyes. I don't believe it! I am so ready...I could have come in an instant! I haven't been this ready this fast in ages. Oh God, he is good. She tried to ignore the throbbing between her legs, and around her nipples, and the glow of the beating on her ass. I will be good, she reminded herself. And when he is finished with me, I will get what I've wanted all my life.

Dimly, she heard him speaking again, but not to her. It again took him a long time to get back, and she was amazed that in that time, she had not lost the edge of her passion. She was still as excited upon his return as she had been when he left.

"Come here," he said. Robin looked toward him. He was standing by the window, his foot resting on the edge of a low, narrow table positioned underneath it. She crawled to him, not sure what other way might be permissible.

"Good. Now come up..." He guided her with a hand in her hair again, and pointed at his boot. "I want you to straddle that. Yes, get your cunt over it, nice and comfortable. Put your legs on either side of the table, and wrap your arms around my leg."

Robin did as he instructed, and the feel of the polished leather between her legs sent a shudder throughout her body. She gladly wrapped her arms around him, feeling the warmth and strength of him, the smooth fabric of his pants.

"That's it. You know what to do now, girl. I want to see you get off. So move your body, hump my leg, just like the little hungry pet you are. I want to feel you fucking yourself on my boot, bringing yourself off just like a bad dog in front of company. And you're going to do it quickly, girl. You have three minutes." He gripped her hair and showed her that he was looking at his watch. "Begin."

Robin couldn't think; she didn't dare think. Every word he said, the images he invoked, the incredible humiliation of it all was too overwhelming to believe. But the need within her was also overwhelming, and the need to obey, to do as she was told, was also incomprehensibly strong. Slowly, she shifted her position, trying to figure out how to do it. The first time her weight settled back onto his boot, the leather pressing against her, opening her up, she moaned at the intense surge of joy that raced through her. The position was odd, and the command heavy, but she moved her hips and body, and grasped his leg and whined, and soon she had built up a rhythm that would satisfy.

"Ah, such a good girl," Chris murmured encouragingly. "Such a good little pooch. Come on, hump it out; let me see how much you need it, you're just like an animal in heat, you need to fuck it out."

"Oh, oh, nooo!" Robin whimpered, clutching him even tighter.

"Yes, yes, that's it. Do it. You may come at any time, girl, but if you don't before the time is up, it may be a long time before I permit it this opportunity again."

"Please! Yes! Yes! Ungh! Oh God!" Robin writhed against the leg and against the boot, feeling the leather grow slippery underneath her, and feeling the wetness of tears against the cloth she was leaning into, and then the rush hit her as fast as lightning. Her entire body, aching, hot and tight, drew tightly against Chris's leg and her cunt ground into the top of his boot and she seemed to explode! Her eyes tightly shut, she still saw bright bolts of light, her hands gripped compulsively, her toes dug into the carpet, scraping back, pushing her forward. She panted, and thrust herself forward again, only slower, and felt the shudders rise into pleasure again, only this time fainter, and as she drew back, she felt Chris's hand lightly stroking her head.

This time, she let the tears come and knew they were there, and she sobbed and gulped air as he gentled her down, putting her back onto the floor. When he lowered his leg, and nudged her with the boot that was now covered with her own essence, she didn't hesitate, but raised her head up and began to wash it over with her tongue. She didn't stop until she covered every inch, and her tears added a different taste to the leather where they fell.

He took it away when he was satisfied, and she felt something light fall across her shoulders.

"There is money on the table by the door. Give it to the housekeeper when she comes, and then lock up again and come into the bedroom."

As he walked away, Robin sat up, still a little dizzy. The object across her shoulders was a shirt…the one Chris had been wearing. She pulled it on just in time to hear the gentle knock on the door, and she followed his instructions, giving the five dollar bill to the woman in return for the blankets she bore.

Chris, his muscular shoulders now more evident in the white t-shirt that was tucked into his pants, pointed at the floor at the floor of the king size bed. Robin nodded, and, feeling more then a little bit disappointed, laid them out on the floor. I should have expected this, she thought, folding them into a semblance of a bed. It's in all the books, isn't it? I've dreamed about it, haven't I? But somehow, the cold reality of a hard floor next to a wide, soft bed with plump pillows and the warm body of a man who had just given her a magnificent orgasm was just too jarring. She trembled slightly, trying to form the words in her mind, trying to decide whether begging for the privilege of sleeping next to him would be presumptuous, and then just allowed the thoughts to subside. She would not...could not!...tempt fate. When Chris came up behind her, she knelt absolutely still.

"Do not remove this during the night," he said, slipping a soft blindfold over her eyes. "If you must rise to answer a call of nature, you will manage to find your way without removing it. Do you understand?"

"Yes, sir. Please...I'm sorry, sir, I should have thanked you. After...I mean, thank you, sir."

"Yes, you should have. But I'll make an allowance this one time, because of unfamiliarity. Go to sleep. I will tell you when to remove the blindfold."

He guided her down into her cocoon of scratchy wool. She pulled the blankets around her, and despite the strangeness of the place and the circumstances, fell at once into a deep, deep sleep.

Chapter Two

Robin awoke to the sound of a shower running. For a moment, she felt confused. Where was her pillow? Why did her body ache so much? But the entire evening flooded back into her conscious memory, and as she stretched a little bit, she fairly purred with satisfaction.

Of course I'm sore, she thought with a grin. I was well used and slept at the foot of my master's bed, like a good slave. Immediately, she curled back with a rush of embarrassment at her own thoughts. Why not just rush things, she asked herself angrily. As far as I know, last night was just a little test of my reactions, and I am not a good slave, and he is not my master. But he has to be pleased! He did accept me. He could have thrown me out. I don't even know if camping out on the floor is supposed to be a reward or a punishment! Troy thought it was silly. And Maria would just send me home...

Home! How am I supposed to take care of my apartment? I should have packed more stuff. I should have given notice. I have to call the super! Robin turned over onto her belly and leaned her head into her folded arms. Oh God, I am such an idiot. Ken Mandarin told me to get ready to leave right away, why didn't I listen?

Because you didn't think you'd get in, answered the voice inside her. Because you figured that the Marketplace wouldn't be interested in you. So you didn't even warn them at work, and you didn't talk to the landlord, and you only packed up some of your things, leaving days of work that will have to be done before you can just pick up and leave your life behind.

They never talk about what happens to a person's life when they just vanish into thin air, Robin reflected. They just start the story with the slave arriving at the master's house. You never really find out how many people they had to say goodbye to, or if they just decided to leave everyone they knew with this mystery.

16

I guess there aren't a lot of people who really have to know anything, she reflected. People leave jobs for better jobs all the time. And it's not that I have loads of personal friends who are going to miss me. She grimaced at the self pity that swept through her, and continued her inventory. The landlord won't care, all I have to do is leave my security with them. And if I never attend a meeting of the WISE Women again, no one will ever know the difference. But there are a few people who will want to maintain contact with me, even if I told them I was taking a new job and moving away, she knew, not wanting to think about them. How am I supposed to tell my family? Oh Mom, don't expect to see me at the holidays this year; I'm going to be a full-time slave, and slaves don't get vacation days.

Her stomach twisted into a knot, and she slumped down. This business of creating a reality out of what I assumed to always be a fantasy is too hard. Of course I didn't prepare, and of course I never really tried to think about what to tell everyone. I might as well have been trying to figure out how to tell people that I was going to Mars to live with little green men. At that moment, she realized that the shower had long since stopped running. Without thinking, she held herself still, and listened.

Rustling and clinking noises, the sounds of a man getting dressed. Around the corners of the blindfold, she could tell that the light in the room was artificial. Was it still very early morning, or did Chris Parker just dislike sunlight? He walked past her, into the other room, and she heard him open the outer door. She stopped trying to figure out what he was doing, and just remained still.

When he came back, she felt and heard the bed shift as he sat on the edge. The heavy sliding sound and the light thump could only mean he was putting his boots on. Robin decided that she had wasted enough time feigning sleep, so she raised herself up on one elbow and tilted her chin up.

"Good morning, sir," she said, her voice slightly cracking. Oh, I need a cup of coffee, she thought, clearing her throat. At least they'll have good coffee here, it's a great hotel.

But there was no response from the man, only a moment of silence, held suspended as she realized that she had just done something that was very, very wrong. She tried desperately to think of what it was. And then, Parker was off the bed, and she heard a sound like a long, ragged whisper, and felt his strong hand close around her upper arm.

She yelped, but he merely pulled her up and halfway out of her wrapping of blankets. Her feet were caught and tangled, but it didn't matter, because he pushed her powerfully against the bed, forcing her head down to the sheets with one hand, bracing her body against his leg. She barely had enough time to gasp when he brought his doubled over belt across her ass cheeks, hard, with an explosive crack! that filled the room.

Robin's yelp of surprise became a wrenching cry of pain, and she buried her face into the bed, pushing her mouth against the surface to try to contain it. Chris paid her no attention. He merely used that belt on her bent over form, again and again, each stripe glowing white and then red and then fading back until he struck her in that same spot once more. She writhed, and clenched her teeth into a crumpled wedge of sheets, but never tried to escape him. And when he stopped, and the ringing in her ears and the pounding in her chest threatened to send her toppling off the bed, he solved her imbalance by pulling her back and letting her fall to the floor, her feet still tangled in her own bedding.

He began to slide the belt back onto the loops around his waist.

"When you awaken," he said, his voice betraying just a hint of breathlessness, "you will only speak when spoken to."

"Yes, sir," she managed to whisper. Her ass glowed with a painful heat.

"I have left instructions for you in the other room. You may get up and remove the blindfold when I have gone. Do you understand?"

Robin drew in a deep breath. No! she wanted to say, no, don't go! What comes next? Do I have time to make my arrangements? Can I call the auction house? Can I go home? But she drew all the questions in and held them tightly, and concentrated on trust. She had to trust him! "Yes, sir."

She felt him pushing the toe of one boot next to her face, and she twisted to kiss it gently. She felt him change his posture, felt the nearness of his body as he squatted down next to her, and shivered when his hand gently stroked her hair.

"Good girl," he said. "That's a good girl."

And as the tears came and dampened the inside of the blindfold, she felt him rise again and leave her. Minutes later, she heard the outer door close, firmly.

"Oh my God," she whispered out loud, curling into the blankets as shudders drove their way through her body. "This is so good. This is so right!"

The instructions were precise, and Robin read them while she ate the bagel and strawberries that were left on the breakfast tray in the outer room. If Chris Parker had actually eaten anything, there was no evidence. Not a crumb or a wrinkled napkin to be found. But then, Robin thought mischievously, he was so neat and proper, crumbs probably sprang away from his body and self-destructed. He did leave an empty coffee cup by the window, though, leaving her to wonder just how long he had been awake before she stirred. She had to shift in her seat from time to time, favoring sore spots on her rear, but this only made her smile.

The note was written on hotel stationary in (of course) a steady, refined hand. It read:

You will pack my personal belongings and deliver them to the address below. I will not expect to be there until eight o'clock this evening, whereupon you will deliver yourself and one personal bag. You do not need to pack a wardrobe.

In the meantime, you may consider yourself free to conclude whatever affairs necessary to facilitate your exit from your current life. You will of course conduct yourself with utter discretion concerning your future plans.

Parker

It was nine o'clock in the morning. The address on the bottom of the page was on the Upper West Side, in the low 100's, and there were two keys on a silver ring in the envelope. Robin thought for a little while, lingered over her own coffee (it was good, as she had guessed earlier), and then got up and got to work.

There wasn't a lot to pack. Chris had left one change of clothing and his suit jacket and several ties. There were no personal items in the bathroom. In the closet, she found a garment bag. He had already checked out, via the computerized system in the room, so after she showered and dressed, she picked up the bag and left. She couldn't resist looking at her rear in the mirror. It was still blushing slightly red, and several marks crossed both cheeks from his belt. If she didn't have so much to do, it would have been nice to stretch out on that bed and pleasure herself for a while, pressing those sore spots down to get the most satisfaction. But she contented herself with the knowledge that she had things to do, and left the room awake and slightly aching and perfectly happy.

She left the garment bag with the bellman downstairs and took a cab all the way home. It was extravagant, but soon she would have no need for the money she had so painstakingly saved over the years. Why not splurge, she thought, sitting back and watching the traffic. I should go to town! Have lunch at Lutéce, maybe. If there's time.

Home was a modern building in the financial district, not far from the South Street Seaport. She looked around her one bedroom with a moment of indecision, and decided to make her calls first. Might as well get the really hard part out of the way. She changed into jeans and a t-shirt and pulled her rolodex out and started calling.

It was a regular roller coaster ride of reactions. Of course her boss at the auction house was pissed. Couldn't she at least give them two weeks notice? And who was it? Was it Christie's? Would she at least give them a chance to match the offer? Robin bit her lip and lied, and felt a little guilty. But in reality, she knew that they would have no problem filling her job, and that after a few days her co-workers would get used to her absence as they all got used to the eternal shuffle in the art world.

That done, she called the super and told him that she would be vacating within the week. As she thought, he stuttered and shouted his own outrage and swore dire circumstances should he have to place a call to the owner corporation, but her willingness to let the security deposit go caught him by surprise.

This is not so hard, she thought, dialing the third storage company and getting their prices. I guess it's really kind of easy to leave town in a hurry. Not that I know I'm leaving town. Hm, that's a thought. Do Marketplace slaves ever go out? What if I don't leave town and I end up seeing people I know? What would I say if they invited me out for a drink, asked me what I was doing?

"Hey, lady! You still there? I said you can get the lease as long as you want."

"What? Oh, yes, yes, thank you. I'll call you back later," Robin said, returning to the present.

You think too much about the wrong things, she scolded herself, laying the phone down. You didn't think about how to manage this properly, but now you're thinking about what might happen if you get accepted and if you get sold and if that person lives in town and if and if and if. And meanwhile, the next name on the list was her Mom and Dad's.

She decided to spend some time packing.

That job wasn't easy at all, and by lunch-time, she knew that Lutéce was out of the question. She called one of the Chinese places that delivered menus under her door every week and ate General Tau's Chicken right out of the box while she divided her belongings into Pack, Give Away, and Throw Away piles. Then, she spent more time on the phone, calling various charity organizations that provided pick-up service. Only one could send someone today, so they got several boxes and bags of clothing, kitchen items, books and office supplies. The young men were very friendly and grateful, and she was even more pleased with herself when they gladly accepted $50 to take her "throw-aways" as well, and dispose of them somewhere.

And it was only after they left that she realized that not once did she imagine them overpowering her and ravishing her on the floor of her apartment. She giggled and dove back into her work, trying to get as much finished as she could. The rolodex remained next to the phone, stubbornly flipped open to the card she left it on.

By 5:30, she admitted defeat. There was no way she could get anything else out of the house today. So she showered again, dressed simply, and threw a carry-on bag onto her bed. She had thought all day about what to take, and the items she put in the bag were gravid with memories. Three books went in first. One, an anonymous Victorian novel, the second a fairy-tale romance, the third a collection of short stories about gay men. All were about surrender and mastery. All of them were worn with handling. A leather collar, bearing a golden "M" in gentle scrollwork followed. A small box of jewelry. A woven leather wrist-cuff, worked into a complex mystery braid. Her favorite pillow-case, dusky rose in color, a whispery cotton that felt smooth and comforting beneath her cheek. Then, she tossed in her latest journal and a box of her favorite pens, her address book, wallet and banking items. Her passport and ID. Her prescription medications she tossed in just in case, and followed them with her spare reading glasses.

It was such a minuscule collection, really. Hardly the markings of a complex life.

The rolodex seemed monstrously huge next to the phone.

But there was no time now! Robin locked the door and ran to the elevator, trying to close out all thoughts of the one job she hadn't even thought of all day. Maybe tomorrow, she said to herself, waving down a cab. Or the next day.

She stopped at the hotel, as she had planned, and picked up Parker's garment bag, and then continued on uptown. The west side traffic was hellish, and she kept glancing at her watch the whole ride. But she arrived in the neighborhood with plenty of time to spare, and the doorman in the beautiful old building only gave her the slightest look as she walked into the stately lobby.

It was a beautiful pre-war building, and as she admired the scrollwork inside the elevator, she idly wondered about the costs of living up here. Nothing I could afford, she noted while she looked for the apartment number. She used both keys and let herself into a spacious, airy home with a long hallway leading to a living room that had a magnificent corner view of the river. Below her, trees swayed in the park and cars rumbled past on the expressway, but the river gleamed, a dark, sparkling line of reflections.

This is beautiful! Robin dropped the luggage and ran over to the windows to look out and down. I could never, never afford a view like this! She turned into the room to look around. Whoever decorated this room knew enough not to take away from the visual centerpiece. Woven rugs lay scattered across a pale, polished wooden floor, and the furniture was arranged to that no one needed to sit with their back toward the scenery. Natural canvas and heavy wooden frames dominated the look, rather southwestern. A desk stood in the corner opposite the windows; it would never lack for natural light.

Robin spotted several genuine pieces of antique painted pottery on a shelf in a glass fronted cabinet, and the framed photos on one wall were classic (if somewhat standard) Ansel Adams. On the other hand, there was a definite lack of western kitch in the room; no bronze replicas of Remington statues, no horseshoe mandellas strung with colored yarn and rabbit fur scraps. It showed not only an interest, but a knowledgeable one, guided by a sense of authenticity and money. It could have been brought together by a good decorator, except that some of the collectible pieces were just slightly out of period and style, something a perfectionist wouldn't stand for

Slavery must pay, was her first thought. Funny, though. I hadn't figured Parker for the southwestern type. I would have guessed he was an anglophile, and had a place filled with big comfy chairs and a zillion books, all arranged by topic, author and edition date. And, thinking of the man…well, I guess he's not here yet. A glance at her watch showed that he wasn't due for another fifteen minutes.

OK, that leaves me a few seconds to learn my way around. First, grab the garment bag and search for the master bedroom.

All in all, the apartment was one surprise after another. The larger bedroom was dark and subdued, almost as though it knew that its own view of the building across the street was rather pitiful. But the decadently huge walkin closet and dressing room which most New Yorkers might have comfortably used as another bedroom, held clothing for a man and a woman. And the man, judging by the length of the raincoat hanging behind one door, had to be taller than the shorter-than-average Mr. Parker.

And the dresses are just not his style, Robin added mentally. She followed that disrespectful thought with a slight nudge of shame, but hung the garment bag up without any more immediate speculation. And on her way out, she did notice that there was what seemed to be a single-sized futon folded neatly on a rack in one corner of the room. There was no corresponding futon frame, but neither was there a chest or anything to take up space near the foot of the bed.

The other bedroom door was locked. With visions of pirates and secret rooms dancing through her brain, she went to investigate the kitchen, where to her delight, she found a fancy Italian cappuccino machine on the counter. Oh good, I've always wanted to use one of these things, she thought, examining it. It doesn't look that hard. Mmmm, café latté for breakfast. Espresso after dinner. Looks like life as a slave won't be too terrible.

Her musings were interrupted by the sound of keys in the front door, and for a moment she panicked. He was right on time, but she had no idea what to do! Should she go out into the hall and greet him? Stay where she was? Kneel? Be relaxed and casual? She heard the click of his boot crossing the threshold and a jingling sound of keys, or maybe that was his jacket, it had two chains looped around one shoulder...

His jacket! I should go take his jacket!

She dashed out of the kitchen, bumping into the swinging door with one elbow and rounded the corner, trying not to look rushed. Chris was in fact standing with his back to her, and already starting to shrug the jacket off his shoulders. She came up behind him and caught it, drawing it down his arms.

"You should have been here a little earlier," he said, pointing to a rack affixed to the wall. She hung the leather jacket up and blushed.

"Yes, sir, I'm sorry."

"Not nearly as sorry as you will be in the future if you fail to meet me at the door. Make some coffee. Have you eaten dinner?"

"No sir, I haven't. Would that be regular coffee?"

"Yes, leave that monstrosity alone and use the Krups. There are beans in the freezer. Have some ready for me in the living room as soon as possible. Milk, no sugar."

Damn, another bad guess. I would have thought he took it black. But Robin inclined her head in an acknowledgment bow and went back to the kitchen to do as she was told. He looked interesting tonight, a cross between the two looks she had seen on him so far. His polished engineer boots looked very correct with the black jeans, and the motorcycle jacket was the only correct outerwear to accompany them. But again, he wore a fresh-looking tailored business shirt and a tie. Yuppie from hell, she thought without warning. Ivy-league Angels, their motto is, Think Yiddish, Look British and Ride American. Good thing she had to grind the beans and figure out where the gold filter was and find the coffee cups, or else she might have actually giggled in front of him.

Soon, she was sitting on the floor, cross-legged on one of those wool throw rugs, while Parker sipped his coffee and watched the lights across the river. She did not pour a cup for herself, and was not invited to, and she was embarrassed to the core of her being when her stomach complained about the lack of dinner. She would have been fine if Chris hadn't asked!

"I've sent for some food," the man commented, stretching his legs out. "It will arrive soon. In the meantime, let's hear what you've done today, and what is left to do."

"I'll need another two days to finish emptying my apartment, " Robin began. "I resigned today, called my gym, and got rid of a lot of stuff I don't need to store away. I need to visit my bank to store some of my artwork in the safe deposit box. I figured I'd send the rest to...my family, I guess."

"So you haven't told them yet."

Robin tapped her nose and tried to smile. "On the nose, sir. I have no idea what to tell them."

He nodded.

"It's just that I've never really vanished on them. I don't keep in contact that often, really. A call every once in a while. I try to make it home at least once a year." Robin grimaced. "Jeeze, it sounds like they'd barely miss me, doesn't it?"

"My guess is that they would miss you at least once a year," Chris said. "Some Marketplace entrants tell their family and friends that they are leaving the country. I would not advise you to rely on this falsehood. Although you may very well end up doing exactly that, you may also end up being sold to someone who lives right here, which may leave you encountering people you know, who will then want an explanation."

"I was thinking about that today. I don't suppose you could guarantee a buyer outside of the area, huh?"

The corner of his mouth rose slightly. "No, I'm afraid not. But the market is international. And the northeast is rather a small part of it."

Robin shivered for a moment and drew her knees up. "I don't know," she said softly. "I don't know what to say."

"To them, or to me?"

She looked up. "Both."

"Of the two, I would spend more time worrying about me. Because if you somehow fail to assure me that your behavior and dedication is perfect for the block, you won't have to say a thing to your family, other then perhaps explaining why you suddenly left your old job. But if you manage to get into the Marketplace, at the very worst, you can always simply tell them the truth."

"Oh sure. 'Hi Mom, just wanted to call and tell you that your daughter has run off to be a slave! Love to Dad!'" Robin's sarcasm sprang forth without thought, and the horror came immediately after. Her mouth dropped open, and her hand flew up to cover it. "Omigod, I'm so sorry, sir, I didn't mean that!"

Chris only smiled. "Yes you did. Apparently, you are so used to hiding everything about yourself, the very thought of openly declaring it is utterly ridiculous to you. But I tell you that almost half of the Marketplace appli-

24

cants do actually tell their spouses, parents, lovers, or best friends about where they are going. Now go get the door and our dinner...we will eat informally, in here."

She had been so overcome by her embarrassment that the light chiming in the background had gone entirely unnoticed. Now, with a contrite nod, she leapt to her feet and almost ran down the hallway.

Of all the stupid, dumb ass things to do! Why can't I watch my mouth? Why can't I concentrate? Stupid, stupid! You have to watch yourself, girl, or you're back on the streets with your resume and a lot of explaining to do, to an awful lot of people.

There was a man at the door, bearing a covered tray. He was tall and slender, with long blonde hair, wearing a light silk shirt that was open halfway down his bare chest. Obviously, he had to have come from somewhere in the building. But Robin focused upon his throat, around which was wrapped a heavy gold chain, linked through a ring from which a golden lock was suspended.

"Hi, you must be Robin!" he said in a friendly drawl. "Here's dinner...watch it, it's a little hot on the right side. Please give mah respects to Chris, will you?" His voice was as light as his attitude and clothing, and as he handed a tray to her, he grinned. "And don't look so worried, chile, you'll get all wrinkled up, like a prune!"

"Thank you," Robin managed to say. "But...but...who should I give respects from?"

"Heavens! Where have mah manners gone?" The man drew himself up and bowed politely to her. "I'm Leon, ma'am, and I belong to Mr. Reynolds, 14c. I 'spect we'll be seeing each other a few times while you're here. Chris does like mah cookin'!"

"Thank you," Robin said again, taken slightly aback by Leon's ease and friendliness.

"You're right welcome! My pleasure to be of service." He bowed to her again and headed off to the elevator.

He sounds like he's from far away, Robin thought, taking the tray into the kitchen. Texas? Arizona? She opened the covered dish, and a luxurious scent filled the air, making her mouth water. Dinner was couscous, with spiced chicken and grilled vegetables on the side. Not exactly what she expected from the blonde cowboy at the door.

Let's face it, girl. Nothing is like you expected it to be. The only thing you know for sure is that you are *not* using the furniture in this house. At least that was something that she had read and heard about that seemed true.

"No, sit up here and put your plate on the table," Chris said, when she seemed ready to take her place on the floor again. He patted the seat of one of the comfortable chairs. "But you are correct to seek the floor until invited to do otherwise."

This time, she managed to catch the exasperated sigh before it came out.

"Leon sends his regards," she told him, cutting into a piece of eggplant. "He seemed very friendly."

"Yes, he is. I used to liken him to a large golden retriever." Robin could easily see it; she nodded. Chris continued. "His skill as a cook and a household manager made him an excellent bargain, too."

"Then, he is…"

"Oh, yes. He's been in the Marketplace for about six years. With his current master for almost two. Before that, he was with a rather large family, and I think he misses caring for a lot of people." Chris indicated the food. "So, I indulge him. And at the same time, his owner gets to show him off. Now…while we eat, and for some time afterward, I want you to continue your story. This time, I do want it from the beginning. You've told and lived lies for too long. You must now get used to exposing yourself, in many more ways than the obvious."

Robin blushed, but at least she knew that this was coming. She drank some water and composed her thoughts and began to tell him just how much of a liar she had been.

Chapter Three
Robin's Story: Games of Youth

From the age of five, Robin lived a life of deceit. There were no warnings, no hints that those thoughts and dreams she was having were wrong or bad. But deep in her heart, beyond any understanding that she could put in words, was the knowledge that no adult should know what she was thinking. And no grown-up should ever, ever know what she was *doing*.

It started with the games she played at family gatherings, with cousins and friends. Their feverishly charged, impulse-driven antics ran from quiet playing with blocks and dolls to dashing through the rooms of the house, crawling under tables and through the legs of the grown-ups, creating havoc until their goal had been achieved. Temporary banishment, until their silence became too mysterious, at which time they would be called back to eat or nap or go home.

During those times of banishment, their imaginations gave way to games that were shrouded in mystery and secrecy. And although some of them were as uninteresting to Robin as any of the earlier frolics, it was during those serious moments that someone could suggest games that involved the kinds of stories and play that she was so taken with.

For then, they played Pirates, or House, or Spies, or any variation of a game where some of the kids turned into some kind of authority figure with the power to judge some of the others and cast sentences upon them. They used roles from Saturday morning cartoons, and they used comic book heroes and villains. They pulled their stories out of the books that their parents read them and the ones they got in school. Some of the older kids brought in ideas, characters and scenes from their favorite movies.

And then Robin could relax. Because she was one of the youngest kids there, and they never let her be the evil Princess, or the Lady Pirate. She couldn't even be Natasha the Spy. But she could be the Little Princess, the maid, the youngest daughter (or the oldest one, when it seemed that she was the one that was going to get ritually blamed for everything), or the hostage taken by the evil villain to get the good guys to have to come and rescue her.

And as kids do, they used their overwhelmingly powerful imaginations to come up with scenarios beyond the pat and G-rated endings they were subjected to. They used their own experiences with parental discipline to create fantastic, silly and sometimes all too accurate portrayals of threatened torments and fear. They were children.

They feared being abandoned, so they acted out scenes of banishment. They feared being lost, so they blindfolded each other. They feared being discovered, so they hid in dark places and whispered. They feared adults and their mysterious one sided world, so they played at being tyrants and victims.

Without having to say that she longed for the times when cousin David would tie her to a chair and pretend to be her kidnapper, Robin could throw herself into the role so easily that there evolved quiet agreement that these were the kinds of parts she played. It was just as natural as when her older cousin Pete also found himself to be always playing the part of the family dog when they played house, or being the villain whose plots were foiled and then had to be captured and pummeled ruthlessly with pillows and plastic swords before he was finally defeated.

But as the children grew and the generation was sealed for a while, the older ones drifted away from such games. With no new young kids to initiate, and more sophisticated games to tempt the participants, the imaginative scripts of evil and good gave way. When cousin David got his own Nintendo, that destroyed them forever.

And no one ever spoke of them, except to laugh. How silly we were, they could say, so embarrassed at their past play. By age 12, they started to forget.

Or at least most of them did. But Robin never forgot. Because in many ways, Robin never outgrew those fantasies.

I am different than everyone else, she once observed, looking at herself in the mirror. I don't look like it, at least I don't think so. But I have thoughts that no one else does. I think of things that no one talks about. When the other girls are talking about make-up and hair, and which boy likes them, I'm thinking about being kidnapped. While everyone watches the same TV shows, I still like to watch those movies where bad guys tie their prisoners up in dungeons and people get whipped. Why am I so weird? Why can't I just talk about what happened on TV last night? There must be something wrong with me.

So she hid her secret perfectly, growing up to be the perfect middle child. Her older brother was the star of the family, her younger sister the baby.

Robin herself had a little of her brother's charm and magnetism, and some of her sister's sweet nature. But she was also the loner, the bookworm. She read precociously and voraciously, earning excellent English grades in school. She had to be prodded towards athletics, and endured girlish sports until Junior High School, where she discovered track and field. Running, especially alone, gave her even more time to explore her secret thoughts.

To the rest of the world, she was perfectly normal, smarter than average, good natured, and maybe a little strong willed from time to time. No one could have guessed that as she studied Greek and Roman history, she became a barbarian slave, brought to Rome in chains, to be sold to the highest bidder. No one knew that she deliberately sought out books about slaves and prisons and societies which maintained second and third class citizenships. She was always careful to mix these books in with books on other topics, so that the librarians wouldn't suspect that she was having evil thoughts.

By that time, she knew that these fantasies of surrender and degradation weren't only unusual, they were very bad. She knew because she read all these books. Slaves didn't talk about their former slavery in glowing terms. People were hurt, families destroyed, and people died because of slavery. The whole country went to war over it (or so she understood it), and the good guys were the ones that *didn't* want it.

To make things worse, she became aware of the social realities of her time and life. When she read about the beginnings of women's emancipation, she decided to do a school paper on women's lives in earlier times. And much to her dismay, it seemed that her mind had divided into two distinct parts which were absolutely incompatible with each other.

One the one hand, she was absolutely horrified at what women had to live with in the past, and even right now, in different countries. She had taken much of her life for granted. But the thought that few women ever attained the level of education that she had right now, that they couldn't vote, or own property, that they couldn't go to college or be doctors or lawyers, this was all amazing to her. It made her angry.

Now she understood the news stories about the women who marched in Washington, or through other city streets. She extended her research to modern feminism, and liked what she read. She was as good as any boy! She could be whatever she wanted to be!

She was a teenage feminist.

Who had evil thoughts. Thoughts that were just not acceptable to her political beliefs, that were in fact betrayals of the simple feminism she had been exposed to.

Because even as she began her tentative reaching out to the world of feminism, she also retained those intense fantasies of her childhood. They invaded her dreams, and they waited for her to lie awake at night, tossing and turning until she knew that only one thing would let her sleep.

By now, those thoughts had evolved into full-fledged, soap opera style stories. In one, she was a Greek slave, clad in a short, diaphanous tunic, utterly owned, totally dominated, available to the members of her master's household. In this one, she grew to a position of some authority, getting to manage the other slaves. But when that became too threatening, she imagined that the other slaves planned a revolt and that she was terribly punished for not seeing it early enough, and demoted as well. That scenario lasted for years.

In another, she was a rebel spy in some mysterious, futuristic government. (This one came about after she discovered science fiction.) She was captured by the ruling forces, tortured, and often, brainwashed into joining them. That fantasy was full of fetish images, boots and capes, cuffs and collars. She imagined that they had drugs to make her fantasy character pliable or confused, or to cause her pain. It was a much darker fantasy than her Greek one, but it had its rewards.

She didn't know how to masturbate to orgasm yet, not quite. But she did know that thinking of these stories made her feel good, and that when they were accompanied by select touches and pinches, she felt even better. And the enforced silence of her nightly explorations only added to their power. She couldn't afford to let Mom or Dad hear her as she experienced the pleasures of her fantasies.

And she knew, absolutely knew, that her new feminist heroines would never, ever approve of such visions and dreams. They shamed her. But she could not reject feminism because she had secret evil thoughts! The best that she could do was master the thoughts and put them away.

Robin found a refuge in academics, burying herself in more books and more studies. No one was surprised when she skipped a grade; everyone was proud when she received special honors in graduations. She discovered fine art and spent weekends strolling through museums and going to different libraries and galleries for showings. She wrote pages and pages of journals, recording every thought but the most disturbing ones, pushing them back with new strength and knowing that they would return with new cunning. She ran, sometimes faster, sometimes further, never an award winner on the track, but keeping it up for the release of energy it promised.

Sublimation, she wrote one day, in a rush of frustration, *is as exhausting as pursuit.*

She found herself starting to drift off into daytime fantasies from time to time, while watching someone else or while waiting for something to happen.

Standing on line at the supermarket led to lurid fantasies about being dragged into the dark, cool stockroom and humiliated and ravished by the hulking stockboys and their leering supervisor.

Lying at the side of a pool over summer vacation with the sounds of splashing and the sensation of tightness as water droplets evaporated from her skin invariably led to thoughts of pirates, their hands and mouths all over her helpless body.

Then, one afternoon when she was sixteen, she was fooling around with one of her girlfriends in the attic of the girl's house. They had already gone through a wedding album two generations past, and giggled at the clothing and gasped at the small waists of the women in the bridal party. Then, Cheryl, the friend, found someone's old army stuff and put on an officer's cap, standing straight and saluting in the mirror. Although it was old, it had been packed away in plastic with some care, and although it was large for her, her silhouette made Robin gasp. Cheryl, still silly over the pictures, swung around and barked, in her rough estimation of what a soldier might sound like, "What are you gaping at, girl? Stand at attention when I'm talking to you!"

And that caused another, much more disturbing reaction. Robin flushed and tried to cover it by laughing. She excused herself not much later, saying that she had work to do, and went home feeling nauseated and dizzy. And moist between her legs.

I'm not only perverted, she thought, holding her pen above the journal page, not daring to write. But I'm a lesbian. That's impossible. Lesbians love women. They're feminists. Feminism is the theory, lesbianism is the practice, wasn't that what someone said? How could I possibly ever tell a woman that I loved her when she'd recoil from me in horror if she knew what I was really like?

I will certainly never find a true lover, she finally wrote, a new pain growing in her chest. *I am even an outsider among outsiders.*

Of course, nothing was ever that easy. Her late night and midday fantasies, now bolstered with a much more complete understanding of how her body worked and what it needed for release, did not suddenly cease to have male characters in them. And as she found herself looking at classmates and people on the street, or even at movie and rock stars, she realized that she could be attracted to men or women. This did nothing to help things, but only complicated them to such a ludicrous degree that she managed to avoid dating as much as humanly possible, looking for events that required group participation and hobbies that didn't allow her time on the weekends. She became involved with school plays and newspapers and student councils. And then she turned her attention to college.

"She'll be a teacher," her father assured friends. "She's always reading, and she loves libraries and schools. We're gonna have a teacher in this family real soon."

"Definitely a lawyer," her mother confided to her friends. "So bright! All these awards! And she's so political! Who knows? Maybe one day she'll be the governor. She's going to go out and change things, that's for sure!"

"I want to be an art buyer," Robin told her college counselor. "I know I'm no artist, but I want to work for museums or galleries or auction or restoration houses. What do I have to do to get the right training?"

Her confused and slightly miffed parents wanted her to go locally, and there were certainly plenty of quality schools nearby. But she negotiated a scholarship to one far away, were she could live on campus and be part of a new community. She also wanted one within easy distance of a major city. It was important to her that she be separated from her family, because whatever happened, whether she gave in to these fantasies or not, there was no way she was going to want to come home and sleep in her nice single bed with the pink coverlet.

If I'm going to be a pervert, she wrote at last, just before packing her journals, *at least it'll be where no one knows me.*

And, was her less conscious thought, as she packed up to head east, where there might be more people who are like me.

"So what's the deal with you and Greg?" Donna asked, combing her fingers through her long blonde hair. She flipped a few strands over her forehead, where they would fall in that sweet, slightly stylish way that drove some of the young men to distraction. She smiled at the effect, knowing how it looked. "Are you guys going out or what?"

"It…didn't really work out," Robin answered. She had a textbook open in front of her, and she was making notes on a yellow pad.

"Aww, too bad. He was cute, too. But what was it? Was he, like, all dick and no brain?" Donna cocked her head and rolled her eyes. "Du-uh, wanna pizza? Wanna watch me sweat with a buncha other guys? Wanna fuck, bay-bee?"

Robin giggled. Donna was just too funny sometimes. "I guess you could say it had something to do with his intelligence. Or at least his imagination."

"Oh yeah, ain't it the truth? Like some of these guys think that foreplay is when they squeeze your tits a little first. And where do they get this?" She raised her hands and mad pinching movements with her fingers. "I mean, did you ever have a guy just grab your nips and twist them around like knobs on an old radio? It's like, who taught you how to make love, the TV repairman?" She snorted and checked her hair one last time.

Robin was so used to being flooded by these feelings that she didn't do more then raise an eyebrow at Donna's mimicry. But under her sweatshirt, her nipples ached for someone to grab them and yes, squeeze them and twist them around. Well, thank goodness Donna was going out. There was always the box under the bed.

"It's too bad you don't have a guy, though. Ramon says he's got extra tickets to the game tomorrow, and we could'a gone together. You can still come if you want to."

"No thanks, Doni, I've seen enough games for a while." Robin tapped the book. "And I have to finish my research for this paper, anyway. But say hello to Ramon for me, and tell him thanks for those magazines. They really came in handy."

Like Robin, Donna's boyfriend was taking a series of courses in art. He had seen Robin's books on pre-Columbian paintings and mentioned that his parents had a series of magazines that had some great color illustrations and photographs, would she like to see them? He seemed to treat her like a younger sister, which was fine with her and just peachy to Donna. Especially since Ramon was a sexy hunk of manhood who spoke three languages and came from money.

"He's perfect for me," Donna often said. "Older, smarter, richer, and utterly fascinated by my big tits. Latin men, you know. Give 'em blonde hair and big tits, and they're all yours." Certainly Ramon did nothing to disprove her theory

"Yeah, I'll say hello," Donna said as she got up to go. "And don't be such a nun, OK? Get out and do something. It's Friday fucking night. Go out and get blasted or something. Meet some guy on the track team, they're more intellectual then the ball players. I got safes in the basket, help yourself. And I shouldn't be back until two or three!"

"I'll consider your advice," Robin promised with a wave. But as she eyed the garish woven basket that held Donna's endless supply of colorful prophylactics, she only sighed. She never wanted to see one again. Especially not in the hands of a jock.

But an hour later, as the silence in the room grew oppressive, Robin finally closed the books and stretched. With a cool deliberation, she closed the curtains and locked the door. And pulled the box out from under her bed.

The box. It was a rectangular cardboard box about twenty inches long and five inches deep, designed to be used as storage. It came to school packed with her journals. Now, there was only one volume in it, her current one. The rest of the space was taken up by her slowly growing collection of toys and books and magazines. She took them out with a ritual slowness, touching them and laying them out so she could decide what to do.

First, the two tabloid newspapers, with garish, horribly drawn caricatures of women in bondage on the cover. She had gotten them when her train passed through the city, along with several of the books underneath them. The only woman in a dimly lit store inside a huge bus and train terminal, she had hurriedly made her selections and paid for them as sweat broke down the middle of her back. She had been positive that every man in the place was watching her and that everyone on the train she later boarded would look at her with disgust if they knew what was in that stapled brown bag.

She had purchased the two papers and two softcover books. One was about a woman who trained men to be her slaves, the other about group of men who abducted and tormented young girls, who invariably grew to love it. Robin knew that the stories were shoddy, the writing awful, the sexism unbearable.

But they made her hot. They got her so wet that she couldn't stand it. Filled with more shame, she had written to the companies and gotten their catalogs and ordered more. And their arrival made her even more humiliated; held captive by her own twisted libido.

That was when she had just gotten to school, though. She wasn't that bad about these things any more. Now, she just accepted her fantasies for what they were, and indulged herself as needed.

Like right now. The books she stacked to one side, leaving her current favorites on the bottom of the pile. Then, she took out the collar.

It was a normal dog collar, purchased with a load of munchies at a local supermarket. But as she put it on, she felt a new rush of heat flooding through her. It felt so *right*.

Carefully, she piled pillows on her bed to make support for her shoulders. She undressed slowly, her eyes closed, hearing a voice whisper the commands to her. When she was nude except for the collar, she opened her eyes to look at herself in the mirror across the room. This always served to excite her more. Her curly hair cascaded around her shoulders, and her fit body seemed so pale. The collar stood out sharply, defining her. *I am a slave*, she mouthed silently. *I am* your *slave*.

She put the box on her nightstand, pushing the clock out of the way, and eased back into the bed. For about a half hour, she read through the newspapers, with their fake letters and fake stories. She read everything, from the token editorial to the ads for professional mistresses, and everything went straight to her loins. This was a world made of her fantasies.

She spent time trying to imagine what it would be like to visit a professional. How she would go there, what she would say? Would the woman be tall and thin? Would she be powerful, and stately? Would she wear these clothes, like in the magazine pictures, the corsets and the stockings, the high boots and long whips?

Carefully, Robin reached over to the box, not looking at it. This was to add a touch of unpredictability to the session. She pulled out the first thing she touched, and sighed as she trailed it cross her body. It was a plain pair of clothespins, which she had tied together with a leather shoelace. She had gotten the idea from one of the magazines. She pinched one nipple and slipped the jaws of the pin around the base, sighing when it was on. The other went on easily, and she let a low moan issue from between her lips.

The newspapers fell to the floor as she shifted to get her next toy. It didn't matter; their part in her ritual was over. Now, she looked specifically for the heavy piece of black silk she used as a blindfold, and she tied it around her eyes. Now, with her hands and the power of her imagination, she could truly pleasure herself.

Running her hands quickly over her body, she imagined someone examining her. Their hands would be cool, hard and impersonal, stroking her to catch her reactions, pinching and squeezing to test firmness. She gathered the leather string between the clothespins and put it in her teeth, so she could pull on them by jerking her chin back. The sensation was doubly thrilling, since the thong tasted salty and rough and the hands-free movement of the pins made it easy to imagine foreign fingers manipulating them.

She spread her legs apart with both hands on her thighs, one leg going off the side of the bed. It made her feel wide open. One, two quick, hard pinches on the lips of her sex, and she knew that she was already more then prepared for coming. But it would be a while longer before she permitted herself that release.

With a deliberate slowness, she stroked the insides of her thighs and her belly. She cupped her breasts, brushing her fingers alongside her nipples, tapping the clothespins. She didn't have a pattern. In fact, she tried to vary her actions as much as possible. Sometimes, she would reach up and twist the pins sharply, so that she couldn't help but gasp.

Finally, she let the pins go, and carefully pulled them open and off, hissing through her teeth as blood rushed back to her nipples. Then, she slipped the blindfold off, and reached over the side of the bed and picked up the book on top of the pile. She scanned it quickly, stopping at favorite passages and folded over pages, and read about the things that made her breath quicken and her clit thrum like a guitar string. But she didn't touch herself, no, not yet. With a growing impatience mixed with her need to make it last as long as possible, she picked up, read through and tossed aside each of the books.

Scenes played themselves out in her mind; leather cuffs around her wrists and ankles, a heavy black whip in a gloved hand. Bending, bowing, lapping her tongue across smooth leather. A slap across her face, angry words thrown at her in contempt. Rough hands squeezing her breasts, long, slender, cool fingers with gleaming red nails cruelly pinching her nipples. A hand pulling her head back, forcing her mouth open, thrusting into her with passion and fury! Her own mouth pulled down, buried in another women's cunt, commanded to please, worked until she gasped, and then pulled back for more. Hands, many hands, upon her body, pulling apart her ass cheeks, preparing her for another violation...

Time had lost all meaning when she finally dropped the last book and grabbed blindly for her vibrator. Arching her back, she lowered it to the exact right spot, directly on her clit, and with her other hand, she pinched one nipple, hard. There was no teasing now; she had reached the end of her limit on arousal. At the first touch of the insistent toy, she jerked against the bed, and clenched her teeth together to still her cries. Oh this would be a good one! She reached across her body to pinch the other nipple and moaned, and then yelped, and with a burst of wetness and an explosion of body-shaking tremors, she came, her hips thrusting at nothing, her eyes tightly shut.

"Oh God, oh God," she whispered, collapsing back onto the bed. "So good. So...so good."

Chapter Four

Robin awoke with a start, knowing immediately that she wasn't in her own bed, and feeling the disorientation that comes with darkness and deep sleep. Then, she turned over and remembered; she was in the room that had been locked, and Chris Parker was presumably sleeping in the room across the hall. That's twice in two days, she thought, stretching a little. I guess I really haven't spent that much time waking up in strange beds, have I?

She had never been one for one-night stands. Predictably, plain sex, 'vanilla sex', as she came to call it, became something she just avoided. She stopped going to the singles hang-outs that her friends from school and work crawled through, except when she had a large group to insulate her from unwanted attention. And if sometimes her reputation seemed to be somewhat prudish, well, there was ample evidence that she did have relationships with other people. Somehow, it just didn't seem that she met them dancing, drinking, or while conducting the dating and mating rituals of her class and culture.

Two mornings waking up in different places was already something new.

Disappointingly, the locked room turned out to be another bedroom, at least to casual glances. Before she turned out the light, however, she realized that there was a distinct spartan atmosphere to the room, a lack of heavy furniture and a lot of wall space. There was a small bathroom, with a shower stall. Large closets with locked sliding doors lined one wall entirely, and unlike all the other rooms, this one had heavy drapes to close out the light.

Or to hide the interior from voyeurs with binoculars across the street, she added. She had made a note to carefully examine the room the next day if she had time, but she was pretty sure that it was a playroom.

But there had been no time this night. By the time she finished filling Parker in on her erotic life up until college, it was already getting late. Her trainer did not touch her or use her in any way, but merely sent her to bed with a wake up time and a wave of his hand. Still trying for best behavior, she had gone, and dove into the single-sized guest bed within the ten minutes Chris had suggested.

She glanced at the clock. God, was it really only three in the morning? She flopped back down into the sheets in frustration. Insomnia would be damn hard to combat now. She had been given some very simple instructions concerning her sleeping arrangements.

"You will sleep naked," Chris had ticked off, looking her directly in the eye. "You will remain in bed, unless you have a physical need to leave it. You will keep the lights off; no reading, no watching television, if there is one present. And you will not, under any circumstances, give yourself pleasure. That right belongs to me now. If you even absently stroke yourself for the calming effect, you will be stealing from me, and will be punished."

Her hands itched to do just that. Just thinking of the instruction caused a twinge of excitement to run through her, and she moaned, turning over onto her stomach to trap her hands under the pillow. There was a part of her mind clamoring for attention, a strong and determined segment which demanded satisfaction. How would he know?, that part of her screamed. You know how to keep it quiet! And you are going to take a nice shower in the morning, plenty of time to make sure there's no evidence, not that women really leave anything men know to look for. It'll calm you down, it'll get you to sleep, it'll be all right, just this once!

But I'm trying to live this way, she hollered back. There's no point in me doing this if I don't do it all the way!

Somehow, she managed to fall asleep again, and the buzzing of the alarm clock seemed like an explosion when morning came.

Chris seemed disgustingly alert when he came out of his bedroom, his curly hair wet and his body clothed in jeans and a t-shirt. Robin caught a better look at him while she poured coffee. He was stocky in build, heavy shouldered and short waisted. She imagined him fighting a lot in his youth, short boys get picked on as a matter of course. So, he probably bulked up his body with weight lifting, put some muscle power in his reactions to their taunts and provocations. She wondered if his height cost him any dates in the gay community, or whether the shoulders and the jacket made up for a lack of inches.

I wonder if he even cares, she thought, hesitating before pouring herself a cup. She glanced over to him.

"Yes, you may," he said, not looking at her. "Normally, you should assume that you take your meals or drinks in the kitchen, before or after your owner. You may or may not be used for domestic services; my assumption is that most slaves are. In the case of a single owner, you may have to snatch something to eat while they do; your attentions may also be needed immediately before and after a meal. Individual owners will, of course, have their own tastes. Some may treat you like a member of the family; I understand it's all the rage in California."

Robin grinned and casually took a seat on the floor, leaning against the wall. Cushions scattered around the apartment took on new meaning. "And you don't approve, sir?"

"No, I don't. And neither do you." He sipped and nodded his approval. "If you did, you'd be looking for a position as a domestic, not a slave. You really shouldn't try to be too clever, Robin. I don't appreciate it unless it's excellently judged and timed, and others might take it for impertinence."

"Yes, sir," Robin murmured. She buried her concentration in the coffee for a while, to cover her embarrassment.

"You will have a total of three days to complete your business in the outer world," Chris announced suddenly. "Wednesday of this week, next Sunday, and the following Monday. You will live here, except for next Sunday night, which you may spend anywhere you like. Consider it your last night in freedom for quite some time."

"It sounds like you have a lot of confidence in me," Robin said, trying not to appear too eager.

"I do. But I must admit that I also have a great deal of confidence that your shortcomings can be mastered in a relatively short amount of time due to my training. You're hardly the first applicant I've handled, you know."

"Ken Mandarin said that you've trained hundreds."

"Mandarin exaggerates. I have participated in the training of over one hundred slaves, yes. Personally, I believe my standing is twenty-six to the block, four back to their owners. That's not an extraordinary number for a trainer who has been doing this work as long as I have. Some of my methods have achieved some minor professional notice; perhaps Ken was merely trying to express that my influence has been felt to that extent."

Robin cocked one eyebrow, masking the move as soon as she felt it. Chris Parker wasn't exactly lying, but what he was saying seemed in direct opposition to what Mandarin had told her. In fact, Ken seemed to be excited by the discovery that Chris was "in town." And there was absolutely no reason to doubt Mandarin: in fact, Ken seemed supremely confident that Robin could be in luck if she could only get Parker to see her. So was everyone else they had spoken to while they looked for a potential trainer.

But there was no reason for Chris to pretend that he wasn't as successful and respected as these people seemed to think he was. And you can't reach that kind of level in your field without knowing your relative value, Robin noted. So what reason could he have to be so self-effacing with me? You'd think he would inflate his experience for my sake, to make me feel more in awe of him.

"We begin your training today," Chris said, bringing her attention back to the real present. "You should attempt from this moment on to behave as though you were my property - your body, your responses, your services, your mind, your thoughts. You will eat, drink and wear what I give you, sleep where I direct, and do whatever work I assign. You will accept my direction in all things, and never hesitate to inform me of any physical or emotional limitation which may hamper you in the performance of your duties. Is this all understood?"

"Yes, sir!" That familiar rush of pleasure covered her, and she drew herself up to listen.

"I want you to ask me questions concerning any aspect of your time with me; by the time you get to the block, I do not want there to be any mysteries about your position or the potential in your future. Your confidence will be what sells you, if your passion for slavery is real. And to that end," he focused his eyes on her, the morning light glinting off his steel framed glasses, "should you ever experience real doubt as to your wish to be sold, I want you to come to me immediately and inform me. Is that understood?"

Robin nodded. "Yes, yes, sir."

"Good. There are a few other rules you need to know besides the ones I've already explained to you. This apartment does not belong to me, in case you have not already guessed. You will treat it and its contents with respect and courtesy, and keep it clean and straightened. While inside, you will not wear clothing, unless I have directed you to do so."

Robin blushed. She had put on the same clothes she had worn last night, not even thinking. But Chris went on without pausing.

"You will wake up at the time I indicate every morning, and keep such hours as I direct. You may, as I've indicated, ask questions, but you must learn to limit small talk; speak when you are spoken to, and answer any of my questions quickly, honestly, and to the best of your ability. As a trainee, an applicant, you have no status in my world, and therefore you will treat any visitor with the utmost respect and courtesy.

"You will keep yourself clean and available for inspection or use at all times. You will submit with dignity to any punishment or training exercise I

40

prescribe for you, and I expect that you will show the proper attitude toward correction and reward at all times."

He didn't have to ask again; she understood. "Yes, sir, I will."

"Go into my room. Strip, and leave your clothing there. Bring the object you find on the bed back to me and present it to me properly."

Robin bowed her head in a nod and sprang up and into the hall. Her cheeks burned as she tore open the buttons of her shirt. I should have asked, she cursed, pulling it over her shoulders. I should have asked before I went to bed! Or when I woke up, I should have just come out and waited for him to say something! God, where did my brains go?

Chris made his own bed, and quite neatly, too. Laying on the bed, centered on the luxurious patterned quilt, was a leather strap. It looked like a doubled over belt, with two ends formed into a handle and riveted together. It had a loop strung through the handle for fastening to a belt ring, and it looked very old and very used. But in the way of good, rich leather, its use had made it glowing and supple. Unlike most of the SM toys she had seen and felt over the years, it wasn't black with silver studs or anything like that. It was a deep but light brown, British Tan, she thought, having read the name over and over again in catalogs.

Dumbly, she thought, what do you know? Maybe he is an anglophile. Focus, damn it! Pay attention!

And then she stripped off her jeans and folded her clothing in a pile. It had been a long time since she had been self-conscious about her nakedness, but suddenly, she felt a shiver of fear. It was daylight now, and she was in a large, beautiful modern apartment with a stranger. It wasn't the weekend, at night, in some darkened place, whether a bedroom or a playroom. And when she picked up the strap, a tingle ran up her arm, as though she had picked up a live wire.

Suddenly, she didn't know how to hold it. In one hand, her arm hanging down? Both hands? Across her lower body? No, that would look like she was trying to hide herself. Both hands held out? No, that would look stupid!

I'm panicking. What's wrong with me? I can do this, I used to bring stuff to Troy all the time. And Ken told me how to present it. I'm OK.

Repeating that to herself all the way down the hall, she balked only once, when she crossed into a shaft of light. But she forced herself forward, and reentered the dining room, where Chris was standing, draining his coffee.

With a calm grace that she had no idea was in her, she went to him, lowered herself to her knees, and offered the strap to him with both hands held above her eye level. He took hold of the handle and snapped his fingers, and she looked up.

He was pointing to the edge of the table. Robin bit her lip and glanced up once to be sure, and then rose and carefully stood at the edge, lining her belly up with it. She gasped when his hand came down in the center of her back and pushed, hard.

"You should have assumed the command to present," he said, stepping back. "Ten more for that hesitation. Do not count."

She didn't, at least not out loud. The strap landed on her ass cheeks like a broad band of pain, not as intimate as his hand, not as sharp as his real belt, but heavy and punishing, the way a good strap is. Each swing brought it hard against her, covering her ass, driving her slightly forward, washing her with stinging pain and solid whumps of impact that drove the breath out between her clenched teeth.

Like the beating she had experienced yesterday morning, it was devoid of teasing, touching, or even the gradual increasing of pressure and speed that an erotic beating manifested. No, this was punishment, pure, almost dispassionate. She clenched her fists as well as her teeth and rested her head against the smooth surface of the table, raising her shoulders when the impact drove her to unsteadiness, shutting her eyes and trying desperately to keep quiet.

But her body never felt so alive! Each heavy slap of the old, polished leather, each careful swing, each wonderful drive forward, sang through her entire body. Waves of pain, yes, covering her, washing over her, until sounds were wrenched from her, sighs and groans, and then whispered, desperate sounds that started as words and ended as whimpers.

And of course, punishment or not, her sex opened for the music, and she could feel the dampness of her excitement, the delicious humiliation of her state. She moaned once, loudly, and then wailed out her frustration and her agony, the fire spreading outward, upward and down, catching her again and again, over sore places not yet healed, over the backs of her thighs, around the curve of her buttocks.

The strap fled her and returned with a rush of air, over and over, increasing in speed and strength only by the smallest of increments, and when her whimpers became little explosions of sound without meaning and her every breath was punctuated with the forcing of air, in and out, she wished for bindings to cling to. It was so hard to simply bend forward and hold her body still for this abuse!

And then, sharply, it stopped, and she realized that the glowing in front of her eyes were the tear drops on the table, shining in the morning light, so clear and so precisely placed beneath her. Her own breath seemed ragged and harsh, and heat covered her from behind.

Chris' hand suddenly came up between her spread thighs and took hold of her there, cupping her pussy again, taking it all into his hand, and holding her tightly. She wailed again, it was too much! Then, as the sound seemed to echo in her brain, she stifled it, brought it back inward, and coughed out humiliating little snuffles and gasps as she brought herself back under some measure of control. The silence in the room grew to such an intensity that she heard the distant whooshing sounds of the cars along the highway.

"What have you learned?" His voice was supernaturally loud in her ear, and she jumped. She hadn't even realized that he was leaning forward, over her, next to her.

"To…to not wear clothes without your direction," she managed back.

"What else?"

"To…ah!" He had seized her even tighter, curling his fingers into her, making her body squirm under him. "To make sure I know what is proper, sir! Before I do something!"

"Good." He raised his body away from hers and placed the strap on the table next to her head. Then, he placed one firm hand at the back of her neck, while his hand remained nestled between her legs.

"Don't try to bring your legs together. Spread them wider apart. That's it. Never try to close yourself to me. Next time, I'll use something you won't like at all. But admit it, you did like the strap."

Oh, how did his voice go from matter-of-fact to sultry? Or was it all in her mind, the gentle lilt that she heard now that wasn't there before? She did as he instructed spread her legs wide, and whimpered slightly as he played with her.

"Yes, sir," she whispered, clutching at the air. "Yes, I like it."

"Tell me about something you don't like."

"Paddles," Robin answered, a little too fast.

He chuckled. "But paddles are common things. Every player of sex games has one hidden in the lingerie drawer. Surely you've learned to endure the touch. Now, tell me something less common. What, if given the option - and I am sure you have been granted this - would you remove from a player's arsenal from fear or knowledge? What makes you squeal and cry and surrender utterly? What frightens you?"

His hand never stopped, in fact, it demanded more reaction from her. Gently stroking, it opened her and retreated, circled and pressed, flicked and massaged at her, until she really bit her lip and tasted warm salt in her mouth. Groaning, she tried to still the jerking movements of her hips, and her desperate efforts seemed to amuse him even more.

"I asked you a question, girl. Answer now."

The hand left the back of her neck and went toward the strap and she gasped out, "Canes! I'm afraid of canes!"

"Really?"

"Yes, sir!" She moaned, and gasped, and her breath started coming in those light rhythmic waves that signaled an approach to ecstasy, and then his hand stopped.

"How interesting. What about knives?" His hands left her all together, and she moaned again, from their absence.

"No," she whispered, her voice now more then slightly strained. "No, sir, I've played with knives, they scare me, but not as much as canes. Canes are…different." Her entire body seemed to ache again. But the ache circled around her clit, and spread outward. Even the burning pain of her glowing ass cheeks couldn't compare to the erotic agony between her thighs.

"Bring me more coffee. And a damp towel, and the telephone. And then clean the table off, I think you might have marred the polish a little."

Feeling slightly faint, Robin managed to push herself off the table. She had indeed marred the polish a little, with the marks of her body, her sweat, her little pool of tears. Her nipples were tight, compressed by her own body against the wood, erect with the pleasure of Parker's expert probing. Robin fled to the kitchen with a flush covering her face, and her hands trembled when she took a coffee cup down from a shelf. In the reflection of the oven door, she could see the difference in color between her legs, back, and that area between them.

Oh God, she thought, reaching back to touch the heat. Oh God, I can't take this.

But she followed his directions, and watched him wipe his hands with the damp towel, as dispassionately as a terrace gardener who had pulled up a very small weed before coming to dinner. Would she never stop blushing?! Then, he tossed her the towel to put away, and dialed a long number on the cordless phone she brought him from the kitchen.

"Good morning, Rachel," she heard him say, as she deposited the towel back in the kitchen and searched for cleaning rags. She listened carefully, no real need to eavesdrop, but her curiosity was almost as strong as her frustration.

"No, I'm fine. Yes, as a matter of fact, there is. I'm going to be staying at Nancy and Lawrence's apartment, the West Side one. Would you please arrange to send me some clothing, a copy of the workbook, and a collar?"

Robin shivered as she walked back into the dining room and ran the soft cloth over the table top, wiping up her responses and rubbing out her image. Chris ignored her; he had a slight smile playing around his lips.

"Well, you're right my dear. What can I say? I have to do something to keep busy. How are things at the house?"

There was a long pause as he listened, and Robin saw him nod a few times.

"Fine, fine. Let me know if you need any help. Oh, and Rachel? Include in that package three of my canes, will you? There's a good girl." He paused again, and laughed suddenly. "Anytime you like, my love. Take care." He

44

clicked the receiver off and handed it to Robin to replace.

"Now," he said, when she returned, "you're in serious trouble."

Robin felt the blood drain from her face.

"What did I do?" she asked.

"What didn't you do?"

She looked around. The coffee was in his hand, the phone was put away, the table was polished clean again…what?

"On your knees while you think," Chris snapped.

She knelt immediately and not knowing what position to take, brought her hands behind her back. What had she forgotten to do? She ran images backward in her mind, from the current moment back through the beating. It was the second time she did this that she realized what she hadn't taken care of.

She immediately pushed her shoulders forward and down, lowering her face to the floor in front of Parker's feet.

"I'm sorry, sir," she whispered, blushing to her ears again, and this time slightly shaking as well. "Oh God, I'm so sorry. Please sir, please accept my thanks for teaching me, for disciplining me. I'll be better in the future, sir."

"Incredibly, unforgivably sloppy. What did you think I was waiting for when I stopped beating you?"

Nothing, she thought furiously, raging at herself. I wasn't thinking of any damn thing except how good it felt, and how awful it was, and how hot I was! But she pressed herself even lower, unable to speak these things out loud.

"Your punishment for this one will not be as simple as a beating," Chris said, nudging her shoulder. She picked her head up, and seeing his nod, drew herself up on her knees again. "Most of it will have to wait until later this afternoon, however, because you have an appointment in about an hour. But for now…"

He turned, leaving her kneeling on the floor, and left the room. She heard the jingling of his keys for a moment, and shivered again. How could she be so stupid! That was one of the first things you learned, you thank someone for disciplining you, you thank them for letting you please them, you thank them for pleasing you, damn it, you practically thank them for every kind of attention!

But she was so overwhelmingly distracted by the specter of the Marketplace, the looming reality of it, taking over her future and erasing her past. Although she tried to contain it, tears formed in her eyes.

Chris returned, and leaned over her from behind. She caught a glimpse of the object her held before he pulled her head back and forced the gag into her mouth. It wasn't huge, but it felt like it filled her, and the shame of it crashed through her with a powerful violence. He spoke as he buckled it on.

"Since you haven't learned to be polite, I don't see any reason why you should speak at all for now. Perhaps this will remind you that speech is a privilege, not a right." His voice was slightly angry, enough to add another needle of fear to her emotional state. When he raised her up and turned her to face him, he seemed content with the tears which had trailed down her cheeks, but showed no sign of pity or compassion. Instead, he told her to wash his coffee cups and the pot and last night's dishes, and clean the kitchen.

Later on, when the doorbell chimed, he went to answer it. Robin was now standing in one corner of the living room, her hands behind her back, still gagged, posed with her back and shoulders straight, her head bowed. She had been there just long enough to feel a little cramped. She tensed and felt another shudder of shame and fear run through her.

"Chris, good to see you!" It was another man's voice. "Got yourself another project, hmm?"

"It keeps me out of the bars," Chris' voice sounded lighter. "I'm glad you could come on such short notice."

"How pretty!" The new voice belonged to an older man, only a little taller then Chris, but well into his fifties. His hair was a thick, wavy white and silver, and he was wearing an exquisitely tailored business suit; Robin could spot old money a mile away. She tried to keep her eyes cast down, but her curiosity fought her every inch of the way.

"But misbehaving already? What a shame, what a shame!" He looked her over with frank but friendly appraisal, and snapped his fingers, and a third person entered the room.

Robin felt a moment of dizziness. Her eyesight almost seemed to waver, as though someone had smacked her hard. Because the woman who joined this man entered with an *aura*. And there was not a shred of doubt in Robin's mind that this woman was a slave, that she was utterly owned, meant to be that way, and that she carried with her a sense of intense joy that permeated her being.

It was as though this new woman were alive, and Robin a shade. Robin moaned behind the gag, more ashamed then she had ever been in her entire life. This wasn't simple embarrassment here; it wasn't going to make her blush. This was true shame, the sense of worthlessness felt only in the presence of awe, and the power of it was overwhelming.

Without thinking, Robin sank to her knees and bowed her head. It was so hard to think, she couldn't really determine if she were bowing to the slave or to the implied power of the man who owned her. At this point, it barely made a difference.

"Oh, that was nice," the new man said, walking into the room and examining her.

"And entirely unnecessary," Chris added dryly. "Not that I blame her. She's had a trying morning. Would you like something to drink?"

"Oh, some coffee would be lovely, lad, with a small dollop of something single malt. And some for Greta, if you don't mind. We'll conduct the exam in here then? The light is perfect."

"Make yourself at home, Doctor."

Doctor? Robin's curiosity easily defeated the shock, and she was surprised when she realized what position she was in. She peeked up out of the corner of her eye to see the older man smiling down at her.

"Yes, yes, that's right," he said easily, bending down. "You can come up for a while. Let's have this off, shall we? Greta?"

The woman crossed into Robin's sight, and put down two cases she was carrying, a slender portfolio style briefcase and a Gladstone bag. Then, she came over to undo the gag, and Robin got a real look at her.

Greta looked to be in her mid to late forties. She had short, wavy blonde hair, streaked with silver colored highlights and cut in a rather severe, mature style. Her face was a little long, with arched cheekbones and a pointy chin. Gold hoops hung from her earlobes, dancing in the light. Her ice blue eyes were deep set and kindly, noticing everything. When she reached her arms around Robin's head, Robin could smell something light and floral, a perfect scent for such a woman. Under the collar of the burgundy silk blouse she wore, the herringbone edges of a heavy gold chain flashed.

The gag slipped out of Robin's mouth, dripping with spit. Robin flushed and shut her eyes, working her jaw to shut and open again. "I'm sorry, ma'am," she managed to whisper.

"That's all right," Greta responded, depositing the gag onto the coffee table. Her voice was carefully controlled, like that of an actress or someone whose native language had not been English.

"Yes, it's impossible to wear one of those things without getting a good helping of saliva down your chest, isn't it?" The doctor sat down in one of the chairs as Greta opened the briefcase and presented him with a file folder and a gold pen. It was so seamlessly done that Robin felt even worse. Was she expected to compete with people like this? To be so graceful and so perfectly attuned to someone that you can slide something into their hands the minute before they started to move toward it?

I'm a clog dancer at the ballet, she thought, the ludicrous image establishing itself in her mind.

"Now for introductions. I am Doctor Emil Kaufmann, and this is my slave, Doctor Greta Mueller. And you are?"

Slave-Doctor? Robin nearly lost herself again, but struggled and held on, and coughed to clear her throat.

"I...my name is Robin, sir," she said, not knowing whether to give him her full name. It suddenly seemed so odd to be totally naked in a room of clothed people who didn't seem to pay any attention to that fact at all.

"Excellent, excellent. We are here to examine you, my dear, to establish that you are in good emotional and physical health, and to create your medical file for the Marketplace records. As with all your files, the contents will be considered confidential, although they will be released to your owner when you are purchased. Do you understand, and give your consent to be examined?"

"Yes, sir."

"Wonderful! Then we shall begin." He opened the file, and Greta opened the Gladstone bag, and they started the most comprehensive examination Robin had ever heard about, let alone experienced, in her entire life.

Chris went back and forth, serving coffee with a style and ease that Robin knew came from long acquaintance with such tasks. And Dr. Mueller...Greta...worked with a cool efficiency and a wonderfully assuring bedside manner, testing reflexes, taking up instruments to peer into Robin's eyes, ears, nose and throat. She listened to the heart and lungs, probed Robin's body with expert fingers, took hair and saliva and blood samples. At one point, she conducted a simple gynecological examination, with a level of gentleness and care that Robin had never experienced in a table fitted with stirrups, and the irony of this didn't escape her.

"No evidence of past trauma to the area, developed and healthy external organs, patient is shaven," Greta said when she finished. "A lovely cunt. You are erotically functional, yes? You experience clitoral orgasms? Multiple? G-spot?"

"Yes, ma'am," Robin admitted, almost bashfully. "All of them."

"How fortunate," the woman said back, flashing a bright smile. "Mr. Parker, would you like her pierced?"

Robin froze.

Chris looked as though he was considering it. Then, the corner of his mouth turned up and he said, "No, Greta, it's too much in vogue. If her owner wants her pierced, then they can outlay the money for the gold. Leave her with the holes she already has."

Robin nearly fainted with relief, and Greta gave a short, light laugh and continued her examination. You bastard, Robin thought, closing her eyes. She opened them again as Greta began to ask more questions.

She probed Robin's medical history for almost an hour, finding out about childhood injuries and diseases, and adulthood experiences. As she asked,

48

Emil kept that beautiful golden pen flashing, taking notes, marking off boxes on lengthy lists, and interjecting questions from time to time.

Robin was asked about everything from vaccinations to allergies, from venereal diseases to whether she performed regular breast examinations, and if she knew how. She was asked for the prescription for her reading glasses, and the names of her doctors. Greta even asked her about her family medical history; heart problems, high blood pressure, cancer? Did she exercise regularly, and what did she do?

At their request, Chris brought out a step aerobics block and Greta instructed Robin in doing a series of movements stepping on and off it in cadence. Her heart rate was measured before and after, and her recovery time was noted.

And then, as lunchtime approached, they took a break. Leon came by again, this time with vegetable soup and chicken salad sandwiches. Robin, still being punished, ended up sitting on the floor in the corner while Leon served up the food and some light, bantering chatter.

Robin was not allowed to speak, except in answer to a direct question.

It was as thoroughly agonizing as any beating she had ever taken. She watched them out of the corner of her eye, watched as Greta took a seat at the table with the two men and spoke and laughed at perfect ease. Was she being treated the way Chris talked about this morning? Like a member of the family? Were there no consistent rules regarding how slaves were treated? Emil reached out and touched Leon intimately once, cupping the young man's ass cheek in one hand and making a joke about its supposed tenderness, and Leon seemed neither surprised nor upset. In fact, he sighed just a little and moved away with a slight show of reluctance. Was he being teasing?

So many questions! And she was ordered into silence!

But after lunch, she was given the opportunity to talk as much as she liked.

After lunch, Dr. Emil sat her on the floor and began to ask her questions about her life. And not in the abstract, as Chris wanted to hear about her, but specific questions. When was she first aware of sexual feelings? How were her relationships with her parents? Had she ever been arrested, and for what? What did the word friendship mean to her? How often did she masturbate, and how? Who did she think was the best president in her lifetime? What percentage of her life would she say she was happy? What were her favorite books? If she had a penis, what would it look like?

And the questions came at her seemingly at random, never staying long on one topic. Emil did allow her to think for a moment before answering, but encouraged her to speak off the top of her head whenever possible. Now, it was Greta who was taking the notes.

They only finished with her in the late afternoon. She hardly realized that it was over, until Greta began to gather papers and instruments and put them away, and Chris came back into the room with what looked like sherry in two small glasses. Emil took one and nodded before Chris offered the other to Greta.

I might never have noticed that, Robin marveled. It's all so natural for them.

"Would you like to stay for a while longer?" Chris asked, giving the tray to Robin and pointing at the kitchen. She rose, her knees more then a little stiff. "Robin is at your service, of course."

"Thank you, Chris, your hospitality is as generous as your employers'. But I'm afraid that we have another engagement tonight, and cannot see to your charming new acquisition." Emil sounded jovial. He sipped his sherry with a murmur of approval, and laughed at the Robin's retreating body. "You know, I can see that you have a shy one in your hands. So delightful! So enticing! She must be exhibited, and as soon as possible. Can you not see her, mounted in some well-lit corner, her thighs spread, her body opened and unprotected, inviting glance and touch?"

Robin returned to the room, her face flushed, her body shaking, despite all efforts to keep it under control.

Chris didn't even look at her, but pointed to the corner she had been sent to before Emil and Greta arrived. From there, she watched as Chris chatted amiably with Emil. Shortly thereafter, the two doctors took their leave, without a single word directed to her. Chris saw them out, holding their coats for them, closing the door behind them.

The gag sat on the table where Greta had left it.

But Chris walked past it, and without warning, brought his fingers up between Robin's legs, and opened her. She was wet, a steamy, heated wetness which parted for him, invited him. She moaned, suddenly, and the sound seemed to shatter the silence of the room.

Chris smiled, and brought his fingers up to her lips. She didn't need a command to lick them clean, tasting her tangy moisture.

"Go and drink some water," Chris said, retreating to a chair. "And bring the strap back with you."

He posed her with her hands braced on her knees, her head down, and used the strap on her in sets of ten strokes. For each ten, he had another reason; pausing too long before responding to a question, looking sulky, delaying before obeying a direct order, sneaking glances at the doctors when she should have kept her head down.

Tears came soon; the day had been long and confusing, and she had no idea that she had been watched for these seemingly petty errors in behavior.

But Chris ignored the tears and the sobs which soon followed, and continued going through his mental list and his almost mechanical beating.

When the force of one blow sent her stumbling forward, Chris came in close, and clenched the hair at the back of her neck in one fist, holding her pressed down and forward.

The blows were steady, of an even force and crack, but as they built up redness and then bruising, they landed again and again on sore spots and over past stripes, and Robin's sobs were interrupted with gasps of pain and shock. Each time a blow landed, heat rushed up to the skin and then burned intensely until the next one came. Before too long, Robin's mind was completely taken over by a desperate bargain: only these few more! I can take just three more! And then I'll beg for mercy, just two more, or three!

And each time, she found some inner strength to keep holding on, even though she was dizzy from the position, stiff from being on her knees most of the day, even sore from her beating that morning. And through it all, still agonizingly wet, still as hot as she had been a few minutes ago.

"And that is all for now," Chris said, letting her go. The strap hit the table.

Robin hit the floor at once and sought out his boot-tops. She kissed one and then the other as gracefully as she could manage. "Thank you, sir, thank you!"

"Good girl. You remembered." She could feel the sting of his tone, which only drove her back down to press her lips against the polished leather again. When he made no move away and failed to raise her, she continued her adoring thanks, covering the boots with her kisses, and feeling the intense heat that spread over her ass and the backs of her thighs.

And then the doorbell chimed again.

"Get that," Chris said, nudging her.

Robin pulled herself up, and wiped at the tears and the slight sheen of sweat on her face and stumbled slightly on her way out of the room. She was still dizzy. What a state to answer the door in! But it had to be Leon, with dinner, although it seemed a little early. She ran her fingers through her hair, pulling it back a little and wiped at her eyes again, and opened the door.

It wasn't Leon.

Standing in front of her was a woman, taller than she was, with thick, long, curling hair, and beautifully arched eyebrows. She had fine, prominent cheekbones, and dark, glittering eyes, and her cheeks were flushed with wind. She was wearing a rich, long woolen coat, and beautiful high heeled boots, and carrying what looked like a leather architects' blueprint case slung over one shoulder and a garment bag hanging from her outstretched hand.

"You'd better take it if you don't want *another* pitiless beating," she said. "I'm Rachel."

"I don't believe that you're giving up your vacation for a mere woman," Rachel said, once she had been properly welcomed and settled into a chair, a cup of tea at hand. Robin, after putting things away and taking her coat and making the tea, had been positioned on her elbows and knees on the coffee table, so that Rachel could see the evidence of Chris' discipline.

"I have no prejudices," Chris answered. He was going through a stack of papers and envelopes Rachel had handed to him, placing them in different piles.

"Humph," Rachel made the sound as though it were a declaration in itself. "She doesn't look like much."

Robin's ears turned bright red. Why was it always so much more affecting when women criticized her? Why did it matter so much more?

"I will show you her folder later, if you like. She would not be refused at our house."

"Yes, well we take everything!" Rachel laughed. "And, we spend more time with them. What do you have, two weeks?"

"Exactly."

"Impossible!"

"We shall see."

There didn't seem to be any annoyance from Chris at Rachel's skepticism. In fact, he was remarkably calm. I wish he would be more angry, Robin thought, furiously. He chose to do this! He knows it can work out!

"Well, thank you for bringing these," Chris said after a long silence. "You could have sent it all by some messenger, you know."

"No, I wanted to see this paragon of yours, maybe try her out. And I've been wanting to spend a night out of the house for a while, too. Besides, there was some bad news, too; I figured I'd better bring it myself." She reached into a pocket and withdrew a fat envelope addressed in an ornate hand. "I spoke to the bosses today. They said that you should go." She passed it over to him, and on her way back, trailed her fingernails along the insides of Robin's thighs. "Such lovely bruises. I don't think she'll want to sit down for days." Robin shivered, and Rachel smiled.

Chris took the contents out of the envelope and sighed heavily.

"Yes, I know," Rachel said soothingly. "But it's only one night. And it's close by. I brought your winter tux."

"Wouldn't you care to attend?"

"I might, sure. But they said that *you* should. I even told them that you, well, that you found a new project. But Alex said that this should teach you to take your vacations like everyone else does."

Robin stiffened in confusion, despite the scratching pleasure of Rachel's stroking fingernails. Every new sentence seemed to raise new questions, and her curiosity seemed ready to strangle her.

"Then I shall handle it," Chris finally responded. He put the envelope on the side, with the others. "But now, you're here. And, I do have a new toy, at least for a while. Of course you are welcome to stay the night, and to make use of her. However, according to my schedule, this little chit should be giving me some more of her personal history, and Leon will be arriving within an hour or so with dinner. So I suggest that you sit back and enjoy your tea while she continues her tale, and then we can have a civilized dinner together."

"Leon! Oh, I haven't seen that boy in ages! Well, maybe I was too harsh in judging your vacations." Her laugh was low and slightly sultry. "OK, boss, it's in your hands." She pulled her own hands away from Robin, who moaned in their absence.

"Get up, Robin," Chris directed. "You may sit there while you speak." He pointed to a spot on the carpet. And when Robin was in position, Chris prompted her.

"You were in college. You had not yet managed to find a partner with whom to practice or even discuss your sensual desires, but had accumulated a collection of sadomasochistic literature and a few toys to use when masturbating."

"How sweet!" Rachel mocked.

"You may continue from there," Chris ordered.

"Yes, sir," Robin whispered back. The wetness between her legs was maddening. How often had she dreamed something just like this, submitting to a strong man and a strong women at the same time? How many times had she pulled out her box of toys to exactly that image?

Her box of toys…

53

Chapter Five
Robin's Story: The Soloist

I have become a connoisseur of coming, she wrote one night, after an enormously good session of solo sex. *I am a master masturbator. And good thing, too. Because that's going to be the sum total of my sex life forever and ever.*

Months later, dating seemed as hopeless a past-time as it was during the night she gave her unmourned virginity to the unaware Greg. There had been two more boyfriends since then, one she gave blowjobs too, then another one she never let get past making out. Neither one seemed to have a clue about what she was really into, and she never managed to be as direct as she now knew she would have to be in order to get through to them.

Even Marty, the guy who taught her how to suck cock, (if you could call his insistently pushing her head toward it any form of teaching) seemed utterly unaware of the slightest possibility that she might like something a little more then "Oh, baby, you're the best!" in the way of encouragement. And he was so passive, just lying or sitting back and not even touching her, except to stroke her hair absently once in a while.

She had tried a little harder with him, maybe because he was an English major and she figured that words might have more of a trigger effect for him.

"I love being your personal cocksucker," she had whispered to him one night.

"Oh, I hate that word," he responded, looking vaguely shocked. "It's so dirty. I mean, you say cocksucker, and I think *faggot.* You're my lover, baby, my sweet lover."

And I thought that sucking cock would make me gag, she recorded in her journal that night.

She wandered into the lesbian and gay student association on campus, but found herself not quite fitting in there either. For one, the president of the association also played on the basketball team, and he knew that she had dated Greg. That branded her as a bisexual, and she was immediately viewed with suspicion. And although she was willing to get involved in on campus feminist activities, one day she found herself at a meeting planning a protest in front of the bookstore for selling Penthouse and Playboy.

She thought guiltily about her stash of porn under her bed, and didn't return to the next meeting. Hell, if these women didn't like Playboy, which had the lamest, softest smut she had even seen, they would just heave at the sight of one of her newspapers.

But one thing that she did get from the association was a list of gay publishers and bookstores. She wrote away for more catalogs, and discovered the world of gay and lesbian SM. She loved it all, even the male/male stuff, and bought as much as she could afford. The box under her bed filled, and she started throwing out things that didn't work for her any more. And she was very, very careful about when and where she tossed her rejects.

So she turned her attention sharply onto school, taking extra classes when she could. She started running again, to work off any excess energy, and pretended to be going out on dates so Donna wouldn't try to set her up with someone. And she jerked off, whenever she could, getting better and better all the time.

It was a Saturday night in late winter, and Robin had such a session in mind as she returned to her dorm after working on a special cataloging project she had volunteered for. It was guaranteed to get her into a special class with the professor who headed up the arts department, and it was giving her the skills she would need when she left. It wasn't enough to be able to appreciate art in order to work with it. You either had to be an artist, a critic, or a business person. And business seemed the way to go.

But the work was hard and tedious, and crammed into an already crowded schedule, so she needed the release of orgasm more than she seemed to before. Luckily, Donna was home for the weekend, not due back until Sunday night. There would be plenty of privacy for a deluxe session. Maybe she would come twice, or three times. She had two new newspapers to read through, that she had been saving for a night just like this.

So within minutes of getting in, she was stripped, collared, and lying on the floor, the short, rough carpet abrading her nipples. With sighs of pleasure, she read through the letter columns, full of patently false personal adventure stories, and then continued on to the features, some of which were illustrated. They were, without an exception, awfully written. She could usually ignore much of the clumsy, ham-handedness of the writers. But for some reason, tonight of all nights, the stark vacancy of the words made the images behind them ludicrous. Robin flipped pages in frustration, trying to get the proper frame of mind back, and ended up tossing the cheap newsprint onto the floor in front of her.

I'll just switch to the books, she thought, feeling the pang of more money wasted on this trash. But as she reached for the box, her eye fell on an advertisement on the back page of one of the newspapers.

It read:

"Find the mistress or master of your dreams tonight!"

She pulled it back over and read. Under a drawing of a physically impossible woman wearing boots that could earn a mention in the Amnesty International annual, was a series of phone numbers. Some were in different area codes, some were 800 numbers. In fine print below each one was a description. She read, "Hot Masters and their Rough Boys for Wild Masculine Encounters," and "Large and Lovely Ladies for Mounds of Pleasure!," and "Threesomes, Foursomes and Moresomes; the Swingers Line," and then, finally, "The Dial-In-Dungeon, Masters, Mistresses and their Willing Slaves."

All this, the add promised, for 10¢ a minute.

Ten cents a minute? Robin thought. That's not much. If it's just a stupid recording, it'll still cost less then calling home to say "hi." She dug her toes into the carpet while she considered. What could it possibly be? What would she say if someone actually answered? Could they trace her number?

Oh, don't be stupid. It can't hurt, not for a few minutes. No sense in getting paranoid over this. So she reached over to her table and pulled the phone down on to the floor. When her call connected, she heard:

"*Welcome* to the Dial in Dungeon, where your *hot* Mistress or Master awaits. Your call will be 30¢ for the first minute and 10¢ each additional minute. If you are under eighteen years old, hang up *now*. And if you're old enough and *bold* enough, you may *now* enter the Dungeon!"

What is this, a computer game? Robin asked herself. I wonder when I have to tell them whether I want a master or a mistress? But before she could actually giggle, she heard someone speaking.

"...so we ended up going to the movies while she had a plug up her ass. I kept pinching her nipples all through the show. Thea was wet as a fucking river! Weren't you, babe?"

The voice was masculine, but slightly muffled. Robin pushed the phone closer to her ear, fascinated.

"Yeah!" Came an enthusiastic response. Thea's voice also sounded slightly muffled. Robin figured that it must be the connection. "I was so sore when we got back! Master had to soothe me all night." She laughed, and her laughter was joined by several other people on the telephone line.

"So what did you do this weekend, Cutiepie?" Another man's voice cut through the laughter. For a split second, Robin thought that he meant her, although how he would even know that she was there was a mystery. But a different woman, her voice making her seem older then the first, sighed and answered.

"I stayed home, Roy. And did the fucking dishes. I tell you, life's a bitch when a slave can't get a good master."

"Awww, poor baby. You can come over and I'll be your master."

"Yeah, right. Roy, you're a fucking slave, honey, and you just wanna get laid."

"Well, a man's gotta try, right?" More laughter sounded out.

"All you guys gotta try. I swear, one night you're all masters, but let one mistress get on the line and you're all foot slaves. I need a real man," Cutiepie whined. "Someone who's really the boss. Like Mark."

"Thank you, Cutie," responded the man whose voice had welcomed Robin to the line. "But I have my hands full."

"Anything more then a handful is wasted, buddy!" someone added.

Robin sighed, heavily. That line was tired among the freshmen. God help any adult who thought it was witty. And this was where she was going to find a master or mistress? Not bloody likely. She was going to hang up when she heard yet another voice.

"Hello! Any submissive sluts out there who need some phone domination?"

"Hi Bob," chorused a few of the voices on the phone. Robin drew her knees up to listen for a little while longer. What on earth was phone domination?

"Hi, Master Bob," purred Cutiepie. "When am I gonna get to meet you?"

"Anytime you want, Cutie. On the phone. Care for another session with my toy bag? Call me right now, and you'll get it all." His voice was very deep, and compared to the others on the line, much more assured.

"Oh, you tease. You know I'm on the courtesy line. Lemme call you later."

"No. Now. I want to see how much you'll give up for me."

"And what will you do it I get off...the phone I mean!" Giggles and muffled laughter flooded the line. "Will you do all the things I like?"

"I'll do whatever I want, Cutie. Take it or leave it."

"Whoa!" came several exclamations. "Such a tough guy," someone muttered.

"Well, be that way. There's no one else out here except for me and Thea anyway, so you wasted your call!" Cutiepie did actually sound miffed.

Robin swallowed hard and said, "I...I'm here."

"Hey!" "Who was that?" "Is that a new girl?"

Voices crowded each other, and Robin almost slammed the phone down. But she held onto it, hoping that Bob hadn't left.

"Who's out there? Is that you, Destiny? Or is it Lola?"

All the women seemed to have made-up names, Robin thought. Quick! What do I call myself?

"Um. This is…" Her mind shut down on her. What could she say? Oh God, what a time to freeze, isn't it just like her, the pervert who couldn't say her name! Then she drew a deep breath and said, "I'm Perverse."

That got a hearty laugh. "So are we all, honey, so are we all!"

"Hey, Perverse! Waddaya look like?"

"Waddaya into?"

"Are you dominant or submissive?"

"What are you wearing?"

The questions were fired off in rapid succession, all of the inquisitors male. Robin bit her lip, trying to figure out what to say, when Cutiepie's voice cut through the noise.

"Hey, cool it, fellas, cool it! You'll scare her away with all your fucking questions! Perverse, you still out there?"

"Yes."

"Well, speak up, honey, we all wanna hear ya. What's your story?"

Robin panicked again. "I…I don't know what to say."

"For starters, are you dominant or submissive?"

"Submissive."

"Oh good!" Some male voice said. "Wanna call me?"

"Um, I don't know," Robin replied. "Why should I want to?"

"Oh! You're a virgin!" Cutiepie laughed, and Robin flushed. "Tell the truth, Perverse, you never called this line before."

"This is my first call," Robin admitted.

"Well, welcome to the line, sweetie. And don't sweat the little boys; they'll back off after a while. What are you looking for?"

"I don't know." Robin barely got the words out. How can I answer that? she thought furiously. I'm not ready for this. I shouldn't have called.

"Why don't you give me a call?" It was Bob. "I won't bite. But I can explain how this all works."

"I don't know," Robin repeated helplessly.

"Oh, give him a call, Perverse, he's OK. And you never have to worry about meeting him!" Cutiepie declared. There was a tone in her voice that sounded slightly derisive.

Bob gave out a telephone number, but Robin was sitting naked, in the middle of her floor, with nothing around her but newspapers and books. She sprang forward, reaching for her desk. "Wait a minute! Wait!"

Bob repeated the number for her, and the other people online all yelled out various good-byes before she hung up.

That, she thought, staring at the piece of paper in her hand, was weird. What did these people do on this toll call? Chat about what they did on the weekend? And how was it that they all seemed to know each other? Why did the men have real names and the women have phony ones?

She called the number, her heart pounding.

"Hello?" His voice was the same as it had been on the line, but much clearer. Deep, but friendly.

"Um. Bob?"

"That's right. Hi, Perverse. Do you know what you've gotten into?"

Robin laughed suddenly. "No! That's why I called you."

"Well, before we start, just get comfortable and relax. No one's going to hurt you. Are you OK?"

Robin pulled her pillows down and did as he suggested. "Go ahead," she said when she was comfortable. "I'm OK."

"Good. Are you into dominance and submission?"

"No. Yes. I mean, I think so." Robin found herself flushing again. "God, you know I'm usually not so moronic."

He laughed companionably. "Relax! Let me rephrase it. What do you like to think about when you come? You do masturbate, don't you?"

"Boy, you just come right out with the personal questions!" Robin laughed again. "Whatever happened to 'So, what are you doing tonight?'"

"I'm hoping that you'll masturbate," Bob easily answered. "That's one of the benefits of paying six dollars an hour to talk to a couple of fellow S&M devotees. You may find a few who like the same things that you do and would like to share their fantasies with you until you want to explode from pleasure. You might even meet people if you want to, and maybe hit it off in person." He paused. "So to speak."

Robin snorted in amusement. Bob was turning out to be a good bet. "How do you do this?" she asked. "Phone domination, I mean. Can I stop it if I don't like it?"

"Of course, silly. You can always hang up."

Duh. Robin sighed. "OK, never mind me. Please go on."

"There's nothing much more to say. Except that you shouldn't use your real name on the line, or ever, ever, give out your phone number. And you shouldn't agree to meet with anyone who no one knows. If someone wants to meet you very badly, try and find out if they've met with anyone else on the line, and ask if they're safe. You can always call me, any time, to ask about someone. I've been on this line for a long time."

"Yes, but how do I know if I can trust you?"

"Good! Now the brain is on. You ask the other women out there, like Cutiepie. She knows me."

"But she said she never met you."

"That's true. I don't meet people at all. But I do talk to them a lot, and I hear what everyone says about everyone else. Enough about me. Are you naked?"

Robin jerked up a little. "Um. Yes."

"Good. I like my submissives naked. And you are going to be my little submissive tonight, aren't you?"

Robin froze for a moment. Ohmigod, she thought, clutching the phone. Ohmigod, this could be so good. But this is so silly! On the phone? How can I do this on the phone?

"Come on, my little slavegirl. Tell your master how much you need to be a good girl for him."

"Yes," Robin whispered, sliding back down onto her pillows. "Yes."

"Say 'Yes, master,' sweetie."

Robin sighed. "Yes, master."

"That's a good girl. Now, tell me what little toys you play with when you're naughty all by yourself. Do you have any dildos? A vibrator?"

"Yes." Robin blushed deep red, but felt a complimentary warmth reaching up from her loins.

"Yes, what?" Bob snapped, his voice suddenly harsh.

"Oh! Yes, master."

"There's a penalty for being so slow, slave. You have to learn to respect me. So I'm just going to have to take you over my knee and spank your ass very hard. So think of your body bent over my knee, slave, your cunt right up against my leg, and your tits hanging down. Can you see it? Can you feel it?"

His voice was deep, and soothing, but hurried. It hit her in a hypnotic rhythm, and she moaned unexpectedly.

"Yes," she whispered. "Yes, master!"

"I'd take one arm tightly in my hand and pull it up behind your back so you can't move, slave. And then, I'd stroke that pretty ass of yours, and get you ready for your spanking. Have you ever been spanked, slave? Spanked by a master?"

"No," she moaned, closing her eyes.

"That should have been 'No, master,' slave. I was going to give you ten smacks. Now, it'll be twenty. And they'll be hard ones. They'll be so hard that you'll be tender there, and you won't be able to sit. Are you going to be a good girl and take them for me?"

"Yes, yes, master!" Robin rolled over on to her stomach and pushed her ass up into the air. With her eyes closed, she could almost imagine the feeling of being over someone's knee.

"Then here they come, slave. Feel them!" And suddenly, there was a loud, sharp slapping sound coming through the phone. Robin jerked in surprise, and then realized that Bob was clapping, or slapping something down. But when she closed her eyes again and rocked her hips with each striking sound, she began to draw her breaths faster.

"Count them, slave!"

"Oh! One! Two!"

"That should have been 'One, master.' We start again!"

The slapping sounds continued, and Robin allowed her body to react to each one as though it had actually fallen on her. She counted desperately, moaning between each count, clenching her thighs together and pressing them apart. By the time they got through the first ten, she was already in a state of intense excitement. Her nipples were hard, like little stones, and there was a steady dampness between her legs that almost frightened her. She had never gotten so hot so fast.

"Do you remember what this is for, slave?"

"For not calling you master, master!" she choked out, pressing her body into the pillows. Another slap. "Oh! Twelve, master!"

"So what do you say, slave?"

"Uh! I...I don't know, master!" Slap! "Thirteen, master!"

"Yes you do, slave. And if you don't say it by the time we finish the twenty, I'm just going to keep going until you do." Slap!

Robin gasped, and hurriedly counted, but her mind wasn't ready to start working on what else she could be saying. She moaned and squirmed, and counted, never forgetting the 'master,' until the number twenty was reached, and Bob paused.

"Have you figured out what to say, slave?"

"No, please, I don't know, master!" She was surprised to find that part of her was absolutely getting into this absurd game! She was actually concerned that she didn't know! The tension grew within her and it was an incredibly powerful catalyst. She wanted to reach down and touch her cunt lips, squeeze her whole hand around her pussy, but she didn't, held captive by the commands of the 'master' talking her through this amazing experience.

"Maybe you'll figure it out before my arm gets tired, little slave. I hope you do, because when I get tired, I'm switching to something much nastier. You can stop me anytime, my dear. All you need are the magic words!" Smack!

That one was loud, harsh against her ear. Robin moaned involuntarily and pressed her thighs together. The smacks continued at a new pace, not bothering to wait for her to count, and she began to grind her hips into the floor, truly feeling...something. She panted, and almost dropped the phone, but held onto it and tried to think. Wait! Magic words!

"Thank you! Thank you, master!"

"You're welcome, sweetie." The spanks stopped. "Now what are you thanking me for?"

"For correcting me, master!"

"See? That was easy. You're good at this, slave. A natural." His voice became soothing again. "And now, I get to have a little fun with my new submissive. I get to play with her body for as long as I want. So stretch out on your back, and spread your legs."

Robin followed his voice and the commands which came to her. She touched herself, her breasts and belly. At his commands, she stroked her throat and thighs, pinched her nipples until she whimpered, drew wide circles of scratches across her skin. This stranger was directing her to do things she did when she jerked off, but they were in his order, according to his tastes. As her moans and sighs built up, he chuckled and addressed her in gentler tones. Soon, she could feel that the wetness between her legs had become raging, creating a sense of overwhelming weakness and tension.

"Now I'm going to bring you off, slave. For my amusement. I like to see beautiful slavegirls squirming under my touch, begging to come for their master. Can you feel my hand on you? My fingers finding your clit, sliding along it, back and forth, until you can't take it any more? And I'm going to push my fingers inside you, slave, two, and then three fingers, pushing you wide open for me. Do it, do it…"

Robin let her fingers stand in for his, and closed her eyes.

"And you're not going to come until I tell you that you may, you little slut. You're going to lie there and take it all, until you can't stand it any more, and you have to beg me to bring you off, beg to come all over my hand, to jerk your body around and cry out and drip your sweet juices all over your legs." Bob's voice picked up tempo again, and Robin matched him with the motions of her hand. She found the places she liked best and the pressure that worked, and her fingers swept around her clit until her body did in fact begin to shake and tremble.

"Now, slave, now, I want you to feel me pushing my cock inside you, while my hand works on your stiff little clit, I want your whole cunt wide open, naked for me, as I fill you up and make you whimper and beg…you want it, don't you?"

"Yes," Robin whispered, pushing her hips up a little. "Oh yes!"

"Beg me! Tell me that you want to be fucked!"

"Yes! Fuck me, master! Fill me!" Robin pushed up again and again, pressing against her hand. She was breathing raggedly, and sweat gathered in the hollow of her back.

"That's good! Good! Because you need this, don't you, slave?"

"Yes! Please! Please fuck me! Make me come, master, please, please…Oh, I can't hold it, please!"

"Then come, slave, come for your master, wrap your cunt around his dick! Come on, I want to feel you!"

Robin gasped, and her whole body straightened out and shook for that final moment before ecstasy. Then, her fingers slipped to that perfect place, and her hips jerked convulsively, and she felt a new urge of wetness accompany the series of wonderful, shuddering waves of pleasure coming from her loins. Her moans became inarticulate groans and gasps, and she whimpered, "Oh, master, master, master!," riding each exclamation with another sob of joy.

When she lay back, her breath slowly returning in long, shuddering inhalations, she realized that she had dropped the phone. She picked it up gingerly, and held it to her ear. Her heart was pounding.

"H-hello?" she whispered.

"You have to figure out a way to come when you're holding a phone," Bob said. His voice sounded normal again, his manner relaxed. "Did you really come?"

"Yes!" Robin giggled, and then took a deep breath. She hadn't recovered yet! She tried to control her breathing a little more, and then realized what he had asked. How curious, she thought. "Why would I fake it?"

"Don't ask me, sweetie. Some do. Probably to end the call that much sooner. But you did great! And now you know what phone domination is. Or at least, my style."

"It was hot," Robin admitted. She pulled herself up, and leaned against the side of her bed. Why on earth would someone want to end the call even faster? "I liked it a lot."

"Well, you can call me any night after eight at this number. If it's busy, I'm probably with another one of my little slaves. But you could try looking for me out on the line."

"Oh, I don't know if I could afford that. All those minutes could add up real fast."

"Call the courtesy number, my dear. Women who call and talk to those poor, frustrated men out there don't have to pay. It's part of the economics of SM; hell, it's the politics of sexuality in general, according to Betty Dodson. Women, whether they're mistresses or slaves, are at a premium. Men, also regardless of role, are deeply discounted. You get in cheaper at the SM clubs too." He sighed, and sounded like he was stretching. "Yes, you have wandered into a whole new world, sweetie. Take it nice and slow. It's been known to swallow people up."

Robin nodded to herself. "I can believe that."

"The next time you call, ask for the operator. They'll give you the local number to call. And they know me, too. So if you're looking for me, you can ask the operator if I'm on, and she can put you on my channel. I've got to go now, sweetie. You were a good girl, for your first time."

"Good night," Robin said.

As the phone clicked, she laid it down, and threw her head back with a sigh. Her entire body was tingling. She pressed a hand to her chest to feel her heartbeat, and then weakly gathered up her materials, to hide them away.

That was fun, she thought, pulling a t-shirt on over her still stiff nipples. That was better than reading anything. And it's so convenient! Just call and pick someone up and do it! What a great invention it was!

But not what you'd call a real sex life. After all, it's just an extension of what I'm doing by myself. It's…masturbation by media.

Oh God. I am so pathetic.

I'll never actually do this stuff with a live person. But what else can I do? At least it's better then being totally alone. It's the best I can hope for, now.

Chapter Six

Leon arrived again, this time with a splendid paella, shrimp, clams, mussels and scallops over saffron rice. There was a light herbal broth with soft, hot bread to begin, and a spicy tomato salad on the side, and even a bottle of white Burgundy, compliments of his master. This time, Leon stayed to serve the meal, and Robin ate with him, standing in the kitchen, and watched when he served. She also listened carefully as he gave her instructions on how to hold her body, or turn her head, or respond to more then one request at a time.

"You try to place yourself so's you can keep an eye on the dinner," he said, scooping up some of his own creation and savoring it. "That way, you can see if the water glasses are gettin' low, or if a plate's gettin' too empty too fast. Some masters, they like you to stay by the table the whole time, in case they need anything."

"If I have to stay in the room for the whole meal, when do I eat?"

"Ain't their problem, sister. You catch it when you can. But don't worry; they can't really starve you. You just gotta be clever about it, an' find out what they have in mind. Friend of mine, he's with some folks that like to see him eatin' outa their hands at dinner, begging for food, but he always gets to eat as much as he wants when he's in the kitchen."

Robin shuddered. "Oh, I don't know if I could do that! Beg for food like a dog at the table?"

"Oh, you'll do it, sugar. If that's what your master wants, that is...OK, they're ready for more wine. Now, Mr. Parker ain't gonna want seconds. You watch me close!"

And Robin did. Sure enough, Chris raised one hand to indicate that he didn't want any more of the wine, but Rachel allowed Leon to serve her. And before he returned, she took a pinch of his shirt between her fingers and said something softly to him.

"Now here's another thing," he said when he got back to the kitchen. "You gotta get used to bein' dressed up and stripped down, over and over again."

With a grin, he shed his shirt and trousers and shoes and piled them neatly in one corner of the kitchen. His body was long and slender, but hard in places, his stomach tight and rippled. His cock was held suspended in a sheer black undergarment that looked like a jock strap, but left even less to the imagination. His body was shorn of all hair under his chin, and he had a very even tan. The golden necklace/collar seemed stark and powerfully attractive against his throat.

"You're very handsome," Robin whispered. He was. There was a beauty about him, a grace that defied ordinary language. He didn't have the same almost mystical aura that Greta possessed, but Robin could see that the two of them had much in common. They both attracted her, grabbed her attention aggressively and held it like a mirror holds the attention of a child.

"Why, thank you, honey. You're a sweet little beauty yourself. Now eat up…we're gonna have to get the coffee out soon!"

And when he returned, there were sounds of pleasure and appreciation, and Robin watched as he did his work around the table, stopping to pose when Rachel told him to, submitting to her lingering touches as he passed. Chris seemed to ignore Leon's state of undress.

He's made of stone, Robin thought, taking one more succulent scallop and washing it down with cold water. She hadn't been offered any wine, and despite wanting some very much, she didn't even try to ask.

There was no dessert, but Robin helped Leon serve the coffee, trying to follow his every move. It was an utter failure. What motions he made naturally seemed awkward to her body. She couldn't even keep her arms steady when carrying the tray, although she didn't make a clatter when she set it down. Even standing still seemed difficult; while Leon became a golden statue, her chest rose and fell with exaggerated power, her fingers clenched and relaxed, and she became itchy in places she really wasn't generally aware of.

When Leon was finally dismissed, amid laughter and fond teasing, Robin was left with the clean up, which she dispatched in an almost mindless fashion. It was getting hard to think now. There were more questions then ever, and fewer options that she really wanted to consider.

Was Chris serious when he offered her to Rachel? And who exactly was Rachel anyway? Did they work together? Who were the bosses? Ken Mandarin had said something about Chris working for someone else, Grendel Elliot? Was that the name? So who was Alex?

And all the things that Leon spoke about! It wasn't just how to set the

66

damn table and which wine to serve with which course, but dammit, it was how to smile, how to turn your body, how to be unobtrusive, yet utterly available. It was a million rules about asking questions, or answering them, carrying drinks or food and setting them down. It was information about where you knelt if that was what was required of you, and how to take food from someone's hand.

"The stories I could tell you!" Leon had said once, gulping water down to wash away his mouthful of food. "Why, between gettin' the house cleaned, gettin' the owner fed and keepin' body'n'soul together, why you'd think we never had time to have any fun!"

Fun. Was that what this was all about, Robin half wondered, even as she washed and rinsed. Was this fun? There's nothing fun about doing domestic chores, or working your tail off for what comes down to room and board and a cash salary that comes two years down the road.

But at the same time, there she was, buck naked at a kitchen sink, and dammit, she was still on the edge of arousal. Walking into the dining room and holding something for Leon really *was* as thrilling as a stroke from a caring lover. Thinking about the possibilities inherent in Chris' invitation to Rachel were both amazingly, powerfully erotic and stomach-clenchingly terrifying. She had once offered such a license to one who touched her submission deeply, but somehow it was different then. She had known her dominant lover, and known his friends. After her first full day with Chris, she didn't know him any better then she did last night.

And what was worse, there were no safety nets here, no friends waiting for her to call and make sure she was all right. There were no safe words, no negotiation beyond what was to go into her contract…if she got that far.

Her ass cheeks still glowed hot with pain, and each move reawakened it. How could she be any good to play with? Would they continue, despite these bruises? Would there be no time for her to surrender and receive mercy?

It was far better to allow all these questions and worries to collide with each other until they obscured thought altogether.

When she finished, she closed the cabinets and stacked the trays to return to Leon tomorrow, and felt rather then heard the presence of Chris in the room. She turned to him.

"All done, sir," she said lightly, her voice failing slightly when she looked at him. He was serious, a thoughtful dispassion that made frivolity unspeakable. He raised something in his hands, and she saw that it was a plain silver chain.

"Are you still determined to do this?" he asked.

"Yes, sir," Robin heard herself respond.

"Then receive your training collar." He stepped toward her and looped it around her throat and placed a small lock on it. The weight was almost negligible, but it was heavy enough to make its presence known. The lock lay about an inch below the hollow of her neck.

"Now, you have truly entrusted your body and your mind to my direction," Chris said. "I see no reason why my original expectation of your training should not be fulfilled. This is a symbol for you, so that you remember why you're doing this. But it's also a warning. If I take my key out to remove this lock upon your request, I will not ever return it. Do you understand?"

Robin understood completely. She nodded.

"Good. Then go to the playroom, Rachel is waiting for you." He stepped aside so that she could pass him, and it was only that move which impelled her forward.

The cabinets were unlocked. The sliding doors were drawn back, and the drapes closed, and the room lit by soft, indirect lighting. Rachel was sitting on the bed, her skirt tight against her hips. There was something in her hands that glittered silver, and new things scattered around the room, almost in disarray.

"Come here, kitten, and let's get to know you better."

Robin moved in cautiously. She was suddenly aware of how her body must appear to this strange woman. She hadn't showered since the morning. Since then, she'd been beaten twice, brought to sweat and tears. She had on no make up, no scents, and spending the entire meal in the kitchen with the steam and Leon's harried directions didn't help her hair one bit. Her hands were soft from washing dishes. And she had been close to coming too many times to speak of.

And Rachel noticed. She beckoned Robin to her, and ran her hands over the smaller woman's body, lifting her arms, tapping her legs apart, posing her. "Don't you know how to show yourself?" she spat angrily, after Robin fumbled her posture.

"Yes, ma'am," Robin answered, blushing again. "I'm sorry ma'am, I didn't realize that was what you wanted!"

"Then do it."

Robin took a deep breath and stepped slightly back to give herself the room. Showing oneself took precision, and a lack of things to bump into.

She stood straight, spreading her legs in a wide stance, and lacing her fingers behind her neck. This posture thrust her breasts out prettily, left her entire body open and inviting. At a nod from Rachel, Robin executed a neat turn, to display her back, and then bent over, placing her hands just above her knees.

"Mmmm. I like you like that. But finish it up."

Robin swallowed, half rose, turned back and knelt, her knees and thighs spread wide. She placed her hands behind her back and bowed her head, her hair spilling forward around her ears.

"Not bad, little kitten, not bad. Tell me, have you ever served a lady before?" Rachel took the silver thing in her hand and attached it to Robin's new collar. It was a leash, a very short one. She let it trail down between Robin's breasts, and Robin shivered at the touch of the cool metal.

"Yes, ma'am."

"Oh, good. I would hate to think that all your experience was jerking off to cheap porn and strange men." Rachel laughed and pulled something else off the bed next to her. "I think it's time you prepared yourself to be well used, dolly. And I want to watch you do it. Let's go."

Robin felt the tug of the leash and rose with it, keeping the pressure light but steady. It was a good move, a perfect response to being leashed, but Rachel seemed unimpressed. They went into the small bathroom, and Rachel unhooked the leash and leaned against the door jamb and pointed.

Robin showered, keeping her body turned toward Rachel as much as possible. She soaped herself up, blushing and wincing whenever she felt the soreness of her ass and upper thighs, and whenever Rachel snickered. And when Rachel handed her the object that she had brought from the bed, Robin bit her lip. There was a silver extension that attached to the water valve in the shower; Robin had originally thought it was one of those hand-held massage units. But it wasn't. The thing in her hand was a nozzle, long and shaped somewhat like a narrow cigar case, with holes stamped into the end. It screwed into the end of the silver coil.

"Do you know how to adjust it?" Rachel purred, moving forward for a better look. "I don't want you to hurt yourself. I'm saving all the hurt for me."

Robin almost dropped it in her nervousness. "I've never…I mean, I only…never with something like this, ma'am," she managed to choke out.

"Then I'll have to show you." Rachel attached the two parts with speedy efficiency, and showed Robin the safety valve which prevented the water pressure from building past a certain point. Robin's heart pounded in her ears; it seemed impossible that she was actually going to have to do this in front of someone else. No one had ever asked that of her before. Oh, certainly she had given herself cleansing douches and enemas, but never, never in front of another person.

"Cunt first," Rachel said with a cheerful smile, handing the nozzle over. "Shall I pass you some lubricant, or do you think you're wet enough?"

Robin did as she was told, no lubricant necessary. The slender tube rose up into her by her own hand, and she shivered at the cool invasion, and then at the slow jets of water inside her body.

"Turn! Let me see! Spread your legs, wider!" Rachel was leaning into the room, her voice hard despite her smile. And she laughed again as Robin did as she was told, and the water cascaded down her spread thighs. Robin moaned, the pressure and the sensations so nice, the shame so terrible! She wanted to lean that silver penetrator against her clit, rock it back and forth, pull it out and let the water batter away at that little scrap of flesh that was feeling so abandoned and so needy. But she kept it where it should be, and withdrew it when Rachel's voice commanded, and with a groan that almost ended in a sob, accepted some slippery wetness from Rachel to open up and penetrate her rear passage.

"Do you like to be fucked up the ass, dollface?" Rachel asked, keenly watching Robin push the nozzle in.

"Ahhh…" Robin clenched and unclenched her teeth, drew herself together and spoke through shudders. "Yes, ma'am. Yes, I do."

"Oh, that's good. That's very good. That's it, dolly, open up and let some of that water out…yes, pull it back, let it run in and then right out again, yes, that's it…now put it back and take some more…"

Every humiliating second seemed to last forever, down to the final washes that emptied her out and cleaned her up. When she stepped out, she collapsed into a little kneeling, soaking wet bundle at Rachel's feet, kissing them as though she had just been punished, and the echo of Rachel's delighted laughter stung her.

Dried off, she was leashed again, and brought back into the room. Rachel looked at her for a minute, and set herself in motion. Before long, Robin's wrists were cuffed together behind her back, and a posture collar was up high around her throat, forcing her shoulders back and her chin up.

"You need some decorations," Rachel murmured, pulling out something new and silvery. "You're much too plain by yourself."

Little clamps, wide mouthed with fat, heavy heads, were carefully placed on Robin's nipples. Robin couldn't look straight down, but by casting her eyes downward, she could see that they were cleverly made to press but not to pinch. Their pressure was constant, but not unbearable, and the chain that connected them glinted. But Rachel was not finished. She brought out two weights, shaped like tears, and attached them to the clamps. As the weights were added, the clamps tightened.

"I wasn't going to let you off that easy, little dolly," Rachel whispered. "Oh no."

She lifted a tangle of more silver so that Robin could see more clamps like the ones on her nipples. And then, Rachel sank gracefully down, and began to attach them in rows of three to each of Robin's labia.

Each pinch of flesh made Robin want to jump. Each gathering, each compression, and each addition of weight was like a lightning bolt through her pussy. The pain was exquisite, as only this kind of intimate pain could be. And Rachel's warm breath against her bare lips was a sweet agony in itself, one that made her whimper, even as she struggled to stand still and keep her legs spread.

"Much better," Rachel said, stepping back to admire her work. "I might even let you near me now."

"Yes, ma'am," Robin whispered, feeling the stiffness of the cuffs, the weights swinging softly against her thighs, against her breasts, a tiny trail of sweat working its way behind the collar. "Oh, yes, please, ma'am!"

"Eager dolly."

"Yes! Yes, ma'am!"

"You have to learn to be *patient*," Rachel stepped back and fingered the button at the collar of her blouse. "I'm surprised Chris hasn't already beaten that into you." Carefully, slowly, she unbuttoned the conservative blouse, and let it fall open. Robin panted in some air as Rachel's firm breasts came into view, each one with a thick, luscious nipple, and each nipple bearing a golden ring.

"Do you like these?" Rachel asked teasingly. "If you want them, you'll have to earn them. Show me how much you want me, dolly. Make like you want me to fuck you, like your hips need to push up to me. Yes, that's right, shake them, girl, make them rock."

Robin moaned and closed her eyes. Slowly, she began to rock her hips back and forth, each sway causing the weights to swing, the clamps to pull at her flesh. She whimpered again, but didn't stop, planting her feet wide, and trying to undulate, working her body to thrust her hips out, present her splayed lips to the woman in front of her, a desperate plea for any kind of touch. They jangled as they struck each other, and that added to her sublime shame.

"I don't know," Rachel said, watching. Her eyes were dancing, but the smile on her face was thin and cruel. "I think you could do with a little more, don't you?"

"If you wish, ma'am!"

Each new teardrop added another degree of pain. One on each nipple, and one on each of the foremost and aft-most clamps on her pussy lips. These hung down lower now, pinching cruelly even when she stood still.

When Rachel walked over to the cabinets and came back with a short, stinging whip, Robin moaned, and felt tears growing.

"Now you're really going to dance for me!"

Robin tensed and bit back a cry when the first lash fell. It was like being burned in a thin line, quick and shocking, and Rachel delighted in catching

71

her unawares. Robin bet her knees into a half crouch and began to gyrate her hips, moving them upward, and moaning with every tug on the clamps. The weights bounced up and down, hitting her and each other before falling into place and pulling on the wide mouths which pinched her flesh.

And Rachel laughed with delight and walked around her, snapping the little whip in unexpected places, like across the inside of one thigh, or around the upper arm, or across the belly. It never struck hard enough to throw Robin off balance, but it did serve to keep her moving, and to stimulate the arrival of tears.

I can't bear it, Robin thought madly, clenching her fingers behind her. *Not one more minute, I just can't!* And the pounding in her head and her chest was matched with the trembling of her body and the agony between her legs, still hot, still demanding a touch, as wet as she had been before.

And then it stopped. "Not bad, dolly. You wouldn't pass muster at any dance club I go to, but all you need for that is practice. Down."

Robin hit the floor heavily, and gasped. The weights spun and danced between her legs.

"Thank me."

Each kiss on each boot dragged the weights on the nipple clamps across the carpet, took pressure off and then returned it, but Robin was too flustered to care.

"Now, really thank me." Rachel unhooked her skirt and let it drop behind her. Stockings adorned her legs up to her thighs, but her own pussy was bare of any covering but a tangle of dark hair.

Robin froze for a moment, and then carefully wet her lips. Controlling her body so she could keep her balance, she sank lower and arched her back a little. Craning her neck, cursing the stiff collar which prevented her from being as flexible as she should be, she placed a soft, respectful kiss at the top of Rachel's cunt, right over the clitoral hood.

"That's it, keep going."

New kisses got placed all along the lips, and as Rachel obligingly spread her legs, Robin sank between them. The rich, heady scent of a woman filled Robin's world, and she whimpered just a little before her tongue came from between her lips to gently caress the flesh above her. Her heart was pounding too loud to hear the responding purr, but she continued nevertheless, licking at the soft folds of flesh, covering them a kind of worshipful attention.

She went slowly, that much she knew. Up and down, along the sides and dartingly between them, returning to the hood and licking alongside it, and then gently probing at it. Rachel's clit was already pushing it aside, and Robin struggled with the urge to go for that little bundle of nerves, that tightly wrapped center of pleasure that she knew would respond so well to the thrumming of her tongue and the soft pressure of her lips. But she held back, opening the labia, taking that soft flesh between her lips and licking, planting wet kisses along the sides, sending her tongue gently into the wetness inside.

Abruptly, Rachel stepped back. "That's enough for now," she said, her voice just a little hoarse. "Up!"

Robin struggled a little for balance, but rose in one nice movement. As soon as she was back up, Rachel kissed her, hard, pressing their bodies together. The compression of the clamps on her nipples hurt, but the ecstasy of a kiss from someone who was so clearly dominant and forbidding washed away the discomfort. Robin moaned and received the kiss, letting Rachel probe the inside of her mouth with a hot tongue. And when she felt Rachel's hand between her thighs, her moans got louder, and she thrust her pelvis forward into Rachel's hand.

With one hand, Rachel gripped Robin to her. With the other, she released the clips on Robin's labia, one by one, and dropped them to the floor, each new agony adding to the desperate, muffled cries beneath Rachel's mouth and lips, each new absence of weight and pain a shuddering of relief and regret.

Robin trembled as Rachel pulled herself away. Indeed, all of Robin's body was shaking, from her head to her toes. There was a burning sensation all along her cunt lips, and a steady pounding from her heart and clit. She had to take deep breaths, and even so, she felt slightly dizzy. *No, not dizzy*, she thought, *heady. This is what it's like. I'd forgotten.*

She expected Rachel to remove the clamps on her nipples, but Rachel took the posture collar off instead, and then she pushed Robin back down onto her knees, guiding her with the neglected leash.

"Stay," she said, the tone of her voice reflecting her amusement. And as she left the room, leaving the door open, Robin shivered, both from the unexpected draft of cool air that swept in and from the sensations that were struggling within her body. Even these little shivers set the weights still on her nipples moving, and she muffled back a whimper. Between her legs was a tangled pile of clips and weights…all of which had been suspended from her own pussy lips just a moment ago. She closed her eyes and opened them again only when she heard the voices in the hall.

"Of course," Chris was saying, in a warm tone of voice that was clearly not meant for Robin. "Of course my invitation included that. But you aren't finished with her already, are you?"

"No, no, I want to bring her in. Don't be cross! Let's have some fun tonight!"

"You'll get your fun!" The two of them laughed softly together and Robin felt a new ache, one in the pit of her stomach. This one was also familiar, the

73

desire to be with a couple, the intense fantasy of having a pair of powers to serve. It was classic and poetic, such a natural thing to her. Instead of being a partner, which always seemed inappropriate, to be the adjunct, the addition, to serve the balance instead of making it. Please, please, she silently begged, oh please! She kept absolutely still.

"But this little chit hasn't earned it," Chris was saying, closer to her now, actually inside the room. "She's barely gotten used to her collar. She's been a veritable list of imperfections since arriving here. Haven't you, Robin?"

Robin's head dipped low in shame. Keeping her thighs apart was a tremendous effort; she felt that if she didn't concentrate, she would be clenching them together in a desperate effort to stop the moisture that threatened to spill from her body. "Yes, sir," she whispered in response.

"Well, I want to take her to bed *now*," Rachel said, standing so near to Robin's body that Robin could feel the heat from her legs. "I'm in no mood to wait and see if you ever drag her there. I'm here *now*."

There was a long pause. Bent forward as she was, Robin couldn't see either of them, and she squeezed her eyes shut to help her concentration.

"Blindfold her."

A heavy, shaped blindfold was slipped over her eyes while she knelt, and hands came around to the front of her body to remove the nipple clamps. Robin gasped as blood returned to those sensitive knots of tissue, and gasped again as her hands were released and she was pushed forward on her hands and knees and fingers ran up between her legs and entered her without warning.

"How sweet! She's a river!" Rachel chuckled and withdrew her fingers. "Come along, kitten, follow me, that's a good girl."

Robin moaned as she crawled, feeling the humiliation build up inside her, but trying to concentrate on keeping the leash taut but not to pull against it. To remember the layout of the room, to estimate where the door was, to follow Rachel's upward leading, to keep her head level, her limbs smooth.

Her nipples ached, begged for soothing touches.

When she was pulled up again, on her knees, her hands were jerked behind her again, and the cuffs linked. Something touched her lips, and without thinking, she kissed it. It was a small piece of warm skin, a finger? No, it was smaller, and on it, through it, was a ring.

Finally! Robin's breath came out in a small whisper of heated air against Rachel's breast, and then her mouth gently caressed the nipple with all the adoration she could express. Her tongue snaked out and flicked at it, firmly, and then retreated, as Robin's lips pursed around it. In front of her, she could hear Rachel's sharp intake of breath and feel the rising of her chest.

"So sweet," Rachel breathed, pulling Robin toward her.

"So bad," Chris chuckled from behind Robin's back. "Keep those legs spread, girl!" His hands parted them further, and Robin whimpered, because that brought her further away from Rachel's breast. Her two tormentors laughed.

"You just have to learn to reach a little more," Chris prompted, one heavy hand at the back of her neck. "Up! Now forward…don't lean! Don't fall!"

When she had a nipple before her again, Robin renewed her gentle teasing, lapping at it, circling the ring with her tongue, or with her lips. When Rachel pushed her head, she eagerly reached for the other nipple and gave it similar treatment.

"Come here, Parker," Rachel sighed at one point. And Robin could feel the man leaning over her back, hear the wet sounds and the low, throaty murmurs of kissing above her head. It was almost too erotic to bear. The fabric of Chris' jeans brushed against her hands, and she clutched at it, shivered at the feel of the denim, the closeness of the two bodies.

When Chris pulled away, Rachel leaned back onto the bed, leaving Robin with empty air. But not for long. Chris firmly guided her back to that delta between Rachel's thighs, and whispered hotly in her ear, "I want kisses, soft kisses, all the way up and down her thighs. And then I want you to pleasure her as though she were your one mistress, the woman who owns you body and soul. You'd better impress me, girl!"

And then he joined Rachel on the bed, and took hold of her and the bed shook for a moment. Robin swore curses she had never said aloud as she began her row of kisses on Rachel's soft inner thigh. What she would give to be able to see what they were doing! As it was, she could sense that Rachel was feeling great pleasure. The shifts in position of her legs and lower body, the tensing and relaxing, all these things were familiar. And when the kisses reached back up to her cunt, Robin found that Rachel was more then ready to be pleased, her lips open and wet, her clit engorged and sensitive. It was no hardship for Robin to dive in; in fact, it was hard to hold back and be as gentle as she felt she must be. Above her, on the bed, creaks and rustles told of other things happening, but Robin couldn't even imagine what they were.

"She's good," Rachel murmured to Chris. "Oh, shit, she's good." She moaned softly and pushed her hips up a little. Robin flushed with pleasure, and wondered why Rachel's movements seemed to be curtailed. Other women often moved their bodies more, or at least relaxed. Rachel's hard body was all tension, as though she…

As though she was being held down, Robin thought with a new rush of confused pleasure.

"Do you want her to make you come?" Chris asked, his voice also low. He shifted his position slowly, and his weight moved away from the edge of the bed. Robin knew he was leaning over Rachel now, and the sounds of kissing, deep, hard kissing, swept down to her. When they stopped, Parker asked, "Shall I hold you down until you come all over her?"

"No, damn you! I want…I want you in me." Rachel tensed and arched her back, and in one powerful move, almost dislodged him. It surprised Robin, but only for a moment. She was back at her pleasurable work almost at once. And what an amazing thing this was, this struggle above her! Robin breathed out hard and hot across Rachel's cleft.

"Not that easy," Chris said, moving again. There was a sharp movement, one that rocked the mattress, and a hissing sound that could have only come from Rachel. "*Never* that easy. Try again, and you'll regret it. Why don't you relax, and let this new toy suck her way to your heart?" He leaned down again, and when he moved back up, they were both gasping for breath. And when Rachel jerked suddenly, in what Robin imagined to be a struggle against Chris' hold on her, the dark woman immediately yelped, and snarled, and Robin moaned in sympathetic pain. Whatever happened, it led to new wrestling, and new shifting, and then a tangle of exchanged laughter, low and breathless…

I wish I knew what was going on! Robin thought desperately. But no instructions came, so back she want, lavishing more powerful affection into her task, taking the swollen pussy lips up into her mouth and sucking on them, washing them back and forth with long swipes of her tongue.

"Now what was it that you wanted?" Chris teased.

"Fuck me, goddammit, I want your cock!" Rachel relaxed suddenly, moaned as Robin began working steadily on her clit. "Do me. Come on, let me have it, Parker, I want to feel it all the way in me!"

"Then take it out."

That, Robin heard clearly. Anxiety ran through her as positions shifted on the bed again. Would she be pulled up anytime soon to show Chris how she was at cocksucking? She felt a brushing across her face, a swirl of air as Chris moved. Under her hungry lips, Rachel clenched just a little, and then relaxed again, and even above the beating of her heart and the muffling of Rachel's thighs and Chris' body, Robin could hear the appreciative sigh that Rachel made.

"Oh yes," Rachel murmured, "That's it. That's what I want. Ease back, dolly, mama's got a new toy to play with."

And with that, Rachel pulled away from Robin, leaving her kneeling at the foot of the bed, blind and bound. Robin moaned, slightly, keeping back the wail that threatened to explode from her. She trembled, and her pelvis shoved forward in a futile attempt to calm the driving need between her legs. Oh please, please, please! One word, no images, no hard desires, just that one thought, reverberated within her. She could not have asked for a specific favor if she were forced to, but her need for some kind of attention or direction was maddening. Robin cocked her head, leaning her forehead against the side of the bed, trying to listen for an invitation or command. She heard a tearing sound, and then jerked up in surprise as something light brushed her face, falling across the edge of the bed and landing on her chest. She shivered and pulled back, and as it fell, realized that it was an open — and empty — condom package.

She felt another wave of dizziness hit her. *It's perfect*, she thought, tears beginning to dampen the blindfold. *Oh, it's so terrible, so perfect.*

Above her, in front of her, the sounds of fucking became clear. The bed was firm, but the shifts in position and the rocking movements of the bodies caused the mattress to compress in places, and Robin felt each movement. The rhythm was established early, and as Rachel gasped and urged Chris on, Robin bit her lip. And clenched her fingers so hard that they burned.

"Oh yeah, Parker, do me, fuck me, slam that fucker in me!" Rachel's voice was low in fierce joy, and she laughed as the shaking and the tempo increased. And when there was a long and sharp change in the positions on the bed, and Rachel's voice now came from higher up, Robin knew that they had switched positions and Rachel was on top, riding Chris, thrusting her body down against him. Robin couldn't help it any more; the combination of her personal heat and the images of what was probably happening before her, her gentle bondage and the warm stinging of her pussy lips and nipples, it was all too much. She leaned against the bed and pushed her hips against the crumpled mass of bedspread that had been shoved off the edge by the energetic fucking. The first touch of the heavy fabric between her legs was electric; she gasped and humped forward again, trying to capture more of it. Above her, she could hear panting and smooth heavy breathing. She barely realized that she was the one panting.

Rachel moaned and urged Chris on with sounds like growls, until they built up and up in range and volume. Finally, she was not so much urging him but holding herself back, and the strain of that frustration drove her growls to grunts and then to hard, slamming exhalations. Beneath her, Chris breathed as he thrust upward, and clenched her body down to him, each time pulling her down, only to let her rise.

"Now, Parker, now!" Rachel demanded. Below her, a man complied with her wishes while down on the floor, a woman thrust her way pathetically against the fallen bedclothes. Rachel arched her back in an explosive erotic convulsion, taking her own breasts into her hands, screwing her body down onto and against the manly tool between her legs.

Chris pulled her down one more time with a sigh of his own, and then pushed her onto her side. Carefully, he eased out of her, letting her collapse back and stretch her limbs out.

"Oh, you sweet fucker, oh, I needed that," she said, her voice a little hoarse. She coughed to clear her throat. "But you better stop the little dolly, she's humping the linens."

"Yes, I know. You relax. I'm not finished with you yet."

"Good, I hoped you weren't. G'night, dolly!"

Robin had frozen the moment she realized that the activity on the bed had stopped. Her heart sank as she heard Rachel so casually report on her forbidden activity, and she trembled again as Chris moved off the bed and took an agonizingly long time to get around to coming to her.

"I'm sorry, sir, I'm sorry," she whimpered as he dragged her across the hall and into the other bedroom, half on her knees, half struggling to get her feet under her. When he unfastened the cuffs but didn't remove them, she panicked and pulled away from him for just a second. He ignored her and pushed her down onto the bed.

In a minute, her wrists were securely locked to the sides of the bed, making it impossible for her to do anything but lay on her back. He took the blindfold off, and she blinked. He was still dressed, the t-shirt no longer tucked in. His hair was slightly rumpled. You would never know he had just come from such passionate sex.

"Please, sir, please, I'm so sorry, don't leave me like this all night!" she managed to get out, desperate in her fear of his anger and her own self recriminations.

"It's very uncomfortable to sleep in a gag," Chris said, laying a finger across her mouth. "So shut up."

And he left her there, closing the door behind him.

It took an inhumanly long time to fall asleep. She had rarely been left alone and in bondage; she could remember each time with a sharp clarity that made it impossible to relax.

Chapter Seven
Robin's Story: Maria's Girl

Robin stretched her limbs out to the fullest she could reach, and lessened the tension on the ropes which held her wrists down. As she arched her back for a moment, she sighed in pleasure. It always felt good to stretch every once in a while, even if it lessened the illusion just a little bit. She knew that if she moved just slightly more, one of the ropes might slip from the hook and accidentally free her. It had happened before, and although she had been punished delightfully for her transgression, the feeling of being able to slip your bonds that easily really ruined the feeling of the scene. And it kept sliding back to annoy her, like a gnat, an insistent little buzzing reminder that it was really just another game.

She couldn't know what time it was, but she could feel the warmth of the sunlight on her belly. It might be her imagination, but that warm spot seemed higher then it was before. Again, she could easily rub her head alongside the pillow until the blindfold shifted a little and she could peek under it, but that would ruin things too.

Damn, she thought, wiggling her toes. *It takes as much effort from me to continue this as it does from the top! Whoever said that slaves just lay back and take it and get all the pleasure was full of shit.*

But then, what kind of source am I talking about? Desperate men who would just love to have a girl named Bambi wait on them like a late model June Cleaver. A woman who looked like she walked off the cover of the swimsuit issue, or at least from some porn rag, dressed like a Frederick's of Hollywood window display, who could suck a golf ball through the proverbial garden hose, and lusted mightily for their masculine essences. And would bring them a cold one in a long necked bottle afterwards, of course.

She tried to control the little giggle that escaped her lips. How many times had she sat on the phone with the other women who called that old trusty phone sex line and complained about the lack of suitable play partners? Their complaints about the men they talked to and met could fill volumes, as long as you didn't mind the eternal repetitions. Thank goodness for the courtesy line; if she hadn't gotten it, she would have spent a small fortune for all the hours she utilized. And all the numbers she had in her little phone book! Dozens of them, men and women, with notes under each listing, describing the kinds of scenes each one liked.

But as she predicted, it helped to get her through some nights but didn't do much for her sex life on the whole. And the more she spoke to some of the regulars, the more familiar she became with the "scene" — the SM world outside fantasy and pornography. And the more she spoke to people who actually did these things with each other, the inevitable moment came closer. She would have to get out and meet someone.

A finger came out of nowhere and lightly stroked one nipple, and Robin gasped in shock and pleasure.

"Are you OK, slave?" A warm and sultry voice asked.

Robin sighed and pushed her body up to meet the hand. "Yes, mistress," she sighed.

But Maria would check anyway, brushing a cool hand over Robin's palms and feet, making sure they weren't lacking for oxygen. Robin suppressed a sigh of exasperation, and immediately felt guilty for feeling that way. *But how should I feel?* she asked herself furiously. *I told her I was fine. I'd tell her if I was getting cramped or something. But she still has to check; it's like she doesn't trust me to be honest with her.*

Or, an even less charitable thought intruded, because the rules say she should check anyway.

Rules. Even as the world of phone and computer sex (and dominance) were full of their own rules, so was the new world of doing-it-for-real. And some of these new rules, (OK, most of them, Robin admitted) were just as silly as the ones she had learned and followed before. Safe words, for example. Magic words that when said by the bottom, stopped a scene so that some kind of inconvenient or dangerous activity could be halted. Robin had nothing against the concept. In fact, she heartily approved, and tended to like other people who used them. But you could go too far with them. One safe word for "slow down." Another for "don't use this emotional pain on me." Another for "I'm uncomfortable, my bondage/posture/whatever needs to be changed." And then the one for "stop."

Having a code to use so that you're free to pull against the bondage or whimper "no, no, no" seemed to be a great idea. But having all these possible ways to orchestrate what was happening seemed, well, contrary to the point.

I have nothing against all the good reasons to do things that way, Robin wrote in her newest journal. *It makes sense for most people. Hell, it probably keeps them from all kinds of sad and angry scenes that have nothing to do with SM. But I want to feel that I can't stop it. I want to be really mastered, taken over by someone who isn't going to stop doing things because I'm not getting off on it. Someone who knows enough not to endanger me, unless that was what was intended...*

But still, feeling another person's hand, listening to their voice as it whispered hotly into her ear, pulling against restraints and moving with the thudding impact of a whip were all so wonderful! Her first spanking taken as an adult was electrifying, an experience in blinding joy. The first time sturdy leather cuffs were buckled around her wrists, she had nearly melted with the rush of heat that sped through her. Every new episode made her shake with excitement, made her literally drip with her neophyte lust.

She had tried to find potential partners through the phone line. Taking Bob's advice, though, she had been extremely wary of meeting anyone, especially any of the men.

"Once they get you alone and in bondage, they can do anything they want," Bob had cautioned her, his voice earnest and harsh. "And you know what happens if you get hurt. You'll get all the blame. No court will want to hear about a woman who was willing to meet a strange man and let him abuse her. And that's assuming that you survive the experience."

There was a part of Robin's mind that rejected Bob's paranoia. It all sounded like the advice that her mother gave her before going out on dates, minus the bondage, of course. But there was a kernel of truth in what he said, enough to keep her from ever giving out her real name or her telephone number to any man.

But Bob never said anything bad about any of the *women* who used the line. So, when a woman with a girlish voice and the phoneline name of Dominique volunteered the information that she didn't live far from Robin's campus and that she could easily drive down for coffee or lunch one day, Robin accepted. It seemed all right. They would meet in a public place, and Robin still didn't have to give out her name or where she lived.

How deeply Bob's warnings had sunk into her became apparent only after "Dominique," who turned out to be a middle-aged woman in a battered Volvo who insisted that Robin call her "Peggy," sat down opposite Robin in the coffee shop and asked, innocently, "So, Perv, waddaya want for lunch?"

Robin stifled a giggle and shook her head in exasperation. "Robin," she said firmly, reaching across the table to shake Peggy's hand. "Please call me Robin."

Lunch led to a long afternoon of discussions, as the two women revealed their interest in their sexual subculture. It was a real eye-opener for Robin, who finally found out that Mistress Dominique was a lab assistant in a clinic, and a divorcee with two kids and a houseful of cats. And that Mistress Dominique, who had a whole stable of phoneline slaves, had only actually *met* two of them.

"Oh, it's all a scam," Peggy said at one point, amused at Robin's astonishment. "We're only doing this to amuse ourselves, right? These guys don't really want a woman who really has the power to order them around. They want a women who will order them to do exactly what they want to do, no more, no less. But I like telling them to do things like put clamps on their dicks and ice cubes up their butts, and I like hearing them whimper and whine and say 'Yes, mistress, right away, my mistress, thank you, goddess!' and stuff like that. So we both get what we need, it only costs a phone call, and we don't have to clutter up each others lives with reality."

"That's very pragmatic," Robin admitted. She couldn't keep the disappointment out of her voice

"Hey, it's not all that way, kiddo! That's just how we handle it on the phone." Peggy took a piece of paper out of her purse and began to write on it. "Now if you're looking to meet more people who really do this shit, 'stead of just yakking about it, try these places. I got friends in all of them."

And that started Robin off into the world of "people-who-really-do-these-things."

At first, it took more bravery than it did to call the phone line. The list that Peggy had made included three organizations that were accessible with a train ride into the city. Two had mixed memberships, men and women. One was all women. Robin kept their names and addresses and meeting times sandwiched between her campus ID and her social security card in her wallet, and wore the paper thin folding and unfolding it. She talked to other women on the phoneline, asking if any of them had ever gone to these places, and what they were like.

And instinctively, she avoided discussing it with Bob. Somehow, she knew that he would tell her it was a bad idea. In a way, she felt like she was betraying him. He had, after all, taught her so much about his particular world. And he seemed genuinely concerned about her welfare and happiness. But Bob never met people; he couldn't be a master for her, not really. So she kept him out of her discussions about going out into the real world and hoped that when the news got back to him that he wouldn't be hurt.

But his repeated warnings about the dangers involved when meeting men had done sufficient damage. Every time she tried to imagine what meeting a whole group of people with these interests would be like, images of overbearing, domineering and abusive men came to mind. Other people told her about meetings, bylaws, dues, and tedious details, or they enthused over parties and events. But no one could really tell her what the people were like. And there was no way to find out but take the plunge and go herself.

Finally, she heard about a Saturday evening event hosted by the women's organization. Her mouth so dry that she could barely ask for the train ticket, she purchased a two way fare and stared at the ticket and the address all week.

She decided to tear them up at least a dozen times. But she found herself at the train station anyway, and rode the way down into the city in an absolute daze.

What a waste, she was to say to herself for weeks afterward. So many hours of anguish, all that panic, tearing through my closet for the "right" clothes to wear, wondering what would happen when I walked into the room, all of this over a Saturday night at a bar, with mostly women instead of mostly men.

Because that was what the evening turned out to be. The woman at the door, dressed in black jeans and a halter top with a leather jacket over it, had taken Robin's money, stamped her hand, and given her a drink ticket without a second glance. And once inside, there was nothing more terrible then a long, polished wood bar with three bartenders wearing white t-shirts and leather vests energetically pouring drinks for a crowd of mostly young women who were mingling, feeding the jukebox, playing pool, or trying to dance in the narrow space that could only laughably be called a dance floor.

In her black jeans and black blouse, Robin hardly stood out. She went to the bar to get her complimentary drink, and while the server tipped a glass under the spigot for a draft, Robin glanced around her. No one was paying her the slightest bit of attention.

Well, she thought, pulling the cold mug into her hand, so much for walking in and feeling all the eyes in the place on me.

Most of the evening faded into a blur. She drank, got change for the box and played some music, and even danced a few times, each time exchanging nothing more then first names with the woman she danced with. No one offered any more information, and Robin couldn't bring herself to ask.

But she did begin to notice more and more during the night. Some women wore small whips on their belts, some of them small enough to be thought of as key chains. And among the labrys and Venus symbols on necklaces and earrings, there were also little knives and tiny handcuffs.

Some women were more explicit. There were women there in leather vests with "colors" on them — patches proclaiming their affiliation with a motorcycle group or another leather-related women's group. One symbol had a medusa on it, her eyes glinting bright green, her chest almost bursting out of a leather jacket. Another had the double Venus symbol with riding crops standing in for the vertical line, and a pair of handcuffs acting as the two circles.

Handcuffs also hung from belts and jackets.

This is so great, Robin thought. I can't say a bloody word to any of them, but it's so great just to watch them! Just to know that they're here, that they come out and party. But how can I actually meet one of them? What do I say? Hi, I'm new here? Say, have you read this magazine? Where did you get those great boots?

In the end, it was Maria who solved that problem. Robin was turning back to the bar, debating on whether or not to have another drink, when a gloved hand caught her wrist. Robin looked up sharply, directly into the bluest eyes she had ever seen, and gasped.

"Good reaction," Maria had answered, withdrawing her hand. Her hair was cropped cruelly short, and was the intense, thick color of fresh cream. Her lips were slightly pursed, drawing their natural tightness in to a sensual knot of crimson flesh. When those lips moved again, Robin froze to watch them.

"What are you looking for, sweetness?" Maria asked, drawing each word out.

Robin knew what the set up was for, and resisted it with every bit of strength she had, but knew when defeat was imminent.

"You," she whispered.

"Correct!" Maria leaned forward and gave Robin the first passionate kiss she had ever received from a woman. Robin, who had gotten quite enough stimulation for one night, smiled when Maria released her and then to her utter horror, fainted.

People talked about it for months, of course. What a fairy tale way to start a romance, more then one wit offered. Of course, in the case of Sleeping Beauty, a kiss woke her up, not made her fall into a dead faint.

But it was nothing less than destiny which brought them together. That one kiss in a bar led to a date, which led to another one, and then another one. Maria didn't live in the city either, but she had a car, and by the time she came up to Robin's little college town to visit her, they already knew that they had something going. That night, in a cheap motel off the expressway, Maria tied Robin's hands together for the first time, wrapping them in many layers of a long cotton scarf, and Robin finally felt the rapture of surrender under the touch of another human being. And learned all about the kinds of love that two women could share.

Several weeks later, at Maria's house for the weekend, Robin bent carefully over her new lover's knee and took her first spanking, a long, hard ritual that made her cry and kept her sobbing, her face buried in Maria's lap, her arms wrapped around her legs, for longer then she could have imagined. That night, in bed, Maria was able to coax Robin to orgasm with the lightest of touches, and it became harder and harder for Robin to go back to school during the week.

Other things seemed to pass out of her life as well. It took weeks before she realized that the box under her bed hadn't come out at all since she started actually sleeping with Maria. And when she thought about it, she took the phone book with all her notes about numbers from the phone-line and tossed that into the box as well. She had no real use for any of it. She felt a little guilty about leaving some of her "regulars" without a word of explanation, especially Bob. But she had a real relationship now, no more fun and games over the phone.

But she joined the group that had hosted the bar night. Its name was WISE, Women Into Sadomasochistic Expression, and their symbol was a witch silhouetted against a full moon, riding her broomstick while whirling a long whip over her head. They had monthly meetings, most of which Robin couldn't attend because of the travel time it would take. But now she would get their newsletter and be able to say she supported the organization that Maria belonged to. The mailings were regular, but despite Robin's deepest hopes, were not filled with fascinating instructional essays and stories about women and their SM activities. Oh, there was always a brief synopsis of their last meeting topic, but most of the space was taken up by announcements for future events (especially fund-raisers), and notes about which actions had or had not been taken by which committee. There always seemed to be some upcoming crisis, something that required the members to show up and vote.

Robin didn't much care. She stopped eating at local restaurants and forced down cafeteria food in order to afford more train tickets to go and see Maria. She vanished every weekend that she could, and noted long weekends with joy. Over winter break, she went to live with Maria instead of going home for the entire time, cutting down her Christmas visit to three days and talking vaguely about a ski trip with some girlfriends at school. The family believed every word, filled her suitcase with their presents and sent her back into Maria's arms for the happiest New Year she had ever had. That New Year's Eve, Maria gave her a little box that contained a narrow black leather collar, with golden "M" on the front. Robin received it on her knees, with tears of gratitude and happiness streaming down her face.

"I never accepted a slave before," Maria told her, bringing their bodies together in a long, hot embrace. "You're Maria's girl now."

"I'll love you forever," Robin vowed.

The tail end of her junior year and the entire senior year seemed to mesh together into a crazy pattern of work and study and her life with Maria. Maria was always more than supportive of Robin's schooling and her eventual job. "Despite," she would say, her blue eyes dancing in irony, "my overwhelming lack of artistic appreciation. Luckily, I can just sit back and appreciate the appreciator."

And Robin would blush.

But Maria's support proved to be priceless in that all important final year of undergraduate work. She would gladly drive Robin to art shows and galleries and studios and auction houses, where Robin could not only look at the actual works, but talk to the artists, restorers, dealers and clients. She spent patient hours wandering around and looking at anything from broad canvases splashed with bright colors to boxes and files full of ancient photographs, from kinetic sculptures made of found materials to authenticated masterpieces of Impressionist origin.

When Robin spent three weeks in Italy with several other students, touring more museums and galleries in those days then she had in the past six months, she still found time to write to Maria every day. She had to! Maria had instructed her to do just that before she left. And each envelope she posted made her sigh in pleasure. She was being good. She was doing what she had been told. Every day, from dawn until long after nightfall, she belonged to the world of art. But every night, her mind and body existed only for the memory of Maria's touch and her voice.

Robin graduated with more honors than seemed appropriate. Her parents flew in to watch her, unaware that in the same audience, not far from where they sat and applauding wildly every time their daughter's name was mentioned, was a woman with short cream-colored hair and intense blue eyes who just that morning had beaten their smart, pretty daughter so hard that Robin's every shifting movement onstage was accompanied by twinges of delightful pain.

It had been Robin's idea. "For the rest of my life," she had explained to Maria's amused patience, "I want to remember this day as a day where even though I was getting out of school and receiving all this attention, underneath I was still your slave."

"Oh, I'll give you something to remember," Maria promised. And she did, with a beautiful braided flogger, its tails a bundle of black snakes, its touch a massive, heavy thump! which sent Robin's body pressing against the edge of the couch she had been braced on too many times to count.

"We're so proud of you," her mother said at dinner, smiling as her father laid their generous graduation present before Robin, the slender envelope containing what would become moving expenses and first month's rent and security. "We always knew you'd be the smartest one in the family!"

They spent the next day together, Robin acting as a tour guide through the campus. She introduced them to some of her teachers, all of whom had nothing but those warm, glowing words that seem to come out only on sunny graduation days. She rarely left them alone, and rushed back to their sides when she was called away by some business they assumed to have to do with getting out of school. They protested that they could just be on their way and leave her to her work, but she insisted on making sure that they had a lot of her company and attention. And when they finally had to leave, Robin grinned and kissed them and bade them farewell, waving at their taxi as they went back to the airport.

They never knew that all during their day with their daughter, her few absences were to meet with Maria in some semi-private space so that Maria could add other delightful torments to Robin's day. By the time she lowered her arm from energetic waving, she ran back to find Maria sitting on Robin's bed in the dorm (a single room at last). And only after some truly abject begging would Maria consent to removing the dildo and butt plug she had inserted earlier, and only after Robin showed some absolutely devoted attention to Maria's boots and then her cunt did Maria give her the cream that would take the burning sting away from Robin's aching nipples. Maria had massaged them with a heavy coating of something used to soothe aching muscles. For the final hour with her parents, Robin's nipples had ached so much that she could barely keep still. The sensation faded, but it was still more the thought which held her attention.

Maria had indeed given her something to remember.

But now there was a new adventure to embark on. There was the studio apartment in the city, where Maria had brought some of her friends from WISE, who came with their tools and a bag of hardware. In one day, they installed hooks and rings in all sorts of places, along the baseboards and from the ceiling, and of course in the frame of the bed that was Maria's graduation present to Robin. Robin barely had one week to move in before she had to show up at work, a nice, middle range auction house and gallery. She was an assistant to their second best appraiser and buyer. Her hours were going to be long and sometimes erratic, but she knew that she was already ahead of the game. Many people in her position spent years doing other kinds of work before they could even get such an entry level position in a good house.

And of course, now that she was on her own and in the city, there was no question about her ability to join other dominant and submissive pleasure seekers in their little underground worlds. With the safety of her collar and Maria's company, she could finally dare to venture into the mixed gatherings and meet some men as well as women. Maria had no interests in that direction; she was comfortably, wonderfully gay. But she had long ago discovered Robin's bisexuality, and liked to use it as a tease, asking Robin questions about who she found attractive or not, and what she would do if Maria loaned her to one of the dominant men.

Robin was never sure if what she felt at that suggestion was horror or shock; either way, it made her feel threatened and vulnerable while dampening her between the thighs.

Together, they attended parties, held in the basements of private homes and in empty rooms in theaters and schools. They went to WISE meetings together, where Robin sat on the floor in a rented room in the Gay Communal Association's building, and leaned her head affectionately against Maria's thigh. So what if the meetings seemed to be one problem after another, or one debate after another? So what if things always ended up being issues about the patriarchy, and the overculture, and this racist/sexist/classist/homophobic society and the need for consensus? Robin didn't need to pay that much attention. She knew what kind of a world she lived in; she was aware and registered to vote. She signed petitions and sent checks to the causes and campaigns she supported and thought that she was generally attentive to her local community politics. But when she was collared and seated on the floor, in the presence of people who would appreciate the image she was presenting, she was too engaged in how she behaved and appeared, so that Maria would look like the excellent mistress that she was. Robin was always concerned about helping to make Maria look good.

She couldn't believe her luck, after all. Years of anxiety and all those nagging feelings of guilt had been blown to pieces, shattered in the moment it took to meet a woman's eyes in a bar and say one word.

I can't imagine anything that could make me happier, Robin would think, sliding her cheek against Maria's leg, adoring her, adoring the place she had at her side. I could live like this for the rest of my life.

Maria finished checking the bonds before she ran her hands lightly over Robin's bound body. Carefully, listening to the minute gasps of pleasure, she attached sharp little nipple clamps, and then a row of similar clamps along Robin's thighs and belly. This would go on for some time before Robin's body would betray her, as it always did, and she would writhe and stretch, and earnestly try not to dislodge the bondage while doing so. And when Maria thought that Robin had had enough, perhaps she would fuck her. Or, maybe she would climb up on the bed and let Robin's eager mouth go to work on her, and take her pleasure that way.

Robin struggled again and again throughout their session, but her struggles were inside of her, and not against the ropes which would be so easy to slip.

I love her, Robin thought, sighing and moaning in proper reactions to Maria's touch. *Oh God, I love her so much my heart could just explode of it all. But there's something missing.*

The guilt that swept through her made it even more poignant when Maria's fingers lightly touched between Robin's spread legs, and Robin's moan was doubly strong. This encouraged Maria, and her fingers' dancing was a reward that only intensified Robin's regret and shame. The bound woman shut out as much thought as she could and tried desperately to concentrate on the scene, and on Maria, and even on her own pleasure, until Maria seemed satisfied and slipped the blindfold off and kissed Robin sweetly, waiting for their heart-poundings to subside.

But Robin couldn't get away from her own private thoughts when the scene was over. She tossed and turned trying to get some sleep later that night.

I don't believe how fucking ungrateful I am, she thought, fighting with herself. I wait my entire life for someone like her, and when I have her, and I have a life together and a collar around my neck, all I can think of is what I don't have.

But let's face it, what I don't have is pretty strong.

For over a year and a half, I've been made love to by a woman who thinks I'm attractive, smart, and sexy. She likes me as a friend, she supports me in my job, and she enjoys my company. We're lovers, like a million other lovers, except that she ties me up a lot, and the kinds of things we do to get off aren't exactly commonplace. For most people, I guess that would be about the best thing you could hope for in this life!

But I'm not really her *slave.*

And that's the core of it all.

Oh, she likes it if I carry her bag of toys, and I like getting her coffee in the morning, or helping her out with shopping and things like that, but she really doesn't use me the way you'd think. I don't do any real work for her, only little token things, like the way a gentleman used to treat his date.

And even when we're playing, there are all those reminders that it's just a game. The hooks instead of rings, so all I have to do is stretch to get free. Cuffs without locks. Even my collar doesn't lock.

She lets me get away with almost anything, Robin admitted, sitting up in bed and forgetting any thought of an easy sleep. I don't have to call her by any title, even at meetings and parties. If I tell her I don't feel like playing, we don't play. And isn't that a kick in the head? I'm upset because my lover cares about me too much.

But it's more then just caring about me, I know it is. And I haven't been facing it. When we played early on, she used to train me, tell me how to act and punish me if I did things wrong. Now, she never does anything like that, and I know I'm not near being a perfect slave. It's just that she's lost interest in that aspect of play. Now, the only time I get punished it when she uses it as an excuse to be a little rougher in our sex.

I'm wearing a collar with her initial on it, but I really don't feel like I belong to her, at least no more then any person belongs to their lover. All it seems to mean is that we're monogamous. And we're a "couple."

But we do have great sex! She's so sexy, and so sensual. All she has to do is look at me thoughtfully, the way she does when she's thinking about what to do, and I start to melt inside. And she does do the things I need. I do get tied up and beaten and tormented and pleasured in all these wonderful ways. So what if it's not as often as it was at first? All I need to do is let her know I want it more and I'm sure she'll try to accommodate me.

But I don't want to be accommodated, that inner voice screamed. *I want to be owned!*

She's the best I'm ever going to get, Robin thought, hugging her knees and feeling the tears come. She pushed that inner voice back and down, until she silenced it again. I can't fuck this up. I can't afford it. She deserves better than to have me whining at her. I can learn to deal with not having these things. And maybe one day she'll get back into being more of a mistress and less of a lover.

And maybe I'm just drowning in all the lies. I thought I stopped all the lies.

Chapter Eight

Imagine that you found yourself going to hell for a week, Robin thought. She was always composing for her journal, even when she couldn't add anything to it. *But then, you found out that you liked living in hell. What would that do to your value system? Or your self image?*

Hell might have been an exaggeration, but not much of one. Early Sunday morning, Chris unstrapped Robin's bonds and physically threw her across the room to the shower. Standing in the doorway, just like Rachel did the previous night, he barked commands at her for her morning rituals, how she was to wash, and to what degree of thoroughness. And then, on to when and how to present herself to him, and her chores and responsibilities.

And by the time she could pass his inspection for cleanliness, and she had answered his directions with crisp "yessirs," she was taken back across the room, bent over the edge of her bed, her knees against the side, her hands braced on the coverlet, and Chris savagely caned her.

But no, savagely wasn't the right word. Like his other punishments, it was cold, icy cold and precise. Each stripe felt like he had laid a line of acid across her buttocks, and when she couldn't hold back the screams, he gagged her, a heavy, thick tube pushed into her mouth and held in place with a leather strap. She could breathe through it, but the sounds she made were muffled and distorted, and she couldn't bring her mouth to make any meaningful sounds. It was humiliating, but much, much easier to take than the next few cane strikes. The strikes themselves seemed even harder, as though they were supposed to check the efficiency of the gag. When she fell forward, twisting her body away from that terrible, burning pain, he pulled her back in place, pushing her head down lower, making her thrust her ass back and up.

No safe words, Robin managed to think, fighting back the flow of tears and panting through the air hole in the gag. *This is real! No safe words! No mercy!*

When he finally did stop, and he took the gag out of her mouth, it was the most natural thing in the world to kiss the cane he presented before her and then to sink to the floor and cover his boots with kisses, thanking him again and again for both the punishment and for stopping it.

But that was just the beginning.

Sending her scampering into the kitchen on her hands and knees to prepare and serve breakfast was the start of her real day. Kneeling in one corner, ass up, to show off her stripes while Rachel and Chris chatted and drank their coffee, was the immediate follow up.

Cleaning and polishing Rachel's boots came next, on her knees in the kitchen, rubbing and brushing until her arms hurt and the boots gleamed with a mirror-like finish, and then scrubbing her hands and arms and spots on her thighs and her chest which were all touched with oily, black polish.

"That took too long," Chris told her, when she delivered the boots back to the bedroom. He put a pair of nipple clamps on her again, and attached the chain connecting them to her collar. "Try again." This time, he gave her a pair of boots from out of the closet. Out of the corner of her eye, she could see that there were plenty of shoes and boots in the racks of that closet, and she compressed her lips together to stop the moan that threatened to come out.

The entire day was like that.

Nothing she managed to do turned out right. And Chris was all over her, always there to spot clumsiness or hesitation, always quick to point out a gesture missed or a display of a forbidden emotion. Rachel acted like a guest and sat back to watch, laughing from time to time, but mostly ignoring what was going on. She and Chris went over some kind of business for hours, and Robin could never figure out what they were talking about from the snatches she heard. All Robin knew was that Rachel had become distinctly uninterested in her.

And Robin couldn't decide whether that was part of her training or not. In fact, Robin was far too busy to give it much thought, and by the time she realized that Rachel had actually left the apartment and she was alone again with Chris, there was only a little confused sense of gratitude and regret. One demonic trainer was quite enough, thank you.

But it was so nice having a woman near!

Two days passed in a blur of pain and humiliation and constant erotic agony. Chris ran her ragged, setting her alarm for pre-dawn hours so that she could exercise before he woke up, and keeping her up late at night, asking her questions about her previous experiences and her feelings. When there really weren't chores that had to be done, he was the master of make-work, and Robin knew that when the owners of this place got back, they would be coming home to an apartment that had literally been scrubbed and polished from floor to ceiling and back again. Every shoe or boot in the closet, every toy on their racks, every piece of artwork, every dish, glass and pot, every inch of wood floor and furniture and every piece of metal in the house will have been personally and perfectly cleaned, polished and buffed to within an inch of its life.

Chris would make sure of that, even if it did make Robin's body into a striped work of art. It didn't take long for the bruises to start showing through the constant pink and red of the beaten flesh, and Robin could never remember being so carefully and perfectly marked.

Nor could she remember the near constant pain of a body under such treatment. Her movements from waking to sleeping were all accompanied by sharp stabs and thrumming aches; all reminders of her mistakes, both recent and aged.

On Monday, a thick envelope was delivered, which Chris opened and examined while Robin was kept busy. In the afternoon, he summoned her and placed the folder of documents before her, neatly spread out.

"These are most of the results from the examination you underwent on Saturday, plus the medical records you requested for me. You need to read them and check for accuracy, and then sign a release form allowing the Marketplace to keep them as part of your records."

Robin grinned at the pile of papers before her. "You folks certainly are thorough, sir."

"We've learned to be. If there is anything in there which you want removed, let me know. You are released from protocol to discuss the contents. Will two hours be enough to examine everything?"

It was. Robin went through her history from childhood up through the previous Saturday with slow amazement. Everything was there, from her early childhood diseases to shin splints to the first time she had a yeast infection. Plus breakdowns of all sorts of tests run on her blood and urine, and notes concerning the availability of the test results from a few that would take a bit longer. There was a rather long and involved psychological report which, when she got through all the big words, came down to this:

"Subject has a series of finely developed paraphilias for behavior which suits her placement within the Marketplace."

"It means that selling you should be a great turn-on," Chris commented.

"No kidding," Robin replied. "I could have told them that years ago. In plain language, without all these tests. Chris…may I ask you a question?"

"You may always ask."

"What was so special about Greta?"

He raised one eyebrow, and looked mildly pleased. Robin had already gotten so dependent on his approval that she blushed even at that faint sign of it.

"Do you mean besides being a highly skilled physician whose value is extremely well rated?" he asked, leaning back.

"You know what I mean," Robin answered softly, "There's something different about her. I would have known it if I passed her on the street. Is it that she's so happy?"

"I suppose that's part of it. Happy slaves do tend to give off an aura of contentment which usually serves only to confuse people. Our culture is not used to dealing with any individual who is so comfortable with their station in life. Leon, for example, is constantly asked what he has going for him which makes him so happy; outside of the Marketplace, there is no answer that will suffice, and he is often forced to shrug and offer some lame excuse. But Greta is, as you noticed, somewhat different."

He paused, looking thoughtful for a moment. His eyes seemed to focus on some spot out the front window, hovering so many feet from the ground. Robin waited patiently.

"Greta spent six months training with Anderson," he finally said, as though that would explain everything. "And what you felt is the mark of such training. You, however, lack the opportunity for the same, and therefore must do your humble best to get the most out of what I can offer you. Which today, after you sign and initial these papers where necessary, will consist of a lot of fetching and carrying. You need to work on rising in one fluid motion and stopping with grace."

And when she wasn't demonstrating her skills at all kinds of domesticity, she was being tested for all the movements, postures, and the nuances of service. During the day, at any time, Chris would come up behind her and ask things like, "Two guests at your owner's house each request something of you. One wants to see you clothed, and the other does not. Assuming that your standing instructions are to obey any reasonable request of a guest and that both of these requests fall into the category of reasonable, what will you do?"

When he wasn't giving her verbal problems, he was running her through the ritual positions which all Marketplace slaves had to know, and making sure that she was perfect in them. When she commented that she felt like a show dog being posed for the judges, he replied, "Yes! That's exactly the image you should think of. Sleek, still, disciplined. You want to be a possession worthy of acquiring, worthy of training and grooming and showing off. And at the same time, you want to be available, open for every touch and caress.

Ready to be examined, poked and prodded. Braced for any sort of pain, whether it's erotic or not. Owners may do as they like to you, and need not seek your consent, approval, pleasure, or even your reaction. And they will not owe you explanations or words of encouragement or comfort or praise. You will just be a person who belongs to them, and nothing more."

"Oh God," Robin had murmured, stretching her muscles and bending into the posture demanded. She was dizzy again, flush with the excitement that Chris brought up in her whenever he spoke of such things. And when he beat her shortly after, braced against his knee, she had to verbally beg him to choose some other method, because she was ready to come the next moment he touched her.

Naturally, he listened, and chose to punish her with some more stripes, leaving her standing, cuffed and blindfolded, for at least two hours. Tears streaked her pretty face and filled the blindfold.

Leon came and went, bringing food for them both and bits of advice for her. She soon came to look forward to her appearances, eager to taste his culinary delights and more then eager for his encouragement and gentle corrections. He was the real thing: he was a slave, purchased and owned and completely happy. Whispers in the kitchen informed Robin of the life he led, his daily chores, and his master's passions. She envied him and sighed appropriately when he spoke of the love he had for his owner and for his life. She also blushed when Leon enthusiastically described his frequent sexual uses, and the state of his body when his master was in a particular mood.

It was a very sore issue with her. Because except for the touches she received as part of her training, Chris never used her. Or, to be precise, she would remind herself, Chris has never fucked me. Never asked for as much as a blow job, despite the explicit sexuality of her position. Being gay was one thing, she supposed. But if he's interested enough to train me, why wouldn't he at least try me out? He had enthusiastic sex with Rachel, after all, so he apparently wasn't *all* gay, despite the evidence she had gathered during their brief introduction in the leather bar. So if he could get off on screwing women, why was he keeping such a distance from her?

The question shamed and infuriated her, and she tried her best not to think about it.

But in the one day she had been given to go back to attending to her business, she could barely concentrate on what she had to do. Even while she visited her bank and locked up her small valuables, when she called the storage facility and made her arrangements for pick up and storage and paid the fees for three years, and when she packed up the list of clothing that Chris had given her, all she could think of was eight o'clock that evening. When she was due back on the Upper West Side. When she could get out of these clothes and get back into what was real.

Her rolodex remained by the phone, untouched. Her answering machine had several messages on it, one a clear job offer from a major auction house.

She erased them all with a casual tap and left the apartment without looking back. Tonight, it was time to tell Chris about Troy.

Chapter Nine
Robin's Story: Troy's Real Thing

Robin was on the floor, paddle in hand, when she realized that the gentleman in the tan blazer was staring at her. She didn't allow him to distract her from her duty; she was already far too much a professional to take such frank appraisal as unnerving. There would be time enough when her business was complete to find out what his problem was. She focused on what was in front of her, keeping her ears and eyes sharp, and raising the paddle with a swift confidence that intimidated lesser creatures around her.

Finally, interest wavered, and one man's hesitation got tangled in the rush to complete the transaction, and Robin heard the auctioneer call out her number, pausing only to take a breath before starting to describe the next item in the catalog.

All in a days work, she thought, jotting down her final bid with satisfaction. That last fake Goya would seal up the exhibition contract she had signed last year, and all brought in under budget. It was hardly standard to purposefully seek out forgeries for exhibitions, but it had been a fun contract to fill. She got to spend a lot of time in restoration rooms, watching artists use solvents and neutralizers and all sorts of sophisticated methods to expose what some owners had truly thought were original Goya works. It was a pity, for some of them. But it had been a bonanza for her. A staff of three people had worked for almost a year, tracking them down and talking, begging, threatening and once, bribing the various owners to allow the testing. Robin had been personally to over twenty places which had offered genuine articles for sale just on the supposition that they might have sifted through known fakes in order to verify their true finds.

It was exhilarating. Fascinating. And just the thing to show her employers how valuable she really was. Putting this exhibition together (or, she reflected, just getting the pieces in one place), was quite an accomplishment. But she hadn't wasted her time out of the country; if her Goya searches came up empty, she was always purchasing assorted other pieces and lots and having them shipped to the prestigious New York auction house for their eventual arrival in the next season's catalogs.

The irony of the entire search was that the final two pieces she needed to fill the contract came on the block at the auction house of her chief rival. Well, she tried to get them to deal exclusively with her, but they chose to put the fakes up on the block. Now, she had them both, for just slightly less then the original offer she made them. In fact, this was such a simple transaction that she could have sent one of her assistants to finish it up, or simply called her bids in from the comfort of her office, but it gave her a sense of satisfaction to come out and handle this last little detail in person.

"You're good, kid, you're good," Taylor murmured as he gave over the paperwork. She knew him from way back; working for different employers didn't stop art people from socializing in the same circles. And she liked him. He was always friendly and never took on the snobby air that most of their fellow workers put on to protect their egos and keep the rivalry sharp.

"Well, this seals it for me, Taylor," she said, signing her name and clipping the shipping instructions onto the sheets. "I'll see you next month? At Ray's party?"

"Wouldn't miss it for the world. Be good!"

Yeah, right, Robin thought, a sudden cool wave of sadness passing through her. She turned her paddle in and went to claim her coat with a sigh of frustration. It had been a long time since someone had told her to be good and really meant it.

Breaking up with Maria had taken a horribly long time. Robin had struggled with her discontent for months, wavering back and forth through all sorts of convoluted arguments with herself.

She had loved Maria, and there was no doubt about that. But as their relationship slipped further and further away from mistress and slave and deeper into the state of lovers, Robin never knew what to feel. It was secure to be so loved, to have a stable partner who was interested in pleasing her and being pleased, who was supportive and nurturing and had just the right amount of personal interests and projects to keep her away from the borders of clinging over-protectiveness.

Robin concentrated on doing things like offering submissive gestures before being asked for them, and found the Maria was generally pleased by them. She also took comfort in the fact that Maria didn't stop playing with her; she was still being tied up and she still got some beatings and some sessions with all sorts of toys. They still went to meetings and parties where

Robin got to wear her collar and sit on the floor. As long as these things continued to happen, Robin decided, everything else was just great. She should be grateful and happy with what she got, and she should be glad that she had the opportunity to show off just how submissive she could be.

It was when Maria suggested that they begin to live together that matters got too entangled for Robin to be able to neatly compartmentalize. Suddenly, conversations shifted from the world of romance and fantasy into real world things like apartment size and location and budgets and the possibility of a domestic partnership agreement.

"Why don't we just do this," Robin had suggested one night, her stomach and chest full of butterflies that threatened to strangle the sounds coming out of her. "I'll start to turn my paychecks over to you. I'll put my savings into your accounts. You find a place you like, wherever you want it. And, and, when we do this, I'll become your real, full time slave. You can decide how much to spend. I'll agree with anything you want."

Maria had looked at Robin as though the younger woman had taken leave of her senses. Robin sunk into her chair and felt her throat and mouth dry out.

"What the hell are you talking about, Robin?" Maria had demanded. "What, do you think you don't have anything to say in this relationship? Do you think I'm some kind of mommy figure who's going to take over all the responsibilities for you? We're a partnership here! Or are you just trying to get out of my suggestion? Is it that you really don't want to live with me?"

It was a long night, stretching into a longer day. Before it ended, they had both cried and been comforted and shared their ambivalences over their relationship and what to do and where they were going. And they agreed to give it another try and to trust each other.

The second time they had such a discussion, the ending wasn't so congenial. Robin still stung at the accusations that Maria had flung at her in the heat of their most painful shouting match.

"You're still a child, trying to find someone to run your life for you! Well, real people who do that aren't into SM, sweetie! They're pimps and pushers and abusers who would love to have someone who wants someone else to run their lives for them! And you're walking right into their arms! Because you can't handle the responsibility of your own fucking life!" She had tears in her eyes when she tore those words from her throat, and her fists had been curled so tightly that the knuckles were white.

Robin took her collar off and left it on the table before leaving the house, hot tears of her own streaking her face.

Now, the collar was at home, wrapped in tissue paper and tucked away in a box. Months after that final confrontation, it had arrived at Robin's door, with a brief note inside.

> I'm so sorry about the cruel things I said to you. You know they weren't true. But I knew that I was going to lose you eventually and I hated knowing that I couldn't be the person you need in your life. Please forgive me.
>
> This really belongs to you. No one else could come close to earning something like it from me, and you deserve a better remembrance of our years together than my bitter words.

It was signed simply, with an "M."

And that had been almost a year ago. And since then, there had been no one else. Or rather, Robin reflected, no one else who lasted more than one date.

Feeling uncomfortable at WISE, Robin had turned to the mixed gender groups in town for entertainment and in desperation. She found a little of the first and a lot of the second. In one group, the men seemed so intimidating, especially those who had seen her in public submission to Maria and who spotted her uncollared throat at once. And even the male slaves seemed a little overwhelming. Several of them tried to convince her that her real destiny lay in becoming a mistress, specifically, their mistress. At least that was better than the male "slaves" who told her that *they* would be the best possible master for her.

The women there seemed to think of her as either a rival, or insignificant.

In the other organization, she found the situation somewhat less oppressive, but stupifyingly dull and dominated by quasi-charismatic leaders who had their own sycophantic followers. She was eagerly welcomed and pressured to join, and prodded to all sorts of volunteer work on projects that she had no interest in. The rest of her time was taken up by meetings where whatever the ruling council wanted was done and whatever they wanted to discuss was discussed. She felt alternately patronized and used, to no specific purpose.

Between the two organizations, Robin began to feel a genuine longing for a capacity for suicide. If this was what the future of her sexuality was dependent upon, she was heading for a destiny filled with trivia, shallow thinking and the endless struggle between the more manipulative members of groups of people whose only real purpose in organizing was to create a space in which people could meet and get laid.

She did her best to ignore the pettiness and the senseless power-plays, and tried to gravitate toward those individuals who seemed to at least radiate a core of responsibility, balanced with the capacity to take the whole SM "lifestyle" with a grain of seriousness and dignity. But eventually, she realized that there too, she was lacking the crucial element to her satisfaction. It was one thing to treat SM as an enjoyable way for lovers to expand their sensual repertoire. It was something entirely different to contemplate living a life based on a dominant and submissive relationship.

In time, she stopped going to the endless meetings and discussion groups and panels and seminars. The lives and goals of these mostly closeted men and women were nowhere beyond what she had with Maria, and, in the end, much less interesting.

Out of her own closet came her old box of personal toys, and into her life came a new collection of terribly written pornography. She even called the old phone sex line again, and picked up a few voices who seemed promising, only to discover that she couldn't go back again. The limitations of phone sex just couldn't make up for the majesty and the rapture of the real thing. And when she heard Bob's familiar call for submissive ladies one night, she hung up the phone with a solid click and never called the number again.

Thank goodness she had such a big project to oversee. It kept her traveling, it kept her occupied, and it kept her mind off of her loneliness. It didn't stop her from visiting clubs in Europe that catered to the SM and fetish scene. But it did stop her from establishing any regular contacts with people, which probably saved her from even more heartache.

And now, her project was done. She had almost a full month of vacation time coming due, and no doubt there were proposals and assignments being stacked on her secretary's desk even while she waited on line to get her coat. Maybe she could just dive into them when she got back to the office and start something else that would be time consuming and thought devouring.

"I didn't know there was such a market for fake pieces of art," a strange voice said behind her. "And I wouldn't have guessed that you were the type to collect them."

She turned and looked up into the face of the man in the tan jacket. A moment of recognition struck her. She had seen him somewhere before. His warm, hazel eyes were dancing in some kind of private amusement.

"That's an enigmatic statement," she said finally. "Why wouldn't you suppose that I collect art forgeries?"

"Because I know that you're the real thing," he said, leaning slightly forward. "Something our mutual acquaintances at the EC would never realize."

The EC...the Equivocal Coalition. One of the SM organizations. Robin took another look at him. Yes, she had seen him there. A few times, not regularly. She had never spoken to him.

"Your coat, madame," the man behind the counter said. She turned away from her new almost acquaintance and took it, and then turned back, her heart pounding.

"I was about to go to lunch," she said, astounded at the casual sound of her voice. "Perhaps you would care to join me and tell me about your theories about real things?"

"It would be my pleasure," he said, nodding his head a little forward. "But if we're going to lunch, we'd better be introduced. I'm Troy."

"I'm Robin."

He smiled. "I know."

Compared to Maria, Troy was pure lightening. Where she was exotic on the outside and warm and cozy and comforting inside, Troy looked like a slightly absent-minded mathematician whose friendly eyes and carelessly groomed hair guarded a steel-trap mind with a strong appetite for misdirection and games of torment.

Over lunch, they laughed and talked about themselves like any two people discovering a common interest. They shared their disappointments with the scene in the city and some of their experiences at the clubs. They compared lists of mutual friends. By the time they were dawdling over the third serving of coffee and lunch time was long over, Troy captured Robin's eyes with his and said, "I'm strongly attracted to you. Would you like to take the rest of the afternoon off and get to know me better?"

"Yes," Robin answered, embarrassed by her too-quick response. "I think I'd better call in and let them know I'm going to be out."

"Good. And while you're up, you can decide something." A flash danced across his eyes. It was a look that she was to become very familiar with.

"Oh? What's that?"

"After you suck my cock, I'm going to beat your ass until it's bright red and tender. What I want you to decide is whether you will then bend over and pull your own ass cheeks apart so I can fuck that tight hole, or whether I should tie you securely down and gag you while I do it. Think about it."

All this was said in the same slightly amused but calm and friendly voice he had been chatting in all during the meal. He raised his eyebrows as she sat shock still in her seat, breath quickening, color rising into her cheeks.

"Do you need change for the phone?" he asked, reaching into his pocket. Robin shook her head and almost leapt from the table. The phone banks were far away, thank God, and she strode right past them into the corridor leading to the ladies room and locked herself in a stall to think.

She was so needy it was almost ridiculous. Her pussy was already moist with excitement, her nipples erect under the blouse and jacket. A million thoughts cascaded, and questions. How could she trust him? She didn't even know him! No one would know where she was or who she went with!

But wait. People did know him. He did go to these silly clubs with their oh-so-serious meetings and agendas.

And he was so…compelling. For such a plain looking man, with his soft eyes and broad forehead and clean-shaven cheeks, still he was one of the most charismatic men she had ever spoken to about these things. And he knew something about her, he sensed that she needed something strong and direct.

You're reading too much into this, she cautioned herself. You're so damn horny you can't think straight. You haven't even discussed safe sex with him for crying out loud. You can't be thinking about just going home and having sex with him on a moments notice!

Oh, yes I can. Even if it turns out to be another date with a guy who thinks he's God's gift to women and doesn't have the imagination of a planarian worm, it'll be *something*.

And with that pessimistic but rational attitude, she returned to the table, cool and confident. She slid into her seat and smiled comfortably at him. "I guess I just have one point to discuss with you," she said, opening her purse with one hand. "This being the age of safety concerns…"

"Of course we'll use safer sex," he interrupted, with another grin. "So with that out of the way, which of the two scenarios did you prefer?"

Robin froze for a second. Well, that had been her biggest concern, right? So, she broke free of the stillness that settled inside her and blushed and lowered her head just a little bit.

"I like the bondage idea better," she said softly.

"Nope. Wrong answer." Troy stood up and scooped up the check. "You should have said, 'Whatever would please you most.'" He leaned over her, whispering hotly into her ear. "Just for that, you'll be holding those red cheeks open for me, begging me to fuck your asshole."

And, three hours later, that was precisely what happened.

She was much more cautious with Troy than she had been with Maria. After the initial thrill of their first three or four meetings, Robin deliberately pulled back and began a more controlled approach. Troy turned out to be perfectly agreeable to this; in fact, he seemed to think more of her for it.

"I hate people who can start calling themselves slaves after the first date," he said one night, while they waited on line for a movie. "You see them hopping from relationship to relationship, always sure that this one is more real then the last one. And I guess it makes me feel like the words get cheapened. If everyone who plays bottom is a slave and everyone who plays top is a master or a mistress, then where's the romance of the titles? Where's the element of the extraordinary?"

"It's in the people who really make you feel that they're different. The ones who don't make a point out of telling you about what they're doing, but who just do it." Robin thought about it for a moment, running the names of people they knew through her head. "Like those two guys at the Fetish Frolic? Dave and…"

"Mike. I remember them. Mike had his nipples pierced."

"Right. But what I really remember about them was that the minute they walked into a room, even though they were both dressed and you couldn't see Mike's collar, you could tell that Dave was his master. When Mike sat down on the floor, it didn't look staged. It was just what he did. When they talked about how they lived at home, you really believed it. It wasn't like they were making it all up to impress other people."

"I like the way you can sense things like that," Troy said, looking into her eyes. "It keeps me remembering that you're the real thing."

Lines like that made Robin blush and move the conversation along. But they also kept her coming back.

He was as different from Maria as two people could be. Where Maria had started with ritual and elaborate scenes, Troy built upward from good and hot sex to a gradual inclusion of rules and formalities. Where Maria fell in love and loved wholeheartedly, Troy kept a certain distance, never touching the border of "boyfriend." He never brought flowers, or used endearments. He didn't hold her hand or kiss her gently and playfully. When they went out, he never placed his arm around her, or encouraged her to move into that closeness that people associated with couples.

Where Maria used her skills in dominance and erotic torment as a lover would, Troy used them more as parameters for their growing relationship. Some forms of attention were rewards. Some were punishments. Some were entirely for his own amusement and pleasure. Robin became aware that they had entered a period of negotiation where the two of them traded expectations, fetishes and needs, without actually coming out and saying everything directly.

In time, they passed through those awkward stages of semi-negotiation.

He encouraged her to talk about her fantasies. She encouraged him to take the lead in determining when, where and how they would interact sexually. They rewarded each other with their eagerness to go into their respective roles, until it became more natural than anything else.

And without a collar like the one she wore before, Robin slowly became Troy's "submissive".

He was demanding of her in ways she delighted in. He began by teaching her exact postures and positions to take upon the utterance of a word or a flick of a subtle hand signal. He utterly dominated their sensual explorations, planning what they would do and not altering it unless it was his pleasure to do so.

And rather than keeping the physical side of their relationship private, he introduced Robin to semi-public play, at SM clubs and parties, where she would find herself stripped and bound and tormented for the pleasure of an audience as well as for the pleasure of her "dominant". The sheer exposure, the humiliation of her responses, and the amount of strength such performances robbed from her all combined to make every public appearance into a test of her endurance. But it was all just another way for her to add luster to her chosen master's image. It was wearing Maria's collar and sitting at her feet, but multiplied by ten.

Experiences began to accumulate, making a kaleidoscope of sensations that swept Robin into a period of complete acceptance of her role. She followed Troy's training with the same sharp attention which served her so well in her profession, and earnestly tried to do everything he demanded of her with flair and an inner expectation of perfection.

Sucking his cock became a regular duty which she transformed into an art, watching videos and reading about techniques and even clumsily practicing on one of her dildos.

Silky, lacy costumes from expensive lingerie stores began to fill her wardrobe, carefully chosen for the way they accentuated her curves and allowed instant access to any part of her body.

She learned everything she could about his tastes and preferences, from the way he took coffee (black, one sugar), to which colors he preferred in his SM toys (in this he was typical, black on black). She anticipated his movements and desires whenever they were together, and learned that such behavior would almost always be followed by some kind of attentive reward from him.

As weeks fell into months and months gathered into seasons and they fed into and upon each other's desires, Robin began to sense that she was finally feeling something that answered the emptiness inside of her since she was a child. This was more real than anything she had ever felt before. She was making a difference in Troy's life, giving him face, pleasure and service. He was possessive of her, and nurturing and demanding, the way she always imagined a master would be.

So, blinded by her own pleasure and satisfaction, she didn't realize anything was wrong until the night of the video camera.

Bound inside a doorway with chains, her breasts wrapped in loops of soft rope, her body crisscrossed with a harness made of the same material, Robin could only moan when Troy set up the camera and lights and taped her writhing and moaning as he steadily beat her. Then, as she gasped and whimpered, he used a vibrator on her, making her jerk and thrust as he touched and retreated, teased and pressed. All the while, saying, "Look into the camera, baby. Smile for the camera."

She came, again and again, and he captured it all on tape.

And made her watch it while he took her from behind, on her hands and knees in front of the television screen.

Whimpers of pleasure became screams, became inarticulate sounds of pleasure mixed with shame mixed with a perfect sense of something that she might have called contentment if she were capable of thinking.

And much later that night, as she lay wrapped in his arms, she murmured to him, "I would love to be marked by you."

"You are," he chuckled, tracing the area over her ass cheeks and hips that was dotted with little marks of his earlier whipping.

"No, I mean a real mark," she whispered, snuggling closer.

"You mean, like a tattoo?"

"Yes, if that's what you'd prefer. Or maybe a brand..." And she smiled and kissed him and immediately felt the shift, the slight stiffening of his body that was as chilly as an icy mist sweeping through the sheets.

"Go to sleep." His voice no longer held amusement. Nor did it permit discussion.

With a sinking feeling settling over her, Robin couldn't help but disobey. Closing her eyes, she lay awake beside him long into the night, wondering what she said that made him suddenly so distant.

And what that would mean in the morning.

Chapter Ten

"An owner may wish to alter your physical appearance, and has every right to do so, barring an alteration which places you in physical danger. Therefore, you may be expected to grow or trim, remove, style or color any or all of your body hair, or to have its texture changed. You may be expected to use or not to use cosmetics, clothing, adornments, jewelry, or anything else to conform to what your owner expects from you. They may have you pierced in any number of places. My standard contract includes a restriction on any alteration considered permanent; in this category I include tattoos and brands. Would you like to alter that?"

Chris was making notes on a legal pad while Robin knelt motionless on the floor, trying to hold a perfect position while looking natural and relaxed. Her knees were wide apart, her back straight, and her palms resting lightly on her thighs. She spoke carefully, trying to keep herself from bobbing her head and turning it from side to side, the way she normally did when having a conversation. If she wanted to be sold without a gag filling her mouth, she would have to learn how to speak properly.

She had no intention of being gagged on what might be the single most important day of her life.

"Sir, may I please ask a question?"

"You may."

"Sir, should an owner wish to mark me and I am willing to be marked, will that clause prevent it from happening?"

"No, it will not. It only applies to situations where a permanent mark would be against your will."

"Sir, then please allow it to stay as you have written it."

Chris smiled and ground out his cigarette. "Good answer. I was sure you were going to say that you would like the clause kept in. Good girl."

Robin flushed and tried to keep her position.

"You've learned quite a bit in such a short time. I'm beginning to think you might actually be worth it." He jotted down a few more notes. "On your back and masturbate for me."

An erotic jolt flashed throughout Robin's stiff body, and she leaned backward with a barely stifled moan. That kind of mood switch was so typical of her trainer, yet so unpredictable! She slid her legs out underneath her body and brought her fingers down to her bare cunt, finding the wetness already there. It was almost always there, or waiting for a moment's notice to start flowing through her.

She had not experienced the joy and release of orgasm since that first night. But she didn't let that get in the way of performing exactly as she was instructed to. In fact, since Chris had added "for me," she tried to be even more direct in her self-stimulation. She pulled gently at her cunt lips, sliding her fingers along the sensitive flesh and trailing lines of sweet moisture up and around her clit, coaxing it erect. And Chris actually watched her, leaning forward, instead of leaving her to moan and twitch while he paid attention to still more paperwork.

Robin felt complimented by the attention, and deliciously embarrassed. She moaned as she brought herself closer to the edge, and then backed down, controlling herself, keeping herself primed to cum, but not so close that she would let it get away from her.

And then the doorbell rang.

"That will be Leon, I suppose," Chris said, leaning back in the chair. "Stop and tend to your duties."

Robin allowed the slightest of groans to get past her compressed lips, and blushed at the look of disapproval Chris flashed her. Damn it! She had been so perfect all afternoon! With a slight nod which served as an exit bow, she scrambled up and ran down the hallway to answer the door. She licked her fingers and drew them across her belly to dry them and pulled the door open without checking to see who was there.

It wasn't Leon who greeted her as she opened the door with a grin on her face. It was an older man, perhaps in his mid-forties. His skin was the color of dark ground cinnamon, his tightly shorn hair inky black. His eyes focused upon her immediately, and Robin felt the intensity of a gaze that could only be called calculating. As in her value.

Robin knew that her mouth was open and she snapped it shut. Before she could panic, she saw the familiar golden halo of Leon's hair just over the stranger's shoulder, and realized, first to her relief and then to her horror, that this was Mr. Reynolds, of 14C. Leon's owner.

She was relieved because here she was without a stitch of clothing on. If it had been some unexpecting delivery boy, that would have been most improper. She was horrified because she hadn't made any gesture of welcome or respect. Her mind flooded with instructions, and she stepped back, bowing her head as gracefully as she could. This seemed to be acceptable, because he brushed past her and continued down the hall, followed by a grinning Leon, his arms full of dinner fixings. He winked at her as he passed, and then hurried on to the kitchen. Unsure of what to do now, Robin locked the door and walked gingerly toward the living room, hoping that Chris would send her to the kitchen as well.

"Mr. Reynolds," Chris was on his feet when Reynolds entered the room. "Thank you for coming."

"Gordon, Chris, please call me Gordon. We're on your turf now." The two men laughed and shook hands. Robin wondered what the comment about turf meant.

"Thank you, Gordon."

"So, this is the new project, eh?" Gordon Reynolds turned around to point at Robin, who froze and tried to look calm and shy and alluring. His voice was deep and strong, and she suddenly remembered all the adoration in Leon's voice when he talked about the man he called master. She suddenly had a flash; the sight of Leon's golden paleness kneeling before this powerful dark man, taking his cock into his mouth…and felt the wetness return with a surge of pleasure.

"This is Robin," Chris said, a slightly amused smile on his face. "Wondering which of her instructions apply to the situation and failing to do anything as a consequence."

Robin gasped and immediately dropped to her knees and lowered her head.

"Well, that was done with some grace," Gordon Reynolds commented.

"But it doesn't help matters, does it? Go and fetch our drinks from Leon, Robin and bring back the strap. I'm really pleased that you could make it over, Gordon. Leon told me that you're working in Canada now…"

Robin fled to the kitchen wanting to cry.

Leon was just corking a bottle of single malt when she entered, her eyes bright with formed tears.

"Now, now, don't you muss up that sweet face," he said softly, dabbing at her with his ever-present kindness. "But if you're gonna cry, be sure to cry real nice."

Robin managed to smile despite her distress. She signed and took a deeper breath and then picked up the tray. Then, with one more glance at Leon, she whispered, "You never said he was so good looking."

Leon winked and turned his attention to unpacking the food.

The strap was on the hall table. Robin picked it up and then went into the living room to serve the drinks. That, at least, she managed to do with competence. When she put the tray out of the way, she presented the strap in a neat, elegant movement which brought her back to her knees before him, her head bowed.

"That's more like it," Reynolds chuckled.

"Up and present!" Chris snapped his fingers and pointed, and Robin leapt. In a moment, she was positioned kneeling on the sturdy coffee table, her ass jutting up and out, her hands braced on the table surface. She was facing Mr. Reynolds, who uncrossed his legs and eased back into his seat with that same frank look of appraisal on his face. She swallowed hard, and dropped her eyes from his.

The first stroke of the strap caught her across the backs of her thighs, and she whimpered, clenching her eyes and teeth. As Chris raised and lowered the doubled strap over and over, Robin felt acutely aware of every move her body made in reaction. The tensing of her rear cheeks, as they tightened in a futile attempt to dim the spreading heat and pain; the arching of her back as she thrust her ass cheeks out again and again, meeting the wallops with the same earnest shame she felt in all of her punishments.

Having such an attentive audience only made the experience sharper. As the blows drove into her, blazing through her skin, she dipped her head lower and lower, and gasped when Chris' hand grasped a handful of her hair and jerked her head up, so that her red and tear-streaked face was displayed for the visitor.

She had expected to see a smile on his lips, expected to hear him laugh or make some comment. But he reached out and touched a finger to her cheek, tracing a line across the tears, and trailing it down to her chin. All the while, Chris' arm never faltered; it rose and fell in the same terrible rhythm until Robin's breath became ragged and choked.

When he finally stopped, she kissed the strap with passionate thanks, and did the same to his boot when let her get down from the table.

Through all this, Gordon Reynolds said nothing. When Robin picked up her tray and returned it to the kitchen, she could hear the two men going back to their discussion as though nothing out of the ordinary had happened.

This is a life where your time is divided into two distinct areas, she thought as she and Leon served dinner. *Either you're invisible and ignored, or you're the center of attention. And there's no middle ground.*

It was so difficult. And so wonderful.

Her wrists were cuffed and clipped together over her head, stretching her body up to the fullest, so that she could rest only on the balls of her feet when Gordon pushed her legs apart. It turned out he liked her thighs spread as wide as she could hold them. The stinging rod in his hand attested to his annoyance when she drew them even an inch closer together to regain her balance. Her inner thighs were crisscrossed with pink and red stripes.

Chris watched from the bed, one knee drawn up, his right heel resting on Leon's back. Leon was on his knees, his own legs spread over Chris's left leg, his cock and balls pressed against the floor by Chris' boot. Occasionally, Leon made muffled sounds and writhed a little, but Robin had really lost track of what was happening to him.

There was too much happening to her.

Gordon had already "warmed her up" with a hand spanking that brought up all the pain from her earlier strapping and then added to it. She could actually feel the heat almost radiating from her before the man made a gruff sound of satisfaction and turned his attention to other parts of her body.

When he had enough time to thoroughly weave a thick pattern of lines across her thighs and inner thighs, he stepped back to admire her. She was stretched out as far as she could stand it, her body slightly arched, sweat trickling down between her breasts, her breath coming in shallow gasps. With a slight smile, he nodded.

"That's better," he murmured. "Nice to see a girl worked over good."

"Do you want the boy back?" Chris asked.

"Yes, for a little bit."

Chris unhooked his right leg and pushed Leon away from him with it. Leon scrambled across the floor on his hands and knees, his cock swinging low and hard between his legs. His face was flushed pink.

Robin had a clear view of the action as Leon attentively helped his master disrobe, taking the clothing and folding it neatly and placing it out of the way. As Gordon's hard body was revealed, Robin bit back a moan. He was a beautiful man, with that natural grace that comes from an active life as opposed to a structured gym schedule. And although there was a hint of softness around his middle, his chest was broad and deep. His cock, when it was freed from the briefs that held it close to his body, seemed to almost extend itself toward her.

It was unbearable to even think about how much she wanted it.

But he kept his distance and stood while Leon carefully put the last of his clothing away and brought back, without direction, a gold colored foil package shaped like a coin. The blond slave waited on his knees, his head up and his hands cupped around the coin until Reynolds made a gesture so subtle that Robin missed it in a blink. Dry-mouthed and shaking from the strain and tension of her bondage, she watched as Leon sheathed his master's cock in latex, smoothing the translucent cover along the flesh with his lips and tongue, taking it all into his mouth with practiced ease. His blonde hair fell back over his shoulders as his body sank lower, taking that cock deep down, covering it until the head was lodged in his throat.

And Reynolds drew it out with a sigh and walked back to Robin without a word. She felt the warm wetness of him touch her hot and aching inner thigh and moaned.

He caressed her, taking her breasts gently into his hands and cupping them, lifting them up, and away from her body. That slight movement made her shift in her bonds, one foot dragging along the floor as she fought to keep her legs apart. He paid no attention to her efforts, but continued playing with her flesh, compressing his fingers around the soft roundness, trailing them forward to brush her erect nipples. Back and forth, always gentle, always teasing, until once again her breath came in gasps of pleasure and she pressed up and toward him, her sex starved for a touch.

And then, suddenly, he lifted her with two strong hands on her hips, and brought her up into the air. A flash of heat between her legs, and she parted them even more, astonished by the release of tension from her arms and legs, now desperate for the promise of his cock.

And she took it into her, with one strong, smooth motion, sliding along her slick, velvety walls until it was buried in her body up to his heavy balls. He laughed then, a startling thing, but Robin was beyond noticing. She cried out and wrapped her legs around him, climbing up the back of his body, and thrust herself back at him, her entire being filled by his thrusting organ. He brought his body in closer and settled her comfortably onto him, and then took her breasts into his hands again.

"Now work for my pleasure, little one," he said, pinching her nipples sharply. "Make your hips grind into me, make me feel you sucking my cock into your hot cunt. You can do that, can't you?"

Robin moaned and fell backward a little, resting against the pull of the cuffs. Oh she could do as he asked, but for how long? Already, her sex was pulsating with need, and her legs were tight with the strength of her passion. Reynolds gave her nipples another twist and then lowered his head to take one in his mouth. As he jerked down, his teeth clamping around the tender bud, she cried out and threw herself into him. With another laugh, he let the trapped nipple loose and wrapped his arms around her, pulling her in tighter. Her hips thrust against his body, taking him in, and pushing herself away again. And when he crushed her against him, cupping her inflamed ass cheeks in his hands, she could easily see what was happening across the room.

Chris was now seated against the wall in shadow, and Leon's head was in his lap. She could see the darker outline of Chris' hand in Leon's hair, a tight fist, keeping the slave's mouth moving back and forth over a stiff cock jutting out of Chris' open fly. Robin could even see the glint of the silver buttons catching the little light there was in that corner of the room. Leon's pale body was shuddering against the surface of the bed, his hands tightly clasped behind his back.

Suddenly, the room seemed to spin! The churning combination of sensations and the vision of this act across the room, the stretching of every muscle of her body and the fullness of her cunt, all of it swept through her and over her, drowning her in ecstasy. Gordon Reynolds pulled her head back, and met her eyes with his, dark and blazing with passion.

"Come for me, baby," he growled, thrusting up against her. "Make me feel it."

And the explosion that followed made Robin scream!

Her entire body thrust back at him, engulfing him, feeling every inch of his body where it pressed against hers, her nipples crushed against his chest, her heels drumming against his back. Her fingers grasped the chain above her leather cuffs, clenching and unclenching in spasms of release. And her hips ground against the man in an incessant rhythm, yes, yes, yes, YES!

She could barely hear Chris' dry chuckle from across the room. Her heart's pounding was drowning out the other sounds in the room, including the slapping of flesh between her legs. Her head fell back as she gasped for air, and Gordon leaned forward and caught her lips against his, taking them into his mouth, tasting her as she gasped and moaned her pleasure.

By the time he released her and let her legs fall back to the floor, she was unable to stand on her own. He unsnapped the hook holding her up and let her go down to her hands and knees. On her way down, she kissed his hands, and glimpsed, out of the corner of her eye, his glistening cock, still wrapped in its protective sheath, covered with her juices. He was still hard. He had not taken his full pleasure with her.

"She's nice," Reynolds' voice cut through the roaring in her ears. "Very responsive. She's ripe for another round or three." He laughed again.

There was silence for a moment, and Robin dipped her head down to try to catch her breath. Should she thank him for the compliment? No, he wasn't speaking to her directly. Thoughts ran through her head and got tangled in the wave of pleasure still sweeping through her.

"Turn around, Robin," Chris' voice finally cut through the threads. She turned slowly, carefully, staying on her hands and knees, until she faced him again.

Kneeling on the floor in front of her, his hands still behind his back, was

Leon. His cock, pale and smooth, hard and curved slightly away from his body, was directly before her eyes.

"Kiss it," Chris said softly. The room seemed to shimmer with heat around her. She leaned forward and pursed her lips gently, and touched them lightly to the soft round head, feeling a tremor run through him in response.

The next command was only natural.

"Suck it. Just a little."

Carefully, she pushed her body forward to take the head of Leon's cock into her mouth. Washing it with her tongue, she slid forward, ducking and turning her head to ease herself down over it, to cover it with her adoring lips. She heard a shuddering moan come from above her.

She continued, moving her mouth and lips, flicking his cock with her darting tongue when she drew back. Drawing her breath in, she allowed it to rush out in heated waves along his shaft, until his hips started to thrust against her and he was pulled sharply away. She almost fell forward in surprise.

"Get this on him. You saw how he did it for his Master. Do the same."

Her hands trembled as she picked up the little foil coin, but she managed to keep a grip on it, despite the weight of the cuffs still around her wrists. Leon's face was unreadable, caught between rapture and frustration. But his cock jutted out, wet from the touch of her mouth. She obediently covered it, caressing the tight latex down over him, feeling the shivers that came with that compression, that promise. His chest was tight, his shoulders shaking with the strength he needed to keep his arms behind his back.

When Robin pulled back, having smoothed the latex down with her lips until it wrapped him from crown to root, she glanced shyly at Chris. He was standing in the light now, his cock back inside the buttoned fly of his jeans, and he was holding a robe for Mr. Reynolds. Something in the way he performed this common, homey task resonated in her.

Robin instantly knew more about Chris than she could have ever dreamed he would reveal.

She gasped, and he turned to her, his face as stonily disapproving as always.

"Easily distracted," he snapped, even as Reynolds belted the robe and walked back over to stand above the two slaves.

"No, she completed her task," he said, examining Leon over the boy's shoulder.

Chris' voice was gruff. "Turn and present your cunt."

A simple turn, and then her head went down, and her ass up, and her thighs spread apart. An easy pose to remember, with that added thrusting of her hips that put a slight arch in her back and raised the soft mound of her cunt up for inspection or chastisement or penetration.

Or all three.

"Go to it, boy," came Gordon's deep voice. "And hard."

And in an instant, that cock she had so gently kissed and covered was sliding into her, filling her from a different angle, thrusting deep from the first stroke. She mewed like a cat, and buried her mouth against her clenched hands as Leon began to rapidly slam his cock back and forth along her moistened walls, the friction pulling at her lips.

She felt the waves growing again, and with the punishing speed of his rutting, she cried out again. Like master, like man, she thought with a dizzying wave of pleasure. Oh yes, take me, fill me, fuck me!

His own climax came shortly after hers, as he extended his body against her back, pushing his knees against hers, opening her up further, and pressing her down to the floor.

And there they lay, gasping together, wet with their sweat and Robin's juices.

And Robin dared, as she felt the weight of Leon move from her back, to shift in her position long enough to raise her head just a little bit, her mouth open and panting, to look toward the bed. Once again, what she saw was like an electrical shock through her body, sending tingles of awareness to parts of her she thought were finally sated.

For Gordon and Chris were kissing now, Gordon leaning forward, one arm wrapped comfortably around the younger man's shoulder. Chris had one arm wrapped low, around Gordon's waist. The other hand was inside the robe. It was strikingly erotic, like watching something you've only dreamed of.

When they broke their embrace and turned to the two slaves, it was Chris who broke the silence.

"You may play with Robin if you wish, Leon. But we will have coffee and brandy at one o'clock in the living room, with the two of you nicely displayed. I'm leaving the details up to you."

"Yes, sir! Thank you, sir." Leon's smile returned to his face in all its glory.

And the two men left, without another word. Robin stared after them, her mouth still open, her eyes bright with confusion. Then she looked at Leon, who was getting up to examine the wall of toys exposed by one of the locking cabinets. Bouncing on the balls of his feet, he picked up a riding crop and a gag shaped like a bit. With that same familiar grin, he turned back to her.

"Play?" Robin managed to gasp out.

"Yep! Ever play horsy with a Texan, darlin'?"

Robin could only shake her head.

"Oh, good! Been a long time since I broke a filly!" In an instant, he was down next to her again, turning her forcefully over onto her back and pinching her nipples roughly. She gasped, but submitted to his touches, even when he brought up the evil little clamps that bit into her and hurt so much. But on they went, despite her whimpers of pain, and she only bowed her head as he put her back on her hands and knees and pulled her ass cheeks apart. She felt him press some lubrication into that tight crevice and moaned.

"Why?" Her voice was ragged, overrun with lust and fear. "Why are you doing this to me?"

"Because I *can*, sweet stuff. I ain't had my pole in a hole since....hell, at least since Christmas. And you'll see, darlin'. Once you're in the service, you'll love takin' care of the new puppies." He came around in front of her and slipped the bit into her mouth and licked playfully at her tears. "Oh yes you will, sugar. You know we all do."

Chapter Eleven
Robin's Story: First Contact

Much later, when the two visitors had dressed and gone back to their apartment and Chris had freed her from the stringent but decorative bondage that Leon had devised to display her well marked and well fucked body, Robin finally collapsed in harsh tears. Her shoulders shook as the sounds of crying wrenched through all of her self-control, and the very fight against them made the tears flow even faster.

To her numbed surprise, Chris did not stay in the room when she cried, but left her silently, offering neither chastisement nor comfort.

But when she raised her head and sniffed and wiped her tears on a napkin, he returned, holding a glass of water. With a gesture that instructed her to keep her hands at her sides, he allowed her to sip some water while he held the glass. And when he sat down and crossed his leg over his knee, she eased back into a comfortable kneeling position and sniffed again.

"I'm sorry," she said softly.

"You should be. Losing control like that is almost inexcusable. Almost, of course, because some owners not only expect it, but cultivate it. Others may use it as an excuse for more sex play. But most would consider it to be an act which effectively barred them from being able to make productive use of you." He looked around, patted his pocket absently, and then glanced at the hallway. He turned back to her. "Go get them."

Robin got up, her knees still shaky, and went to the master bedroom. The huge dark bed held a tangled and rumpled pile of blankets. One pillow was on the floor, and two condom wrappers. The cigarettes were on the nightstand, next to a cock ring. The room smelled like salt and tobacco and something slightly sweet. It was heavy, oppressive and utterly masculine.

She shivered suddenly, and went back to the comforting light of the living room. Chris lit up immediately and waved the smoke away, pointing back to where she had been sitting. "Now tell me about the tears."

There was a comfortable silence between them while she thought. How normal this little ritual had become, she on her knees, shorn of any covering, talking about things which she had held as tightly as secret oaths while he sat in fully clothed comfort, his head crowned with smoke.

"You couldn't have known..." she stopped, blinked, and organized her thoughts again. "It was always a fantasy of mine. To be given away. Or, not really given, but loaned."

"Go on."

"It was something that Maria used to tease me with, but I always knew...really knew...that she wouldn't do it. I used to imagine what might happen if she did, but I couldn't suspend reality to see her actually do it. So I tried not to think about it any more. I figured that the less I used it in my fantasies, the less I'd be disappointed when she teased me about it again."

"But we've spoken about Maria," Chris interrupted. "This is more than your memories of her."

"Yes. Yes, it is." Robin prodded herself a little, searching for more tears. But they had all been cried out, she was calmer now. She took another deep breath, rubbed her reddened wrists absently and met Chris' eyes with her own

"It was Troy," she explained. "When Troy mentioned one day...and it was an idle thing, just off the cuff, 'I'm thinking of loaning you to her,' I believed him. Utterly.

"I suppose I should start at the beginning. This happened while we were still a strong couple. We were at his place one night and he started talking about an old friend who was living in another state. He hadn't seen her in a few years, but it sounded like they'd had a little history together. He mentioned that she had contacted him and that she was going to be in the city on a certain weekend, and that he was looking forward to seeing her again, to catch up on what she'd been doing. And then he said that. That he was also thinking of loaning me to her, to let her play with me.

"The first thing I thought was, Oh, no! I couldn't do that! The next thing I thought was, but that would show that I really belonged to him, wouldn't it? And in that instant, I felt a need I never had before. He voiced it, and his intention became my desire. Even though I never met the woman, even though she might have been of no interest to me sexually. All that mattered was that he had set a new boundary..."

118

The woman never materialized. Whether she had changed her plans or Troy had forgotten his intentions, Robin never found out. But the idea stayed behind. Robin remembered Troy's casual announcement with a combination of anxiety and contentment. Anxiety over how it would eventually happen, and with whom. But content in the knowledge that Troy had such confidence in her obedience to him and in his ownership of her that he would so casually suggest such a thing. She could hardly wait for the opportunity to come up. She would have a wonderful way of proving her loyalty and devotion to him.

And certainly, she thought at the time, Troy would not loan me to someone without some mark of ownership on me. Perhaps a collar. Perhaps…something else.

As time passed, Robin kept herself aware of Troy's friends, making notes about their preferences and habits in her mind whenever she had a chance to learn them.

Not only will I be obedient, she thought with a sense of satisfaction, but I will be on my best behavior and whoever gets me will think that Troy has to be the best master in the world. They'll think I was the best trained, most eager slave they ever met.

But Troy never brought up the subject again. And as their relationship continued, Robin began feeling a familiar sense of doubt. Unlike Maria, Troy always maintained that certain distance, keeping them apart as master and slave. There was very little of the slipping of roles that had threatened and finally ended her previous relationship. But at the same time, there was little forward movement either. As soon as she learned certain things, Troy's regular training sessions halted.

"You're just about perfect," he told her one evening, when she dared to ask him why this was so. "If I trained you any further, there wouldn't be enough left for you to be punished over." He chuckled and she had smiled, blushing.

But when she thought about it, it was clear to her that she was nowhere near perfection. Her behavior did vary, sometimes depending on her mood and sometimes because she just forgot something. And even though Troy could usually be counted upon to notice and react, his reactions started to shift toward acceptance of her faults and forgiveness rather then reinforcement of correct behavior.

One night, at the ending of yet another seminar about their sexuality (during which Robin struggled to stay awake and look intelligent and happy), Troy and Robin ended up involved in a discussion with some other couples about roles and behavior. Robin was surprised to hear Troy bragging about how well schooled and behaved she was, and how genuine she was compared to other women he had played with in the past.

"No, this one's for real," he had said, placing an arm around her shoulders in an uncharacteristic gesture of pride. "I don't know how much longer she'll be content with me! I've already made her perfect."

And the people had laughed and the topic turned to someone else's relationship. And Robin went home that evening with a profound sense of confusion.

The questions compounded with every minute of thought she devoted to her situation. Why did Troy believe that she was perfect in her role when it was patently clear to her that she was not? And why, if she was indeed so "perfect," did he not choose to make their relationship more formal, to place some sort of visible claim on her? Thus far, the closest he had come to that was using a high training collar during some of their sessions. But it was a toy, and not a mark of ownership.

Among their friends, they had seen many examples of such distinctions. Collars were common to be sure, but even they varied in form and substance. Simple leather bands that fastened with buckles, silver and gold chains with delicate locks on them, steel bands, woven and beaded chokers; each one showed the nature of the people using it as well as the style of relationship they had.

But collars were only the most obvious. Other people wore everything from bracelets to body chains to nose, nipple, cock, labia, or even belly button piercings. Still others had markings made on their flesh with tattoo inks or scalpels or even heated iron. In fact, they had been to at least two demonstrations of such arts, and acted as formal witnesses to the binding pact between two friends of theirs.

(Who subsequently broke up three months later, but that seemed somewhat beside the point.)

And what about the things that Troy spoke about but never did? One was his announcement that she would or could be loaned, but there had been others as well. He spoke about extending his control over her to such a point that she would be going to work with some kind of harness beneath her clothing, holding some kind of penetrating toy within her body during the day. Or once, he spoke of the possibility of their attending some kind of fund-raising mock slave auction, where he would offer her to a crowd of strangers, stripping her on a stage under bright lights and showing her off.

At the time, the very suggestion filled her with horror. But the event came and went, and Troy never brought it up again.

Troy, who had sought her out because she seemed "real" to his eyes, always seemed to stop just short of behaving in any manner which would demonstrate that she belonged to him.

She wrote one night:

It seems obvious that he is insecure about some aspect of our relationship. It could be that Joe and Susan's break-up hit him harder than he's showing, and he thinks that setting up a similar situation will make a fool out of him if it doesn't work out. Or it could be the standard male attitude toward commitment. But either way, here I am feeling like I'm missing something and getting trapped in the same old game! I don't want to mess up what I have now. But I can't see that I'm going to get anything much better by giving up. I have to keep trying. Maybe he'll come to his senses.

She decided to try, gently, to remind him of the things he had spoken about but had never acted upon. She was always careful to be non-irritating and cheerful, always acting as his eager to please and easy to satisfy submissive, backing off at the slightest sign of anger or disinterest. And when he actually listened, the responses were one disappointment after another.

About the day-time intrusions, the clamps on her nipples or labia, the dildo in her body?

"We don't need that shit," Troy said, waving his hand derisively. "I know that if I ordered you to do those things, you would. And that's all that matters to me."

About the auction?

"That's just a show for tourists," he had sneered. "I think more of you than to put you through that kind of humiliation just to make a couple of wannabes squirt in their shorts. If we had a better quality of people out there, I'd do it in a minute."

And finally, after that night of uncomfortable silence over her suggestion concerning some kind of mark, Robin approached the last thing that Troy had mentioned but never acted upon. It was the last chance for her to somehow prove her sincerity, or so she saw it.

Barry had been Troy's buddy since college. They had joined together for various sexual adventures, including a brief bout with swinging, and then had settled back into doing SM with their lovers. Unlike Troy, Barry was a switch; he could be top or bottom as the situation required, and frequently enjoyed both in a single evening's entertainment. He tended to stay away from long term relationships, preferring to keep his sensual activities casual or brief. For all those reasons, plus the fact that Barry was a safe and skilled top, Robin decided that he would be ideal for her purposes. Her idea was to gently remind Troy that she was amenable to being loaned, and to then add the suggestion that Barry seemed a likely candidate for such an honor.

She wasn't stupid enough to link the two ideas together all at once. But when Troy raised his eyebrows and told her in no uncertain terms that yes, he knew she could be loaned, and indeed, he had never lost track of that fact, she

121

became almost tearfully eager to move things along. It was the first sign from her man that he was interested in doing something they had never done before.

It happened on a Sunday, over at Barry's apartment. They had finished their bagels a little over an hour before, and were relaxing in the summer heat. Robin was working her way steadily through the Times while the guys talked about baseball. It seemed all very natural and familiar, but Robin wasn't in the least bit surprised when Troy snapped his fingers and made a hand gesture.

She was instantly wet; a thrill shot through her body as she dropped the paper and rushed over to his side to kneel in a formal position, her head bowed and her wrists held behind her back.

"Nice trick," Barry chuckled. "Does she roll over and play dead, too?"

Robin turned a dark red with blushing. Barry had never been so casually insulting before, and he had certainly seen her do similar things on many past occasions.

"If you want her to," Troy said amiably. "I've got to run a few errands, it'll take me until four or five. You wouldn't mind keeping her for the afternoon, would you?"

"Keeping her? You mean, would I mind if she just hung out here for a while?"

"Well, I wouldn't be so ungenerous," Troy said, dropping one hand to her head. "So that you don't feel inconvenienced, why don't you do whatever your heart desires with her. She'll obey you as if you were me, won't you, slave?"

Robin's throat closed against her. She could barely get the words out. Troy had called her slave in front of someone else…but at the same time, he was offering Barry *carte blanche*, and even leaving the apartment!

She glanced up at Barry and saw clearly that he was neither surprised nor confused by the offer. So the two men had already discussed it.

Somehow, that thought simultaneously pleased and worried her. It was nice to know that Troy had given the matter thought and had contributed some advance planning. But it was unnerving to think of exactly what the two men had concocted between themselves.

"Yes, master," she managed to whisper. She hadn't spoken that word out loud in a long time.

"Then, sure, I'll keep an eye on her," Barry said cheerfully. "Take your time."

As soon as the door clicked shut behind Troy, and even while his footsteps were still audible in the hallway, Barry was on her. One hand reached for the curve of her breasts, searching and squeezing, while his other hand whipped to the back of her neck and pulled her up and into his embrace, his mouth covering hers. The faint whimper of her surprise was lost in his fumbling around her blouse buttons, freeing her soft breasts so that he could run his palm over them. Her nipples were stiff and already tender, and she moaned into his mouth.

"I've been waiting so long for this," he groaned as their lips separated. "You're so hot! But first, let's warm you up a little!"

Quicker than she could have imagined, Barry pulled her blouse off, threw a pair of cuffs on her wrists and hooked them to the chain he had installed in one corner of his living room. She was familiar with the position; Troy had put her there many times before for private play parties. Barry lost no time in admiring her, but stripped off her skirt and panties and began to spank her, one hand cupping her tits, the other swinging wide to bring up a slight warmth from her rear cheeks.

"Oh God, this is great," he murmured, moving around her to mouth her nipples. "Do you like it, baby? Tell me you like it."

His voice was desperate to please.

Robin felt the beginnings of disappointment and frustration.

"Come on, baby, tell me you love it!," his insistent voice demanded.

"I…I do," she answered hesitantly. "Please…I love it when you spank me. Please keep doing it?"

It was almost comical how quickly he seized on her nervous query. "You want some more spanking? Coming right up! Man, I love this!"

And he ducked back around her shoulder and started spanking her again, this time with slightly more enthusiasm and force. But the damage had been done. Although the steady tapping and cupping of her ass cheeks was as pleasurable as it always was, Robin had already lost her passion for the scene. She bit her lip to keep from sighing when he stopped spanking and leaned in to lick her ear and ask her if she would like a little paddling now.

When she said that she didn't like paddles, he asked her what she would like. In despair, she tried the answer that Troy had taught her. "Whatever would please you, master."

"Yeah, I like to hear that. Well, how about…some whipping? You'd like that, right? I have a nice whip…it's so soft…you'll love it! Wait right here…slave!" With a cackle, he ran off to his bedroom to bring out his toys.

This was not one of my better ideas, Robin thought.

Barry proceeded, in his friendly and genuinely eager to please fashion, to do precisely whatever Robin wanted. Or at least what he supposed she wanted. He brought out the lightest, most sensual whips he owned and trailed them over her body, and then slapped them gently across her shoulders and ass to no great effect. At the first sign of discomfort from her, he was immediately caring and tender. He only paused between "whippings" to kiss her mouth or suck gently on her nipples. He returned to spanking her, slowly and lovingly, cupping her ass cheeks between each smack, and asking whether she liked it. When she finally lost her patience and urged him to hit her harder, he did so for about three minutes and then praised her lavishly for her ability to take "pain."

When he freed her from the chain and laid her down on her back so that he could massage her wrists and then work his way down her entire body with his hands and mouth, she sighed and tried to relax. This would have been great, she reflected, if it happened three years ago. But now, with the need to prove herself to Troy so strong and the drives within her so directed to dominance and control, submission and surrender, it was like making out in the back seat at the drive in. Sweet, but ultimately unsatisfying. There was barely a glow of warmth on her backside.

If I were a normal woman, she thought, feeling slightly tickled as Barry kissed her belly, I'd want to get fucked. Or at least, I'd need to cum. Being who I am, I really need to get dragged out of here, strapped until I cry and made to feel utterly used.

Instead, Barry brought her into his bedroom, went down on her with glee if not great skill, and showed off his erection with all the pride of a teenager who never realized it could get so big. And it *was* impressive; nice and fat and tubular. As he unrolled a colorful condom over it, smoothing the latex down over the skin, it reminded Robin instantly of a red-skinned kosher salami. She held her breath as his words came tumbling out.

"See what you do to me baby? Look at it! It's all for you! How do you want it?"

Sliced thick and pan fried with eggs.

Amazingly, different words came out of her mouth. "Fuck me!" she cried, fighting to keep the giggles back.

And Barry threw himself on her with exuberant passion, driving into her with a satisfying ease that filled her and kept her mind off that last image. It was the same vanilla fucking that dear old Greg had introduced her to, but by now she knew more about her own body and responses. She lifted her heels up and hugged Barry to her, making him grind his cock against her body, pushing her ass up off the bed and putting pressure right where she liked it, his cock pushing down, his body pushing in. She rocked against him, moaning when he finally took the hint and began to match her rhythms with his own. And with the help of a brief fantasy image of having Troy come in on them and thrusting his own hard cock into her ass, sandwiching her between their two bodies and using her until she was limp and covered with sweat and semen, she did come, a nice, long, drawn out orgasm that engulfed Barry's salami and literally milked his own cum out of it. Unlike Troy, who gasped when he came, Barry whimpered.

His saving grace was that he did not ask her if it had been good. Nevertheless, aware of the fragile male ego, she assured him that the earth moved. He was so thrilled that he went out and brought her a glass of water and insisted that she "rest" after her "workout."

Robin took the opportunity and feigned sleep until Troy came to pick her up. The two men had a brief conversation in front of her where Barry made a big deal about how obedient and responsive Robin was, and what a pleasure it was to use her. Then Troy made a big deal out of thanking Barry for his attention, and they parted with friendly reminders about some upcoming event they were all going to.

That night, Troy fucked Robin with a single-minded passion, turning her body and pushing her into different positions so that his cock could literally assault her from every angle. She cried out, she wailed, and came for him, over and over, and when he finally shot his cum, he was rigid with strain and harnessed power.

But the next morning, things began to fall apart in what Robin instantly knew was such a cliché that she should have seen it coming months ago.

"You liked it, didn't you?" Troy's voice was as insinuatingly hostile as it had been the first time he asked that question. And the fifth. And the tenth.

It had started with Troy's insistence that Robin give him a detailed description of everything that had happened at Barry's. He interrupted her frequently, asking her questions about how this or that felt, and whether she enjoyed everything that happened. And she was honest with him, as was only right; she told him how disappointed she was in Barry's un-master-like attitude, but admitted that it was nice to get such soothing, caring attention.

And then she figured that the incident had ended. She was sure that Troy was now aware of the full spectrum of power he had over her, and he knew that she desired only him. She was completely wrong.

For Troy had manufactured some impossible scenario, wherein she had manipulated him into allowing her to sleep with his best friend. Despite repeated assurances that she was not interested in Barry emotionally or physically, he used her own words against her in a relentless inquisition concerning her reactions and thoughts and present and future desires.

The man who swore that he would not be bound to any sort of formal commitment fell victim to the common lover's malady of jealousy.

In public, he turned hostile to anyone who showed even the slightest interest in Robin. Even other submissives learned to keep their distance when Troy was around.

In private though, he was simply cruel. He wavered from angry passion to cold disinterest, and returned always to the same questions. She *did* like sleeping with another guy.

"It was just that one time," she insisted. "If you don't want me to ever be with anyone else again, you have that power!"

"Until you see another dick you like," he sneered back. "Then all of a sudden it'll be, 'Master, please lend me to him!' won't it? Any excuse to get another cock between your legs!"

Robin's eyes narrowed in fury. "If that's what you believe, then I don't see the point in continuing this discussion," she said. "You can call me if you want to talk about this like adults."

"Oh sure, turn cold on me, you bitch! Well, just remember, I made you fucking crawl to me! I was your only *real* master, you're never going to find another man like me!" He rose too, his slim body suddenly threatening. "If you walk out that door, you're making the biggest mistake of your life!"

"Then tell me what I should do!" Robin thundered back. "You think I don't want you; you believe that I'd use you to sleep with other men! What am I supposed to do, sit here and wait until you go insane with jealousy? It was just an experiment that went bad, Troy. You're the one who's dwelling on it. We don't ever have to do anything like it again!"

"Until you want to," he repeated stubbornly.

She stared at him, feeling the anger subside a little bit and sadness flow in. "I'm really sorry," she said. And then she left, his dire threats and insults echoing down the hallway until the elevator closed and she slumped against the back wall. No tears, not yet.

The tears didn't come until three weeks later, when he called her and apologized and promised that he would behave better if she came back. "I'm so, so sorry," he had said, his voice sincere and soft. "It was all my fault, I should have never done that to you!" And as she heard him, she realized that even in the immediate loneliness of their short separation, she had not missed him as much as she had missed being beaten regularly.

He had done his damage. She was no longer interested in him.

That night, the tears flowed like rain.

But her story with Troy wasn't over yet. Although she made it clear to him that she was not going to come back, she also told him that she was not angry

126

with him. In fact, she emphasized that she was appreciative of their relationship, and that she would remember it always as a pleasurable and positive part of her life. And while he resisted the "let's be friends" approach as well as any rejected lover would, he realized that he had predicted her eventual absence on many past occasions. It was to his credit to be clear headed and rational about the whole thing.

She was even pleased that he found himself a new girlfriend/slave. In her opinion, Susie, Joe's ex-slave, was a bit of an airhead, but she seemed to make Troy happy.

In contrast, her own search for companionship was as frustrating as ever. Now hampered by her public roles as a slave to a man and a woman, she became pursued beyond her capacity to even contemplate. But the inherent quality of her suitors had not changed. The vast majority saw their interest in SM as an imaginative kink in their otherwise straightforward sex lives.

And so it was that nearly a year from the end of their relationship, in the ballroom at a large east coast fetish gathering, Troy came looking for Robin and found her engaged in a discussion about the comparative merits of several works of SM fiction. Interrupting the conversation, he drew her aside, politely but with firm enthusiasm.

"What is it?" she asked, smiling. Around them, the crowds chattered and milled, the crinkling and creaking sounds of leather and PVC and crinoline adding a steady undertone to the evening.

"There's someone I think you should meet," Troy said, gesturing across the room. Robin glanced casually over and saw a black haired woman, dressed in a tuxedo, standing near a pair of men in pony harness, bits firmly in place and headstalls wrapped around their ears and foreheads. She confirmed the target with Troy.

"Yes, the oriental lady," Troy nodded. "Robin, I don't know what exactly's going on, but there are some people here who seem a little bit more serious then the average pervert. Can you tell?"

Robin nodded. She had begun to be aware of a subtle difference in a small percentage of people she met. It attracted her, in ways she couldn't exactly put a finger on. This gathering was no exception. Mixed in with the weekend sexual warriors, the bedroom frolickers and the organization and contest celebrities was a small number of people who seemed unaffected by the posturing and the presentations. Or perhaps amused by them.

"Well," Troy said, taking another glance at the woman across the room, "I think she knows what's going on. And, moreso, I think she's willing to talk about it. But not to me."

"Then what makes you think she'll talk to me?"

"She told me so."

Robin turned to look at the woman. Even across the room, she could see her careful nod. She turned back to Troy. "Why am I scared all of a sudden?"

"Because you might be that much closer to getting what you really want." Troy said this without rancor, and Robin loved him for it. "Shall I introduce the two of you, or do you want to just go over by yourself?"

Robin first felt the urge to walk over and talk to her. But she hesitated, feeling that perhaps such a move wouldn't be proper. So she allowed Troy, resplendent in his leather pants and black shirt, to escort her across the room, there to formally introduce her.

"Robin, please meet Ms. Kenda Mandarin."

"Ken," the woman said smoothly. Her voice was light, but serious, and her eyes were predatory. "My friends call me Ken."

Chapter Twelve

Robin struggled with the knot over and over, until her fingertips felt numb. It resisted her diabolically, remaining tangled where it should be smooth, tight where it should be loose, sloppy where it should be crisp. It never came out even.

She never realized that so much went into tying a simple bow tie.

But she had to get it right before Chris came back from wherever he had gone. His tuxedo hung, freshly aired and dusted, his shirt was crisp in white tissue paper on the bed. A box containing the braces and studs and cufflinks was on the edge of the night stand. Robin had been struggling with the tie for almost an hour. Nothing that she knotted seemed even close to the ideal that was pictured on the instruction sheet she had gotten from the formal wear shop.

That had been an inspiration. When Chris had left her, all he had done was hand her the tie and tell her that she would be expected to act as his valet that evening; she *did* know how to deal with one of these, didn't she?

Robin's sole experience with bow ties had been seeing them around the throats of professors, or on the boyfriends of various girlfriends on their wedding days. And those particular ties had an adjustable band that clipped on. So as soon as Chris left, she opened the yellow pages and called the nearest formal wear shops. One of them did indeed have a prepared sheet that they gave out to their customers, and yes, they could give her one if she came by. So she had dressed and gone out (Chris never told her that she couldn't), and, feeling odd to be so covered, picked up the hint sheet.

Now, with Chris due back any moment, she was only a little closer to tying the damn thing correctly.

When she heard his key in the door, she shook the band of silk out and smoothed it over the shoulder of the tux. Luckily, it showed no great sign of the abuse she had put it through. She hit the hallway as the door started to swing inward, and was ready to receive the large package out of his arms when he extended it toward her.

"We're going to do something a little different tonight," Chris said as he walked into the apartment, letting her close the door behind him. He almost never said "hello," or "good morning." She'd gotten used to it, especially since she realized that on some mornings, he went to a gym and came back all ready to tear into her at the slightest sign of sulkiness. He shrugged his jacket back over his shoulders, and she had just enough time to put the package (a long box) down on the table before she neatly caught the garment and hung it on the rack. "In the meantime," he said, "try this on, and make sure it fits."

Robin eyed the large box and picked it up again. "Sir?"

"You may use the dressing room in the master bedroom. You'll need the mirrors. But first, make some coffee." He walked into the dining room without another glance.

Robin rushed competently through preparing and serving the coffee, and opened the box with trepidation. But as she brushed aside the layers of tissue paper, she revealed a simple but lovely black dress, suitable for a formal party. Separated from the dress by a partition was a small cloth envelope that held stockings and a garter belt, a box containing a pair of gold earrings, and a larger box with a pair of fashionable shoes.

I'm going to a party! Robin thought deliriously as she rushed into the dressing room. Of course everything fit, allowing for the stiffness of new shoes. There was no reason why anything would be unsuitable, she reflected. Chris knows every inch of my body, he has all my measurements.

The dress was long sleeved, with touches of layered black lace where they would add dimension without color. It was high necked, but cut to wrap around her sensuously. It was deceptively simple, as all little black dresses should be. There was no designer label on it, which said more than the presence of a label would.

With her hair done up and the earrings and a little make-up, she'd be very pretty. The heels would help a lot, they would make her legs look longer. She stared at her reflection in the mirror. It was conceivable that someone would pay an awful lot of money for the woman who looked back at her. The thought was amazing; it was unlike anything she had felt about herself since she was a little girl.

Taken by her musings, she didn't hear Chris' approach until he slid back one of the doors. She turned to him with a blush.

"It seems adequate," he said.

"It's wonderful," Robin gushed, turning for him. "It's beautiful, sir. Does this mean that I'm going with you tonight?"

"It does. So take it off, and do whatever it is you would normally do before a black tie affair. When you come to dress me, I want you naked, as usual. You'll dress after me. We have to leave at 6:15. Will that be enough time for you to get ready?"

It was. Chris wanted her to be able to complete his dressing, not oversee it from socks up. So, she fastened the braces, did up his starched collar and French cuffs, and standing behind him, tied the bow-tie into the neatest, most even knot she could have imagined coming from her fingers. Chris glanced at himself in the mirror, flipped his hair in place with his fingers and grunted, releasing her to dress.

The recognition for a job well done doesn't seem to apply to my situation, Robin thought as she rolled a stocking up past her knee. But then, I know it was done well. And I know he knows. And...that's enough.

Her make-up box, one of the things she had brought back from the apartment, seemed alien to her after only a week without it. She used it sparingly.

When she came out of her room, Chris had another surprise for her: a long, black coat. She was relieved that it wasn't fur; she had always maintained a distaste for the sensation of fur. But it was a lush, thick cashmere, with a silken shawl collar. He was wearing a black men's trench coat, with a white scarf tucked into the lapels.

It was all too, too classy. She giggled as she slid her arms into the warm embrace of the coat.

"What?"

"It's just that this doesn't feel like a regular night, sir," Robin said. "I used to go to formal parties all the time. Hell, they were part of the job. Openings, shows, anniversaries, birthday parties for big clients, museum fund-raisers...I have lots of dresses in storage for this kind of thing. But tonight, I feel...different. Almost like I'm going to the prom. Or to Cinderella's ball."

Chris shrugged. "In a way, you are. Tonight, you are going to your first function which takes place within the Marketplace. The event," he took the invitation out of his pocket and glanced at it, "*is* an anniversary. The house which manages the New York Autumn/Winter auction, which is the one I would like to show you in, is celebrating their fiftieth year of business."

"Do you mean..." Robin paled. "Is there going to be...? Will there be buyers there?"

"Certainly." Chris slid the invitation back into his pocket and checked his watch. "Now come, the car is waiting."

The car, of course, was a limousine. The driver was already waiting for them as they exited the building, and he ushered them into the back without a word. As they pulled away into traffic, Chris leaned back with a sigh.

"Normally I don't attend such things," he said casually. Robin, who felt uncomfortable sitting by his side, tried to relax her posture. "But my employers, who would have attended, are away, and they have appointed me to take their place. Upon reflection, I realized that it would be valuable for you to meet some other members of the Marketplace in a setting less intimidating than your first sale. It will also serve as your last chance to interact on conventional social circumstances. Although a few individuals may know that I am training you, you are not considered a slave per se. I advise you to take advantage of this evening. Tomorrow and Monday are your last days to settle your common affairs before embarking wholeheartedly into this life. Tonight, you can catch a glimpse of some of the people who are living it."

"This is really living in style," Robin commented.

"Well, this is a formal occasion. Certainly not all of our functions are this elaborate. You will discover that our average one or two slave owner is only moderately well off by the national standards. Some wealth is necessary to be sure; it is not cheap to purchase and maintain a slave. In addition to the sale price, an owner must provide quality health care and room and board, and in some instances, vocational training or some form of higher education. But we are seeing a new generation of buyers emerging, those for whom their slave is an investment in their occupation, as opposed to a conspicuous way to display their erotic tastes."

"Tell me about that, please," Robin prompted.

"It is analogous to a situation in an ancient society utilizing slavery as a method of debt management. A partnership, or perhaps a family, purchases a talented slave to fulfill an aspect of their small business. Today, that might be an accountant or a lawyer perhaps, or a skilled carpenter or electrical engineer. That slave becomes a part of the business, an unlisted asset in a way. They may be registered as an employee or not, depending on the usefulness of that description. But instantly, they become an integral part of these people's lives, a worker whose energy, commitment and loyalty are without question." Chris paused.

"But they're still treated like slaves, aren't they?"

"As I've mentioned, the treatment of property is highly individualized. The situation may vary as much as having a slave become a defacto member of a family, to being a do-it-all whose duties begin hours before their masters rise and end late into the night when everyone else has gone to sleep. It would not be uncommon to have a slave who works in the family business but is also expected to cook, clean, perform child care duties including elementary education, drive the car and run errands, and then entertain the owners sexually as the mood came upon them."

Robin blew out a heavy breath. "That's some workload."

"Yes," Chris agreed. "But, in fact…" Chris smiled, the corner of his mouth turning up, "Such a situation used to be fairly common in this country. It was called being a housewife."

Robin made a face. "That doesn't make it sound very appetizing."

Chris shrugged. "Yet it makes eminently more sense to have a class of persons willing to commit themselves body and soul to such work rather than depend upon society to pressure half of the adult population to conform to such an unrealistic cultural expectation. And within the Marketplace, we do maintain the added bonus of requiring that foreign born slaves hold valid green cards, and that all of the merchandise is protected legally and fiscally within their nation of ownership. In fact," he smiled again, a little wicked twinkle of amusement, "I'm sure that the IRS is aware that Marketplace nannies and housekeepers are among the best paid and the best provided for in the country."

"What about other situations? Not every slave ends up being a housewife, right?" Robin didn't try to hide desperation in her voice.

"No, they don't. Many are, as I've said, purchased for their professional skills. Take, for example, Greta."

"OK."

"Greta is a skilled personal physician. She entered the Marketplace shortly after her internship, and bidding was fierce. For her first contract, she was purchased by someone who owned a small tourism and cruising business. She spent two years acting as ship's doctor on a cruising vessel which services Marketplace members on one out of every three voyages.

"For her second contract, she returned to open bidding and ended up serving for three years as the private physician for a Californian wine merchant and his household.

"Then, upon her request, she spent six months training with Anderson, and was sold to Dr. Kaufmann." Chris ticked off each sale on his fingers. "Emil is a psychologist, whose practice was split between servicing the Marketplace, which he preferred, to seeing clients from the outside, which he only did to maintain his standard of living. By making a substantial investment in the acquisition of Greta, he added a physician's skills to his services and now fills a specific niche in the scheme of things.

"Since physical check-ups and supervised medical care are specifically provided for in every standard contract, it is to the Marketplace's benefit to have doctors available who will be able to treat patients and make examinations without being surprised or outraged or even embarrassed by the existence and appearance of slaves. And since psychological profiles are considered highly desirable, this team of two doctors has become enormously convenient. The fact that Emil still insists upon doing on-site work also gives him a competitive edge."

"I guess so. Finding two doctors who make housecalls period is pretty amazing."

A chuckle. "Yes, there is that."

"But what about the other things? What about the bondage, the punishments, the sex?"

"Oh, they're almost always present," Chris assured her. " I hey may be less emphasized, because of a slave's usefulness in other areas, or they may be curtailed for lifestyle or disciplinary reasons. But slaves are rarely, if ever, permitted to forget or put aside their primary function: which is to be utterly available and useful to their owners for whatever purpose the owner identifies."

"Which sounds very hot," Robin admitted, "until you realize that an owner may have something in mind that a slave would never expect. Like putting them to work in the family business."

"Exactly. The mark of the fetishist is the pleasure received in the sadomasochistic attention. The mark of the slave is in their devotion to their duties, regardless of their master or their work. It is not a common factor in humanity, although it is a recurrently persistent one. Greta has it. You might." Chris glanced out the window. "Tonight, I expect you to be my companion, not my attendant. Use every minute you can. Learn all that you are able. Because if you return to me on Monday night, you must leave behind your old life with no regrets. Remember, Robin. Not every master will be Prince Charming."

"I was never very interested in royalty," Robin replied.

"That is to your credit," Chris said. And they rode in silence for the rest of the trip.

It was exactly as she had imagined such a gathering to be.

The long private drive with a liveried servant instantly available to open the car door. The matching couple at the door who took coats and hats and murmured responses to questions in perfect upper-class accents. The guests, resplendent in evening wear, floating in and out of a large ballroom with a skylight exposing an inky night sky. And the servants…exactly as she had pictured them.

Men and women, of years ranging from college age to grandfatherly. A few were stunning, absolute perfection in their bodies and their gleaming smiles. There were at least two types present, and her hungry eyes took in all the details possible.

134

Some were totally clothed. She was drawn at once to the servants' manager, who maintained a discreet distance from the guests, but directed the workers when they scurried back and forth carrying trays and running errands. He was dressed in a working tuxedo, but his collar chain was draped over his white shirt, the lock centered on his chest like a European order.

"The best majordomos are still trained in Great Britain and Ireland, as he was," Chris said to her as she watched the man send a pretty little slave on her way with a light swat to her rear. "Or so the majority of owners believe. The trick is to find someone with an absolute faith in organized hierarchy, who can both give and receive orders with maximum efficiency."

"Sort of like a Marine Lance Corporal in fancy dress," Robin quipped.

"Exactly!" Chris raised an eyebrow. "It should come as no surprise to you that many slaves had either served or wished to serve in various armed forces, looking for that precise manner of living. Of course, the Marketplace is a more equal opportunity employer than most military organizations."

The servers themselves were dressed (if you could call it that) in brief costumes which seemed designed to force the viewer to acknowledge and appreciate the form of the slave beneath. Low-slung bands of black silk caressed the hips, falling into a breechclout which dangled just above the pubis, hanging almost to the knees. The silk was weighted by a line of beaded fringe which danced in the light of the room, and made the band of silk fly and shimmer around the legs. Behind them, a narrower matching band fluttered, just an inch or so between the cheeks of the buttocks. Their flanks were bare. And each of them also wore a vest, the same color silk as their breechclout, clasped under their nipples with cross-crossed white ribbons.

The hurried through the guests, bearing trays and messages, their smiles flashing and their voices low. Robin took a fluted champagne glass from a tray and smiled back at the man who had offered it, and he blushed, just a little.

"I could really get used to living like this," she said to Chris as they both admired the retreating form of the server.

"Could you?" Chris sighed, and patted his pocket absently for cigarettes. "I couldn't."

Before Robin could ask why, she noticed something red swoop down upon Chris from behind.

"Parker! What on earth are you doing here?"

The woman who was now hugging Chris with a warmth that made Robin blink in surprise was tall and attractive and ever so familiar and homey. Her burnt russet colored hair was pulled back into a bun, but stray wisps framed her face and bounced with every move. As she pulled back to look at the man at arms' length, Robin realized that the woman was a lot older than she would have originally guessed. Her long, straight body and the thickness of her hair screamed thirties. But her mischievous deep brown eyes and the faint lines around them told a tale at least ten years older. Or more.

"Ali," Chris said amiably. "It's always a pleasure."

"Then you should call me more often," Ali said, swatting at his shoulder. "Instead of making me embarrass you at stuffy parties."

"You could never embarrass me. Please, may I present Robin, who is accompanying me tonight? Robin, this is Allison Cruz." He performed the introductions with a semi-formal move that Robin had been practicing all week, a discreet nod of the head and shoulders that looked as natural as a handshake. Robin extended her hand, knowing that she still wasn't nearly good enough at those little motions.

Ali's grip was firm and cool. "Pleased ta meetcha," she said in an exaggerated accent. "Call me Ali, everyone does."

"Thank you."

"Don't mention it. Say, Parker, are the bosses here?"

"No, they're still in Europe."

"Oh, too bad! Wait, here's my date…listen, Robert's here. You gotta see him, he's been asking about you forever…" Ali half turned and waved to a slightly shorter and more buxom woman who was making her way through the crowd. Robin had to admire the view; it was quite substantial, but all in proportion to the woman's other gifts. Reubenesque would actually be accurate for her, Robin reflected. Ali turned back to them and flashed a quick smile. "That's my latest project. I better go keep her company. Good to see you, and great to meet you, Robin."

"She seems nice," Robin said as Ali returned to her date. "Is she an owner?"

"She is more of an agent than an owner. She handles a specialized corner of the Marketplace."

"Oh yeah? What's that?"

"Transsexuals, or, to be more correct, the gender dysphoric. Which you could have probably surmised by the appearance of her date." Chris gave a slight nod toward the two people now speaking in animated tones, fighting the muted sounds of the string quartet in the background. Robin really looked this time, and was amazed. If the tall woman who was Ali's date was once a man, only her height might suggest it.

"That's some specialty."

"We all have our favored fields of endeavor." With that, Chris offered no more on the topic, and led Robin through the party, making nods and introductions as he went. Robin lost track of about one third of the people she met, all a blur of tuxedos, shimmering gowns and dresses, and a sprinkling of people dressed in ways to display their property status.

None of the guests were accompanied by a naked or obviously scantily dressed servant, which seemed a little strange, despite how out of place such a person might be in such company. But nevertheless, throats bore chains, or chests were bare under a formal jacket, or perhaps a skirt was cut very high, or slit deliciously to reveal nude flanks. It was tantalizing, playing a kind of identity game and spotting the owners and the owned. Could she imagine playing that role, standing behind such an elegant woman, and unobtrusively having that lighter at hand, or ready to take that drink with one sweeping movement of the arm?

Oh, yes.

Chris always introduced her simply as Robin, and no one asked a single question about who she was or what she was doing there. She was even introduced to someone that she knew, a Matisse owner who collected sea coast watercolors. But he merely smiled, met her eyes knowingly, and continued on without commenting on their past acquaintance.

Before she could ask Chris why, she saw that he was about to be accosted by a formidable man who was obviously pleased to see him. The newcomer was over six feet tall and broad around the chest. His receding hair was cut long, with locks dropping over his powerful shoulders. He would have looked somewhat like a professional football player, or perhaps a wrestler, if there wasn't a hint of softness around his chin.

Which made the sight of him kneeling in an almost full prostration before the much smaller man almost comical. But instead, Robin felt a shiver run through her. Around them, several people nudged out of the way, but no one seemed to pay any real attention beyond a quick glance.

"You may," she heard dimly. Chris was looking down, and after he released those two soft words, his lips compressed tightly.

The man kissed Chris' polished shoes quickly and lightly, not marring the gleaming surface, and then raised himself up to his knees. He was smiling, a pink flush showing around the close cropped beard. "Sir, I've been waiting for some time to be able to do that."

"And so you have. But you have forgotten how to address me, I see."

"Please, sir, I am under instruction by my Mistress to so address you, sir."

"Then of course you must. Please rise."

The big man rose again, and stood with his head slightly lowered. Chris reached out one arm to touch Robin lightly and said, "Robin, meet Robert. He had the opportunity to be tutored in his slavery for six weeks, by my employers. Robert, this is Robin, who is undertaking that training in two weeks' time."

Robert raised his eyes slightly in surprise and respect, and gave her a friendly smile. Robin flushed, knowing that she was not expected to shake his hand,

and feeling that such a nice, normal ritual might help her to gain some sort of serenity.

"You are here with…?" Chris prompted.

"Mistress Janelle and her friends," Robert said smoothly. "Mistress has loaned me for the evening, sir. Please, may I ask a question?"

"You may."

"Are Mr. Elliot and Ms. Selador here tonight?"

"No, they are not. But I shall convey your respects to them if you wish." Robert beamed. "Thank you, sir!"

"And you may do me a service, if you are permitted, Robert."

"I would be honored, sir."

"Then stay with Robin for a bit. I will go and make my own respects to Janelle." Without turning to Robin or waiting for an answering nod, Chris took off into the crowd, leaving Robin with a man who dwarfed her. He looked down at her, still friendly and obviously cheerful.

"May I get you a fresh drink, ma'am?"

Robin eagerly traded her barely sipped but already flat champagne for a still sparkling flute, and then eyed Robert carefully. He seemed comfortable under her gaze.

"Hi," she said lamely.

"Hello, ma'am!"

"Um." Robin put her brain in gear and found the phrase she needed. "I wish you would feel free to speak with me as a peer."

"Oh, thank you! That's very kind. Are you in training now?" He moved a little closer, so that she wouldn't have to speak up to be heard.

"Yes. For one week."

"You must be very excited. I was. I was also terrified."

"You? Terrified?" Robin rolled her eyes. "Of what? A Panzer Division?"

Robert blushed again, and Robin was amazed at what a charming thing it was.

"Well, you wouldn't have recognized me when I was accepted for training." His eyes left her for a moment, following the path that Chris had taken. "I was a totally different person. I was confused, miserable. I still don't understand why I was accepted at all. But they took me, and they helped me to change. Gave me a new way to look at things, a new perspective, if you will."

"That was a nice show of gratitude."

"It was less than what he deserves." Robert fixed his eyes on her again. "I believe that if it were not for Chris Parker, I would have never made it through the training. He encouraged me every step of the way. He listened to my problems, and counseled me, and he was relentless in his discipline. In fact," the man smiled, lost in his memories, "I used to think of him like a Drill

Sergeant. He even gave us the same speech about what to call him. Have you ever heard it?" In answer to her head shake, he continued, "I knew a DS who started out every platoon with the same lines, about how they don't call him "Sir," but "Sergeant," because he *works* for a living. Well, Chris settled that right from the beginning. It confused some of the others, but I knew what he was doing."

That was a fascinating bit of information, especially since she was supposed to call Chris "sir."

"What about the other two?" she asked. "His employers?"

"The best people in the world! Mr. Elliot and Ms. Selador are amazing, just amazing. Why, they took one look at me, and knew immediately what I needed. And Ms. Selador, why she…she…" Again, his eyes glistened with memorable pleasures. "She is the most intuitive, wise and just plain intelligent women I've ever had the privilege to serve. She had no patience for dissembling. But she understood so much about me. I will love her always, and Mr. Elliot, too. They have my respect, and my gratitude. But Chris…I don't know. Words don't really exist to describe how I feel about him." He seemed distressed at not being able to find those words, and Robin felt a stab of guilty compassion.

"That's all right. I didn't mean to put you on the spot. It's just that Chris doesn't talk about himself or his employers very much."

Robert nodded. "Yes, that sounds like him, all right. But he wouldn't have left you alone with me without expecting you to question me. You always have to take advantage of any opportunity to learn. When you're allowed something that might be forbidden later, take it, do it. That's the most important thing I could tell you."

Robin took the advice eagerly, even though she had heard it before, from Chris, as a matter of fact. It seemed wonderful to hear it as a teaching and in practice as well. "It must have been great having other people in training with you," she mused. "I have no one to talk to about these things."

"Oh, it was an experience with its benefits and drawbacks," Robert said. "In the long run, I'm glad I had the opportunity to meet the people I trained with. They taught me a lot by example, good and bad. And one of them gave me a magnificent gift." He blushed again. "But we spent far too much time not getting along with each other and complaining. Why, there was this one woman—" he cut himself off, and lowered his head with a shameful grin. "I mustn't gossip. Please forgive me. The real point was that we became very aware of each other in six weeks, our histories, and our hopes, and then we all lost contact. That's what happens when you get sold. So I don't know what happened to any of them, and it's not something I can ask about."

"Oh? Why not?"

"Well, because they aren't family, and my Mistress can't be expected to know about them. And I think it would be poking into their confidentiality to ask Chris about them. The best I can hope for is to run into one of them at an event like this." His face fell. "But that hasn't happened yet."

"Well…" Robin glanced away with an almost automatic move. How had she known that Chris was returning? She could see him now, shaking someone's hand, obviously on his way back to them. She looked back up into Robert's eyes, and asked, quickly, "Are you happy? I know, it looks obvious, but I need to hear it."

Robert grinned. "Oh, yes, Miss Robin. I wake up every morning and thank all the higher powers for what my life is now. And I think you will, too."

"You may return to your Mistress, Robert."

"Thank you, sir." Robert turned easily with one of those eloquent nods, but Robin spoke quickly before he could move away.

"Chris? I was just going to ask Robert what happened to the other people he trained with."

The trainer's eyes narrowed, and his mouth twisted sardonically. "I see. And were you about to answer, Robert?"

The tall man turned his body back to face Chris and brought his hands behind his back, lowering his head. "I would be unable to answer that question, sir."

"As is only correct. After all, it would be none of your business that Claudia is at this moment the treasured companion slave and ruling hand in her Lady's household. Nor would it be proper for you to know that Brian has entered the service of a much esteemed gentleman whose western estates are known for the talented and exceptionally hard-working young men who populate it." Chris kept his voice steadily cold and harsh, as if delivering a lecture, and Robin couldn't control the twitches of mirth that played around her mouth. But Robert listened with a serious hunger, keeping his eyes downcast.

"And of his other companion in training, well, the less said about that one, the better. The situation turned out to be unfavorable for her and the house, and she was freed from her contract, and so we do not discuss her. Of course, Robert would be informed of that fact only if it had something to do with his current or future position. Robert…hadn't you better be on your way?"

"Yes, sir. Thank you, sir." And he was gone in a flash, darting through the crowd like the linebacker he resembled, his long hair waving gently behind him.

"He seems like a nice man," Robin said after Chris had sent Robert back to his Mistress of the evening.

"He has grown considerably in his new life." Chris fixed one of his raised eyebrow looks upon her and she blushed. "I hope that you will not be in the habit of lying for much longer."

"It wasn't really a lie," Robin protested. "I was asking him about them. He said he couldn't talk about it because it might be considered gossip. And that he was afraid to ask because he didn't want to intrude on their confidentiality."

"And he was correct. I'll punish you for lying later." Chris scanned the room while Robin gulped some champagne to cover her embarrassment.

Most of the rest of the evening passed into a comfortable blur of faces, names, and more guessing games. Unlike the many SM-themed parties she had attended, there was no moment where the host stepped out and started some sort of erotic play, and there were no general announcements that a dungeon or bondage area had been arranged for the guests. There was just the constant stream of charmingly scantily clad slaves, bearing drinks and food and the amused but mild attentions of a very few guests.

"Who are these people?" she asked once, waving one hand. "Are they all owners?"

"No. Many of them are agents, trainers and spotters. A few of them are professionals in other fields who provide services for the Marketplace without actually participating in the business of slave training, use and sale." Chris pointed out a few. There, in one corner, was an architect who took time off from developing commercial properties to design sleeping and living quarters for human chattel, and had also designed some very stylish and durable torment devices. Across from them at one point were two women who were fashion photographers. They also took the artistic and necessary photos for a slave's personal file, and for the catalogs used in the larger international sales. One of them had achieved some attention recently for her advertising work, now featured on billboards and kiosks throughout the country.

"So many people know," Robin marveled. "But no one tells."

"Oh, someone always tells," Chris answered smoothly. "But very few will believe them. The ones who believe, come and find us."

Regrettably, Chris was no party animal. He stayed just long enough to be polite, and directed Robin away from the affair before it really started to wind down. Robin had noticed that he rarely stayed in conversation more than a few minutes, and that most of his time was spent explaining where his employers were, and introducing her. In a way, she felt bad. She would have liked to stay some more, and maybe get a chance to talk to Robert again, but it was obvious that Chris was only taking care of a chore. She sank back into the cushions of the limousine as the ride started, and then sat up again.

"Ken wasn't there."

"No. She is away on business. But she may be back in time for your sale."

"Really? How do you know?"

"She told me." Chris covered a slight yawn, and at the end of it, made a subtle gesture. The dim lights of the passing cars almost made it invisible, but Robin acted on instinct, pushing herself carefully off the seat and curling her knees under her on the carpeted floor of the car. Under her legs, she could feel the pulsating vibrations of the frame.

"Tomorrow, you go back out to finish your business."

She nodded.

"When you come back, I will allow for no imperfections, do you understand? All this past week was a test, to see how much you knew, and how fast you learned. Now, there's nothing else to be done but make every move and every twitch or reaction as perfect as you can. Every response to me will be exact and respectful, containing all the information requested with a minimum of hesitation and embellishment. Your most minor flaws will be punished out of you, even if it makes you into one walking bruise. And Robin…when I place you in the list of properties to be auctioned, and I sign my name as your trainer, I am in effect swearing that your behavior and appearance are guaranteed by me. If you fail me, you will have lost your best hope of attaining the status you seek."

"Sir, Ken told me that you were the best trainer I could get. She was right." Robin swallowed hard. "If anyone could get me perfect, you could."

"Ken wanted me because she knew it would mean an excellent opening bid," Chris snapped. "Any trainer could have gotten you prepped for some sort of appearance on the block. But right now, only I could make sure that you were accepted as an experienced servitor, instead of a novice. And that may make all the difference in the world for you, little girl. It may bring you exactly the life you crave. So when you're concentrating on not disappointing me, also remember that your own happiness depends upon your being seen as an excellently schooled and driven slave."

Robin nodded, and sighed extravagantly when Chris reached out and drew her head toward him, pushing her down onto one hip so that she could rest her cheek against his leg. And like that, they rode in silence toward the city. Fighting the urge to cry, Robin never felt more frightened. Or, when Chris's hand strayed to her to smooth down her hair, so happy.

Chapter Thirteen
Robin's Story: Bank Shot

"No, no, Jesú, no! You've got to thrust your hips up, higher! Make me feel you surround me, take me into you, and now! Yes, now! Open your eyes, you stupid slut!"

Robin panted and bent her back into a bow, pulling her body back for a wild, desperate thrust, her legs spreading wider, her stomach rippling. This time, when she brought her hips up, her pussy lips splayed and soaked with her juices, she gasped at the licking of cool air that swept across her flesh. Her clit seemed giant, pounding with an agony that was too furious to be released by one orgasm. Between her legs, Ken Mandarin stood, her dark face even darker with excitement, her hair matted around her forehead. She had one hand taken up entirely into Robin's body, and the effort and strain in getting it there was paying off for them both.

Robin groaned as Ken's hand began to naturally form into a fist. "No, no, Master, I can't!"

"You already have! Feel it! Look at me!"

Robin forced her eyes open, looked down her body and moaned, and then whimpered. It seemed impossible that there was an entire hand in her cunt, the fingers curled and pressed against her internal walls, pressing smoothly up, and down, and back and forth. Robin felt like crying, like laughing, like pulling away in horror. One twist of the hand and she felt a desperate urge to pee, and then it was replaced by that wonderful sensation of fullness.

"Oh, oh, I don't believe it, I don't believe it," she finally sobbed, allowing her head to fall back. "Oh, God, yes, please, don't stop, please…"

"I'm not going to stop, not yet. Answer me quickly, can you come like this? Will you come for me, like this, with my hand inside your wet cunt?" Ken's

143

voice was harsh, like it always got when she was being cruel, and Robin knew that whatever she answered, her orgasm was in Ken's hands. Literally.

"I don't know," Robin gasped out. "It's too much! Please, I don't know!"

"But you like it? You love it!"

"Yes, oh, yes! Ahhh, please, please..."

Ken laughed, and tossed her head back, sending spikes of inky black hair flying past her ears. Her eyes glittered in possessive pleasure as she hunched forward, rocking her wrist back and forth to spread Robin open even wider, and then to press her strength against Robin's exposed clit. Robin panted, and then moaned, and pressed back, her hips shaking, her entire body now trembling with tension and need.

"Tell me, little pet. Tell me if you can come for your Master."

Robin bit her own lip, her head rocking almost in time with Ken's hand. "No, no," she gasped, "too much...it's too much..."

"Then you won't. Today."

And Ken relaxed her hand a little and went back to the rhythmic stroking movements that had enabled her to ease her way in before, twisting her hand comfortably to find the easiest ways in and out, gently now, always gently.

"Can you imagine people watching this?"

"Yesss!"

"And afterward, your owner will allow them to use you. Perhaps they will scorn to use such an open hole, and fuck you only in your mouth, or they will thrust into your arsehole. That is what being a slave is like."

Robin moaned out loud and thrust her hips up again, and Ken laughed.

"You like that, too? Tell me the truth, little slut, there is nothing you would not submit to. You are truly a slave already."

"Yes, Master, yes, yes!"

"I am going to stop soon. Do you want me to stop?"

"Please, Master...please...do as it pleases you..."

"Ha. Then it pleases me to stop now." With a cruel smile, Ken stopped moving her hand, relaxed the fingers, and slowly drew it out. Robin whimpered for every inch, and then collapsed back onto the table with a moan, her legs shaking. When Ken gave her permission, she drew her legs together and then pulled her knees up toward her body, slipping over onto one side. She shivered, and whimpered while Ken went to wash her hands.

Kenda Mandarin. "Ken" to her friends, "Master" to her slaves. All four of them. Real slaves. People who did not have day jobs with paychecks deposited in their own accounts and their own friends and their own activities and their own places to live. Four people who lived only to do her bidding, who used the title of Master in some magical way that Robin could not only hear, but *feel*, deep in her soul.

144

How desperately Robin wanted to be among them, serving this charmingly cruel, hauntingly beautiful, exotic woman. Foreign and familiar. Caring and sardonic. A talented and voracious lover and an implacable sadist. But it wasn't going to happen.

"You are very nice, very natural," Ken conceded early on. "Cute, too, and fun to play with. But I don't need you. I have all the workers I require, and your skills are of limited use to me. But we shall be together for a while, and enjoy each other."

It wasn't enough. "Tell me about your slaves," Robin begged. "Where did you get them? Can I go there?"

"No, no, it takes more than a cute bottom and an earnest smile to be what they are," Ken scolded. "Leave them be and enjoy what you can have."

It wasn't hard to enjoy time with Ken Mandarin. She was fabulously wealthy. She had a large house far away from the city, and kept a duplex apartment on the Upper East Side as well. She was a genuine heiress, a child from an ancient trading family based in Singapore. Her family's heritage was mixed, and rich with fascinating historical tales, which she only told when plied with drink and steady flattery. But she was obviously Eurasian, and spoke Malay, Chinese, French and Portuguese before she had learned English. She spoke her English with a faint trace of a British accent, mingled with French endearments and an occasional Chinese oath. No one, she claimed, could curse as well as the Chinese. No other language even came close. But she never actually translated what she had just muttered. She was a woman of an almost mercurial temperament, rising to extreme heat in passion and anger and cooling to a businesslike exterior that could make a person shiver from the lack of warmth.

Her slaves seemed eager to serve her. One, a slender and somewhat aged man, took care of her houses. He was also the one who applied his powerful hands and gnarled fingers to Robin's body, drawing out every knot and every ounce of tension before Ken would deign to play with her for the first time. When he smiled, his strong, white teeth gleamed against his dark face, and his eyes flashed with pleasure. He almost never spoke, and when he did, his accent was strong. Ken addressed him only as Yaro, and Robin never found out if that was a name or a title. She did find out that he had been with Ken since her childhood, which was a daunting thought.

Two of her slaves, Andy and Cindy, looked as sweet and corn-fed as any midwestern newlyweds, except that they were brother and sister and as sexually ravenous as two humans could be. They served various functions in Ken's life, ranging from cleaning tasks to bookkeeping, secretarial work and errand running. They also served their Master's desires in bed when she was in the mood, or entertained her with their own antics, or their attentions upon her guests. The weekend that Ken had them take Robin, again and again and again, was overwhelming. Robin had to call in sick on Monday, staying home to wrap herself up among her blankets and pillows, not daring to think about what it would be like to experience such repeated pain and ecstasy on a regular basis. Andy and Cindy were always friendly and cheerful, painfully so, and Cindy told Robin that they had been slaves for three years. It was their use of the title of "Master" which had taught Robin the power of the word, so much more than an endearment, so much more than it had ever seemed before. She yearned to use it as they did, with such respect and awe and pride that it became more than a word. Sometimes, she succeeded.

And then there was Celia, who was French by birth and whose English was also a late acquisition. Celia was a chef whom Ken claimed to have belonged to her older brother. The brother apparently traded Celia to Ken for a male slave whose talents were in construction work and looking good. The male slave was even now working on site at a petrochemical plant that her brother owned, leaving work to strip his clothing off, displaying the many rings her brother would have had attached to him, and then squatting to take her brother's prick in whatever hole the man desired. "My brother," Ken would sigh, "is so predictable. If I sent him one such slave every year, for Christmas perhaps, he would love me forever. Personally, I couldn't tell the difference between them, especially with all their body hair off. It looks so…robotic."

But the result of that trade was a plump, happy slave in the kitchen, who regularly turned out masterpieces for the delight of Ken's household and her many guests.

"And she is already a luxury for me, *ma petite*. She is the only one of my people who does not have more than one function. No, no, you must be content with what you have!"

"But I'm not!"

"Then you must learn to live with disappointment."

"But I love you."

"Ah, and I love you, *ma chérie*! Especially when you cry. Will you cry for me tonight?"

That night, and many more.

It took four months of regular begging to actually get Ken to consider the problem.

"Look, you know I'm good enough," Robin insisted. "You've taught me almost everything I need to know, haven't you? All I need is the way to get in."

"You don't even know what it is you would be getting into," Ken scoffed.

She was dressed, as usual, in her exquisitely tailored men's clothing, a designer pin striped suit today, and a tightly knotted silk tie. Her hair was slicked back, spiky on the top, stylishly ragged and long down her back. Robin never knew what she would discover under Ken's mannish dress. One day it might be a pair of boxer shorts hiding a cock of monstrous proportions. On another day, it might be little scraps of delicate lace barely covering her pubic mound. Ken's erotic moods were as changeable as her exposed ones. It was part of what made her so magnetic.

"So tell me," Robin demanded.

Suddenly, Ken's eyes took on that same predatory gaze she had fixed upon Robin back at the conference. "Very well then, listen. Yes, there exists a large network of sellers of human flesh. It is called, in English, 'the Marketplace.' There, we engage in the trading of men and women for vast amounts of money, and for uses which are not limited by our societies and our cultures. This is not for fun. Do you understand that? It is to provide servants for those whose drives require such absolute obedience. It is not to provide boyfriends. Or girlfriends."

"I understand that."

"If you are allowed to enter this world, you cannot choose your masters. Nor may you deny them use of you once they purchase you. If you leave them, or rebel, you will be rejected from the Marketplace and never allowed to return. Even I do not speak to those who have been sent away."

Robin nodded solemnly.

"And it is not like in the novels, or in the movies!" Ken raised one finger, her eyes lightening up even as Robin got more serious. "The masters, they are not always handsome young men or dashing Asian women."

"Ken…I know that."

Ken leaned back and seemed to take a moment to think. But at that instant, Robin knew, she knew, deep within her, that Ken had been waiting for this. That Ken had always expected this. And rather then feeling ill-used, Robin felt relieved, flattered, and tremendously excited.

"This is the situation," Ken said quickly, sitting up again. "There is an important sale coming up, a large one, here in the city. And I know of two people who can train you for that sale, make you presentable. It will take a month, perhaps two. You will have to give up your employment, and your apartment. But they will almost guarantee that you will be accepted and sold to a respectable bidder. Are you that ready?"

A month! Perhaps two!! Robin's mouth dropped open. She closed it again, feeling a touch of vertigo, and put a hand on the arm of her chair to steady herself.

Surely, it was not her voice that said yes.

But Ken had laughed and called across the house for Andy to call Grendel Elliott.

"What do you mean, they're not home?"

Andy cringed slightly, the bearer of ill tidings. "Please, Master, Mr. Elliot and Ms. Selador are leaving for an extended tour of the European continent, and are not expected back until after the autumn sales. Their earliest agreeable date for the acceptance interview is late November. Shall I make the appointment?"

Ken uttered something that sounded like "duuay-ohmo" and then peppered it with a twist of one hand that looked delightfully obscene. "No, you stupid idiot! Give them my regards, the usual felicitations, wish them a *bon voyage* or whatever is suitable." She waved him off and he scampered away, leaving Robin feeling like she had just missed her lottery drawing by one number. She looked up at Ken, who had started to pace, in expectation.

"Winter sales are difficult," Ken was musing. "Unless we go to Hong Kong, or perhaps to Spain. What languages do you speak?"

"Just English and Italian."

"How do you Americans get away with your colossal ignorance?"

Robin ignored the lure. It was one of Ken's favorite ranting topics. It would hardly help her now.

"Italy, Italy, who is in Italy? You are not tall enough for them...and you aren't exotic enough. The Italians love models, anything that doesn't look like the child their parents wanted them to marry. No, Italy is wrong for you." Ken walked back and forth, weaving her fingers together and then tearing them apart. "I know of some other trainers, but at this time of year, they are all busy polishing up their best clients. The Marketplace has its seasons like any other business. And the autumn through winter is the best. You are in trouble, little one. I think your best option is to wait until these people return, enter their training, and be prepared for the sales after the New Year. It is unfortunate, because there is a large volume of sales just before Christmas. But without good formal training, you will never fetch a price that will ensure a good home."

"If you say so, Ken."

"I do! So there is nothing more to be done, and we shall have that much extra time together. In fact, this is perfect, because we have time to assemble your Marketplace file, and make you presentable. And we shall make some more calls, to see if there are any other trainers who might be free, just in case."

"My file?"

"To be presented for sale, you must have a file with your identity papers, some photos, and a history of your time in service. I shall have a photographer come, and we shall hire an excellent writer to describe your positive attributes. And then I shall write my own description of you, which will be most excellent, because you will be even more pleasing to me from now on, hoping that I will be generous and kind in my writings."

Robin had to smile at the look of pleasure that crossed Ken's face. And to tell the truth, there was something comforting in thinking that she wouldn't have to think about it for another couple of months. And as a few days passed, and Ken asked her personal friends and some business contacts about where a good local trainer could be found, they were steered back to the people who were out of town, or to others who were either too busy or not acceptable by Ken's standards.

But Robin submitted to the photographs and the making of the file, and enjoyed numerous fantasies about people looking through it, trying to decide whether she would be a proper investment. Sometime next year.

Two weeks later, Ken invited Robin to accompany her on a weekend of slumming. Ken knew about all the events and places where people who were interested in SM frequented. She often cruised them for playmates, and took great pleasure in attending their functions and pretending to be what she called "merely kinky."

Robin didn't quite know what to do when she accompanied Ken on these outings. Sometimes, she laughed at Ken's wicked observations and enjoyed the thrill of knowing about an entire world that lay within the reach of these people but always out of sight. But at the same time, there was a pathetic element to it all. This was the world that had sheltered her, provided her with her two important lovers. To see it through Ken's eyes was like looking at your childhood and realizing that your parents weren't really all-knowing and loving, that you really didn't have a comfortable home. Ken considered the entire SM underculture to be nothing more than a huge joke. One evening, she described a Platonic view of it.

"It is as though these people were really dwelling in that cave," she said, pausing to make sure that Robin understood. "They cannot see the flames behind them, and they cannot see the other people around them. They are focused upon the shadows of reality, bound in one place by hoods and blinders and chains which they never realize can be removed. So they create a reality that is based upon a wavering, insubstantial, two dimensional vision.

Naturally, this cannot be satisfying, so they create ways of granting themselves another dimension. They make governments, and declare each other leaders and politicians. They form circles of supporters and pronounce that they are outlaws, struggling against an oppressive society. It is great fun to watch them at their work; they are most industrious. But they rarely take the blinders down and bend to look behind them."

"That's not fair," Robin protested. "When it's all you have, you have to make the best of it. You don't know what it's like thinking that you're the only twisted pervert in the world! When I needed them, that community was there, and they welcomed me. Just because you've had access to something better all your life doesn't mean that people like me shouldn't try to get what we can out of what's available."

"Ah, but it is not a matter of better, my pet. You are comparing the apple with the orange. I do not scorn that little world because what they have is inferior, any more then I scorn a man who works for his money. I find them amusing because in their need to assure themselves that they are acceptable, they find many ways to deny that I exist, or that my slaves do. They make it all into a game that lovers play, with their terrible black costumes and clubs and slogans. Look! Here is a three day conference, where they shall undertake to teach me...let us see... 'Humiliation vs. Degradation'... and 'The Basics of Watersports.'" Ken rolled her eyes. "Taught, I am sure," she added, "by those for whom humiliation and urine drinking are the most desired of activities. But only the *correct* humiliation. Certainly, it would be unacceptable to call this one ugly, or that one a worm; they must have the appropriate oaths and curses shouted at them, and only by the most appropriate of partners! Only urine from a person of the proper physical attributes, and in such a context, with such and so amount of the urine, and only if asparagus was not eaten at the last meal." She laughed and tossed the brochure over to Robin, who caught it and sighed.

"We shall go to that one, I think," Ken had said, a twinkle in her eye. "And perhaps we shall attempt to match their recommendations, and see if that pleases you."

And so they had, and Robin was reminded why she had strayed away from the SM community so many times. She found herself looking into people's eyes and trying to spot the dedication, perhaps the obsession, that she knew was reflected in her own. She also tried to listen to some of the presenters with the same openness and gratitude that she had felt when she first encountered them, and found herself being embarrassed for them. With a few forgettable and insignificant exceptions, they were all good intentioned. But next to Ken and her slaves and her friends, they seemed, well...lacking.

"It's like going back to your old junior high school," she said when Ken

150

finally took her back to their hotel suite. Ken was busy marking off other seminars they could go to for her amusement. "It all looks so…small."

"Never mind them, little one. In a few months, they will be nothing to you. Look! Here is a class called 'SM and Legal Issues.' Let's go to that one and ask about slave contracts, shall we?"

And although she still felt some slight resentment at some of Ken's broader and more insulting characterizations, she knew that she could never go back. Not when she knew that there was something so much more suited to her needs just beyond the next ridge.

But when Ken invited her to go out and wander through the leather bars where the gay men went, Robin agreed. There was always something romantic about the leathermen, in their tight jeans and heavy black chaps. They always seemed like knights to Robin, in their colors and their armor and their easy camaraderie. If Ken wanted to go see a few of them strut their stuff on a stage and mill around in tightly packed bars, it was no great hardship to accompany her.

It turned out to be a great night, cool enough for the heavier costumes, warm enough for bare chests under leather jackets. In her own chaps and leather shirt and cap, Ken looked simply too hot to handle, and many of the men appreciated her androgyny with cheer and approval. Robin wore black jeans, her boots, and her motorcycle jacket and faded in neatly next to her more flamboyant companion. Together, they blended into the mixed crowds, buying raffle tickets and admiring the flesh, walking from bar to bar and then to a packed dance club where men stripped down on stage and performed fantasies for the delight of the crowd and the approval of various judges. But Ken didn't bother to stay for the resolution. Taking Robin by the hand, she dragged her out and back to one of the bars.

"But why? Don't you want to know who won?"

"The winner will come to the bar to be admired," Ken replied. "I have no patience to wait while they thank all of their penurious sponsors and stall for time. We shall obtain a good spot for witnessing his triumphant entrance and perhaps get the pool table for a game." Ken grinned wickedly. She was a great pool hustler.

But when they got there, there was someone playing, and upon seeing him, Ken froze and then grinned again. "*Ma chérie,* I think you have just been saved," she said confidently.

"Why?" Robin looked around, taking in the entire bar in one sweep. There were about twenty men posed around the bar, another five or six hunched over tables, idly talking over the sound of the music and the television screen, which showed highlights of last year's contest. Several men were gathered in the back, grouped in twos and threes, and two men were stalking the pool table, waiting for the loser of the current game to get out of the way.

"See that man there? The one who is no doubt winning? He is your salvation. Go and purchase a shot of whatever single malt scotch these heathens have on hand and then come to stand with me. Do not speak. You must be on your very best behavior. You must be most serious. Go!"

While Ken sauntered casually toward the pool table, Robin went to the bar and did as she was told. And from her place slightly behind Ken's shoulder, she got a better look at the man Ken had pointed out.

He was short, and young. He was dressed like almost everyone else, in the usual uniform of jeans and boots and chaps and vest, but his looked well worn and perfectly tailored, to draw his slightly bulky torso in and make his legs seem longer. When he bent and cradled the pool cue, Robin could just see the shifting of flesh on his upper arms that suggested muscles. He had kind of a cute ass, just a little rounded and tight against the edges of the chaps. He moved slowly, with conservative steps and motions, kept his attentions strictly on the table. There was a dark shadow across his cheeks and chin, that artful shading of facial hair that suggested carelessness. Robin's first thought was that all she needed to do it was dress him in fatigues and put a gun in one hand and he would look like a hijacker.

Within minutes of their arrival, he did indeed win the game and collected a strong and somewhat more lengthy than usual handshake from the loser. But as someone else stepped up to rack the balls, Ken made a motion, and the man looked up at her. There was a brief moment, and then he turned and spoke softly to the challenger. The man nodded agreeably and beckoned to another player and the short man came over to Ken and nodded.

"Mandarin. Slumming again?" His voice was as careful as his movements, a mellow tenor. His eyes were partly hidden behind the slightly shaded lenses of steel rimmed glasses, but Robin knew that he had already glanced at her several times. She also realized that he was older than she had originally thought, but it was more a sense than an observation of his face. He was probably the kind of person who looked anywhere from five to twenty years away from his true age, depending on what you wanted to see.

"Home was dull. And you never know what you can find out here: look, I have found you! And such a new you! I like your mustache. And you look so healthy! Your wastrel's life must be paying as well as your pool hustling. Allow me to buy you a drink, in way of apology for losing the table."

Robin knew a cue when she heard one. Gingerly, she extended the shot of whisky, which the man picked out of her hand without comment or acknowl-edgment.

"I accept. You're looking exceptionally well yourself, Mandarin," he said. "But I am forced to disagree with your assessment of what's to be found out here. We both know exactly what's available. Nothing much."

Ken abruptly dropped the small talk. Outside the bar, they could hear sounds that suggested that the contest had ended. Men who didn't wait for the crowning ceremonies were hurrying back to get their drinks ordered. "I thought you were in Europe."

"I decided not to go."

"That may be fortunate for my friend here, and for you."

"I am on vacation."

"Nonsense. With what you can earn from her sale, you can purchase an-other vacation. Surely, you do not intend to spend the next several weeks cheating these boys out of their money."

The man grinned, flashing teeth in the dim light. "They always get the money back one way or another."

"Yes, you no doubt beat it back into them dollar by dollar. Consider a more civilized way to pick up some minor change, if you will."

Finally, the man turned to look at Robin. He beckoned her from behind Ken, and examined her without touching her. With one finger, he made a gentle gesture, and she turned, so he could see all of her.

"She's very common."

Robin turned dark red with embarrassment. She was grateful for the dim lighting in the bar, and for the rising noise of the entering crowd, which had probably drowned out this man's casual comment about her.

"If you're only handling models now, you should change your advertising, white boy. What do you want, quality of form or quality of spirit? She was born to the life."

"I will interview her tomorrow night," he said abruptly. "Five weeks, you spot only."

"She is to be ready for the next sale. Spot plus five percent."

"In two weeks? No spot, and I'll prorate my standard fee."

"Bastard."

He smiled again.

"Your fee against twenty percent, I get spot. If your fee isn't covered, you can take my spot and I'll pay the balance. If there is any."

"My full fee then?"

Ken glanced at Robin, and Robin froze. She hadn't understood a single thing they were talking about.

Ken muttered another Chinese curse. "Fine, and fuck you! You're lucky I like her so much."

"I'm lucky that you don't need the money, so you might as well give it to me. You're not in the business, Mandarin, you just like pulling short hairs." He drank the scotch down quickly, and Robin was barely there in time to catch the glass as he let go of it. "OK, you've got me for a miracle. Let's hope your latest find is worth it."

"You'll be pleasantly surprised," Ken promised. "And you'll call me after the sale and beg my forgiveness for being such a grasping prick."

"Seven o'clock then?" The man pulled a business card out of one shirt pocket and wrote something on it. He passed it to Ken when she nodded. "I'll be in touch if she's acceptable."

Ken took the card and nodded again, and the man turned away from them, to watch the new game of pool.

"Come, my pet," Ken said, leading Robin back through the new crowd of leathermen, pressed together in a morass of polish, oil and sweat. At the door, they were able to see the new winner, a broad sash crossing his chest, and a bouquet of leather roses over one arm.

In the cab, Ken grinned and placed the business card in Robin's hand with a flourish. "You have it made, little slave. He will get you to your paradise. We will have a celebration lunch tomorrow and invite some of my friends, because the next time you see them, you shall be chattel. What *joss*, hey? You've got some luck. And it won't cost me a dime, no matter what he says."

Robin looked down, and then held the card up so that she could read the plain black printing against the pulsating flashes of streetlamps they passed. On one side, it named a hotel and a room number. On the other, it said:

Chris Parker
trainer

Chapter Fourteen

Her apartment was nearly empty now. With the last of her belongings packed off to the storage facility, and the last volunteers carrying away the few pieces of furniture that were left, she was alone with her walls, her empty closets, a table and two chairs, and her bed.

Sitting on the table, by her phone, was the rolodex, still flipped open to the same card. A legal pad sat next to it, with a long list that had most of the entries crossed off.

So easy to do away with a life, Robin marveled, taking another tour of the place. It wasn't that long ago when I moved in. Now everything I have is gone, or packed away. And it barely took two full days.

Have I been waiting for this all my life, that I never placed that much importance on lasting tangible assets? I never even considered buying into a co-op. I never thought of owning a car. I kept my wardrobe to a minimum, borrowed more books then I bought, and never collected anything.

It had been so odd, sleeping in her wide, soft bed again, and waking up when she wanted to. Throwing on jeans and a sweater to go down to a bakery for croissant and coffee, and then getting a newspaper. Watching television. Hell, it was odd hearing people talk about newsworthy events that had happened in the past couple of days.

I've been living on another planet, she thought, touching the rolodex. And now I want to emigrate.

So what do I tell Mom?

Chris had explained to her what the general policy was for Marketplace slaves. If the slave did not choose to cut all contact off with their family, they were permitted a certain amount of contacts per year. Although some slaves insisted on constant communication, most were content with limited inter-action with any member of the outside world. Chris' preferred contract al-lowed for four.

That would allow for two birthdays, their anniversary, plus Christmas. Which was exactly how many times Robin voluntarily contacted them last year, anyway. The only problem in pretending that nothing had changed was that she'd no longer have the same address, and she would probably not be able to receive calls.

Mom, I'm going away for a while, and I won't be staying in one place. But I'll keep in touch.

But Robin, can you afford this? Where are you going? Is it safe? Does it have to do with work? Are you all right?

Robin buried her head in her arms. I can't, I can't, I can't! The less I say, the more she'll worry, and the more upset I'll get. And if I start threading lies together, they're going to come apart somewhere! A glance at her watch told her that she wasn't due back at the upper west side apartment for another five hours.

Five hours is an awfully long time to sit with a rolodex, a table and chair and a phone.

Robin tossed the phone file into a shopping bag and left the apartment for the last time. She dropped her keys off with the super and went out into the cool afternoon to enjoy what would hopefully be her last day of freedom. And if she thought up something she could tell her mother during the day, well, that would be fine. If not, at least Christmas was still a bit away. The fact that her mother wouldn't be able to contact her nagged like the real problem it was, but she refused to let it confound her. Some way, she would find a way to handle things. She always had before. She breathed deep in the autumn air, and smelled the approach of winter. Soon, she thought, picking up her pace and barely glancing at the passing world. Soon.

Robin signed the release forms in four different places and dated her signa-ture. The last of her medical tests had come in, and her professional file was almost complete. The beautiful photographs that Ken had taken of her showed her in profile and full face, clothed and nude. In one, she was kneeling with her back to the camera, looking almost fearfully over her shoulder. She hated it and thought it made her look stupid. Chris Parker tossed it into the folder anyway.

Her medical records had been condensed to three forms which attested to her emotional and physical health. Her detailed reports would only be given to her owner, after she was purchased. Ken's notes were in there, and they were warm and positive. But Chris waved a hand over those pages with disdain.

"They show too much affection," he told her.

"Well, isn't that good?"

"No. Not all owners are interested in being affectionate toward their slaves. Nor will they fail to see that you were not Marketplace trained when you were with Mandarin. The training will make all the difference." He piled everything together, and placed several clean sheets of paper on top, with a blank form. "*My* notes will make all the difference."

Robin pressed her lips together in reaction to his casual arrogance. But he was only telling her the truth. Even Ken said so. She composed herself and nodded.

"This week, we do nothing but refinements. You will move and speak for me, and you will lose every trace of the mannerisms which will tend to lower your price. Tell me what they are."

"Sir. I hesitate too long before answering questions or moving to obey an order. My movements are still clumsy—"

"Be more specific!"

"When I rise from kneeling, sir. Especially after I've been kneeling for a long time. And I am too abrupt in my abbreviated bows, and too theatrical in my formal ones. I rarely anticipate your needs correctly, and I am still too prone to forget myself and daydream from time to time."

"And?"

Isn't that enough? Robin thought. I sound like a real jerk already. How could I have ever really thought that I could be a perfect slave?

"Now, girl, now!"

"Sir, please forgive me, sir. I can't recall any other specific faults which you have instructed me to correct, sir."

Chris stood up and stretched. "That's correct. You got them all. You may place the pallet at the foot of my bed and sleep there tonight. Coffee at dawn, and we shall begin to make you truly presentable."

"Yes, sir," Robin said, barely restraining a grin. "Thank you, sir."

And again, as she rolled over onto her side, wrapped up in a warm blanket and feeling the unyielding floor beneath the thin padding, she almost cried, holding herself and disbelieving the sensations that ran through her. It's so good, she thought, so good. So right.

He turned the heat down, so much that her teeth chattered in the early morning, and lectured her long and hard, a multi-tressed, stinging whip in one hand.

"Discomfort is meaningless. Your comfort comes from?"

"Service, sir—"

Slash! The narrow tresses caught her upper arm with a flick that stung like a wasp and made her gasp. Chris' eyes were flat and angry behind his shaded lenses. "Too automatic, too dull. Believe it, or you'll sound like an idiot. If you don't believe it, this is all for nothing, and you might as well join a secretarial pool to get your required doses of humiliating labor. Tell me again."

Robin clenched her teeth, tried to ignore the chills running over her arms and belly and the heat where the tips of the whip landed. *I am not cold. I am patience. I will wait patiently for the opportunity to serve. I will be warmed by my devotion.*

Somehow, the words that seemed so patently false when said aloud worked again. She drew her breath in and felt the stiffness in her limbs fade into a distant dull annoyance and looked up at Chris again. "Comfort comes in service, sir."

"Better, but still awkward." Another flick of his wrist, and the same spot, only on the other arm, got a touch of fire. "And I want to see more artfulness in your reactions. Don't be stoic, but don't be showy." With maddening calm, he flicked the whip up twice more, now touching each shoulder, and she winced, hissing a sharp breath inward.

"Too melodramatic. Fetch the cane, I think you need a few stripes to remind you what pain is like."

On her knees again, her head cradled in her arms and pressed against the floor, her ass raised, her legs spread wide. Open and exposed, she inched forward to draw herself more correctly in place and waited for Chris' painful correction. But she didn't exactly know what she was being corrected for! She had been cleaning up the dinner dishes when suddenly, Chris marched into the kitchen, seized her by the hair and dragged her into the living room, where she was thrown to the floor with a barked command to assume the proper position. She trembled, waiting for the feel of the cane he had been carrying or the strap, which was on the chair. Instead, she felt his fingers trail lightly along the lips of her cunt, brushing the bare skin there with a tenderness she had almost forgotten.

"Oh God," she murmured, relief flooding through her and the words slipping from her lips before she could stop them.

"You would do better to call upon your master than God," Chris drawled, taking his hand away. When he pulled her up by her hair and pushed a gag into her mouth, she was red with shame and anger at herself. She assumed the position again, and he idly caressed her, opening her and stroking her and teasing her until she cried and writhed like an injured kitten. And then he beat her mercilessly, using his strap, ignoring her muffled screams.

I hate you, she sobbed to herself, wrapped up again at the foot of his bed. I don't understand you! I don't know what you want! Spilling tears onto the pallet, she kept the edge of her blanket wedged tightly in her mouth. If he heard her, he might send her back to her bed in the next room. I am so confused, she thought, staring into the darkness. I don't want to spend one more day with him, but I can't stand the idea of not having the fucking honor of sleeping like a dog on the floor next to him.

I'm not going to break, she swore. *I worked damn hard to get this far. I am not going to fuck this up, no matter what he does!*

The constant burn and ache of the beatings plus her own anxiety and confusion kept her awake most of the night. In the morning, when Chris examined her, noting the reddened eyes and the dark circles beneath them, he slapped her, hard, and she touched her mouth in amazement. His occasional cuffs and light slaps had almost become expected and tolerable. But her mouth was filled with the copper taste of her own blood and she could feel the pounding in her lip already.

"You may not indulge in any behavior that makes you unavailable to me," he snapped. "Your self pity has exhausted you, and made you unattractive. Perhaps you need a reminder that your body is not yours to abuse. No hot water for you, today or tomorrow."

Robin blinked in semi-comprehension, fighting not to burst into even more tears.

"Yes," Chris said, his lips parting in an insincere smile, "that includes the water for your internal cleansings. I will have my coffee after you have finished grooming yourself. And don't bother to make more than two cups. No hot water means no hot water, period."

Later, Robin began to wonder if she would ever feel warm again. The chill of her shower and the biting cold sensation of douching herself with cold water was terrible. Feeling the heat on the sides of a coffee cup, the slight steam coming from hot food, all sent her into shivers and made little bumps rise all over her body. When she stuttered out an improper phrase, Chris beat her again, and the pain and heat from her assaulted buttocks made the chill in the rest of her body even more terrible.

Late that evening, she spent twenty minutes eagerly, entreatingly, washing his boots with the flat of her tongue, her wrists held behind her back and her body arched correctly, until he relented and tossed her blanket back onto the pallet.

And then he opened the window, just a crack, and turned out the light. As she heard him toss his robe aside and climb between the soft cotton sheets and under the thick comforter, she felt the slight wavering touch of cold cross the room to where she was curled up.

"Sir, I may get sick," she whispered the next morning, stiff, sore and still cold. Her legs were still shaking after the morning cleaning ritual, and she hated the way her hair felt when all she had to rinse the shampoo out with was cold water. "Please, sir, I beg you to reconsider my punishment."

"More formal," Chris snapped.

"Sir, this slave begs for mercy, sir. This slave fears that illness may...make this slave less able to serve." It was so hard to speak that way! Already, alternatives were occuring to her, and she struggled to ignore them as she listened to his response.

"People don't fall ill because they are cold," Chris said, his voice neutral. "It is true that it weakens your natural ability to fight off various illnesses, but I am not overly concerned about that." She couldn't see his face because she had assumed a posture that was appropriate for such an impertinent request, kneeling in abject submission, her head down, her body curled into a posture that would be perfect for a footstool. Indeed, Chris had placed his booted foot on her bowed back several times this week, all in order to press a particular point home. Now, he nudged her, touching her arm with one swing of his foot. She raised her head a little.

"So, is your concern regarding your health, or your comfort?" he asked.

"It truly concerns my health, sir."

"I will consider it." And he nudged her away to tend to her morning duties. Then, he returned to her training as though nothing had occurred, asking her questions and drilling her endlessly in movements and gestures.

In the early afternoon, he told her to close the window in the bedroom and turn the heat up. "You will still be slightly uncomfortable, I think," he told her when she returned to his side. "But now you will always remember that punishments may be difficult and unpleasant without leaving you with a single comforting thought or sensation. You may scream at a beating or moan at restrictions, but your body will throb with pleasure as you recover. However, your owners may choose to deny you even that much comfort, by utilizing methods of control and discipline which afford you no luxury of fetish. Your acceptance of that is *vital* to your ability to be a good slave."

And that evening, when Leon brought over a steaming pot of vegetable soup, Chris startled Robin by placing a bowl on the floor next to her, where she sat chewing on a piece of the crusty brown bread that had accompanied the dinner. When he didn't also give her a spoon, she nodded, just a little bending of her chin, and said, softly, "Thank you, sir," before lowering her head to lap from the bowl.

"Good girl," he said, letting one hand drop down to pat her head.

I don't believe I'm doing this, Robin thought, embarrassment and pleasure welling up together. *And I don't believe that I love him again.*

On Thursday night, Chris examined her again, carefully, and pronounced her fit for display.

"I shall not cane you again," he added, tracing the faint lines of her previous canings. "Although I think the marks are an enhancement, there are those who prefer an all-over rosiness of a paddle or a hand or a strap to the lines and bruises that canes and cutting instruments may leave. I wouldn't want that to prejudice a buyer against you."

"Thank you for your thoughtfulness, sir," Robin answered, a touch of color coming to her face. For all of his cruelty, each hour of each day, Chris never failed to remind her that she was scheduled for the sale on Saturday night. He no longer spoke of "if," only "when."

"You mean, 'thank God he's not going to use that blasted thing on me again,'" Chris shot back. "But that's all right. I will be making a note of your reaction to it in my report. Your new master or mistress will no doubt find it to be valuable information."

He continued to stroke her ass cheeks, and pushed her forward a little more. "Although I personally dislike shaved pubics on women, we shall leave them bare, as the look seems to suit you. When you are aroused, your labia spread in a delightful fashion, and are very pretty — a clear asset. Also, the shaven look does seem to remain in fashion." He sighed and stroked her there, pulling gently on her labia to bring them open and engorged, as though to illustrate his statement.

Robin moaned and gently allowed a little of her weight to fill his hand, as he had taught her. She would not be so bold as to actually push back, but she would allow herself to be opened more, to be touched and probed at the slightest hint of interest.

"Very good," he said, sliding two fingers into her. "You would like to be fucked again."

"Sir, if that would please you, yes, sir." The phrase came out with ease, and her reward was a tapping on the hood of her clitoris, a sliding of a wet finger to press over that sensitive and hungry spot until she whimpered with pleasure.

"It would please me to see you fucking yourself," Chris said, sliding his fingers in and out of her, pressing forward and up with every stroke. "When I let you go, you will go to your room and bring back the largest dildo you can comfortably take. Without using your hands, you will cover it with a condom, and then position it on the floor and mount it, for my amusement. And *if* you please me sufficiently, I will allow you to guide it with your hands until such a sight fails to interest me." He drew his fingers from her and stepped away. "Go."

And despite her acute embarrassment and the difficulty of the task, she managed to amuse him for quite a long time before he allowed her to stop her self-inflicted torment and crawl off to bed. Without orgasm, of course.

"You will be so sensitive that the slightest gaze will make you wet," he promised, before turning out the light. "Any touch will make your entire body reverberate with need. It will be very attractive. It should more than make up for your lack of exceptional beauty."

Robin couldn't deny the truth of his words; after all, he was the expert. But the aching between her legs and the constant ache in the pit of her stomach were bound together in her anxiety over the sale and her anxiety over what she could only see as his rejection. And I may not be a model out of the pages of a fashion magazine, she sulked, but I'm nice looking. I guess. But maybe not nice enough for him to turn on to me.

I want him to fuck me. Like I've never wanted it before, more than Troy, more than anyone. I want him to wrap me in his arms and just throw his body against me, make it hurt, just take me, goddammit, until I scream. Why doesn't he? Is it part of the training? Why let others do it, but not try me himself?

Doesn't he want to?

Shouldn't he? So that he can say something about it in his report?

And aren't I trying to make up any reason for him to just roll me over and fuck me blind?

Luckily, the blanket corner was still available to muffle the little whimpers of hurt and confusion and worry that came before sleep finally took her.

Robin read the pages that Chris had left for her several times while she waited for him to return. After a rushed cup of coffee, he had left the apartment, with no instructions other then to consider what the pages meant.

They were essays of a sort. From the language, she guessed that he had written them. They were about dominance and submission, slaves and owners, and the rewards and limitations of those roles and that kind of life. They were abstract, speaking generally as opposed to specifically, but they were filled with personal observations that were almost poetic in their clarity.

Chris had been a slave once, Robin was now sure of it. It was so...classic. He had completed the great journey, gone from apprentice to mastery. That was where he learned all of the things he knew, that was how he so easily slipped into a service attitude from time to time. Flashes came to her, the sweep of his arm as he poured a drink for Dr. Emil, the quiet and firm acceptance of a responsibility thrust onto him, the way he held his body when offering a robe or a coat.

How wonderful! How exciting! It was just like one of her favorite books. He would watch her being sold and remember that same feeling in himself, and experience an emotional flashback, something dangerous and thrilling and a little sad. And then he would go back to his life, training more slaves, and helping them on their journeys.

It's so romantic. So melodramatic.

And it was so hard to believe that tomorrow evening, she would be a commodity, displayed and bid upon like all the artwork and antiques and collectibles she had handled in her years as a buyer and appraiser.

She leapt for the door when he arrived, and took his jacket. "It's cold as hell out there," he said, heading for the living room. "It will probably snow tomorrow."

"Oh! Will that effect the sale?"

"No, not in the slightest. You're still on. Make some tea and come look at your contract."

The contract! He took the leather briefcase he had been carrying and opened it on the coffee table. Robin made the quickest cup of tea in her life and rushed to her accustomed place on the carpet.

"It's a two year contract," Chris said, sipping gingerly. "I know you wanted three, but you can always renew in favorable conditions. I've included all of the standard clauses we've discussed. You must read it all, very carefully, and allow the weight of it to sink in. And then you will sign it, and date it today."

Because it was her last day of freedom, she knew, taking the heavy sheets of paper into her hands. Tomorrow, I'll be considered a slave, and slaves don't sign contracts.

The pages rustled when her hands shook.

Well, it was all there. The language wasn't as difficult as legalese could be, probably because it would never withstand a courtroom examination. But it was very similar to a personal service contract in many ways. She read over the paragraphs that Chris had discussed with her, and nodded several times.

163

And when she looked up and nodded to him, he passed her a gold pen, and she initialed and signed and dated where she had to, on three copies.

"This is it, Robin," Chris said as he opened her file and slipped two copies into it. "You are now an official member of the Marketplace."

"It's hard to believe."

"Believe it. Tomorrow, your body will be sold to another human being, in a manner that the greater outside world can barely comprehend. And in doing so, you will contribute to a society and culture, not to mention economy, that has existed purely to serve the needs of those of us who must see the world in dichotomies of master and slave."

Robin nodded again. But his use of the word economy had triggered yet another nagging question that she hadn't found a way to ask. He saw it flicker in her eyes and shrugged.

"You might as well ask. The worst thing that can happen is that I'll be annoyed."

"I wouldn't want to annoy you on my last day here, sir." But she smiled, and then gently bit her lip, considering how to ask. "It's just that...well...I am curious about the money."

"You should be. I was wondering why you hadn't asked."

"Oh! Well then, um, how much do you think I'll go for? How much do slaves normally go for? Is there a market rating system for them? Is it objective?" She leaned forward eagerly.

"There are several rating systems; they apply to different kinds of property, and sometimes to different styles of markets. But I'm afraid that I'm going to disappoint you with my other answers. It is against regulations to discuss prices, especially particular prices, with slaves." He laughed at the way her face fell. "And no, that doesn't mean I would have answered you before you signed the contracts."

"But what if I wanted to be sure that I would have enough money to get back on my feet when the contract ended?" Robin asked. "I mean, since the money is coming to me anyway, don't I have the right to know?"

"The money isn't all coming to you, my dear. Your spotter, your trainer, the auction house and the regional office all have their cuts. Ken has effectively wagered that twenty percent of your purchase price will be large enough to cover my training fee plus her spotter's fee. She may be right; twenty percent is often split between the spotter, trainer and the auction house, and sometimes even with a previous owner, although that doesn't happen as often as it used to. But this much I can tell you. As a novice, you will not be worth much compared to slaves who have had more training or have been sold two or three times. Your price will most probably fall into a category equal to or slightly surpassing a comfortable living for someone of your education and age bracket, over a two year period. If you were taller, and your breasts fuller and your mouth a little more sensual, you'd fetch more. Even as you are, you are an expensive little chit."

"I don't understand. How can I be cheap and expensive at the same time?" Robin frowned, but then realized the answer. "Oh, because of my upkeep. I'm like a painting that has to be kept in a specially designed box."

Chris' mouth turned up a little. "If you like. You may be purchased as a bargain, but you eat as much as any better trained or more beautiful woman, and you take up the same room, and need the same physical care. But I wouldn't be worried about the size of the payment you'll receive when your contract comes due. If you love this life, you will not see that money for many years to come."

Robin flushed and swallowed hard. "Oh God. I hope so."

"For your sake, I hope so as well. Now I need time to write my report on your training. I want you to take the exercise tape into the master bedroom and work out there. I want you to work yourself hard, stretch every muscle, make yourself sweat. It will add to your edge tomorrow."

"Sir? Won't I be stiff then? Won't it make it harder for me to hold my positions?"

"Tsk. Still don't trust me, do you? Do as I told you. Be glad that I need you well rested for tomorrow, or you'd be spending the night sleeping in an inch of water in the bathtub."

Robin shut her mouth firmly, nodded and ran.

Saturday was a flurry of activity. Robin woke up, as stiff as she had predicted, and when Chris tossed some of her clothing to her, she blinked in confusion.

"We are going to make try to push your price up a little," he said with a smile. "Get moving!"

Mutely, she dressed and followed him out of the building. It was still cold, and there was that hint of something in the air that suggested snow. But Chris didn't stop to examine the weather. He hailed a cab and the two of them rode downtown in silence.

When they got out on Hudson Street, Robin followed him to a private dwelling on one of those short, twisting little named streets that hide some of the most beautiful brownstones and courtyards in the city. They were let in by a young man in a short robe, who yawned and jerked one thumb at the stairs. "She's waiting," he said gruffly. "You staying or going?"

"I'll be back in three hours or so. Robin, strip and go upstairs." Chris gave

165

her a pat on one shoulder and left just as she had managed to pull off her jacket.

He must love doing this, she mused. One mystery after another. The man in the robe pointed at a chair in the hallway and nodded when she started to pile her clothing there. Then, with another yawn, he went back to reading his paper.

Upstairs was a stern looking, powerfully built, dark skinned woman whose hair was shorn close to her scalp, except for a row of dreads that topped her skull like a rooster's crown. She was dressed in dark danskins, with an artfully ripped sweatshirt falling across her wide shoulders and hanging suspended over her taut stomach. The room she was in was almost bare, with a pale wooden floor that gleamed in the morning sun. On one wall was a huge dancer's mirror and barre. On the other, two tables were lined up, and pushed out of the way. Several folding chairs were stacked near the door.

"Hello," the woman said, folding her arms. "I'm Teralia. And you're my latest victim." And she grinned, and then threw her head back and laughed. "Well, don't just stand there, you little wimp! Come on in and shake yourself loose. Parker wants himself a little dynamo tonight, and he's gonna get it!"

Oh dear, Robin thought. What has he done to me now?

Another workout, this one a purposefully graceful and disciplining one, with dancer movements and long pauses. Unfamiliar with some of the motions, Robin felt clumsy and awkward, but as she got used to them, they began to flow with more grace. Teralia spent a lot of time working on breathing and concentration, and then went back to working Robin with some basic aerobic repetitions until Robin's sweat ran off of her body in rivulets.

"Now, we get some of that stiffness out," Teralia explained, leading her victim into a tiny sauna. Inside, the physical trainer made Robin do more stomach crunches, and then more stretches. When the heat became too oppressive, she stopped, let Robin drink some cool water, and then began to massage her.

I like this part, Robin thought, fairly purring under the strong manipulations of the trainer.

Then a cool shower, and back to the sunny workout room, for more stretching, and more massage. And when Robin began to feel that her body just couldn't take another second of being pummeled by this muscular woman, she was swept downstairs, wrapped in a white terry cloth robe, for the now wakeful young man to examine her hair and nails and sigh with exasperation.

"What do you use on this, baby shampoo?" he asked as he started selecting little colorful bottles from a window box.

"Uh, sometimes, sir," Robin answered.

166

"Jeeze. It's disgustingly healthy. No color, no ragged ends, no chemical burns, nothing. What am I supposed to do with it?" He came back to examine her again and nodded. "Okay, here's the plan. How's about we go with a natural style. Kind of layered on the sides, but long in the back. You're still young enough to stand it. And we'll leave some nice wisps flowing down here... and here..." He fingered the hair at the side of her face. "It'll give you that debauched maiden look. Very romantic novel. Okay? Your nails are a disaster. We'll just smooth them down and put a little clear polish on them and maybe you can hide your hands. OK? What am I saying, of course it's OK, you don't get to say anything about it. So close your eyes, sweetie, Glen is gonna make you beautiful."

She did close her eyes, as he pulled her head into a sink basin and washed her hair and anointed it with-who-knew-what. And unlike a beautician's, where she would stare at herself in the mirror while a stylist worked on her hair, he simply positioned her on a stool in some good light and worked away without another attempt at explaining what he was doing or how it would look.

He covered her hair with some kind of lotion after he cut it, and wrapped it all up in a towel. Then he worked on her short nails, doing exactly as he described. Robin had never paid a lot of attention to her nails, she just couldn't justify the time spent on it. When she was with Troy, she would occasionally get one of those five dollar nail jobs for the weekend, but he rarely noticed them or seemed to care much.

In minutes, Glen finished one hand and showed her the contrast between the finished one and the plain one. They looked like the hands of two different people.

"Now, if you can only get a job that didn't have you writing so much, you could get rid of these," he said as he fingered the light calluses on the insides of her fingers and on the pad of her thumb. "Thank God you weren't a secretary, though," he continued, even as she gave him a look of amazement. "Secretaries get the worst calluses on the pads of their fingers, although now, with all these word processors, it's not as bad as it used to be." He looked up into her eyes and shrugged. "Hey, you think Sherlock Holmes is the only guy who can pick up clues? It's all in the hands, sweetie. The stories I could tell you!" And he went back to work, chatting aimlessly.

He uncovered and rinsed out her hair, and styled it with his fingers. "I hate blow dryers, don't you? They're one of the three grooming aids that Amnesty International should be investigating. The others? Well, how about that little machine that catches your leg hairs up in a little silver coil and then rips them out by the root? Oh my God, it's like being set on fire! And for bikini hair? I'd rather stick a porcupine up my ass."

I don't believe this, Robin giggled to herself. Here I am, about to become human chattel, enter the Marketplace and leave the real world behind, and I'm being entertained by a nelly hairdresser in the Village. There has to be some meaning to this. And one day, I'm going to have to find out how Chris knows these people.

When Glen finished, he dusted her shoulders off and led her to a mirror. She glanced into it with some trepidation, but when she saw what she looked like, she almost cried with relief. He was right. Glen had taken some of the weight of her last hair style away, and created almost a waterfall effect of hair that rose around her crown and flowed down her neck to lay in soft waves over her shoulders. The short sides seemed to make her face seem less full, and the wisps of hair that he left long did indeed act as an attractive frame. And what was more, one of his mysterious bottles had apparently added to or enhanced her natural highlights, which were little shots of tawniness among the darker tresses.

"I did everything I could but make you blonde," Glen said with satisfaction.

"It's beautiful."

"Of course it is! Now go back upstairs, it's time for more torture."

More torture turned out to be another energetic massage, which made her moan and grunt until Teralia began to ease off. Then, soft soothing touches turned down the heat on her skin and got her purring again.

When Chris came to pick her up, she felt brand new. Even the faint twinges of pain from her beatings during the week seemed to feel good. And she was flexible, felt light on her feet, and any trace of stiffness had been banished. She almost blushed with shame for her outburst yesterday, but Chris didn't bring it up. He just nodded with satisfaction, and shook Teralia's hand, and without another word, took Robin back to the apartment.

In the afternoon, she had a pasta lunch, eating with Leon in the kitchen. He seemed as proud of her as she felt, and complimented her on the new hair. It was hard sometimes, thinking of the Leon who had been so supportive and friendly and the Leon who had roughly fucked her from behind, smacking her ass cheeks and thighs and dragging her head back with the horse bit he had shoved into her mouth.

But, before he left to go back home, she hugged him warmly and accepted his best wishes with a smile.

Chris packed her chosen belongings and her file copy into a special little case, even while she packed his things for him. She heard him on the phone, talking to Rachel, arranging to be picked up that evening at the house where the auction was taking place. They were leaving the borrowed apartment spotlessly clean, and Chris had two champagne bottles chilling in the refrigerator along with some nice delicacies he picked up while Robin was being "done." Two bottles of twenty-five year old Scotch had already been tucked away in the liquor cabinet.

How odd that this strange apartment had become more familiar and harder to leave then her own. She felt mild regret that she had not met the owners.

"What are they like?" she asked Chris as she watched him seal up a note to them.

"They are good people," he replied, tucking the note in between the bottles of champagne. "Friends of my employers."

"Yours too," Robin added. "It's nice of them to loan you this place for so long."

"Yes. But they'll reap benefits. They're in the market for a new slave, and they know that I will be available for training or touch up work if needed." He turned to her and his eyes looked a little less piercing then usual. "You're terribly nervous, to ask such a social question and forget all of your training. Or are you doing this knowing that I won't do anything so drastic as to muss your hair?"

"No, sir!" Robin protested. "But you're right, I'm extremely nervous. I feel like I want to throw up or faint, or run away."

"Don't do any of those. Breathe, like you were taught. Take a nap if you like." But he smiled at that thought, acknowledging the impossibility. He looked at her thoughtfully as she nodded and tried to take a long deep breath.

"Poor slave. Comfort yourself with the thought that in less then ten hours, it will be all over, and you'll have a completely new set of fears and anxieties to deal with."

Robin stared at him. "Thank you, sir. I feel much better now."

"Oh, good. Now go finish packing and put all of my things in the front hallway."

The afternoon seemed to drag, and Robin found herself looking at a clock every ten minutes. Finally, Chris called her to sit beside him while he read over her file, examining it for the slightest errors. She sat on the floor and leaned her head against his leg and tried to concentrate. All of her remaining questions and insecurities struggled within her, and knowing that this would be the last chance to get them out only made it harder to mentally address them.

"It's time to get ready," Chris announced suddenly. She looked up in panic; had that much time passed? Yes, it had, thank God. She darted off to the master bedroom, where she had laid out a very nicely tailored dark suit. Chris went off to shower and shave, and came back into the bedroom already in his t-shirt and trousers.

Robin had never even seen his bare chest.

She helped him dress in silent valet fashion, but he put his tie on. Her traveling clothes were the same ones she wore to the party last weekend, and he watched her dress, smoking a cigarette with what seemed like great fascination. In his dark suit, with the steel rimmed glasses and his short, almost stocky body, he now looked less like a terrorist and more like a gangster.

"Tell me," he said suddenly, and Robin flushed even as she smoothed the little black dress over her body.

"How do you know?" she asked, not looking at him.

"It's part of my job. Get it out of your mind, or you'll think about it all night." Another slow drag, followed by a thin stream of blown white smoke.

She faced him and knotted her fingers together behind her back. "Sir. I'm sorry sir, but you're right, I can't stop thinking about it. Please, was there some reason why you never…" Words suddenly failed her. Made love to me? Used me?

"Fucked you?" he offered. He smiled as her blush deepened. "It's simple, girl. If I had, you would have misunderstood our relationship. I am your trainer, not your lover or master. You haven't had enough experience to understand the nature of the distinctions, so I made it easier for you by denying you the one thing that you really do expect of your lovers or your future owner."

"I'm sorry," she repeated, looking down. "I wasn't thinking."

"No, but you're excused. This one last time. Just remember; very few people in the Marketplace will behave as your logic or your fantasies expect them to. We are truly a breed apart. We are neither the royalty of fantasy nor the pragmatic poseurs of your comfortable old S and M scene." He used a tone strikingly like Ken's when he mentioned her origins. "It has become a cliché to advise someone to expect the unexpected. But you will learn in time. Now gather what is left and prepare to leave, the car will be here presently."

In the car, he lit up another cigarette, and smoked it with the same thoughtfulness he used in the bedroom. Then, with a final deliberate gesture, he ground the butt out in the ashtray and crumpled up the empty pack.

"That's it for that," he sighed.

"Giving it up?"

"Hm. Yes. My employers are very strict," he paused again, and that wry smile tugged at the corner of his mouth, "about their non smoking policy."

"But why did you take it up?" Robin couldn't help but grin. It seemed ludicrous. "You work there most of the year, don't you?"

He nodded. "I do. But I like to smoke. So when I do take a vacation apart from the house, I do." He turned toward the window, and watched as the limo pulled up to a toll booth.

Robin folded her hands in her lap and tried to keep calm. But she kept sneaking glances at her trainer with puzzled looks. No, there was still plenty about him that was a mystery. Somehow, that seemed a little comforting.

Chapter Fifteen

Robin knelt on the sturdy, padded surface of the altar-like stand that bore the same number that now hung around her throat instead of the elegant silver lock. Chris had taken the old chain and lock away just before leaving her, accepting her desperate kisses on the palm of his hand before he soothed her back down into position.

"Do not look at the other slaves," he had cautioned her. "Do not turn your head, raise your eyes without command, or show that you are eavesdropping. Under no circumstances should you even react to the sound or sight of someone reading your file." He had posed her, firmly and with a demanding expertise, and looked her in the eye one last time before he left her to kneel in silence. "If you embarrass me," he whispered, trailing one finger down between her breasts, "I'll never forgive you. Do you understand?"

"Yes, sir," she had whispered back. Trembling seemed about to overtake her entire body, but his careful "shushes" and calm stroking worked their perversely appropriate magic on her.

When they got to the house and she stripped, they had been surrounded by dozens of people, some slaves, some free, running around in last minute preparations. Muscular men, stripped to stylized jock straps, wrestled podiums into position and set up tables and chairs in the bidding room. Chris had some paperwork to take care of, and she was given a cursory look-over by the man that Chris identified as the regional director before she was allowed to enter the viewing room.

There, she saw the special stands for the slaves to be displayed on, and froze.

The reality hit her like a freight train. *How could I have ever believed I was ready for this?* She asked herself this question over and over again as Chris registered her for a number and was told where her spot was. And when he snapped his fingers, she found herself moving forward out of some automatic response.

There, he made the final preparations. After affixing a pair of nipple clamps on her, he examined her for the last time, smelling her body and breath, touching her skin, and smoothing it with lotion where it was dry. He gloved himself and had her bend over so that he could lubricate her asshole, putting a cool salve into her so that she could be easily examined there. He had smiled briefly when he discovered that she needed no such aid for her cunt, which had already begun to open in its own transformation. In fact, by the time he finished with her asshole, she was thoroughly wet in both of her nether regions. Then, after he discarded the gloves, he fixed her hair, put her on the stand and posed her in the proper position. The last thing her did as he packed the gear away was remove the clamps, leaving her nipples erect and tingling.

She had not been the first slave positioned for the sale. On another stand, to her left and ahead of her, was a young man, dark skinned and wiry. His head was shaven, and gleamed in the bright light of the room, and he was pierced with silver rings in his nipples and through the head of his cock. He knelt tall, with a straight back and tautly held legs and arms, a study in tension. He reminded her of a track runner, poised for the starting gun. His trainer, or perhaps owner, rubbed his skin down with a soft cloth, as though he were polishing a statue.

Robin had her back to the wall, and within her vision could see two stands without turning her head. On her right, just beyond her field of vision, making it necessary for her to turn to see it, was a podium that held her portfolio. People could read it without her knowledge, if she remained in the proper position.

And hanging from the side of the podium was a thick leather paddle.

The room filled quickly. On one combined stand, a pair of twins was posed, pale skinned redheads with dancing bright eyes and playful, wide mouths. To Robin's right, another man was posed, this one in his forties, his hair cut in a standard business style and his body a network of decorative body modifications. Tattoos wound up his back and around his legs, and the clean lines of old cuts in his skin showed as pale scars and raised white skin marking off patterns of careful, painful artwork. She could see some of the pictures, a woman's leg, wearing thigh-high boots, a chained tiger. Like the man on her left, he was also pierced, but more extravagantly, with two rings in each nipple and several barbells under his cock, and rings placed around his heavy ballsack. His belly button had two rings, one on each side.

But dress him in a suit, and he would look like any other businessman on the street. Robin wondered if he was something dull, like a tax accountant. Or maybe something like a banker, or an estate lawyer. And he would do his work and come home to his master or mistress, strip off his power tie, and have all those wonderful places on his body that were made to be tormented and played with, admired and altered yet again.

One slave walked in on a leash and took Robin's breath away. Because she was tall, and crowned with a silvery mass of hair that came down her body in waves. But when she passed within better view, Robin almost forgot to breathe entirely. For although the slave had beautiful, upswept breasts topped with pert nipples, between her legs was a man's cock, laying tumescent over a natural pair of balls.

Two for the price of one, was Robin's thought as she regained her air.

She saw people of all kinds bringing their naked slaves in, and tried to remain still as they passed out of her line of sight. It was true, many of them seemed much more attractive then she was. Damn. She wished she was taller, or blonde. Or had those long legs, or those big, rounded breasts. But there was no point in crying over it now. She flexed her muscles as Chris taught her, and thanked him silently for the workouts and the intense treatments she had received earlier that day. She felt great, energized and relaxed. In fact, if it weren't for the anxiety which still made her want to throw up, she'd be just fine.

Some of the same slaves who served at the party last week flitted in and out of the room, now in a different abbreviated costume that still served to make their bodies available and attractive. *I wonder what their closets look like*, Robin thought, trying to relax some more. *Sixteen different outfits made of less than two feet of cloth?*

The stands filled steadily with one slave after another, until they were all there. Trainers and owners and agents came by for last minute posings, polishings, and to put gags in place for those who were not trained sufficiently to answer a prospective owner properly. Chris brought a gag, but placed it between Robin's knees, to indicate that she was newly voice trained, and that this was her first sale with that qualification.

His eyes told her, "Don't fail." And then he patted her gently and opened her file. Within the room, the only sounds were the light shuffling and rustling noises of paper being arranged, and the light tinkling of chain.

The trainers left the room, and for one minute, the slaves were left alone.

Robin fought the urge to break her position and look around. It was agonizingly difficult. She heard a muffled giggle come from the right side of the room, and clenched her fists in order to keep her eyes forward and down.

And then the wide double doors opened again, and the buyers started to come in.

174

They were as varied as the slaves they were coming to see, old and young, Anglo-Saxon and European and Asian and in all shades of skin tone. Their voices rose in admiration and scorn and in calling each other for greetings, recognition and praise, and English was not the only language they spoke. They were beautiful and poised, and they were dead common and brash. Robin glimpsed formal dress mixing with the worn blue jeans and translucent silk of the intensely wealthy. But she kept her head steady and did not raise it, until someone paused before her.

He touched her chin to lift her head up, and she found herself looking at an elderly man, white haired and slender. His eyes were hard though, with a light of fanaticism, and as he turned her head to one side and then to another, she felt afraid. When she shuddered, he smiled. But without a word to her, he simply walked away, not even looking at her papers.

Which I don't mind one bit, she thought.

Before she got back into proper position, she saw someone out of the corner of her eye and gasped. Chris had warned her that there might be relatively famous people at the sale, but she hadn't expected the steady voiced television newsman who was so clearly examining the red-haired twins across the room. How many times had she tuned to his show to hear him intone some important news story, making that sexy eye contact with the camera, his face a carefully worked series of reactions that acted as their own subtle editorials concerning the issues at play?

What if I get sold to a celebrity? she thought in a moment of heady exhilaration. *Think of all the people I could meet!*

Naked and available, came a sudden reminder. Utterly available to them, and to their friends.

Oh God, I hope he doesn't look my way.

This wasn't turning out the way she thought. She fought off a brief wave of panic just in time to have her attention caught by a woman standing to her right. By the rustling sounds, she knew that someone was reading her papers.

"Oh look, she's new."

"You could tell that from the door," came the sarcastic reply. It was a man's voice.

"Well, there's some charm in having a baby around. Besides, she's from Parker."

"The house?"

"No, just him. Here, look."

More rustling sounds, until Robin would have given anything for just a glance at them, and what they looked like. What their eyes were like.

"Well? What do you think?"

"What could we do with her? She'd have to be retrained, and we have no use for…what is she? An art appraiser, auction buyer, whatever? Please."

"But she's cute. And think of the fun we could have training her."

"Think of the hours of work."

Suddenly, a hand stroked Robin's hip, and she flinched, just a little bit. The hand trailed up, along her arm, and out of the corner of her eye, she could see the man attached to it. He was tall, and had a dome shaped head that was losing its hair. His eyes were a watery blue under heavy lids. He cupped one breast in his hands and pinched her nipple sharply. She hissed in an answering breath.

"Oh, I don't know," he said, pinching the other for good measure. "Let's look at the others."

And they went on without letting Robin ever see the woman.

She saw some of the people she had seen last week. The Matisse owner stopped to examine her, with a friendly and teasing look in his eye. Slipping a finger inside her and finding her wet, despite her fears, he chuckled. Keeping it there, he asked her, in a serious tone, whether she had seen an exhibit last month at the Met. Looking him in the eye and blushing deeply as he flicked that finger in and out of her, she answered, "Yes, sir," and her voice cracked just a bit. He laughed, and wiped his hands on the towel that was rushed to his side by one of the scantily clad slaves in attendance in the room. But he didn't look at her file, and she wasn't sure how disappointed she was about that.

The first person to beat her was a stout man with a southern accent. He examined her roughly and quickly, pinching and stroking her, and then pushed her forward without warning. She didn't even see how the paddle ended up in his hand, but it smashed into her cheeks with a heavy force that made her whimper, just slightly. Bracing herself for more, she took about a dozen of them, all heavy and thudding, and then felt his fingers pull her ass cheeks apart.

The exposure flooded her with delicious shame.

"Are you tight, little girl?" he asked, leaning over her, his fingers poised for penetration.

"Yes, sir," she whispered back. Chris had assured her that she was. And as he pushed into her, she moaned.

Such a slut, a little voice in her head insisted. Such a slut.

"Well now, let's see whatcher good fer," the man said as he walked around her to examine her papers. When he left without another word, she rose back into the proper position, flushed and just a little bit tired.

Don't worry about the time, Chris had instructed her. It will be the longest evening of your life. It'll be over before you know it.

She now knew what he meant.

Faces began to blur, with some coming into sharp focus from time to time. Ali Cruz came by, and patted her warmly, whispering good wishes for luck. A man with deep, dark eyes and a gentle touch was called away from examining her by another man who called him "Your Highness" and Robin nearly fell over with shock and thrilling fear. Two women spent a long time with her, one of them letting her suck gently on two exquisitely manicured fingers while the other used the paddle. They read the papers in silence, and later, Robin was startled to see one of them talking with Chris, across the room.

To belong to two women! Wouldn't that be wonderful?

She didn't get a lot of attention compared to some. The man on her right was constantly having his rings played with and pulled. And she could hear the constant commotion in the direction of the twins and the transsexual. There was also evidence that others were beaten more often, and an occasional sound of someone's suffering contained by a gag.

The evening was endless. But before she could wish fervently for an ending, an announcement was made that bidding would commence in fifteen minutes — would buyers please complete their examinations?

That was when Chris came back to see her. As several people gathered around to look at her folder, some of them asked him some quick questions, mostly pertaining to the speed of her training. He answered with assurances and more than a little arrogance, and no one seemed surprised.

"She is an uncommonly quick learner, and devoted to the life," he said to one woman. "She will be an excellent slave."

Robin glowed with warmth. She could feel the threatening force of tears, and struggled to keep them back. She wished she had another opportunity to thank him, to tell him that she would never forget him or what he taught her. *Why didn't I say it before*, she cursed. *Now, I'll never get a chance.*

And the buyers began to leave the room, talking in animated tones with each other. Chris stayed by her, and she noticed that several of the other trainers had come back as well. He turned to her, and although his face was a professional mask of cool politeness, he winked.

You're right, she thought sadly, meeting his eyes. *If I had slept with you, I would have fallen in love with you.*

Over his shoulder, she could see two people approaching, another buying couple no doubt. She didn't recall seeing them examine her earlier. Well, they'd better hurry.

"So, this is your vacation project," said a man's voice.

Chris Parker almost jumped. Robin was amazed at how clearly she could see his surprise. It was so strong, she could swear that it was mixed with fear. She couldn't help it. After an evening of perfect obedience, she raised her eyes to see what could possibly have that effect on her imperturbable trainer.

Standing behind him were two people, a man and a woman. The man had black hair and a close cropped beard that was salted with strands of silver. He was slightly above average in height, and smiling. The woman was elegant and small, with a softness around her face and blond hair that was swept through with lighter waves of white and covered her head in soft round curls. The man's eyes were touched with humor, and the woman's were harder, more piercing and more direct. But Robin could see that they were both accustomed to being obeyed.

It turned her on, even after an entire evening of being aroused by one contact after another. There was no doubt as to their identity.

And suddenly, although she wouldn't have given up her time with Chris for a date with Prince Charming himself, she wished she could have known what it was like to train under the *three* of them for six whole weeks.

Chris turned his back on her and perfectly executed one of those neat bows he was so good at. "Welcome back, sir, ma'am. I wasn't informed that you were arriving today."

"No, it's a surprise," Alex Selador said, touching him lightly on the arm. "I told Rachel not to tell you. We were going to come back a little early anyway."

"And how could we miss seeing the merchandise you're preparing on the side?" Grendel added, looking at Robin over Chris' shoulder. "Let's have a quick look before the sale starts."

They approached her from two sides, and Robin gasped at the touch of their hands. They had really just arrived, and their fingers were cold against the heat of her skin. But they smiled and ignored her, and under Chris' steady gaze, she responded as she had been taught, with all of her heart and with all due restraint. Alex read her papers while Grendel brought her eyes up to meet his.

The romance seemed ready to overwhelm her. My Master's Master, she thought dizzily.

"She seems like a fine piece of work," Alex said encouragingly. "I'm sorry we missed her."

"Very cute," Grendel added. "But I wouldn't think she was your type, Mr. Parker."

Was Chris actually blushing? No, it must have been the light in the room, the heat of her own body. Robin lowered her eyes again, for once grateful for the opportunity.

"Thank you," Chris said. "She was more than adequate." There was no special inflection in his voice.

"Last call, all buyers to the bidding room, please!"

"All right, let's go," Grendel directed. "I'm glad we got here in time. You'll come home with us, Chris. See you in the other room."

Alex crossed over to Robin and touched her shoulder. "Good luck," she whispered. "And welcome."

Robin's "Thank you, ma'am," was barely out before Alex turned to leave. And then she was alone again with Chris. On one side of her, a trainer was stroking the slave with the tension filled body. Someone else was sobbing.

Chris sighed and his mouth curled up into a little smile. "You have just been approved of," he said softly. Robin nodded.

"Then there's nothing else to say. Be a good girl." And he leaned forward, took her hair in one hand, and kissed her, hard, like the kiss of a long lost lover.

And then he let her go, and walked away without another word.

The slaves would not be present for the bidding upon them. For the time during the auction, the man who managed the slaves of the auction house came in and told them that they could stretch out. Other slaves hurried in with little cups of water, and warm, wet cloths to wipe the "merchandise" off. Robin felt tearfully grateful, but she did not break her instructions to remain silent.

It was another one of those inhumanly long and impossibly short periods of time. When the manager came back and ordered them to get back into their proper positions, Robin could swear that the sense of anxiety and antici-pation had actually become a light mist, permeating the entire room.

When the doors opened, they could all hear the sounds of light applause, and the strong voice of the regional director thanking people for coming.

The first person in the room was the television newsman. With a wide grin on his face, he almost ran to the stand with the twins.

The white haired man stopped in front of Robin and she felt a wave of panicked nausea, but he merely shook his head and continued walking.

People continued to fill the room, and more congratulations and good wishes were filling the air. On her right, the businessman with all of the rings and markings was locked into a collar by a black man with long dreads and a lilting accent. Robin saw the slave clamber down from the stand and pros-trate himself before his new master while others reached in to shake the owner's hand.

Across the room, it sounded like someone was getting another taste of the paddle.

Some owners, Chris had told her, will want to do something to demon-strate their mastery of you right away. Be prepared for anything. Do not hesitate.

But as more people came in, few stopped by her and no one came to claim her.

Oh dear, she thought wildly. *No one bought me! No one wanted me! I'm a failure! Chris will kill me!*

And then, into her line of sight came a pair of long legs clothed in Brooks Brother's splendor. A hand gesture appeared before her eyes, and she snapped her head up to look into a pair of bright blue eyes. Wavy, two toned hair was expertly cut so that it fell across a distinguished forehead, a square jaw set off a firm but sensual mouth. He was about 6'2", slender and graceful.

Gently, he took the sales chain from around her throat, and replaced it with a gold chain not unlike the one that Leon wore. He took a lock out of his pocket and locked the ends together and smiled, showing a mouthful of straight white teeth, practically gleaming against his tanned face.

I've been sold to Prince Charming, Robin thought. *I'm swooning.*

And then another man entered her vision. He was slightly shorter, heavier, and had long straight brown hair, which was gathered at the back of his neck into a pony tail. He was also elegantly dressed, although in a more flamboyant manner; he too had a tan. He was also sporting a pink triangle tie-clip, and two gold hoops in one ear.

"I don't know what I'm going to do with you, Eric," he said, touching Robin's chin and shaking his head. "Of all the things! What the hell are we going to do with a woman?"

"You'll see," Eric said, patting Robin on the head. "She'll fit in just fine, sweetheart. You have to trust me on this one." And then he leaned over to kiss the brown-haired man.

I've been sold to Prince Charming, Robin thought again. *And he's gay.*

Chapter Sixteen

"I don't care if they charge you double, just get it in the air tonight and in my hands tomorrow," Robin demanded, slamming her hand down on the desk for emphasis. "This is the age of technology! Express it! Messenger it! But get it here, or my ass is in a sling, do you understand me?"

Literally, she thought, pausing as the exasperated clerk rattled off air shipment numbers at her. *Very literally.*

When she hung up, she sighed and checked the bill of lading again. Somehow, those jerks back in New York had managed to ship the entire set of Hopi household pottery except for the all-important mortar and pestle assembly which had made the set so noteworthy. And it wasn't just any ordinary acquisition here, but a gift, from her masters to Jimmy's parents, whose wedding anniversary was tomorrow night. Eric had spent hours going through catalogs with her, trying to find the right thing. Jimmy didn't much care. His parents would love anything, he had sighed from time to time. But Eric was ever so conscious about appearances. He wanted everything perfect.

Like he was, for example.

Down girl. Behave.

If I can get it here in the morning, she figured, I can get it messengered to San Diego, or take it there myself. God knows the folks would be happy to see me. She giggled out loud as she flipped through her battered old rolodex for her travel agent's number.

The last time she had made the short flight into San Diego, the old man had greeted her like a daughter and insisted that she stay for barbecue and Sangria. Jimmy's parents were old California and old money. They were both bilingual and Berkeley educated, and considered themselves very hip. Certainly they loved their gay son and his fabulous lover. But they didn't know that the young and good looking staff that their son and son-in-law maintained to run their business and keep their handsome house in order were all slaves. When mom and dad came to visit, everyone got to get dressed for the weekend.

Dad had even mentioned to Robin that he never found such polite young men as those who worked for his "kids."

"They're not like I was when I was their age," he chuckled. "Why, I was quite the bohemian, disrespected my parents and teachers, smoked dope, and ran amok. Couldn't tell, could you?"

"No, sir, I guess I couldn't," Robin had agreed.

"Well there you go! Just like those boys! 'Sir!'" He shook his head. "Now why don't you just call me Jack?"

Because your son would take my hide off if he found out, Robin thought cheerfully. "It must have been the way I was raised, sir."

The pottery would look wonderful in their wide living room, with the wall of windows overlooking a wooded hill. Robin decided to let the messenger pick up the whole set and bring it down. She still didn't know if Eric or Jimmy had any plans for her tomorrow, and it was always better to be cautious with them.

Raul came in, his bare feet slapping against the stone tiles. He put a stack of mail on her desk and winked at her. "New books from those auction houses in London and something in Japanese. Did you get the missing piece?"

"Yes," Robin grabbed at the catalogs and grinned with delight. "Oh, great! Here's that sword collection that Jimmy wanted to look at. Maybe now we can match that piece he got last year and make some money."

Raul shook his head in wonderment. "I dunno how they had the time to do all this stuff before." He bent over her desk to look at the photos of Japanese and assorted eastern weaponry. His body was fluid and graceful, a swimmer and a dancer, done in cream-heavy coffee. He often wore Speedos when doing his housework, especially brightly colored ones. They suited him much more then nakedness, emphasizing his long legs and tight stomach and cupping the cheeks of his ass. Today, it was orange, with black racing stripes.

"They didn't," Robin muttered. And it was true. Before they had acquired her, their acquisition of the various artwork and collectibles that they, their friends, family and clients all wanted were obtained in the catch-as-catch-can method. Eric was the primary collector in the house. He loved sculpture, and three dimensional pieces of artwork that he could touch. He also loved ancient erotic art and literature that mentioned or depicted homosexuality. One of his oldest pieces was a section of plastered wall from an archeology dig that had Greek graffiti on it saying, essentially, "Priscus fucked Lucanus here."

Jimmy, the securities genius, didn't have any special love, although he did like to be aware of some items for their investment value. What he liked to do now that he had a full time buyer to do his bidding, was use her to pick up special gifts for his clients. They were constantly showering him with things he couldn't use or didn't want, and Robin got the job of discreetly getting rid of those as well. Or at least putting them away, cataloging them, and knowing when to pull them out just in time for the client to see them when invited over to dinner.

It had been a very *interesting* year.

Jimmy and Eric did not stage any special use of her before leaving the auction. In fact, they were very low key, accepting complimentary comments and best wishes from several people before getting Robin's clothes and telling her to wait in their car. While she sat alone in the limousine, she watched people streaming out of the great old house, and even saw Grendel, Alex and Chris leaving together. She was still somewhat shell-shocked. Luckily, she did have enough presence of mind to curl her legs under her on the floor just before her new masters reached the car. They slid into seats without making any comment about her position, so she assumed that she did the right thing.

"I'm Eric Parese and this is my lover James Appleton," her "Prince" said to her as the car began to move. "You belong to the two of us now. Have you a professional wardrobe?"

Robin opened her eyes wide in astonishment. That was the last question she had expected. "Um…yes, master, I do. It's in storage."

"You'll have to get it out. There's no reason for me to duplicate it." He looked at his watch and then back at her. "We were going to leave tomorrow. Will you be able to get your things packed by tomorrow evening?"

"Yes, sir."

"Good."

And as if to deliberately frustrate her, he had leaned back into the leather seat and closed his eyes for the rest of the ride back into the city. Jimmy had just gazed out the window. Robin knew all the proper forms for asking if she could ask a question, but there was no way in heaven that she was going to start now. It had been a long day.

Back at the wonderful hotel they were staying in, she slept on the couch in the outer room instead of at the foot of their bed.

It wasn't until she had lugged her suitcase and garment bag back to them and they all made it to the airport (where her collar did not set off the metal detector) that Eric finally told her where they were going. California.

To the hills north of Los Angeles to be exact. Not near the beaches, but where they could have a little bit of property and privacy. Jimmy had snorted;

privacy and a one hour commute to the edges of the city. But between Eric's work as a model and Jimmy's mostly at-home financial work, they never made it into the city more then twice a week. They both stayed with friends or at hotels when they had to do extended projects, and tried to make it home as often as possible.

And who could blame them? Home was a paradise, with a spacious, sunlit designer main building, a jacuzzi that sported a view of the rolling hills and the mountains in the distance, a small swimming pool, and three men who lived to fulfill their every need.

There was Raul, the house manager and general handyman; he was also the cook and the mechanic, and the preferred sexual partner for Eric when Eric wasn't doing Jimmy. Then there was Carl, who at thirty-seven was the oldest member of this youthful household. He assisted Jimmy and acted as a secretary, bookkeeper and social secretary, and had been Jimmy's slave before Jimmy and Eric got together. And then there was Jeff, another easterner like Robin, who was the all-around houseboy and gofer and lowest on the household pecking order. Even Robin had a better standing then he did, although not at first. She had to earn her way up.

Despite their well-off backgrounds, or perhaps because of them, her masters were cautious consumers. Every member of their house did double or triple duty, and everyone was expected to be able to step in for someone else if a crisis occurred. The male slaves were as surprised to see Robin as she was surprised to be purchased. At first, she didn't seem to fit in. There was no job that was left undone to anyone's knowledge, and there was no way to slip her into the scheme of things erotically. The masters showed no interest in suddenly picking up girls; why buy one? She was an intruder in their all-boy atmosphere, a cog in their fantasy paradise. At the beginning, they seemed to do all they could to make her understand that she was unwanted and unwelcome.

First of all, despite Eric's assurances, Jimmy remained sarcastic and unwilling to believe that they could or should incorporate Robin into their lives. It was in the context of explaining to Jimmy what he had in mind for the new acquisition that Robin finally learned what she had been purchased for.

"We just spent that kind of money on a personal antique shopper?" Jimmy had asked in exasperation.

"Not just antiques. My sculpture. Your…investments. She could do the buying for the clients, and for the families. We can use her to agent our trading pieces." Eric remained calm at almost every barb and every lilt of arrogance in his lover's voice. Instead, he ticked off the advantages one at a time, seemingly unaware that Robin was listening to every word with a rising understanding and inner sense of irony. "Listen," Eric had continued. "You hate to go to auctions. I hate to waste my time, too. Now, we have someone who can go to all these things, sit by the phone for who knows how many hours and handle all the stupid little details that are such a pain in the ass. I won't need to borrow Carl from you to do all of the paperwork for me. And you won't have to go out by yourself to get me something fabulous for my birthday."

"You just got something fabulous for your birthday," Jimmy sighed. "And she's sitting right there."

They both turned to Robin as though just noticing her presence. It was her first day in California, her first day in the house, and they hadn't even showed her where to put her things or where she was going to sleep.

"She doesn't know anything about the things we like," Jimmy added. "For crying out loud, she likes Italian paintings and Old Masters. We're going to have to have her tutored to make her useful."

"No we won't." Eric addressed her for the first time. "Are you familiar with Southwestern Native artwork? Navaho, Hopi? Mexican and Spanish Californian? Greek, Roman or Aramaic antiquities? Modern sculpture? Hindu artwork and texts? Japanese swords and military collectibles?"

Robin thought quickly. "Master, I'm familiar with most of them, but I haven't spent a lot of time in their markets. But a few weeks with the new catalogs and a few visits with some dealers and I could easily act as your agent in any field, sir."

Eric smiled triumphantly. He was still princely when he smiled. "There, you see? Great investment."

Jimmy snorted. "You don't even know where she's going to sleep."

"No, I decided that on the ride from the airport. We'll just put her in with the boys. There's no need to make special arrangements here. She can use the second floor office as her workspace, and I'll have Raul empty the closet for her things."

It was amazing. *After spending my lifetime wishing for enslavement, to become the object of the whims and will of a master or mistress who would reduce me to nothing but a useful toy, a sexual plaything, I have at last been sold to two masters who don't have the slightest interest in me sexually, but who are going to put me to work doing precisely what I did before being trained and sold.*

Suddenly, she looked up, and her quick movement attracted the immediate attention of both men. She blushed; Chris had hammered into her that slaves move with deliberation and speed, in order to fade into the background. But she cleared her throat and went forward anyway. "Master? May I use one of my personal contacts today?"

"What, you mean to call home? Sure, sure." Eric waved one hand dismissively. "We're not living in some Dickensonian tragedy here. You may

185

give out the telephone number you'll be using for business to a family member if you like, so long as they understand that it may not be abused." He raised his voice. "Raul!" The man appeared at the door instantly. "Take the new girl up to the room, and give her a bed. Then let her use the phone in the upstairs office. She can help you clean the closet out in there. And then bring her back downstairs to meet the family."

And Robin had gone upstairs, smiled at the sight of pine wood bunk-beds in the small bedroom that the four house slaves would now share, and then was taken to the office that would be hers. It had a set of glass doors leading out to a small patio that overlooked the back of the house and the pool. She would get the morning sun.

She picked up the phone and dialed direct and tried to keep from laughing out loud until her mother picked up.

"Hey, Mom?" she said after greetings had been exchanged. "Guess what? I got a new job, a much better one. And I'm moving to California! And my office has a window with a view, and everything!" She looked casually over toward the figure of Raul, who was showing off his incredibly cute buns as he leaned over to pull a box out of the closet. "The benefits? Oh, the benefits are just *fabulous*," Robin sighed.

That night, her two masters examined her closely as she stood in the middle of their living room. The other slaves were all in attendance. Raul was serving, going back and forth with after dinner drinks and espresso. Carl was kneeling by the fireplace, his hands behind his back, looking studious and uninvolved. And Jeff was laying on the floor, providing a spot for Eric's feet. It was common to see the young man sprawled out and paying attention to those two objects of worship. Eric liked it, a lot.

"You can grow back the hair down there," Eric finally said. "I'm no pedophile. And it'll break up the paleness of the body."

"It'll look strange," Jimmy protested. "The boys are all shaven."

"They're different. What do you think about getting her nipples pierced?"

"Oh, that's so fucking trendy. At this rate, she'll be a novelty without them."

"Good point." Eric turned to Carl, over at the side. "Carl, did you ever fuck women?"

"Yes, sir. Before I was sold to Master Jimmy."

"Well, there, you see. Another use for her." Eric leaned back and stretched. "Not to mention that we'll finally have someone to entertain your het clients with."

"Well, if we're thinking that way," Jimmy said, perking up. "There's also the girls."

186

"Hell yes! We won't have to borrow anyone for the parties." Finally, it looked like the lovers were agreeing on her usefulness. Robin sighed just a little. Her position had seemed somewhat tenuous, and the last thing she wanted was to be the point of contention between her two owners.

"Well then. Now that we're settled, let's settle the rules and make sure she knows her place." Eric leaned over to touch Jimmy's hand in comfortable appreciation, and then turned back to the slaves. "You belong to both of us equally," he said, addressing Robin. "When we are not here, you obey Raul, and then Carl. You will rise with the rest of the slaves, and do whatever business is assigned to you, and make yourself available for whatever other chore or activity we desire. You are responsible for keeping yourself healthy. You must exercise every day, and keep yourself clean. Any problems go to Raul. Hesitation or sloppy behavior will be punished, and so will improper attitudes. You will call the two of us master or sir, and all of our guests are sir or ma'am. You do not use the furniture unless specifically told to. And you accept your punishments with as much silence as you can, or you'll be gagged."

"Yes, master," she replied. It all sounded pretty easy to follow.

"Then let's put some color on you, and see what you're made of." Eric stood up and stretched, nudging Jeff out of the way. "I've never played with a girl before. Want to help?"

Jimmy shook his head. "No, I'll sit this one out. I want to watch." He snapped his fingers and Jeff crawled over to him. Jimmy pointed to his crotch, and the black-haired young man put his hands behind his back and maneuvered his head to open Jimmy's fly with his lips and teeth. But Robin could only see the opening movements of that act. Because Eric came up close to her, touched one finger to his lips as though he were still considering, and then nodded.

"I think I will need you, Carl," he said, beckoning. "And bring me a paddle, and one of those little rubber things we got in San Francisco. Get yourself a couple of safes while you're at it."

He took Robin by the arm and led her away from the sunken seating area to a bare corner where a mission style lamp cast yellow light over a square of bare floor. Over his head hung a single chain.

"I want you to reach up and hold onto that," he explained. "As high as you can for as long as you can. Don't make me waste time with cuffs."

Carl returned with the requested items and stripped off the wide red jock strap which had been his only garment. He stood in front of Robin as she raised herself up onto the balls of her feet and wrapped her hands around with the chain. She looked up at him; it wasn't forbidden to do that with the other slaves. He had a bright look in his gray eyes, as though this were something extra special. She would have admired his craggy, square face had she seen him elsewhere. His dark hair was cut very short, but not like the all over buzz cut that Jeff sported, and it made him look a little bit like a soldier. Of all the men in the house, he had the greatest definition in his chest and arms.

"So show me," Eric's voice came from behind her, "how you fuck a woman. How would you start? Skip the kissing. Just get to the sex."

"Yes, sir," Carl replied, grinning. "Thank you, sir." And he reached out and took Robin's breasts into his hands. As she felt his fingers compress, she shared a gasp with him. He immediately swept his hands down so that he could pinch her nipples, and then began to knead them between his fingers.

"Do they like that?" Eric's voice asked again. He was standing right behind Robin, his mouth near her right ear. "Do it harder. Can they take as much as men?"

"They usually love it, sir," Carl said. "And they can almost never take as much as men." As if to prove his words, he gripped her nipples harder and twisted them savagely, and Robin cried out. Her body shook, but she held onto the chain with all the strength she could muster.

"She'll have to take more than that," Eric commented. "Tell me, Robin, do you like what Carl is doing?"

Robin moaned as Carl backed off a little, and blushed for the first time in her new home. "Yes, master," she replied.

"Well, that's lucky for you. Those nipples of yours will have to take a lot around here. Is she getting excited, Carl? I can see her breath is coming harder."

"Yes, sir." Carl dropped one hand from her breast and pushed her legs firmly apart. Robin gasped again as the spread put more pressure on her arms and legs. But Carl recaptured her full attention when his fingers artlessly spread her cunt lips and pushed their way inside her.

Naturally, she was already quite wet. She moaned as he pulled out of her and nodded to his master. "Yes, sir, she's hot."

"Fantastic. And do you want to fuck her? Put your cock into her pussy?"

"Yes, sir!"

"Isn't that interesting. Your boy wants to fuck girls," Eric informed Jimmy.

Robin couldn't help but turn her head to see what her other master would say to that. Jimmy was sprawled back on the couch, pulling Jeff's head up and down violently on his lap. The boy's body shook as he tried to keep his balance. When Jimmy paused to answer, he pushed Jeff down, probably filling his mouth and throat with cock. Pinning him there, Jimmy made a dismissive gesture with his free hand.

"Oh, he always wants to fuck girls. I guess having one around might be good for him." Looking down, he ground his boy's head down against him, and then pulled him slowly up. Even across the room, Robin could hear the desperate gasping for breath.

"There you go, Carl. Do you want her to suck you first?" Robin glanced quickly back to see the look of panicked indecision that crossed Carl's face. But before the slave could answer, Eric laughed. "Not tonight, asshole. Learn to answer faster when I speak. Now get your dick covered and in her, and right now."

Carl moved with near lightning speed, and when he stepped up to Robin, he had to bend his knees to get his cock into position. But that didn't deter him. He merely grasped her thighs in his two large hands and lifted her bodily off the floor, and then settled her back down onto his cock. His arms reached around her to wrap her about the waist and hips, and he groaned as she covered him and took him in.

"Whoa! Nice move! Get your legs up, bitch, like they do in the movies. Fuck him back!" Eric moved back as Robin did her best to follow his directions. Carl was not above average in size, but he did move against her in a steady and hungry way that made her want to do exactly the movements that Eric was coaching her in. Her legs came up and wrapped around Carl's lower body, and although the pressure on her arms seemed to increase, she didn't care. She had a cock, a warm cock, sunk deeply into her, and a strong man thrusting against her. And just when the pleasure seemed to become too much to bear while maintaining her proper attention upon her master, the man who bought her stepped behind her again and smacked her ass, hard, with a paddle.

"I said to fuck him back!" Eric shouted, smacking her again. "Move those hips! Take him in, all the way, and then pull back! I want to see every muscle in your body moving to fuck him!" He began to hit her regularly, one cheek and then the other, hard and steady, making her wriggle and dance, wonderful, spreading pain behind her and a pole of flesh inside her and a hot man in front of her.

Eric directed the two of them for the next several minutes, leaving Robin's ass to glow with remembered pain only long enough to use the same encouragement on Carl. But Carl was obviously much more used to that kind of punishment. Robin saw Eric bring out a whip made of long black rubber tresses, and hissed in sympathetic pain as Eric used it mercilessly all over Carl's body.

But still, even as a trail of red lines appeared over his shoulders and across his back and along his legs, Carl didn't falter. He continued to thrust and twist his hips and grind into and against Robin until she saw stars. And it was only when Eric used that rubber whip on her that she began to lose her strength and feel her hands slipping in the chain. Her fingers were getting numb.

"What a wimp," Eric said the first time he saw her slip. "Get her down. I want to see her in another position."

"Missionary is always appropriate for boy-girl couples," suggested Jimmy with a laugh.

"All right," Eric agreed. "Missionary first."

On the bare floor, Carl and Robin were coached into position after position, until their bodies were coated with sweat. Riding him while he lay on his back, Robin had to endure the awful pain of those rubber lashes against her breasts, and she started to cry. But Eric didn't stop to examine her tears, he only switched his attention to her back again, and as the welts heated and then cooled to itching lines of pain, Robin felt a new wave of pleasure wash through her.

She was put on her back with her legs up in the air, pushed up over Carl's shoulders. Eric liked that, and kept them there for a long time, instructing Carl to spank her raised ass cheeks while they were so available.

And finally, he pulled them apart, and left Robin on her hands and knees, her most recent position, with her legs spread and her head hanging low as she panted in shallow breaths.

"OK, Raul. Get covered and get in," Eric finally said. "Asshole. Might as well get her used to it."

Robin didn't even hear Raul's answer. To her, only the cool pressure of a new penetration was the answer to Eric's direction. She moaned, but it was no great discomfort. And unlike a lot of women she had known, she loved the feeling of intrusion and the guilty waves of pleasure when someone or something invaded her warm back passage.

Raul began to move gently, pushing in and slowly pulling out.

"Carl, I want you here. When Raul is ready, I want you to do it at the same time. Raul, stop playing and get to the point. Smack her a little, she needs it."

Raul complied, and before long Robin was grunting as he slammed his cock along her narrow channel, building up a new heat that made her want to squirm and reach down between her legs to help a growing orgasm to reach its full flower. But she braced her arms against his relentless pounding and when he suddenly pulled out of her completely, she lost her balance and fell slightly forward, onto her elbows. She heard a slight snapping sound, and then felt the unmistakable sensation of warm fluid hitting her lower back, where it slipped up her spine and trickled off her sides. And then another light shower of fluid struck her right shoulder, to run in thin streams across her back, down her arm and down her neck.

Her new master had had his slaves shoot their cum onto her body.

Not even Troy had done that. She trembled, moaned, and then cried out, a faint cry that was half surrender and half passion. Between her legs, her clit felt like it was red hot, pounding with need.

And it wasn't over. Jimmy dragged Jeff over, and although Robin didn't see it, jerked Jeff's own dick back and forth in a rough parody of a man's more concentrated movements and ordered the young man to shoot. His cum also hit her back, this time to trickle entirely down to pool at the back of her neck and drip, slowly, through her hair.

She was marked the lowest of the household slaves. Even the "boy" had spilled his pleasure upon her. There was surely nothing else they could do that could shame her further. But even as she was dismissed to shower and get ready for bed, she knew that she was going to be proven wrong.

That night, as she lay in her bottom bunk, she was not very surprised when Raul came over to her and showed her his stiff cock.

"When the masters are not around, you obey me," he reminded her. "And there's no master here now. Let's see how you suck, new girl."

In the darkness, she used the skill that Chris had taught her, and rolled a condom over her fellow slave's cock. There didn't seem to be anything else to do. Her masters had said exactly what Raul quoted. Besides, what could she possibly do? Wake them up and complain?

Raul, despite having had one orgasm already that night was quick in his second one. He sighed as he removed himself from her mouth. "You're not bad for a girl," he admitted. "But you have to be a lot better around here. Luckily, you'll get a lot of practice. Carl, you still up?"

"Oh yeah. My turn, cunt." And Carl's bunk creaked as he rose and padded over.

"Please, guys," Robin whispered, "Please don't do this. This is my first night here! Can't I just get a little used to things?"

"This is getting used to things," Raul said, going back to his bed. "'Cause you better get used to us."

Another cock, another blow job, and Carl was rougher then Raul. But luckily, he was just as quick. Robin wasn't to learn exactly why the slaves liked to cum quickly when they had a chance until she had spent several days in the house.

And then, when Carl finished, hissing his discontent with her oral skills, he didn't leave her, but stayed by her head and called over to Jeff. "Come here, dick face, and get some face of your own for a change."

And Robin had to suffer the intrusion of the houseboy's cock as well, while Carl held onto her head and moved her for Jeff's obviously rare pleasure.

By the time the three men had finished with her, her mouth was impossibly sore, her jaw aching and her head pounding. She was exhausted, stressed out, and suddenly scared.

But then, as she stretched out between the soft cotton sheets, she thought about what had just happened. Apart from the knowledge and sight of her two young masters, the three slaves of the household had all ruthlessly used

191

her, without regard for her own feelings or pleasure. They had spoken of her among themselves, degrading her with their words as well as their actions.

Between her legs, a river ran. And to her instant understanding came the one instruction that her new masters did not give her. Slowly, as though she really didn't believe it, her hand crept down to her naked pussy lips, which were barely covering the heated moisture that had gathered in tides of pleasure during the night. Her fingers closed around the sensitive flesh and she pulled gently at it until she could only sigh with pleasure. And then, in a fever of delight, she sent her fingers sliding to that one perfect spot and danced a wild jig on her hungry clit until she came and came and came, muffling her moans of ecstasy with the corner of her sheet.

Perhaps her new life wouldn't be so bad after all. But if only there was even one other woman to share it with.

Chapter Seventeen

It didn't take long for there to rise a certain pattern to her life. Chris Parker had told her that such was the lot of a slave, that their lives would fit a certain rhythm of existence from which they could receive a measure of security.

Early in the morning, she got up with Raul, who had been delighted to learn that she was a runner. Together, they ran, up into the hills and down again. He was faster than she, but she had him on distance. When they got back, they would do a couple of laps in the pool to cool off if the weather permitted, or just shower and get to work. He might be cruel to her during the night, or whenever the masters gave him license to be, but he was always cheerful in the morning.

She quickly established a working office, anxious to prove her worth. She set up her old rolodex and called some of her old clients and contacts and jobbers. She called up all the auction houses and galleries she had worked with before and told them that she was now working as a private agent for a single client, and let them know what her new interests would be. Some of them expressed disbelief. Did she really give up a job that let her handle millions of dollars a year in artwork for a single client with eclectic tastes? What could be worth the switch?

And Robin would rub her sore buttocks against the hard surface of her chair, look out into the yard where Jeff was pruning bushes in the nude and tell them that the atmosphere in her new position just defied description.

As she proved her professional competence, Eric began to let go of the detail work that he hated so much, and even Jimmy got to appreciate the little things that he could just pass on to her without thinking. When he needed a responding gift for a wine merchant who had millions of dollars in Jimmy's expert care, it was Robin who found the Impressionist watercolor of a vine-yard seen through a window that had a wine glass posed beautifully on the sill. The client went into raptures over it, hung it in a place of honor, and sent two of his equally wealthy friends calling.

And although neither master used her sexually at first, both were equally likely to either punish her for some real error or to manufacture some reason to toy with her. Eric especially liked to watch Carl and Raul work on her, and she got used to their touches and desires. It was ironic again; it was almost as though she had surrogate masters.

Raul liked her, and showed it early on. Carl remained suspicious, and it was always Carl who invited Jeff to come and use her after lights out. It took Robin a while to notice all of the workings in the household, but she began to realize certain things in the first couple of weeks. Jeff was never allowed furniture other than his bed, and was also never allowed clothing. He was most likely to be used quickly and pushed away, and least likely to get a treat, like a sip from master's glass or even a pat on the head.

But after Robin had established herself and begun to make a difference in how the house worked, she too began to feel the wonderful pleasure that pleased attention from an owner could give. Eating in the kitchen with Raul one night, she was surprised to be called to the table and fed some of the dessert from Eric's hand. Kneeling beside him and picking up ripe strawberries in her lips, she remembered telling Leon that she could never really do this seriously.

Oh, yes I can, she realized, carefully licking the sweetness from Eric's fingers.

During the day, it was rare for any of the slaves to bother her. There was an unwritten rule that allowed them to do their tasks uninterrupted. After all, they all might suffer if something vital was neglected so that someone else could have their fun. But again, she noticed that Raul and Carl had no compunctions about calling Jeff to them for a quickie during the day, even if it did call him away from whatever menial task he was performing.

So one afternoon, while she was waiting for a call-back from an office in New York, she was more than ready to handle Jeff as he sauntered into her little office.

She had been a problem to dress at first. No one except for Jeff went naked all the time, but swimwear looked more natural on men than on women, at least to Eric's eyes. It was Jimmy who came up with some more appropriate garments, taking them from a spa's catalog. So on that particular day, Robin was wearing hip hugger spandex shorts and a cut off top that held her breasts close to her body. Her throat chain touched the top of the cut-off and gleamed. And while she was still a little too soft around the middle to properly wear that combination, Raul had promised that a month or two of regular workouts would turn her into a real hardbody California girl.

"Except that you're too short and your hair's too dark," he had muttered.

Jeff was a little sweaty from whichever chores he had been doing last. He walked into the room and looked over at Robin, who was doing nothing more strenuous than marking off pages in the latest catalogs.

"You're not busy," he announced, pulling on his cock. It lengthened away from his body and stiffened. His face was a slightly twisted mask of confidence. Carl's invitations had been sporadic recently, and the masters almost never let him orgasm. He was probably horny as hell. He indicated his dick with a jerk of his head. "Come over here and suck me off."

"In your dreams," Robin answered smoothly. "Go away, you little pipsqueak."

"What?" he demanded. He dropped his dick and came forward, leaning over her desk. He might have been a spare youth, without much bulk on him, but he was still taller then she was. "You don't talk that way to me, cunt! I was here before you!"

"But you're still a rotten little no-account jerk," Robin replied. "You don't have any authority over me. Go take a hike."

Jeff drew himself up and frowned, then thought it over. He folded his arms. "If you don't suck my cock," he threatened, "I'll just have Carl make you do it later."

That was the gamble she had to take. If she let him get away with it, she'd have five masters in this house. Robin felt her own lip curling, and thought of the sight of Jeff's body being shaken around by the heavy fucking that Jimmy liked so much. Envisioned the way his ass would turn red and then become bruised if she had one of Chris' damn canes.

And that way, she felt her first twinge of satisfaction in the imagined suffering of another slave.

But she didn't dwell on it. "You can always try that," she said. "You can always try to beg a real man to get you what you can't have for yourself. But in the meantime, get your scrawny ass out of here and get back to emptying the garbage cans or something." Her phone rang, which gave her an excellent excuse to turn away from him and get back to her business.

But there was one other thing she had to do that day. She had to get to Carl.

Luckily, Jimmy was out that night, and Eric wanted to amuse himself by letting Jeff lick his feet for an hour or two, switching off to toe sucking when he got bored. Raul was busy with the household accounts, and Robin found Carl in the room that housed the gym equipment. He was working out on the rowing machine, watching a tape of a flowing river as he rowed. Robin squatted down next to him.

"I need to talk," she said as an opening.

"So talk."

"You were straight before you were sold?"

"That's not talk, that's a question." Carl slowed down and then pulled to an easy stop. She passed him the towel and the water bottle and he grunted thanks. "What's your point?"

"I like you," she said, with some honesty. "You're a kind of man that I'd go for on the outside. So I think we can have more fun if you're interested in my willing cooperation instead of my acceptance of the inevitable."

He smiled. "Good choice of words. I'm still waiting for the point."

"I'm getting tired of the boy. He's getting too cocky. He actually came on to me today and threatened to make you force me to take care of his horniness." OK, so it wasn't exactly what the kid said, but it was close enough.

It worked like a charm. "That asshole is getting too full of himself," Carl growled. "I was doing him a fucking favor."

"So do favors for people who know how to return them," Robin suggested.

"Heh. Cool." Carl grinned again. "Besides, it wouldn't be too cool if the masters discovered the kid acting up, would it?"

Robin agreed.

"OK, Robin, you got a deal. Tell you the truth, it's better for me. I haven't had a girl in years. But Raul, he's still got dibs."

"Raul is cool," Robin answered seriously. And then she broke out in giggles. *I can't actually start talking like them,* she thought. *No one in New York would ever take me seriously again!*

So, starting that night, Jeff learned to keep his distance. In fact, after a few casual and comfortable vanilla fucks, Carl turned a little vindictive. Why, this little asshole jerk almost cost him a fun sex partner! So he began to use the kid less often, and save himself for good times with Robin. Raul saw what was going on and accepted it. He never invited Jeff to make use of Robin anyway, and remained slightly aloof of the whole matter.

It was Robin's first agreement made between slaves for the purpose of her own situation. Afterward, she was amazed at how natural it seemed to her, and how satisfying it was. Raul told her one night, "If things can be done without involving the masters, we do them. The masters must believe that our greatest concern is their pleasure, and our entire attention is upon helping them."

It was all so delightful. And when Raul went off to sleep in the masters' chamber, Robin examined herself and realized that she didn't feel as rejected as she once imagined she would. In fact, nights like that gave her the opportunity to sleep spoon fashion with Carl, the rumbling warmth of his body a comfort. They would never do that in front of Raul. Somehow, it would be improper. And after an initial awkwardness, Robin began to relax and actually enjoy that almost secret intimacy. It was also a good way to remind Jeff that he was still low man on the totem pole.

More than five months after she had entered her service, Jimmy was the first of the two masters to use her sexually.

This time, it was Eric who was away on business. He had achieved some notoriety as a model in a series of ads for a men's cologne; the director had insisted on having him back for the next series, and he would be on location in Nice for two weeks. Jimmy took Carl to his bed for a few nights, and kept Raul busy trying to make up for the more or less constant influence that Eric had on the house. But at the end of the first week, Robin noticed that Jimmy was eyeing her in a speculative fashion more than once, and she felt a combination of wary and excited. But when Carl came into the small bathroom that the slaves shared and jerked a thumb down the hall, she was still surprised enough to panic.

"He's not so hard to please," Carl assured her. His gray eyes danced with amusement. "But your cocksucking isn't gonna make him happy."

"Oh, thanks," Robin snapped. "Just what I needed."

Carl shrugged. He had been with Jimmy for years. And Robin cursed herself when she realized that his ease about her going off to see the master was because Carl didn't think that Jimmy would be amused with her for long. There was something kind of daunting about making her way down the hall. It was like going to see the professor who never gave top grades. She had the feeling that however well behaved and interesting and willing she was, there was still no way she was ever going to be master's favorite. And damn it, it was hard to let go of that hope, no matter how impossible the situation seemed.

Jimmy was waiting for her, cross-legged on the huge bed that he shared with Eric. He was dressed only in a light cotton kimono-style robe, loosely belted at the waist. He had a light cover of brown hair across his chest, trailing down to a narrow column down his midsection. Sometimes, when he and his lover were out by the pool, Robin could see them still as prince and valiant cousin. Apart from Eric, Jimmy was a good looking guy, a little flamboyant and a little coarse. But together, they seemed as natural as any couple, complimenting each other and making the whole more than the sum of its parts.

She knelt in a presenting greeting, bowing her head gracefully. He seemed pleased with the formality and snapped his fingers. "C'mere, I want to take another look at you." She made sure it was OK, and then crawled onto the bed, crossing it to reach him. He brought her up onto her knees to examine her, tapping her thighs and her belly. He brushed her nipples with his fingers and they instantly sprang erect.

"I like that," he said. "It's a nice reaction." Robin smiled, undecided as to whether that was an observation or a compliment. Either way, Jimmy didn't seem interested in any comments from her. He pinched the nipples several times, until she winced, and then nodded. "OK, let's see the back."

She turned and presented for him, and blushed because that position always made her blush. Her pubic hair had grown in again, and under Raul's direction she kept it trimmed rather short and into a tight banner that just covered her pussy lips. Her last beating, just for the hell of it, had actually been three days ago. Raul was good at keeping everything in order, but he wasn't the disciplinarian that Eric was. Eric could find fault in anything. A three day absence from some sort of reminder was almost unheard of.

Jimmy commented on it. "No bruises. And you're not even pink. We're gonna have to correct that. Eric would be all over me if he got back and found out you guys were just lolling around all week. Go get me…I know. A hairbrush. Isn't that what Moms are always spanking their little girls with? Yeah. There's one in the bathroom. Do it doggy style; I wanna see how you look."

The hardest part was getting off the bed on her hands and knees. It took a leap of faith that she wouldn't just fall off head first and then have a tangle of legs follow. But she managed to do it, and crawled mutely over to the bathroom, which, thank goodness, was open and lit. Once out of sight, she sprang up, looked for and found the wooden backed hairbrush that must be what Jimmy wanted, and then wedged the handle lengthwise between her teeth, careful not to get it wet. She looked down at it in resignation: it was going to hurt like hell.

He took it from her mouth when she got back and told her to reassume the presenting posture again.

"I think I'm gonna tell Raul to keep this up every day while Eric's away," he said while he poised the brush. "I think you need it. What do you think, kiddo?"

"I think I need it, master," she said, sinking her head even lower.

198

He laughed and delivered one hard spank. She clenched her teeth together, and drew her hands into fists. It was as bad as she thought. It felt worse than any paddle, because it was so hard and unforgiving and so small. In fact, it stung her almost as much as anything ever had while providing very little of the impact sensation that was the oh-so-good part about a nice beating. And Jimmy used it quickly and efficiently, as though covering her bottom with redness was a goal to be reached with as little fuss as possible.

When she couldn't keep still any more, he switched from her asscheeks to her thighs, until she cried steadily. Then, he flipped her over and used the back of the brush against the slight swell of her breasts, and then the front of her thighs.

Robin felt like each new strike point was a little flash of lightning, and each landing of the brush against an already struck area was like a cane strike, burning and lingering. But her body reacted as it usually did, and she could feel her cunt opening as more and more of her skin became alive with the heat of the beating. When he spread her legs and began to beat the curls of flesh that guarded her cunt, she almost screamed. Whether it was through ignorance or design, he caught the hood of her clit and the emerging bud several times, making her see stars and actually bite her own tongue. Finally, she couldn't keep silent anymore, and sharp whimpers began to escape.

'You still can't take a lot,' Jimmy observed. He reversed the brush in his hand and rubbed the bristles against her pubic mound. "What is that like? Good? Or bad?"

It was better than being hit there. "Good, sir."

"OK. And hitting?"

"Ah!" The bristles raised her own short hairs and parted her now swollen lips, brushing steadily against the tender interior flesh. Robin squirmed, just a little. "Very bad, sir."

"Is it like being hit in the nuts, or in the cock? Do you have any idea?"

Actually, Chris had told her. "It's like being hit on the head of the cock, sir."

"No kidding." Jimmy kept up his brushing movements. "If I do this for a long time, you'd probably hate it," he said finally. "But I want to see you play with yourself. I never saw a girl jerk off. How do you do it? With a dildo? Your fingers?"

"Sometimes, sir." Oh, jeeze, he wanted to see her jerk off. And not for his own titillation, but out of academic curiosity.

"Yeah? Do you like it when people go down on you? Do you come like that, too?"

"I can, sir."

"I wanna see that, too. But not tonight." He pulled his hand away, and once the steady sensation assault was absent, she began to feel the pounding ache of the parts of her body that he had covered with red marks and light bruises. "Turn around and spread your legs and show me what you do to get off."

And so she did. It was fairly easy, after all. She was already hot, and every move and twitch of her body brought a reminder of each part of that comprehensive beating he had given her. Before long, her fingers just found the right spot and the right tempo, and when she told him that she was near orgasm, he just waved one hand and told her to go ahead and do it.

Afterwards, he wanted to touch her and examine her, and seemed delighted to find that she was extra sensitive. But he was also a little disappointed. "I thought maybe you'd be one of those ejaculating girls. Girls don't come as nice as boys do. There's nothing much to see, nothing shooting out all obvious and tangible."

She could only keep her mouth shut and hope that he took that to be an agreement. She was almost relieved when he got through looking at her like a science experiment and opened his robe all the way. "Let's see what that sweet little mouth is like," he said, leaning back into the pillows. "Take it easy and slow. You're gonna be there a long time."

She did, inhaling his flesh and allowing him to feel her mouth surround him without pressing her lips tightly against his organ. He was not at full erection, but he was definitely interested, and he shifted to encourage her to take him deeper. But when she didn't move fast enough, he just grabbed a handful of hair and shoved her face tightly down. She felt his cock twitching and then filling her mouth, jamming into the tight confines of her throat, and when she couldn't bring in another breath, she pulled back sharply.

But Jimmy held her securely down, and sighed as her throat contracted even further on his cock, and the choking sounds began to reverberate on the bottom of the shaft. When he finally let her pull back a little, there were tears streaming down her face and she was gulping air in through her nose.

"You are the worst cocksucker in the house," Jimmy said, pulling her back so that just his round cockhead lay in her mouth. "Get down on the floor, we'll start you back at the beginning."

From her knees, she followed his directions. She seduced his cock, kissed it with the shyness of a virgin and then with the passion of a penitent. She took him in one inch at a time, and licked him up and down like candy. He pushed her lower, to lick, kiss and then finally take his low hanging balls in her mouth. One at a time.

"Carl can handle both," he sneered. "I knew you'd be a waste of time. Get back to sucking. But first, lick that cock shaft. Kiss the head, the whole thing! Now get it back down in your throat, and keep it there!"

But she could never keep from choking around it for a long enough time. And Jimmy never let her forget that he was in control. He always shoved that one inch further, and held her in place for ten seconds longer, or, when he finally just clamped down on her head and fucked her face the way that she had fantasized about for so many years, she gagged and nearly lost control.

But dammit, even as she cursed him, and herself, and the cheap porn that had fed her fantasy life, every minute was an awful delight, a thrilling reminder of what she was, and what he was, and how damn good it was underneath all the anguish and disappointment. When he pulled her away from him, she whimpered to get him back. When he barked some new command, she rushed to obey.

It was still a stinging rebuke when he sent her for Carl and made her watch as Carl effortlessly took the entire length of Jimmy's cock in one smooth motion, or as he stayed perfectly still for Jimmy's ruthless battery of Carl's mouth and throat.

And it was still wonderful when Jimmy ordered Carl to fuck Robin for Jimmy's amusement, and the two slaves scrambled and positioned themselves for their master's pleasure, stopping and starting again at his whim.

"I understand that the two of you got something going," Jimmy said once, standing over them while Carl was holding Robin's reddened and shaking ass cheeks far apart, exposing her tight asshole. Robin held her breath, and then moaned it out as she felt Jimmy's finger penetrate her.

"That's cute," the master continued. "Real cute. But you never forget who fucks who around here, boy."

"No, sir," Carl replied.

"So get her up here and get ready for the ride of your life."

Robin ended up over the edge of the bed. Before she realized what was happening, Carl was in her, slamming down into her anal channel with a strong urgency. But instead of starting to bugger her energetically, which was his usual custom, he stayed inside of her, and she could swear that she could feel the pulsating of his warm cock as it nestled deep inside of her.

And what Robin felt next was a compression of weight from above, and then Carl's whoosh of released breath in her ear. His cock in her ass jerked suddenly, and she heard Jimmy's grunt of satisfaction way above her.

Jimmy fucked Carl in and out of her by making Carl follow Jimmy's thrusts.

She could hear the rhythmic breathing of the two men above and behind her, the shift in pressure as Jimmy pulled back and Carl followed. The dragging of Carl's thickness through her body made her begin to grind back into him, with him, so that the three of them seemed one writing mass of sexual frenzy, back and forth, pushing into each other and wrestling back for another thrust.

Robin panted and pressed her palms against the bed, forcing her upper body up, and Carl reached around her and took her breasts into his hands. The brushing of his fingers against her nipples was all the stimulation she could take before what little restraint she had left wrestled and clawed its way from her. Her voice raised into a series of wails that seemed to encourage Jimmy to speed up. Carl grunted as he was forced to slam into her again and again at his master's rhythm, and when Jimmy snarled out a command to hold still, both Carl and Robin moaned.

But they obeyed, feeling the steady pounding of Jimmy's final thrusts, until he spurted his pleasure deep inside of Carl's body. Robin could feel the answering rush that Carl felt as he clutched her even harder, bruising her with his fingertips.

"Finish up," Jimmy said, his voice tight but calm in the tense moments after he drew his cock out of Carl's ass and walked around the bed to look at them again.

Carl didn't hesitate one second. Relaxing his hold on Robin's tits, he pushed himself back for a better angle and slammed into her just as his master had so recently violated him. Robin mewed and whimpered, and pushed her hips back at him. She wanted him all, every inch, and Jimmy too. She wanted the two of them to use her, fuck her in every cavity she had, until she screamed with pleasure, until she cried with agony and exhaustion. Carl's movements into her reached a steady and tumultuous series of waves that triggered her own pleasure, and she threw her head back to look at Jimmy.

"Please!" Her voice drew the whole word out, made it a wavering song of entreaty, like a hymn. "Oh, please, please, master, let me come, sir, please!"

"Sure," Jimmy said. "Do it."

Robin reached under herself, and bowed her head. In a second, she had her hand right where it should be. In three, Carl had begun those movements that she knew signaled his own approaching orgasm. Robin didn't wait for him. One quick pinch, and her own pleasure rose up and took her, sweeping through her body from that little point between her legs and through her entire delta and up past her breastbone, it rushed through her in wave after wave. Her inner muscles constricted and flexed with every pulse, and Carl gasped and came himself, startled by the powerful contractions. He leaned over her while he came, moving his hips in short jerks, emptying himself out, and sighing in the release.

"Cool," came Jimmy's voice. "Do it again."

And after that, Robin became a more integrated part of the household's sexual doings as well as the professional aspect. Eric was so happy that Jimmy had taken an active interest in making some use of the girl that he even tried her out himself. It was not particularly memorable for either of them, but it marked Robin's transition from utility slave to personal one. It also truly established her at an equal level with Carl, despite his seniority. In time, Carl and Robin got tired of their more or less vanilla relationship, and began to see each other as mutually helpful and available friends.

But before they had entirely cooled down, Carl began to let her know that he was on her side in more ways then just friendship. He told her that as soon as he realized that she had no intention of trying to elbow in on his special relationship with Jimmy, he began to really like her. Then, one night, when he came over to her bunk and she pushed back the sheets to make herself available to him, he just kissed her and held her hands together and called Jeff.

She froze, wondering what she had done to piss him off. But when Jeff arrived, a smirk on his face, Carl merely jerked his head toward Robin's body and said, "Suck her."

"What?" Jeff exclaimed.

"You heard me, shit face. Get your mouth down there and eat her. Lick her pussy."

"No way, man! I don't eat cunts!"

Carl let her go and sprang on Jeff, grabbing him by the back of his neck and forcing him down onto his knees. "And you don't talk to me that way, you snotty little punk. You're dead meat if you don't do what I say, asshole."

Robin watched, eyes wide. Jeff sniveled; it was clear that he really believed that he had to do what Carl told him to. She wondered what his instructions must be.

"But I never did that," he complained, trying one last time. "I don't know how!"

"Now's the time to learn, shit-for-brains. Get your mouth down there and start licking. I'll tell you what to do next." Carl returned to Robin's head while Jeff reluctantly got into position. As Jeff stuck his tongue out and began to lick, Robin giggled; it was almost like being attacked by a perverted dog.

"Relax," Carl said, beginning to kiss her throat and flick at her nipples. "When he gets going good, you'll suck my cock, OK?"

"OK." Robin reached up and gave Carl's nipple a tweak, and when he grinned, they started to play with each other's bodies with obvious delight.

It was over two weeks from that incident when Eric stopped Robin during her work day. When she raised her head from her bow, he shot her a stern look. "Is it true that Carl has been making Jeff go down on you after lights out?"

Robin pursed her lips. But there was no question about how she would answer. "Yes, master."

"And how is he? He's not a bad cocksucker."

"He's…learning, master. He's still…reluctant." Inwardly, she cringed. Chris would have smacked her for not answering the question.

But Eric merely nodded thoughtfully. "Well, we'll have to do something about that."

And that night, for the masters amusement, Jeff ended up servicing everyone with his mouth, one after the other, going back and forth between the other slaves while the owners laughed and threw rolled condoms for him to fetch.

Robin had been firmly established in the household. And the only person who didn't like her was a boy who she could use at will. Life was…good.

At the one year anniversary of her sale, she was supposed to contact her trainer for an update. It was in her contract. So she called Chris at the number she had been given, and spoke to him for about an hour. It was so good to hear his light, sardonic voice, and so good to hear the pleasure he got in knowing that she was working out in her new position.

"You told me that I should expect the unexpected," she said once, when the conversation seemed to drag. "Well, I got it."

"We all do," he replied. "The survivors always seem to be able to make the best of it. And how shall I hear from you in another year?"

He meant, will you be renegotiating your contract with your new masters, or will you want to re-enter the Marketplace through another sale?

Robin sighed, and looked out her window. She was healthier now than she'd ever been in her life. She certainly got her SM play, in abundance, from people who took it seriously and never relaxed it because of affection or love or a bad day at the office. She was doing work she was trained for, and achieving some small rate of success. She even got off regularly.

Could she gamble all of that for something better?

Was there something better?

"I don't know," she finally said.

"Ah." There was silence on the line for a moment. "I do know what you mean. Be good, Robin. And give my respects to your owners."

"Yes, sir," she answered. And then she put the phone down and gazed out the window some more.

It sure was a nice view.

204

Chapter Eighteen

If there was one thing that saved life in California from becoming too monotonous, it was the fact that Eric and Jimmy threw *lots* of parties.

Different kinds of parties to be sure. Jimmy entertained his clients and the slaves got dressed up and became somber and nearly invisible house-staff. Eric partied with fellow beautiful people and their various agents, lovers, photographers and friends, and the slaves became hip, charming waiters in designer outfits who flirted and laughed at everyone's jokes.

Robin was fitted with three exquisite serving outfits, including one maid-style black dress complete with apron and cap and a lovely tuxedo with silver gray trim. She liked doing the servant routine; it was almost like acting in a movie. And the guests were almost always impressed and almost never showed it. If anyone ever wondered why two men needed a live-in staff of four to take care of them, the thought was never uttered out loud. One night, Robin overheard one of Jimmy's guests remarking to another that the servants were all probably hired for the occasion just to impress them, but that was the worst anyone said.

What was ironic about those affairs was that when an occasional guest got out of hand and touched her inappropriately or made a lewd comment, Robin always managed to react the way that any real servant would, with polite but firm refusal and a calm sense of offense. One man even had Eric call Robin aside so that he could formally apologize to her. Afterward, Eric and Jimmy got a big laugh out of it, and speculated that the man had loved the opportunity to relish such humiliation as apologizing to a mere servant before her employer. And Jimmy was especially amused by it, and made mock apologies to Robin for the next week, every time he punished her.

It was more fun to be trendy with Eric's crowd. It was also intimidating as hell. If Robin had felt plain next to other slaves, Eric's friends made her feel like the original Ugly Duckling. But it worked in her favor, because she could be dismissed as a possible distraction; no one would compare her with the absolutely stunning professionals who strutted and lounged their way around the house the same way they did through life. It was at several such parties that Robin actually did meet some famous people, models, directors, actors, photographers, writers and designers.

There, when someone made a move on her, she had to check with Eric or Raul, and let them make a quick decision. Occasionally, to add spice to the event or just to make a friend happy, she was told to allow herself to be seduced, and to take the guest to some out of the way place for a quick screw. When a television actor whose clean-cut good looks made him the cover boy of countless teen magazines slipped into the office he had no idea was really hers and fucked her on the desk, she almost broke into laughter. But he was better than she could have guessed, and despite the tackiness of the situation, she found that looking up into his oh-so-famous soft brown eyes was very pleasant. Afterwards, he gave her his card, and actually told her to contact him if she was ever in Hollywood. Before he left, he had his driver run back up to the house and give her an autographed picture.

Jimmy insisted on framing it and hanging it in her office where she could see it every day. It never failed to make her laugh.

And then there were the more intimate events. Occasionally, either master would bring home a special guest or guests who would be granted the use of one or several of the slaves. Sometimes this was a reward for past services, and sometimes it was a gesture of friendship. Sometimes, especially with Jimmy, it was part of a bribe. These people were never aware of the Marketplace, only of their extraordinary luck in having such an interesting pair of friends.

The slaves were united in hating those events. Raul turned up one lip in distaste whenever one was mentioned (providing there wasn't a master around to see him). "This is surely a case of pearls before swine," he opined with his own brand of self pity. "Let's not kid ourselves. Humiliation and degradation goes with the job. But even a slave has limits."

When Robin cracked up, he only shook his head. "You'll see, girl. Wait until you actually end up doing the funky chicken with a feed store magnate from Idaho. They may be millionaires, but they still have all the charm and sexual expertise they had as a seventeen-year-old prom date in a rented blue velvet tux, driving their polished pick-up truck into town to pick up Mary-Sue-Ellen."

"Not to mention the same BO," Carl had added.

"Come on, guys, it *can't* be that bad," Robin had laughed. "You're scaring me!"

206

It *was* that bad.

Robin's first experience taking care of one of Jimmy's customers started as elegantly as any evening of lust; after serving brandy out by the deck, she had gone up to change into the lacy outfit Raul had tossed to her that morning, telling her that she was up at bat for the visiting pitcher later that night. It was a classic ensemble, Merry Widow in black lace, with stiff ribs caressing her body, g-string, garters and lace stockings, a velvet choker, lacy gloves, and even a matching hairbow. She looked in the mirror and sighed.

Frederick's of Hollywood. Except that she wasn't tall enough. She pulled her breasts up a little more, hoping to make more cleavage. It didn't work. Oh well. At least she looked good otherwise.

She checked the guest bedroom to make sure that the usual supply of sex toys was present, and nodded at the fresh flowers and the chilled bottles of mineral water and champagne that Raul had no doubt placed there. And she waited there, nervously, for the guest to come up. Carl had coached her, "You won't have to say anything. Jimmy will let them know what's going on. All you have to do is look cute and be ready for anything. Don't tell them nothing about real life, but lie your ass off about what they wanna hear. Then fuck 'em, and leave 'em, and forget 'em. But whatever you do, make the fuckers happy. That's what you're there for."

So Robin prepared herself for an evening of making a stranger sexually happy.

What actually happened was that he staggered into the room dead drunk, made astonished and pleased noises at her, opened the champagne and drank some out of the bottle, and told her to dance. After some inspired shaking and wiggling, she watched helplessly while he lurched into the bathroom and threw up, noisily.

He slept for three hours, and she was still too nervous to leave.

When he woke up, he looked around the room, saw her sitting on the floor by the bed, and started tugging at his clothing. She helped him get undressed, and without either of them saying one word, they had a strange, fumbling kind of sex.

Neither one of them came, although Robin put on one of her best orgasm performances. He fell back asleep, and she finally left, feeling that her job was done.

He had ripped the stockings and dislodged two garter straps. But in the morning, he was fresh and chipper and Robin stayed discreetly away from his sights while he loudly proclaimed his visit to be "the best ever!" and shook Jimmy's hand and lumbered back to Chicago.

Robin ended up being punished for not staying with him and doing things that any drunk's caregiver would know, like feeding him water and aspirins and cleaning him up and tucking him in. Also, Raul told her, she should have hung his jacket up and snuck his shirt out to be cleaned. But after Eric finished paddling her for all of these offenses, and she had spent a few hours in bound isolation to think about it, she returned to Raul and whispered to him, "You were right."

"I am always right," he replied. "That is why I am the manager."

As if that weren't enough, the young men also entertained for their friends and contacts who were in the Marketplace. At those affairs, the slaves got to be themselves. They even got to meet and sometimes "play with" other slaves from time to time. It was a great way to catch up on gossip and send messages to other slaves that they knew.

Carl knew a lot of the slaves who visited and had been used by most of the masters and mistresses. He was a treasure trove of information about who did what to whom and how often. Robin loved it when he would come up behind her while she watched some erotic goings-on through the slats in the upstairs banister. "He likes to have his butt-hole licked for hours," he would say, pointing. "And she likes to cane blondes…swears that they make nicer marks. And see her? She says she's straight, but give her a girl to play with and she's all over her, all night. Bet you get her tonight."

And Robin did. And found that Carl was right. The sweet, soft-spoken woman who had an ex-husband in Phoenix and three children in school practically leapt on her as soon as the door was closed. Robin felt the all-over passion that she reserved only for women rise and engulf her, and threw herself into being the most pleasing and exuberant partner in the world.

It was different, being so powerfully ravished and positively devoured by a woman who seemed old enough to be her mother, but it was also comforting. When she led, it was only natural for Robin to follow. When she asked Robin to pose for her, Robin colored, but loved every second of bending, turning and striking one move after another. She shivered and giggled as the older woman trailed her entire body with feather-like touches. And when the guest tied her to the bed and made love to her, Robin had to scream when she came. It was all too wonderful! She had almost forgotten how different a woman felt and smelled. Surrounded by mostly young men who were obsessed with keeping their bodies hard and athletic, she felt herself drowning in the softness of another woman's flesh.

Later, with her hands tied behind her back, she pleasured the woman with her mouth, licking and kissing her way all around her body, over the pale expanse of her breasts and down across her soft belly. She was allowed to suck and lick her temporary mistress until the woman came and came, trembling and crying out with delight. And as if to thank Robin for such a treat, the woman pulled her up onto the bed and spanked her, hard, with her bare hand. Robin ended up coming that way, bent over the woman's lap, with a hard hand against her ass and another one tucked up between her legs.

And there was also the time that Eric and Jimmy hosted a slave owner from the northern reaches of the state, whose property housed a veritable community of male slaves. Raul had trained there, and he was always anxious to find out how things were doing back at the "old school."

"You never forget your training," he had said to her in one of his contemplative moods. "It would be like forgetting your parents."

And while Robin had assured him that she would hold onto her memories of those tightly packed two weeks for the rest of her life, she was nonetheless surprised to find a new reminder of them had arrived with the new guest.

The guest was a vintner who had made a name for himself by writing several books about Californian history. Very few people knew that within the fenced in acres of his estates and farms lived over a dozen men who served him as his slaves. Raul told Robin tales of the tremendously demanding and almost inhuman life lived by those who served under this man's contracts. They were worked hard at basic manual labor, from dawn to nightfall every day, and had to do strenuous workouts designed to build muscles and perfect their physiques. Raul himself had barely made it through his two months there, mostly because his body just wasn't built to bulk up that fast. "I'm no body builder," he added. "I'm built for speed, not muscles."

To supervise the slaves, the man employed three brutal overseers who could use any slave at will in any manner they chose, or order them to use or abuse each other.

"It was a wet dream come true," Raul sighed. "Except that in real life, we had sun stroke and burns, sore muscles every day of the week, and sore everything else as well. And you'd think that being called up to serve big master would be a respite? Why no, not at all. Then, you'd find yourself in all sorts of trouble, tied up, clipped all over, big old plugs up your rear, gags so big they made you want to just die…it reads like paradise, girl, but lives like hell. No privacy, no time off, no freedom at all."

"Gee, too bad it's not open to girls," Robin had remarked in a mock tone of sorrow.

"Girl, you're lucky it isn't. But don't hold your breath. Some big old lesbian is going to open one of those for you one of these days. And you watch out — we'll be seeing your sculpted bod on "Glamorous Ladies of Wrestling," making the big money for your mistress."

The guest himself was entertained by the masters, while his two private slaves were sent off to carry his things and wait for him in the largest guest room. Robin had seen Jeff carrying out the soft pallets that were commonly used by visiting slaves who slept next to their owners beds on the floor. Again,

Raul filled her in on the reason. "When you work that house, you don't get no soft mattress to sleep on. Blanket on the floor, and one of those nasty army surplus things, too. If you're bad, they take away the blanket. When master travels, you sing, because there might be carpeting where you're going."

It was Carl who whispered the news to her as she returned to her own work that afternoon. "One of the boys here trained with your trainer," he said softly, leaning slightly into her office. "The one with the nipple rings. He's going to be on kitchen duty tonight, while the masters play in the back with the other one."

Robin couldn't wait to meet him.

The masters took Carl and Jeff out to use them in the various amusements they had planned, leaving Raul to supervise the general clean-up and prepare the late night snacks and drinks they'd be wanting after the merriment. But Raul, who heard everything, left Robin to supervise the visiting slave while he busied himself with chores that were usually beneath him. Robin made a mental note to be extra enthusiastic the next time Raul came over to her bunk late at night.

The slave was already rinsing things and stacking the dishwasher. Robin slid up to his side and took a dish out of his hands. "I hear you knew Parker," she said softly. There was no one near but Raul, but it always paid to be circumspect.

The man looked at her in astonishment.

He was about average in height, maybe a little tall, and the short fuzz that covered his scalp said that he was naturally black haired. There wasn't an additional strand of hair below his neck. There was nothing about him that was particularly striking, except for the fact that he was very well built; something that was no mystery when Robin applied her knowledge of the activities that he probably spent his time in. He was still pale by Californian standards, and his dark eyes moved too quickly. Robin was getting good at spotting fellow Easterners. There were faint lines across his back, and sharper ones on his thighs. In addition to the rings in his nipples, he had a Prince Albert piercing, and one just behind his balls that looked like putting it in might have been traumatic.

"Yes, he was my training supervisor," he said back. He hesitated, as though surprised that so many words came out at once. Robin remembered what it was like to be restricted to answering questions in the briefest form possible, and smiled encouragingly.

"He trained me too," she said, starting to put things away. "I'm Robin."

"Brian." The man looked out the window over the sink, but it would probably be two or three hours before the masters trooped back to the house. "When did you see him last?"

"Last year. You were with Robert, right?"

"Yes!" he smiled suddenly, and showed a mouth full of strong teeth. "How did you know?"

"I met Robert at a party, and Chris briefed him on what happened to you all. He said that you'd gone to some California estate, but that was before I'd even been to California. I never expected to run into you!" She started to find things to put away.

"It's a small world. I've found that I knew a couple of people before I came into the life who knew all about it. I guess we all did, all of us who trained together, I mean. You know about what happened to any of the others?"

"Not much. Robert seems very happy. One woman is with her mistress, the other has, um, dropped out or something. I never even found out her name."

"No kidding. That must have been Sharon. So she finally fucked up big time." He turned thoughtful for a moment. "Well, too bad. Can't say it's too surprising. And what about you? What kind of a group did you train with?"

"Alone. Chris took me from raw recruit to the auction block in two weeks." It was something she had a hard time being humble about.

He whistled through his teeth in admiration. "Good for you! What an opportunity! Was he as much of a bastard with you as he was with us? Hell, I used to curse him out every night. We all did. But I guess you wouldn't know, not having the comparison to make. But let me tell you, if he was even half as hard on you as he was on me when I stayed behind for more training, I have nothing but admiration for you!" Having answered his own question, he paused and looked at her. Their eyes met and at the same time, they asked each other, "Are you happy?" And then they both laughed.

"It's such a cliché," Robin said when they calmed down. "But it's true. I keep making sure that I should be happy by asking other people if they are."

"Well, who wouldn't be happy here?" Brian asked. "Beautiful house, beautiful men...and you have beds and everything." He grinned.

"I've heard about your place from Raul."

"He left the year before I arrived," Brian said. "But you know, for all the difficulty of this life, I wouldn't trade it for anything. There's nothing that could possibly make me feel more fulfilled. It's really strange. The less I am, the more contented I become. I used to be so obsessed with making a good impression and being the center of attention. It took Mr. Elliot and Chris to break me of that, and show me what I've always really needed." He shook his head in amazement. "I wish they could see me now. You know, last week, I actually pulled a wagon full of shit. Do you believe that? Shit! I used to get a manicure every other week back home." He closed his eyes softly and sighed.

"I was a nothing. Shallow and useless, and directionless. And now, I'm...happy. Happier than I've ever been."

The next afternoon, Robin saw Brian bent over and repeatedly raped by most of the men in the house, including Jeff. They didn't get another chance to talk, but their eyes sought each other all weekend. He winked at her once before he left, and she waved.

Yes, guests who knew the Marketplace were almost always more fun. Some were crueler and more demanding, and all of the slaves had been used by those whose pleasures came strictly from the abuse of human property. But generally, it was an adventure to see what kind of person was going to be granted access to them next.

"It's about time you got a girl," Monica said as soon as she walked into the house. Robin raised her eyes demurely, which was appropriate when acknowledging that someone has noticed you. She immediately met Monica's inky black eyes, which took her in at one glance and then turned their attention back to Jimmy. "I'm tired of playing with dicks whenever I come over."

"We got her with you in mind," Jimmy cracked. "I mean, it was just weighing on our consciences, what can we do about Monica's libido?" He grasped the sides of his head in mock agony. "All she has to fuck with is our three boys when she comes over, oh, what can we do?"

"Yeah, yeah, I get the point. But if you're going to live your whole lives in a boy ghetto, you should at least provide some entertainment for the visitors and resident aliens."

"And so we did." The two of them moved into the dining area, and Robin rushed to pour iced tea. Raul was still upstairs making sure that Jeff had fixed up the guest bedroom correctly. "Actually, Eric bought her. She's an art buyer from New York. He's using her to make sure we can never afford another slave."

"Oh, cornering the market in old gay porn, huh?"

"Yeah, that and some other stuff. She found these old pots that my parents went ape-shit over. If Dad could make any more money to leave to me, he would." Jimmy laughed. "And it hasn't been bad. Carl likes her, and even Eric and me throw her a fuck every once in a while. You know, change of pace."

"Be still my heart. Isn't anyone queer anymore?" Monica examined Robin more closely as she served the drinks, and Robin did what she rarely did any more; she blushed in front of a new guest.

"Cute," Monica said, tapping Robin's retreating butt as she went back to the kitchen. Robin was never so happy to see Raul come back and take over.

212

She fled, catching Carl's eyes as she swept up the stairs. Carl followed her in a few minutes. They crouched in the shadows on the upper landing.

"Well?" she demanded.

"Monica. She's a dyke from Washington. Political fund-raiser, lobbyist, that sort of thing. Knows all the biggies. Wields a hell of a whip."

"Really?"

"Last time she did me, I had marks for weeks. She used a signal whip, the kind they use in sled dog races. Made me cry. Then she called me a wuss, wrapped the damn thing up in a condom, shoved it up my ass and kicked me out. Told me to tell Jimmy the whip was a present." Carl delivered this all in a monotone, and Robin's eyes widened. "Oh yeah. She's definitely the S in S&M."

"Doesn't she have her own slaves?"

"I heard she did, once. But I don't think she does any more. She's real busy, you know? Last time she was here, I saw a list of all the things she's produced and the people she hits up for money. She must be moving around all year long."

Robin looked at the guest again. She was probably just about thirty-five or so, and had the look of a woman who was on the corporate track, despite the fact that she was dressed in jeans and cowboy boots. She looked Hispanic, a little bit lighter than Raul, with the same black hair and eyes. Her mouth was soft, though, and her body was more curves than flat surfaces. She tilted her head a little when she spoke, and exposed a long throat, decorated with a soft tangle of silver chains.

"What's she here for now?"

"Two things, I think. She wants to hit the masters up for some dough, and she wants Eric to show up at some Hollywood glitter party for some charity."

"Do...do you think she'll stay the night?"

Carl looked at her, and then back downstairs. "I don't know," he whispered. "Hope she doesn't."

Robin did, and Monica didn't. And that was the first time that Robin met her.

"I miss snow," Robin said out loud as she helped Raul examine the good china. They were preparing for a New Year's party, and everyone was cleaning or running errands. Carl was making an inventory of champagne and other drinks, and Jeff was washing windows. Raul didn't trust him with the china or the crystal, and Robin was drafted to handle those.

"I don't know why," Raul shivered. "Especially snow in New York. Is it ever white, or does it fall down in that gray-black stuff that messes up the streets?"

"But how can you have winter without snow? Santa in Bermuda shorts, New Year's Eve in sleeveless shirts. It's just unnatural."

"Honey, California is the unnatural capital of the world. Do we have enough for twenty-four?"

"We do! Want me to start on the crystal?"

"Yes, that's a good girl." Raul sighed and consulted his list again. "We've got the catering all ready, the booze is here, the DJ is arriving at six to set up, did Carl get the party things out?"

"Horns, hats and assorted tacky things are all in the big box near the television."

"Good. White folks can't do New Year's without being tacky."

Robin snorted. "My, aren't we brave? Where's Eric, anyway?"

"He's in the city, meeting some of the out of town guests. And don't be impertinent, girl, I still have time to whip you silly." Raul gave her a warning glance and she composed her face and nodded seriously. "And are you ready? Do you have your clothes, and the jewelry?"

"Yes, boss."

"Good. We want you looking nice for Miss Monica."

Robin stopped short, a crystal champagne glass in each hand. "Is Monica coming?"

"That's what I said, girl. And she's spending the night, and *you* are going to be her New Year's resolution." He walked away from her startled face, whistling "Auld Lang Syne."

Chapter Nineteen

"Now, that's what I call hospitality," Monica said wickedly as she threw the door wide open. From downstairs and out on the patio, the sounds of the party continued, interrupted with an occasional horn blast, splash, or a steady slapping sound.

The woman behind Monica peered in. "Oh yes," she agreed. "Much better than a mint on the pillow."

Robin was glad for the blindfold. Not only didn't she know how to respond to that, but she really didn't want to see the looks on the women's faces. It was bad enough being bound and left in the room just like a complimentary after-dinner snack, but it was made even more humiliating by the fact that her costume was a cute version of some designer's idea of what a woman might wear for a sexy romp on New Year's Eve. It looked like a fishnet bathing suit with cut outs for her breasts and a lacing of ribbons over her crotch, and a black satin trim that sort of suggested a tuxedo. Raul had put a clip-on bow-tie around her neck, ignoring her insistence that she really did know how to tie those things.

Teamed with a brief skirt and the fancy jewelry that was provided for her, she knew that it had looked cute during the party. It also encouraged the guests to make free use of her exposed breasts, and her nipples were already aching and itching for more attention. But now, they seemed nothing but slightly numb. Raul had affixed large, decorative clamps to them before leaving, and the weighted ball that hung suspended from the clamps bounced against her pubic mound every time she as much as stretched.

Her fingers clenched the sky again. It was bad enough to be bound. It was always worse to be bound while in high heeled shoes. Before Monica arrived, she had experimented with easing the pain by slowly lifting one leg and then the other and flexing her ankles. Now, she held still and tried to look as dignified as the circumstances allowed.

But she felt like she wanted to die.

"Is this what you wanted me to see?" The not-Monica woman asked.

"Yep. Want to stay for the entertainment portion of our evening?"

"Hell, yes!"

"Good. Look over there in that chest and see what the boys have left us to play with." Robin felt someone move in front of her, and then the lifting and release of the weight that hung in front of her body. It swung out and bounced between her legs several times, and she gave a slight moan.

"Are you having a happy New Year?' Monica asked, letting the weight swing back and forth.

"Yes, ma'am," Robin said. Her teeth clenched as the weight was removed, followed by the clamps. Heat rushed back into her nipples, making them tingle and smart.

"Oh good. It's about to get happier, isn't it?"

Robin couldn't help but smile. "Oh, yes ma'am."

"Cheeky little slut, isn't she?"

"Oh, they all are. What did you find?"

"Good stuff. See?"

"Great." Monica's body pressed against Robin, the warmth and the scent of a woman filling Robin's senses. "But you know, let's try to keep it low key. I want to get as much use out of her as possible before I collapse from exhaustion. The question is…do we leave her here or get her down?"

"Well, she's no damn use to me with her mouth all the way up there!"

The two women giggled, and Robin pressed her lips together to keep from joining them.

"Oh, poor baby," Monica whispered in her ear. "We'll get you down soon enough. Those boys are dressing you up like a little fashion doll, aren't they? Well, we don't need this kind of wrapping on our presents. April; come here and help me raise the boys' costuming budget this year."

With more laughter, the two women stripped the tacky lingerie off of Robin by tearing it in long strips. Each tug forced Robin to pull against it, to brace herself on her stretched legs and the balls of her feet, and the women were quick to use slaps and pinches to get her to move in the right direction. As the material deteriorated into long, tangled strands, they plucked them away, or wrapped them around her limbs, making spiral designs against her thighs and upper arms. Still, the blindfold remained on, and Robin remembered the night she had with Chris and Rachel, which suddenly seemed like such a long time ago.

When two fingers pushed past the ribbons and last remaining lines of netting that barely covered her pubic mound, she unhesitatingly pushed back. They entered her smoothly, and she heard Monica's pleased laugh.

"Yes, she likes it," Monica said out loud. "And after so many months in a houseful of men, who can blame her? Do you like to eat pussy, slave? Do you like to lick cunts, and nibble on a woman's body?"

"Yes, ma'am!"

"What a surprise. And how fortunate for you. I think we're both in that kind of a mood tonight. Would you like to play with her pretty little tits while I warm her up, April?"

"Why thank you, Monica, you're too kind."

Robin felt Monica come up behind her, and then felt the woman's arms wrap around her, pulling her back so that her ass was thrust out a little more. A light tap on the inside of her thigh told her to spread her legs wider, and with a groan, she did.

Monica wrapped her arms around Robin's body and lifted her breasts into her hands, as though offering them to April. While she was that close, the dark haired woman nuzzled the back of Robin's throat and then bit sharply. Robin gasped, and felt a new surge of wetness between her legs. Oh, this is nice, she thought, feeling the slight sting of pain when Monica's mouth moved away.

Her thoughts were interrupted when April suddenly cupped both her breasts in her own hands and squeezed harshly. Robin moaned deeply, and April let go of the captive breasts to begin to pinch the sore nipples and roll them slowly between her fingertips. Robin could feel the bite of long nails.

Gradually over the space of several long minutes, April began to increase the force of her compression, making Robin twitch and gasp with random strong pinches. But Robin hadn't been in this house for a year without a lot of playing on those poor portals to pleasure. As the pressure increased, and as April began to change from rolling to twisting, Robin groaned but also sighed, and couldn't help it as she pushed her ass even further back, to encounter Monica's body again.

"Sweet slut," Monica murmured, biting Robin's neck again. "You're so hot for us." She pushed Robin forward violently, and Robin's body smashed into April. "Bad girl," Monica said, raising her voice over April's laughter. "Should learn to keep your balance! Now, we're going to have to punish you!"

"I'm sorry, ma'am, please forgive me, ma'am," Robin wailed, struggling back onto her feet.

"Too late! On with the punishment!" And with a delighted laugh, as though she had just gotten a long awaited present, Monica began to smack Robin's ass cheeks, alternating sides. "Oh, you're going to get it, my little slave girl. All night long, you're going to get it."

"Hey, she ran into me, I should be spanking her!"

"Well, then get over here and let me play with her tits for a while."

They switched places, and April began a slow and heavy spanking, rubbing her hands all over Robin's cheeks and cupping and spreading them. But in front of her body, Monica began a soft and teasing exploration of Robin's breasts and nipples, being as deliberately gentle as April had been deliberately cruel.

It was its own exquisite cruelty. Monica trailed her fingers around Robin's breasts in soft spirals, first along the sensitive skin of her chest and underneath their swell, and then closer and closer to the aureoles and the sore nipples, and then she would make lazy circles away from them.

April got bored with spanking very quickly and began to use one of the short quirts she found in the chest. For this, Robin couldn't hold still. The two leather thongs on the end of the braided handle whistled and wrapped around her curves as April flicked them back and forth. But now, when Robin's body jerked away, she was bumping against Monica.

Monica reacted by bending down and taking one nipple between her teeth. The sharp pinching was expected and wonderful. But when April continued to lash away at Robin's buttocks and the backs of her legs, Robin couldn't hold herself still. She wriggled and writhed under the lash, only to find that Monica wouldn't move at all.

She was in effect making Robin put more pressure on her own nipple. And meanwhile, her fingers never ceased their wandering; tracing larger and larger circles, they began to drift over Robin's ribs and her sides.

As April's punishing strokes from behind pushed Robin's body forward, Monica met each thrusting movement with a light touch of fluttering fingers and the pinching sting of a bite.

Within minutes, Robin was whimpering steadily, dancing on the edges of pain and delight, her body maneuvered one way or another without her participation or awareness. All she knew was sensation, on one side and then another, a burning touch here and a lewd caress there, the feathery teasing below and the pulling from above. By the time one of Monica's fingers reached the top of her pubic mound, the only thing that Robin could do was thrust her hips forward again, even though this cost her the last of her stability and stretched her body out to the fullest.

"Jeeze, she's having all the fun," April complained as Monica laughed and danced away from Robin's hungry body.

"We can't have that," Monica agreed. "Time to get that mouth down?"

"Way down!"

218

And Robin next found herself lowered to her knees and presented with a wet and musky female delta; the two women stood above her and embraced each other while she blindly caressed the flesh before her. The warmth of their legs surrounding her body was like a secure prison made of bars she longed to throw herself around.

The form before her was soft and round, with a light covering of closely shorn hair. In seconds, Robin knew it had to be April. She remembered her from earlier; a curvaceous, substantial woman who looked as though she had been poured into a long gown with a wide sash around its waist. She had not arrived with Monica, but gravitated toward her during the evening. It had been clear that they were old friends.

Robin concentrated on pleasing. Her tongue darted out and flicked, explored and kissed. She kept it all gentle until one hand grabbed her hair and pulled her sharply in. Above her, she could hear more muffled giggles. She renewed her efforts, this time being bolder and more energetic. She washed the flat of her tongue over the exposed soft inner folds of April's labia, and sucked them into her mouth to lick the edges and work them back and forth. And when April bent her knees slightly and tilted her pubis a little bit more, Robin knew what to do, and nosed directly for the clit.

April's was large, and slightly extended. It was a delight to caress, a swollen knob that made its owner quiver when Robin sucked it into her mouth.

It was a new kind of torture when Robin felt herself pulled away, and hands pushed at her body until she turned around to find a new pussy suspended before her face.

"Get the idea, slave?" she heard from above her. "Keep going back and forth, whenever you're tapped. And keep your mind on what's down there!"

How could she not?

From one woman to the other, Robin was trapped in a circle of steamy musk. She began to cry; it was all too much, being surrounded, being drowned in women's flesh. Her body ached and tingled from her lengthy bondage and the punishing stripes of the quirt, but she kept moving, from one side to another, back and forth, until she realized that she had forgotten which woman was before her. It would always take a few seconds to figure it out, and each new bout of mystery thrilled her even more.

"I need to do this on my back," April finally announced in a throaty moan. It was Monica who pulled Robin from her position on the floor and jerked the comforting blindfold off. Robin blinked as the lights in the room blinded her even more than the heavy silk had, but she was given no time to adjust. April was on the bed, her legs spread and knees pulled up, and Monica simply pushed Robin into place, on her hands and knees, face firmly down into a well of cunt flesh.

Behind her, Monica began to spank again, this time in a quick rhythm. Robin moaned, and began to lick. April didn't have her waste one second where it wasn't needed. As the spanks grew in intensity and stinging pain, Robin's face was forcibly pushed and pulled over the spot that April chose, until the reclining woman began to shudder and rock, thrusting her hips up to meet Robin's searching mouth. She was more than ready; reaching down, she ground Robin's lips against her flesh and cried out, a long, inarticulate cry of pleasure.

When Robin was pulled away, she saw April's look of languid contentment for about three seconds before Monica pulled her off the bed. From the floor, Robin watched while Monica slowly and carefully disrobed, and when the woman sat down in the low wing chair that faced the bed, Robin crawled between her legs to minister to her as well.

It was exhausting, exhilarating. By the time the two women were finished with her, the sounds of the continuing party had all ended, and the rest of the house was shrouded in silence. April and Monica tangled themselves up in the bed, and before turning out the light, Monica had said, sleepily, "You can stay, kiddo."

Which was what Robin intended to do. But first, she crept about the room, picking things up and hanging up the two party dresses the women had worn. It was easy for her to do, now that she was so familiar with the layout and where things were stored. Then, she tip-toed out of the room to get another bottle of mineral water; the two guests had finished the one that was in the room already. Downstairs, she paused to look at the detritus of the party...it had been quite a rocking affair. But she had been invited to stay with a guest; until she was called for work, she had to fulfill the guest's wishes.

Not that it was any hardship.

Happy New Year, she thought to herself as she drifted off. She slept as comfortably and heavily as the two women in the bed above her. Maybe even more so.

Chapter Twenty

Another problem with living in paradise, Robin reflected, was that you didn't have the powerful seasonal changes. The heck with snow, she could learn to live without that. But the fact that the trees and shrubs were never bare made springtime all the more difficult to discern.

But it was only her second spring out West. Two autumns, two winters. Maybe as she spent more time here, she would begin to see the differences that must be there.

She was earnestly trying not to remember that, in the coming autumn, she would have to renegotiate her contract. That is, if Eric and Jimmy wanted to keep her. If not, she could always opt to get back on the block.

But we're not thinking about that, she sternly reminded herself. We are thinking about a pre-Columbian fetish doll and whether it's worth the trouble of acquiring it versus the negative publicity the auction is bound to receive. It was all the rage now for people to acquire such items and then give them back to the native tribe they belonged to. Activists in costume were beginning to attend the bigger galleries and houses, knowing that anyone who actually bought one of the contested items would have to face a press that would ask tough questions about property and value and religion.

It was only worth it for people who were able to somehow donate the items in question to some non-profit organization, like a church or a museum. Then, you could put it down as a juicy tax deduction and get the benefits of some positive press. Get your picture taken with someone in native dress. Talk about correcting centuries of abuse as though attempted genocide could be bribed away by returning stolen property.

Oh boy, you are in a mood today, she reflected. Maybe it's the wrong time to think about controversial acquisitions and follow up on some old business.

She had several investment pieces out on the market now, testing the waters before she brought out the more important items. Art and collectibles went in strict cycles. And now, she had expertise in more fields than she could have imagined in her years back in New York.

It would be so easy to get a great new job if she left slavery behind her. She could even set up her own office and...

Damn. Doing it again. Robin pulled one hand through her hair and took a couple of deep breaths. Got to concentrate!

"Rob?" Carl poked his head in the door. He had taken to calling her that from time to time, a little bit of a joke. "Downstairs."

Grateful for the interruption, she nodded and got up to follow him. He was still a great friend to have, although they had pretty much stopped screwing around on the side. The last time they fucked, it had been for Jimmy's amusement. Anal sex out on the deck, bright lights shining on their oiled bodies. Jimmy idly fucking Jeff's mouth for almost an hour and a half, alternating pulling away and then thrusting violently, easing back and then almost choking the slave.

It had been a hot night all around.

Downstairs, Jeff and Raul were already in attendance, Jeff on his knees with his hands clasped behind him and Raul standing. Carl and Robin joined Jeff on the floor, facing their two masters. Eric looked a little annoyed; Jimmy looked downright exasperated.

Eric got right to the point. "Eve Panski hasn't found the earrings. They must be here."

Well, they were all waiting for that news. Panski had been over to the house the previous weekend with her new husband. It had been a friendly visit, the masters hosting a small celebration of her marriage and welcoming Tom into the society of the Marketplace. It had been just fine until the day the guests were packing to leave, when Eve reported that a pair of emerald earrings, her engagement gift from Tom, were not where she had left them the night before.

A search was launched immediately. Nothing was found. And although Eve was very careful not to even mention the possibility of their being stolen, it was on everyone's mind. What made the situation even worse was that no other guests had spent the night. If the earrings had been removed by someone, it had to be the owners, or the slaves. Both possibilities were beyond belief.

But Tom, who didn't know exactly what kind of an accusation he was making (other than one of simple theft), asked out loud if it were possible to search the slaves' belongings and room.

Eric had colored instantly, but before he could deliver some kind of retort,

Jimmy ordered Raul to empty the room the slaves shared, removing the four small boxes of personal affects, and the bedding. Shushing Eric by asking him to take the slaves outside and see "if he could find out anything new," Jimmy then ushered Tom upstairs to conduct the search personally. Naturally, the search turned up nothing more interesting than Carl's college ring and Robin's old collar. There was certainly nothing which hadn't been seen, handled and approved of by the masters.

The next day, Raul has whispered to Robin, "As if one of us could be a common thief! As if he learned absolutely nothing about us!"

"The man just lost several thousand dollars worth of present to his new wife," Robin had answered. "They were nice pieces, heirloom stuff. If they were mine, and they were missing, I'd be suspicious of everything that moved."

In the end, Eve had tried to rescue the situation by suggesting that maybe she had been mistaken and the earrings had somehow gotten into her luggage. She would search when she got home, but now they had to catch their plane. She apologized and everyone sighed at her attempt to save face.

But now, this. Apparently saving face was not so acceptable any more.

"I've promised her that we will make another search," Eric continued. "But this time, Jimmy and I will supervise. I have to ask you all again; did any of you leave your room the night that the earrings went missing?"

Carl at least had an alibi. He had been chained at the foot of his masters' bed all night.

Three "No, masters" chorused back.

Eric pressed his lips together. "OK. Carl, you can get back to work. Robin and Jeff, you stay with me. We're starting down here. Raul, you go upstairs with Jimmy. We're not going to stop until every square on inch of this place is uncovered, if it takes all week!"

It didn't take more than four hours. But it was four hours of removing seat cushions, patting down pillows, emptying and refilling closets, checking the pockets of all clothing, and going through boxes and bags in storage. It was four hours of removing every book on every shelf, and shaking every decorative pot or vase, and even digging into a potted plant or two.

Resentment seemed to grow in Eric, who was so above the kind of petty labor going on. He was also fuming over the fact that his house had fallen under suspicion, and he let his displeasure show with curses and an occasional smack or kick when nothing turned up.

In the early afternoon, Jimmy came down the stairs, and called to his lover. "Eric, could you bring the slaves up here, please?"

Robin followed obediently, not even curious about what Jimmy wanted. The whole search seemed silly to her, a waste of time. No slave would jeopardize their position in the Marketplace with what amounted to petty theft.

Her stomach tightened as she saw that Jimmy was leading them all to the small room that was her work space. Raul was standing by the door, his head down and his hands folded behind his back.

Jimmy stepped through the door, and beckoned Eric to follow him. Robin crept up slowly, and stood just outside the door. When she heard Eric call her in, she didn't know what she was going to see, but knew that it wasn't going to be good.

Her desk had been cleared off, her calendar and pens and phone directory all on the floor next to the wall. In the middle of the desk, a small pool of water was still quivering. Two red flowers she had picked the day before were scattered at the edge of the puddle, their petals in crushed disarray.

In the middle of the puddle were two metallic things that glittered. Large metallic things with emeralds in them. The ceramic bud vase that usually sat on the shelf above her computer screen was standing on the desk corner.

Robin gazed down at the desk and then quickly back up into the faces of her owners. Jimmy was unreadable; Eric was livid. She opened her mouth to say something, anything, but Eric moved as fast as she'd ever seen and backhanded her across the face. It caught her off guard, and the force threw her to one side, hitting the door frame, which she clung to, fighting to remain standing.

"You ungrateful little cunt," the handsome man snarled, drawing his hand back again. "I'm going to kill you!"

"Master, please, I – ahh!"

Eric caught her with another slap, this one aimed too high to catch her cheek. It hit her on the side of the head and her head seemed to rebound off the wall. The double impact sent her spinning down, and she could feel a warm trickle coming from her mouth and leaking onto her cheek.

The other slaves backed away from her as Eric moved in to kick her viciously in the thigh. She cried out again and shrank down, pulling herself into a ball, even though her training had told her to never do that.

Jimmy had to finally pull Eric away. But it was only the beginning.

And Robin was never given a chance to say a single word.

She couldn't really feel her fingers any more. Which was perhaps a blessing. Everything else she felt was pain. Pure pain, divorced from any aspect of pleasure, and from any sense of security.

The cracking sound of another rod breaking was a momentary respite from the steady cutting and burning of the beating. It might take all of ten seconds to choose the next one, flex it and begin again. But there was no part of her body that didn't already pound and throb with intense agony. Even the soles of her feet had been cut, held aloft for terrifying and excruciating minutes of strain on her arms and wrists.

Eric had not forgotten the line that Chris really had put in his report: that canes and cane-like punishment tools were most effective on Robin because she feared them.

Jimmy and Eric had no canes laying around. But there was a collection of newly purchased garden stakes, still in their wire wrapping.

Eric had sent Jeff to go get them. Then, when Robin was gagged and bound in the corner downstairs, he tossed a bunch of them onto the floor beneath her and pushed one into Carl's hands.

"Use it on her until it breaks," he said. "Not just her ass. Everywhere."

And the torment began. The acute bite of the rods was bad enough on her buttocks and thighs. It was hellish on her breasts and sides. It stung and burned and cut more times then she could count, and when Carl had broken the first rod, Raul was sent over to begin with the second. Carl's face showed a struggle going on; Raul was as placid and efficient as he always was. Both were as merciless as Eric directed them to be.

Heat spread throughout her body, and after some immeasurable time, she could barely tell how often new stripes were added. She could see down the front of her body a mass of crisscrossed red lines, some of them with white edges, others with darker red middles. Every one throbbed and ached, until that was all she could feel.

She wished that she had the power to make herself pass out. In a moment of lucidity, she remembered the Victorian porn she had once collected, and the frequency of fainting spells when punishments got too harsh.

And then a rod would fall again and she would scream into the gag until finally even that stopped. Sweat poured down her face and body and slipped over welts and through cuts, and when she slumped into the bonds because her legs were just not capable of keeping her up any more, they let her hang.

This is not safe, another thought came, ludicrously. By the time they unfastened the cuffs, there was no place on her body that she could rest on comfortably. She was amazed to find the floor a little wet and sticky beneath her, and that the pounding in her bones and muscles was not nearly as bad as the million needles that seemed to be stinging the flesh of her hands.

And still, the worst had not happened.

Because then, after the gag was pulled out of her mouth in a torrent of pinkish spit, Eric looked at her from across the room and said to Raul, "Place a call to New York. Get me Parker."

Robin had thought that there were no tears left in her. But at the sound of that command, and as Raul rose to go to the phone, unaware that she was moving her lips in a silent plea to stop him, to beg for a chance to explain, to beg for mercy, she broke and sobbed furiously.

Now she was finished, destroyed. And over something that she didn't do.

That was when she finally passed out.

Chapter Twenty-One

She was trapped in a little steel box, with burning walls tight against her flesh on all sides. The air was musty and smelled of bitterness, like chemicals spilling over copper. She couldn't see, it was too dark, and no one could get to her, could let her out before the sun burnt through the steel and melted it all against her body, running in rivulets, scorching her, going through her, until she screamed and screamed and ran out of air and couldn't breathe...

Flames touched her and she jerked awake. Instantly, the pain of her dream coalesced into the reality of her condition. She moaned, and something searing touched her again. This time, she realized that it wasn't fire at all, but something cold.

She was laying on her side, and as she drew in one harsh breath, she practically inhaled a mouth full of dust. It didn't make her dry mouth and throat any better. As she began to cough it out, she opened her eyes. Her right eye. Her left eye, still pressed against the surface she was laying on, was swollen. It only opened a slit, and that scared her as much as anything else.

"Hold still, there's a lot to clean," Carl said. She raised her head a little and looked at him. He was crouched down, next to her. She was on a wood plank floor...not in the house. Next to her head she could see the blue trim of a bowl, and the edges of a tray. There were washcloths stacked on the tray, and a brown bottle.

Carl touched her again and she hissed. "It's only ice," he said. "It'll take the swelling down."

"C–Carl." She managed to form the sounds, and heard them inside her head, as though she had a cold. "I didn't...I didn't..."

Carl thrust a hand into the bowl and brought out a small piece of melting ice, which he held to her lips. "Here," he said gruffly. "Suck on this. Don't try to talk."

It felt cool and good for a few seconds, and then it suddenly made her feel chilly. She held onto the slippery sliver though, and tried to look around again.

Behind Carl was something silver and red, with a long black cord. It was the power mower.

She was on the floor of the damn tool shed, next to the garage.

They wouldn't even let me sleep in the house. Just dumped me in an outdoor shed, to lie in the dust and the oil and the dirt. She started to cry again, and found that even that hurt. From the crown of her head to the soles of her feet, she was nothing but a mass of pain. And the only thing that was being done for her was ice for the welts and a bottle of peroxide, administered by another slave.

I want to go home, she thought, clenching her hands into fists. I don't care any more, I just want to go home, where I can have my own bed and sleep with whom I want to and never have to take this from someone who could just do it without any reason! She sobbed heavily, and each movement of her body seemed to awaken another aching inch. Finally, Carl had to go. She made no other attempt to talk to him, and he said nothing else to her.

Somehow, her exhaustion and despair overcame her aches and she slept again. It was a struggle, a twitching of consciousness that kept her wavering from a near dream state to painful wakefulness and then back again.

"You have to understand, Robin, that this is an experience that will make a mockery of everything you have ever believed in," Chris was saying to her. Another lecture, this one after a grueling drill session in behavior and situational problem solving. "Liberty, justice, equality…these are all denied a slave. You will lose every right that you have been taught to believe belongs to you from birth, especially the right to pursue happiness. Your owners can do what they like to you for any reason, and your only alternative is to end the relationship, to quit and go on home. And the price for doing that is losing everything."

"I understand," she replied.

"No you don't," Chris said. He looked somber, and for one moment, a touch of sadness landed in his eyes. "But you will."

I do, I do, Robin cried out, grabbing for his knee. I understand now, make it all go back, make it right, I understand now! But he dwindled, and then vanished, and his voice kept going, a Cheshire cat of a man, she thought. I am crazy at last, hearing people who are not here. Hearing things I heard a year and a half ago.

228

"...been here since?"

"Yes, sir."

"There is a brown leather bag in my car. Fetch it, and bring me a wet towel and a comb."

Damn, but it sounded like Chris.

Chris!

Robin struggled awake again, and groaned. Being in that half conscious state was far preferable to being fully aware. Now, in addition to the pain of her beating, she was stiff from laying on the hard floor for so long. She also felt dirty and was aware of her own smell. She opened her eyes, this time both of them, and saw a black engineer boot by her face. Tentatively, she reached for it, and felt the smooth leather under her fingers.

"Hello, Robin."

Even as relief poured through her, shame followed, and Robin brought her hand up to her mouth and bit her own finger, feeling still more hot tears squeezing their way from her eyes. Chris Parker bent down next to her and put one hand on her shoulder, but suddenly she didn't want him there. Didn't want him to see her like this, to witness her humiliation in this fashion. But he was real, and didn't vanish as conveniently as his phantom had. Instead, he put one hand under her other shoulder and began to lift. She made a sound of protest, but went with him, until she was sitting up, her back against a huge bag of birdseed. She tried to keep her eyes down, but couldn't help glancing up into his face.

He looked different. He had allowed his beard to grow in at last, and although she liked smooth cheeks, it did suit him. He was wearing a white business shirt with the sleeves folded carefully up to his biceps, and she could swear that the flames that had been licking at her body were all over his arms as well. She blinked, and dust and tears made her vision a foggy haze. She tried to look up into his eyes, but they were hidden by sunglasses.

Raul appeared at the shed door with the items Chris had sent him for, and Chris briskly took them and made a dismissive gesture. "Tell your masters that I will be in contact."

"Yes, sir."

Chris looked toward Robin again and sighed. "All right, girl, let's get you out of here."

She kept silent as he wiped her down with the towel. In the brown bag was a pair of her jeans and a t-shirt, and a long sleeved blouse, plus her old sneakers. Chris also had a bottle of water and a few aspirins, which she took eagerly. The water tasted sweet and wonderful, and for a moment, almost seemed to banish the steady throbbing pains that still wracked her body.

Getting dressed was a slow and irritating maneuver. She'd barely worn long pants since she had been sold. The sneakers felt strange, absurdly soft around her feet. But when Chris pulled her up, she was grateful for the softness.

He helped her out of the shed, taking her arm like any gentleman walking an injured lady. There was a gleaming Lincoln parked at the top of the drive, and he led her to the back seat and pushed her gently down, to lay on her side. She didn't know how long it was until he returned to hop into the driver's seat and take off, and she didn't know where he was taking her. But the hum of the engine and the velvety softness of the seat beneath her cheek lulled her back to sleep.

Perhaps, she thought, as she drifted off, this is all still a dream.

"I didn't do it, sir," Robin finally said. It was such a relief to get that line out at last! She winced as the doctor coated another cut, but really didn't mind the sensation. Hell, after the actual beating and laying on a floor for a day and then some, these minor stings and prickles were almost pleasurable.

"That's a problem," Chris answered. He was sitting in a hard backed chair, taken from the desk in the outer room of the suite. Robin was laying on her stomach on the bed, towels underneath her, while the gentle doctor who had already given her a shot and treated her black eye, was busy checking to make sure that her cuts were clean and healing normally. He had actually chuckled when he'd seen her.

"This is nothing," he had said, waving a hand over her body. "Just a few nicks and scratches!"

"Good," Chris had replied. "Then it shouldn't take too much of your time." About the only thing the doctor actually grumbled about was finding several splinters. After removing them, he had cursed owners who didn't maintain proper equipment.

"Damn idiots. Didn't their fathers ever tell 'em, 'right tool for the right job'? What did they use, dowels? Tsk, tsk. And there's such a good quality of rattan coming in these days, too. Not to mention all these plastics they're always coming up with. And they're so easy to keep clean!"

But after that, he fell silent and bent to the task, tsking once in a while. He was almost finished when Chris came in to sit down and look Robin in the eye. Now, he sighed and tapped one finger against his leg.

"Who did it then?" he asked.

"I don't know!"

"Keep calm. Remember who you're talking to here." Robin nodded and cast her eyes down. "Now think. Who had access to the earrings? And why would they hide them in your office?"

Robin thought for a moment. "Almost anyone could have been in that room," she finally said. "Probably, we all were at one time or another that weekend. But they had to disappear between midnight on Saturday and eight on Sunday morning, because Eve said that she'd seen them the night before."

"Meaning?"

"That someone snuck into the guest room while they were asleep. It's not that hard. The door wouldn't have been locked, and we all know our way around those rooms in the dark."

"I would suppose so." Chris leaned back and looked over her shoulder. "Finished?"

"All done. I'm leaving some antibiotics, but the infection is very light, I wouldn't worry. Nicks and scratches, that's all. Ice to relieve the swelling on that shiner, and try not to do any hiking until the cuts on the feet heal. Take aspirin or something over the counter for the pain, unless she's supposed to feel it. Otherwise, she's ready to go back to work." He took his gloves off with two snaps. "I send my bill...?"

"To them. Thank you for coming." Chris saw the doctor out, leaving Robin to stew for a few minutes. When he came back, he took the same seat and looked at her expectantly.

"I don't know what to say," she said softly.

"Well, you'd better think of something. I think you realize what's at stake."

"But it's not fair! I didn't do it! The evidence is circumstantial! How can they just punish someone like this over circumstantial evidence?" Robin bit her lip and guiltily added, "Sir."

"I don't recall ever suggesting that fairness came into the owner/slave equation. Your owners could have done this to you any time they wanted to. Every Saturday night if it amused them sufficiently." Chris folded his hands, and Robin thought, that's another strange thing about him. He's not smoking. He really did quit.

He continued. "Of course, the real issue here is not your physical punishment, but the fact that Eric wants your contract declared violated and you tossed out of the Marketplace. Now unless you have some suggestion for me concerning how to convince him that you are not a thief, or to prove to him who was the real thief, you are about to be in some very serious trouble." He paused and rubbed his forehead. "Let's start with the most obvious question. Is there anyone in the house who would benefit from your removal?"

Robin blinked. "Do you mean that the earrings might have been deliberately planted to get rid of me?"

"That would appear to be the case. Don't you agree?"

She lowered her eyes and thought, ignoring the itchy feeling along her "nicks and scratches." It did make sense, but no one in the house would benefit directly from her absence. Jimmy wasn't perplexed by her presence any more, he even enjoyed having his own personal gift shopper available. Raul was the chief of slaves, he had no beef with her. And although she had stopped sleeping with Carl, it was by mutual arrangement, and besides, Carl was already Jimmy's favorite, so he had nothing further to gain. And Jeff was nothing, what could he possibly have…

She looked up and her mouth dropped open in shock and anger.

"It's that little punk, isn't it?" Chris asked casually. "The houseboy."

"Yes," Robin whispered. "It would have to be. But…why?" She thought about it some more. Jeff alone had not gotten comfortable with Robin, not even in the length of time she had been there. Jeff had renewed his own contract just a month ago, and there had been a state of some tension, as though he had been expecting to somehow move up in rank. But he remained what he had always been — the fuck-hole, the toy who couldn't be trusted with important tasks, the pet and the lowest-ranking slave.

And even though Robin never personally used or abused him for her own purposes, she had never objected to the times when Carl encouraged her to make use of Jeff's body or mouth.

But those times had been rare, and had mostly ended. The most she ever saw of Jeff was when he was emptying her trash basket or sucking someone off in the corner.

But if she were gone, he wouldn't rise in ranking, he'd still be the lowest boy there. It made no real sense. Slowly, she explained the situation at the house to Chris. He nodded from time to time, and gently encouraged her to tell him everything. And when she was finished, she added, "But I can't see any way to prove anything. I mean, if my case is based on circumstantial evidence, then my case against him is based on pure fantasy. There really is no clear motive for him to do it."

"Life," Chris said as he got up, "rarely meets expectations. Criminals don't always have sensible motivations. But nevertheless, your observations have given me some food for thought. Stay here." He stretched and glanced at his watch. "I will be out for some hours. Take your medication, and, if you get hungry, order some food and charge it to the room. If it will help you fall asleep, you may watch television."

"Thank you, sir." She watched him leave, and then stared out the window. In time, she actually did get hungry, and had some soup and a sandwich while she caught up on the world by watching CNN and a little MTV. She didn't recognize half the bands. Then, she took more aspirins, slipped between the soft white sheets and pulled pillows around her for comfort and slept, feeling like a princess.

232

She was surprised when she woke up and saw the digital clock by the bed reading ten thirty. She hadn't slept this late in ages! She pushed herself up, and felt the twinges of the few really bad cuts, but sighed as she realized that she felt one hundred percent better than she had yesterday morning. In fact, her whole recovery seemed somewhat vague and shadowy already, something she felt grateful about. She got out of bed and showered, and was surprised to see that the only razor in the bathroom was an old-fashioned straight edge. Had she never seen Chris shave? Why, no, she hadn't. He'd always gone into the bathroom in the master bedroom, and she was never allowed to follow him in there.

Hm. Well, it suited him. It was also useless to her. She knew better than to experiment with it, and she could live without a shave for one more day. There was just a light dotting of short hairs where she normally shaved on her cunt. Her legs she kept clear with wax. But after one experiment with getting a bikini waxing, she decided it was worth the extra effort with a razor.

Besides, she wasn't sure if it was going to matter. In the mirror, her face looked horrible. On TV, people who got into fights were often shown with only a little bruising and maybe a piece of white tape on their face the next day. By the third, they were all healed. But her bruises looked frightening, dark colored and misshapen. And the cuts from the stakes looked terrible too, with little black marks where every line crossed another and some more where the tips hit. It was hard to look at them. Each one seemed to throb from an individual memory of pain.

She was used to being somewhat clothed, and the air conditioning in the room was chilly, so she did help herself to one of the elegant white robes that were hanging up. Then, she walked out to look for Chris. He wasn't there.

How odd.

But there was a newspaper on the coffee table, and the breakfast menu was propped up on top of it, so she took the hint, and enjoyed the pleasure of being served for a change.

Chris didn't return until slightly after one o'clock. He walked in, startling Robin, who was engrossed in the crossword puzzle. She stood at once.

"You have an important decision to make," he said in his customary no-preamble method. "Do you want to be removed from the house, or serve out the rest of your contract?"

Robin gasped. "I have a choice?"

"Jeff has… confessed." Chris looked positively pleased with himself, and Robin couldn't help but grin. "Your owners have naturally withdrawn their desire to have you shunned. But neither are they interested in dealing with a bitter slave. Therefore, they have offered me the chance to redeem you now, freeing you from the contract as though it had been completed. Their report of you will show great satisfaction with your work and your progress, and will not hurt any potential sale."

While he spoke, Robin wondered at the sudden change in her life's circumstances. Jeff confessed! But somehow, it had taken all night to get to that point; how was it done? I wish I'd been there, she thought. I would have loved to see him break down.

"Or, if you wish, you may return to service, today, and nothing more will be said about the matter," Chris finished.

"Nothing more," Robin echoed.

"You cannot be expecting an apology," Chris said. He walked into the room and sat down on the couch, indicating that she sit down as well. "I told you that justice is not something to expect here."

"Or fairness," Robin added. "But what about courtesy?"

"It is a courtesy that they would consider allowing you the choice of leaving or returning." He leaned back and flexed his right hand thoughtfully. "If getting an apology from your master is so important to you, perhaps you could do with some time off to reconsider your commitment."

Robin stared at him in silence for a moment.

I'm so sorry about the cruel things I said to you, Maria had written.

It was all my fault, I should have never done that to you! Troy had pleaded.

Owners may do as they like to you, and need not seek your consent, approval, pleasure, or even your reaction. And they will not owe you explanations or words of encouragement or comfort or praise. You will just be a person who belongs to them, and nothing more, Chris taught.

And she had been so turned on…she had been so thrilled by the possibilities, the potential.

I was so ignorant, she marveled.

She lowered her head and then took a deep breath. Then, lifting her chin, she said, "Please allow me to finish out my contract, sir."

"Because?"

"Because it's the honorable thing to do."

Chris Parker smiled. "Good girl! Now take that robe off before I take my belt to you; I don't recall mentioning that you could wear it. We'll have lunch before I return you, and you can catch me up on your education and experiences."

"Yes, sir," Robin said instantly, shedding the robe. "And I'm so sorry, sir, that you had to come all the way out here."

"That's part of my job, missy. You may have twenty owners, but I'm your trainer. And always remember…if there's ever a reason why I can't take care of your interests, you can be damn sure that I'll leave you in good hands." He patted his leg and gestured, and she got back into her old position at his feet.

"So tell me what it's like in California. How the hell do you know when the seasons change?"

I love you, Robin thought, pressing her cheek to his leg. She thought about asking him about that "leave you in other hands" bit, but a sudden wave of something new swept through her. If he wanted to tell me more, he would...and I'm comfortable knowing that he'll take care of things. She smiled, and then remembered that he'd asked a question. "I haven't quite figured that out," she said out loud. "I think it has something to do with the arrival of the Neiman Marcus catalog."

She felt the itching and minor aching of her wounds begin to trickle down to a manageable level. By the time Chris drove her back up into the hills, she felt sure she was doing the right thing.

Chapter Twenty-Two

Steve, the new houseboy, was nothing like Jeff. For one, he was big; broader across the chest than Carl, and just as tall, with legs that looked like they were carved from oak and arms that bulged to obscene proportions when he exerted his strength. Also, where Jeff was weasely, wiry, supple, narrow and sexy in a streetwise kind of way, Steve was the true definition of hunk. He was a walking mass of muscles.

"Steve *Reeves* is who he's like," Raul had joked to Robin and Carl before the new addition arrived. "Master Eric has always wanted a body builder."

Robin remembered Ken's descriptions of men that her brother liked to abuse. "But if he's so buff, why is he suited for that kind of scut work? I thought that muscle types cost a lot, and were mostly show pieces." She grinned at her own lapse. Had she actually used "buff," as a descriptive word?

"Yes, if that's what they're sold for. But this one has a nice history of looking for places as master's dog. He'll be just fine in our boy position."

And he was. He arrived with a look of wonder on his comically innocent face and his own set of free weights. And within two days, everyone had used him at least once or twice and agreed that he was going to be an asset. They nicknamed him "Muscledog," because he loved to play puppy roles. And to their amusement and satisfaction, it also appeared that he had a passion for men's feet. Eric was extraordinarily pleased with himself.

One night, Robin sat inside the house helping Carl do some paperwork sorting for archive files. Out on the patio, the masters were playing some kind of fetching game with their Muscledog, involving sticks and condoms and God knows what else. Raul was busy in the kitchen, preparing a menu for an upcoming dinner party.

Carl leaned over and said softly, "You've got a great trainer."

"I know." Robin picked up a new pile of folders and began to pull out the necessary papers. "So?"

236

"So, I thought you'd like to know what happened. Back then."

Robin grinned. "Hell, yes, and why did it take so long?"

"I wanted to make sure it was OK with Raul before I told you."

Well, that made sense. "OK, I'm listening."

After failing to find Parker in one call, Eric had ordered the boys to put Robin in the shed, and they had done so. By the time Carl got back, Eric was dialing the phone himself and tracking the man down. He didn't connect until later that night.

"And did you know where Parker was?"

"No, he didn't tell me anything about it."

"With Anderson. Trainer Anderson. Probably getting some tips or something, or maybe at some kind of trainers' meeting." Carl shook his head, smiling. "Imagine being with the Trainer of Trainers and being tracked down by an owner who has a complaint about one of your trainees. It must have been like shit hitting the fan."

"Oh!" Robin dropped the papers in horror. "He didn't even say a word!"

"Well, I didn't hear all of their conversation. But the next day, he's here. He didn't say much, got the story from Jimmy, and took you out."

"He didn't even talk to Eric?"

"Hon, he barely said three words to anyone."

No one heard anything until the following day, when Parker came back, alone. He walked into the house as casually as any friend or guest and told Raul to make him some strong coffee. And then, when the two masters came to talk with him, they went into the library for privacy.

When Parker came out, he called Jeff to his side and told him to get his sorry ass upstairs.

"Just like that?"

"The bosses didn't even come out of the room!" Carl looked around and grinned and lowered his voice. "They came out after Parker went to the kitchen, had Raul put some coffee in a carafe, and took that and a cup upstairs."

"What room?"

"The same one that Eve and Tom stayed in, naturally."

"And then what?"

Well, then it got hard to piece together. Carl found several excuses to pass by that room, and on two occasions heard sounds that could be interpreted as hitting or slapping noises. But mostly, it was quiet.

Before dinner time, Jimmy went upstairs too. He was soon followed by Eric.

Dinner was postponed for two hours.

Then, Eric came out of the room, calm as you please, and told Raul to get the table ready and set a place for Mr. Parker. Mr. Parker came downstairs with a band-aid over one of his knuckles and was a courteous and gracious guest, complimenting the meal and the wine selection.

"Fuck the wine, tell me what happened!"

"Temper, temper."

After dinner, the three men went back upstairs. When they came down again, it was past midnight. Eric had gone to the phone himself and placed a call to Mr. Lu, who was Jeff's previous owner, and the man who trained him. And Jimmy, dragging a Jeff who looked like he had had the shit beaten out of him, to the same place where Robin had suffered her punishment, and went out to the tool shed for some more stakes.

"They did the same thing to him?" Robin asked, her eyes wide.

"Well, not *exactly*. He was already kind of knocked around. But the worst part came later."

Mr. Lu decided that it was not worth redeeming his former slave. And as Jeff had no other trainer to act as his advocate or take him back for further training, it was decided to just cast him out. Jimmy and Eric co-signed a formal letter saying that he was proven a thief, a liar and a betrayer, and faxed it to the regional offices of the Marketplace. By morning, it would be going out to every training house, every auction business, every private trainer, agent, spotter, seller and owner.

Jeff was the one who was finished now. The next morning, he had begged and pleaded for another chance, offered unlimited clauses in any contract, offered to give himself to any other owner or trainer without promise of future fee. When that didn't work, he tried threats, the usual blustering about exposure, calling the police, calling newspapers or TV muckrakers.

But the bosses tossed him out on his ear, wearing biker shorts, sandals and a t-shirt. He had one thousand dollars of pity money in his pocket and a good hike to the nearest bus station.

"That's terrible," Robin mused. The image was frightening. "That could have been me!"

"No, because you've got a real trainer behind you. Little Jeff was fucked from the beginning. He just jumped into the Marketplace blindly, with no real experience except for one lover and no real love for the work, just a fetish. Turns out he had no training, just a relationship with a Marketplace owner who never put him through what you, me, or Raul got. His contract sucked — not even a guarantee of transportation and temporary housing if the owners sent him away. There's a lesson in this."

"But how is *anyone* supposed to learn it?" Robin asked. "I could have been taken in the same way. Ken could have sold me directly if she wanted to, said that I was her slave."

"But the key is that she didn't." Carl looked over toward Raul, in the kitchen, studiously not listening to them. "You got real lucky, babe. And things worked out fine. Right?"

Robin nodded, thanked him for the story, and went back to work. She didn't tell him that things weren't *exactly* fine.

Of course it was easy sitting across from Chris and talking about honor. She knew that it would get a favorable response from him, and that it was the "right" answer.

But in real life, it was so hard to leave the comfort of his rented car and walk back to the house. Resentment threatened to rise with every step, and it took all of her emotional strength to hold it down.

As Chris had said, there were no apologies, real or hidden. She just returned to her office, stripped out of the clothing that Chris had brought her and dressed in shorts and a tank top and went back to work. The only change was that she didn't run with Raul for another two weeks. But when the cuts on her feet closed and healed and she could stretch out without feeling the tearing of scabs, she began to join him and life went on.

Except that Eric sort of stopped making use of her. Oh, on nights when he and Jimmy put on one of their production number orgies, she was always included somewhere, but he never called upon her for his own use or to perform with one of the other slaves for his titillation.

Robin liked to think that it was guilt, and then wished that there was a way to rid herself of such thoughts. They tainted her awareness of her obedience and dedication. *If I can feel resentment, or happiness because I think my master feels bad, I'm not a good slave,* she would remind herself. *And I so want to be a good slave.*

"What's on your mind, sugar?" Monica asked, laying back in the lounge chair. It was the week after a major series of political meetings in Washington, and she had come out by herself for some quiet time. Eric was out on another shoot, this one in Greece, and Raul was with him — something new. Carl was running the house, and Robin was Monica's personal servant, which suited them both just fine. Muscledog was busy doing the garden work, wearing nothing but a jockstrap and a broad weightlifter's belt.

"Pleasing you, ma'am," was Robin's automatic answer. She smiled. Some of their conversations started out like this and ended up encompassing hours of late night murmurs and secrets shared. But it was a sunny day and the water was sparkling, and it just didn't seem the time to talk about the stories that filled the night.

"That's nice. What would please me would be your telling me exactly what you were thinking of when you stared across the pool for so long."

Robin smiled. "I was thinking of the coming autumn, ma'am."

"Hm. I bet it's real nice out here in LaLaLand. It's fun back on the right coast, too. Congress comes back, the Court comes back, the lobbyists come back, and everyone with money comes back. Lemmings, crawling back up the cliff, forgetting why they were so quick to get away." Robin laughed appreciably.

"You been in the Market long?" Monica's question was startling. People rarely, if ever, asked questions like that of owned slaves. If you wanted to know, you asked the owner. But Robin was getting used to Monica getting what she wanted in unconventional ways.

"For almost two years, ma'am. This autumn."

"Ah. So now we are at the root of the matter. Anniversary time. Contract time?"

"One of my masters would have to be consulted about that, ma'am." That was the general, all purpose answer which meant, "Hell, I can't tell you that!"

"Ah-hah. Another one right on the nose." Monica smiled and trailed a finger through the droplets of moisture on the outside of her iced tea glass. "Going to sign on for another hitch?"

"Ma'am, I'm sorry," Robin lowered her eyes. "I can't answer that question."

"Hm. OK. Who trained you? I know Eric said you were a virgin on the block."

"Chris Parker."

"No kidding? I haven't seen that character in years. Quite a trainer, I hear." Monica eased her legs out and wiggled her toes as Robin nodded in agreement. "Quite a little butterball, too, if I remember. Cute, kind of."

"Maybe you're thinking of someone else, ma'am?" Robin frowned. "The Chris Parker who trained me wasn't tall, but he wasn't, um…he was actually quite built up."

"Really?" Monica pushed her sunglasses back and fixed her dark eyes on Robin. "Well, I guess he could have dropped some excess weight, or built it up in a few years. But just to make sure we are talking about the same fellow…short, light voice, a little scratchy, black hair, kind of thick, glasses? White, with an upper class affectation in vocabulary? Hangs around with Elliot and Selador?"

"That would be him," Robin admitted. "He has a mustache and a beard now, but Ken Mandarin said that the mustache was new…two years ago."

240

"Well, I guess so." Monica grinned. "So? How was training for you? Discover any deep dark secrets about him? He's quite a topic of gossip, you know. Very up-and-coming as far as trainers go. Want to share some insights with me?"

"Ma'am, I really don't...I mean, I don't think that would be appropriate, and I'm very sorry—"

"OK, OK, I'll stop pushing." The older woman patted Robin on the head and sighed. "Ethics. Sometimes it seems like all the ethics have left politics and entered slavery. Did you ever consider the philosophical and sociological ramifications of that? That slaves might someday be the most honorable class in a society and leaders the least?" Robin giggled, grateful for Monica's quick capitulation on the gossipy questions. "Why don't you go inside and get me something really cold, like ice cream or something? I'm feeling a wave of sweet tooth coming on."

"Yes, ma'am!"

But when Robin came back, very little of the ice cream ended up in Monica's mouth. Most of it ended up melting all over Robin's body, and then Muscledog's, and Monica watched and laughed and encouraged as they licked the sticky stuff off of each other. She drizzled trails of strawberry across Muscledog's broad chest, and down to his shaven crotch, and dropped a heavy dollop of the stuff over his cock and balls. And when Robin finished smearing it all over her face while trying to lick it up, she ended up on her back for the same treatment while Muscledog licked his way across her body.

It was cold and it tickled, and it turned sticky in the sun, but the feeling of being eagerly licked all over while she stretched out and pushed her hips out was just delightful. And even though she gasped and giggled when a scoop landed right on her crotch, she quickly began to sigh as Muscledog's talented tongue worked its way through the creamy mass to find a different kind of cream below.

And when Monica ordered Muscledog to bring Robin off that way and he good naturedly applied himself to the task, Robin found herself staring up into Monica's face when she came, her eyes open even as her face was screwing up in the waves of pleasure that ran through her body.

It was a moment of near perfection. Later, while she showered and cleaned off the residue of the scene she sighed and fingered herself under the stinging showerhead.

It would be so nice to belong to a woman. But she had no control over that. If she wanted to stay with Chris, he would not allow such a restriction in her contract. She could hear him saying, "You're looking for an owner, not a lover!"

No, despite the drawbacks, she had something real good right here. She

241

had owners who didn't really abuse their slaves, fellow slaves that she got along with, and an interesting and varied life.

And according to what she'd heard and seen, she lived comfortably, having plenty of time to rest, a bed to sleep in, and a generally undemanding household rhythm. It could be much, much worse.

This *is* as good as it gets, she realized, suddenly losing all interest in jerking off. This is what I've wanted my whole life, to be a real slave, property of a master who could use me as stakes for a poker game if he wanted to. Living a life under someone's complete authority. Giving myself utterly to them.

This really is the best I can hope for, she thought, stepping out and beginning to mechanically dry herself off. How can I even think of taking such a chance with my life, and messing this up? I could end up anywhere. I'll just have to figure out a way to deal with these wrong feelings and get ready to sign up again in the fall. Chris will approve.

That night, in Monica's bed, she worked even harder to please the woman, and was rewarded with an invitation to spend the night in the room again. Yes, Robin thought as she relaxed and got into a comfortable position. This is certainly where I should be.

Chapter Twenty-Three

Chris did the contract negotiation with Eric after Robin called him and told him that she would be pleased to stay if her masters wanted to keep her on. But when Chris asked her if he should add more time to the contract, Robin paused and couldn't get the word "yes" to come out of her mouth. Chris went on to the next question without missing a beat, and when she saw her new contract on the first day after the old contract expired, she saw that it was for another two years. She also noticed that there was an additional clause that identified ANDERSON as a person to be notified for any disputes or renegotiations if PARKER was unavailable.

Well, he said he'd leave her in good hands. She saw Eric and Jimmy glance at each other when they came across that name, but they signed all the same.

Maybe, she thought, they were thinking that they could send me for more training. The idea appealed to her. What would it be like to train under someone who Chris obviously respected so much? I wonder what she is like. I wonder if they are training people together. Wouldn't that be great? But the topic was not raised with her.

She had up to three weeks "off" if she chose. She decided to take two, and went down into Los Angeles to experience the city by herself. The only times she had been there were for various sales and viewings. Now, with fourteen days all to herself, she played tourist, going to Hollywood and making the rounds of the best attractions. In between, she called people in New York, extended the storage contract for her things and spent lazy mornings reading colorful magazines in a soft, wide hotel bed while eating whatever she damn well pleased.

She spent a lot of money on gifts for her family and shipped them with friendly notes that spoke of the wonderful life she now had in California. Remembering that cousin David's wife had been delivered of twins (or so her mother's last birthday card had informed her), she bought a box full of Disney themed toys and hats and little t-shirts and sent that off too. It made her feel good. And it seemed ironic that cousin David would probably never know how clearly she remembered the games she played with him when she was a child, and what her life was like now. She wondered what kinds of games his kids would play.

She played news junkie, reading newspapers and magazines and watching some television. It was amazing how many things could happen without other people talking about them. Reflecting back on her two years, she realized that she probably wouldn't have realized that there had been an important election this past year if it hadn't been for guests like Monica, who chatted about current events. Eric and Jimmy never watched commercial TV, and Jimmy got all of his economic news through various computer services. It was like living on an island, cut off from mainstream life.

In the classified ads of one local newspaper, she found a listing for a meeting of some kind of leather society. It described an "SM Support Group," which met every week. She had been tempted to go; wouldn't it be funny? But then she remembered her disappointment when she had gone back with Ken. If it had seemed so small and sad to her when her only other experience had been Ken and her household, what would it appear like now? And there was also a persistent nudge of old loyalty. She would not put herself in a position in which to ridicule that time which, for all its pain and occasional emptiness, was the best she could have hoped for.

I've changed so much since then, she marveled. *Look at how much I've learned. Think of how much has happened. I am living the life.*

In a way, that started the end of her vacation. By her thirteenth day of freedom, she was more than ready to get back to the quiet house in the hills.

Another autumn. More cycles, artwork here, a statue there, a glorious illuminated depiction of the "crimme af sodomie," probably designed as an early version of a gay men's sex magazine. Eric went into raptures, bought the special airtight frame that she suggested and displayed it under subdued light.

It seemed to settle his discomfort with her once and for all.

Monica started to drop by regularly, sometimes with April but mostly alone. She had established some very important allies in LA and in San Francisco, and was becoming quite the jett-setting businesswoman, her political acumen no longer a well kept secret. She started to joke that now she really believed that "the boys" had purchased Robin for her pleasure. It seemed that whenever she arrived, Robin appeared at her side and didn't leave it until ordered to.

And Monica never ordered her to leave.

Life was good. Usually. But in those moments when she wasn't working, and especially in those moments when the masters were using one or any combinations of the boys but had not requested her, Robin felt those old doubts returning. *Have I settled again?* she asked herself one day, lifting Maria's old collar into her hands and caressing the leather. *Have I become used to something, convincing myself that it's as good as I'm going to get?*

The speed in which these thoughts returned after what seemed like such a strong resolution to banish them depressed her more than she liked to admit.

"Oh, this is beautiful," Robin said, drawing the coiled whip out of Monica's bag.

"Yes, isn't it? Signal whip. As in, 'On you huskies, mush!' and all that jazz."

"It makes noise?"

"Like a gunshot." Monica crossed the room, silver chains jangling around one western boot ankle. She took the whip from Robin's hands, let it uncurl, and then made a strange motion that Robin wouldn't have associated with such a whip: she seemed to throw it, like a ball.

It did indeed make a loud crack that resounded in the room. Robin jumped.

"Impressive, isn't it? It wants to be hung up." She passed it back, and Robin dutifully hung it on one of the hooks inside the closet door.

"You never used anything like that on me, ma'am," Robin casually remarked, continuing the unpacking.

"No. For one, you've never made me angry enough to want to genuinely punish you. For two, I don't think you could take it in a way that would amuse me or get me hot. It's a mean mother of a whip. I tend to use it mostly on boys. They've got the back and shoulder development that's best suited for the trauma, I think."

You'd be surprised at what I can take, Robin thought. But she didn't give voice to that impertinent comment and concentrated instead on putting Monica's things away.

"I'm glad I've never gotten you that angry," she finally offered. Monica laughed in response and stretched. "I think I'll go cook in the jacuzzi for a while, sugar. When you're finished, come down and give me a nice massage, will you?"

"It will be my pleasure, ma'am!"

"You know, sugar, from you, I almost believe that."

Oh, but it is a pleasure, Robin thought as Monica left the room. To be able to touch all of your body, to rub oil into your skin and make you moan and sigh. It's better than having sex, because then you're still paying attention to me. But when I touch you and press into you, you just melt away and let it happen and for minutes at a time...

For minutes at a time...you belong to me.

Blasphemous. Shocking!

But true.

It didn't matter, though. Later on, Monica would take herself back and make sure that Robin would feel nothing but the sensation of being owned and used. Things would be in balance again. The pallet was already at the foot of the bed; the restraints ready at hand and Monica's favorite paddle on the bedstand.

Another weekend in paradise.

But that night, Monica got a phone call that sent her running to find Jimmy. The two of them went into his office, and the sounds of work started to emerge. Robin looked over to Carl, but he could only shrug in confusion. Eric was home, but he only dropped into the office from time to time, seeming to check on the proceedings but leaving the situation in Jimmy's hands.

Carl served coffee and sandwiches, but had nothing new to report when he got back.

And in the hours after midnight, when Monica emerged, all she did was call up an order to pack her overnight bag and get the car ready. As Robin re-packed all the things she had happily unpacked that morning, she kissed the perfect weekend good-bye. When she took the bag downstairs and gave it to Muscledog to take out to the car, Monica was standing by the kitchen doors, hastily drinking a cup of coffee and checking her watch.

"I...I hope everything is all right, ma'am," Robin offered.

Monica turned, and smiled. "It sure is, sugar. Here." She passed the cup into Robin's hands and wiped her lips with the back of her hand. "You go take care of that. I'll be back soon. Be good!"

And with a whirl and a jangling sound, she was out of there, running to the car. Robin stood with the cup in her hands until Raul coughed a warning. Then, with a start, she went into the kitchen to dispose of it.

When she came out, Jimmy and Eric were on the upstairs landing, conferring. She waited politely until Eric went back to the master bedroom and Jimmy ducked back into his downstairs office to go to her own room to sleep. Carl was waiting on Jimmy, Muscledog was driving to the airport, and Raul probably had gone off to be with Eric.

It was the first time she could recall going to sleep alone. But since she couldn't even begin to imagine what the crisis or excitement was all about, she only mourned the lack of Monica's company and went to sleep.

The following morning, Eric and Jimmy did something that they almost never did.

They turned the TV on.

And then, after an hour of watching the news, they turned it off and went back to business as usual. Carl shrugged, his face a mask of confusion. They had been watching the clock all morning, and nothing had been said about the commotion the night before. Muscledog mentioned to Robin that in the entire drive to the airport, Monica hadn't said one word, only listened to the radio and looked out the window.

It took three more mornings before the expected incident happened.

At ten o'clock that morning, a regular news broadcast was interrupted with a "just breaking" story about a scandal concerning two or more senators and a consortium of banks and investment agencies in the southwest. Robin glanced at Jimmy. His eyes were narrow with concentration, but his lips were compressed into a smile. She was firmly pushed back toward the stairs by Raul, whose patience seemed totally unrealistic now; didn't he want to know what was happening? But she obeyed, slowly, taking her time to mount the stairs. To her surprise, she had barely reached the landing when Jimmy's voice reached her, in fact, resounded throughout the ground floor.

"Yes!" It was followed by his laughter, and then a whole string of "Yes, yes, yes!," until Eric shushed him.

Well, whatever it was, it was good. Robin went into her office sure that she'd find out what it was all about later.

She began to find out during her first call to New York. Everyone was talking about it. It was going to be a major problem for the president, because prominent members of his own party were involved. It had also hit the market badly, with money shifting around like mad to remove it from the spheres surrounding the implicated fiduciary institutions. It was another Iran/Contra, another BCCI scandal.

Robin knew at once how it affected her owners. Jimmy had done extensive business with some of the banks in the middle of the mess. She didn't find out until later how much he had pulled back in the past year, all based on Monica's suggestions. And then, three nights ago, she had done him a final, invaluable service by giving him the ultimate insider information, that the scandal would break sometime this week.

"That is *so* illegal," Robin gasped, when Carl filled her in.

"In a way, yes, but in another way, no," Carl shrugged. "If she were a member of some justice department, and she got the information during the investigation, yes, it would be. But she was just making an educated guess. Her sources told her about the time. All they knew was that something big and nasty was brewing. She already knew that these idiots were gliding on thin currents. She was the one who guessed that it was probably the sound of their crash."

"What if she had been wrong?"

"We would have lost a little chunk of money and a lot of good will with the bad guys. Jimmy figured, what the hell. If Monica was right, they'd take a fall anyway."

"How did he do it?"

"Hey, he's the genius, not me. I know he made lots of calls. And you know what the best thing about this is? Jimmy's clients don't know about Monica. All they're gonna know is that he advised pulling out months ago, gradually cut down on his connections with these people, and then pulled out just in time. They're gonna think he's a god." Carl was exhausted, but happy for his master. "Saved again, by the brilliant talents of a financial wizard."

"And the information of a good friend," Robin added.

"Oh yeah, that too." But he winked to show he was just pulling her leg, and they went back to their work.

It was true that Jimmy basked in the compliments and increased business that followed. Robin half expected Federal agents to arrive and arrest him, but nothing of that sort ever happened. Either the money wasn't big enough, the incidence wasn't important enough, or Carl was right and the action wasn't technically illegal.

Robin wasn't much surprised when Jimmy told her to get "something nice" as a gift for Monica. "Something nice" in the price range of seventeen to twenty thousand dollars.

"That's what I call a nice gift," she giggled to the boys that night. Muscledog whistled and looked impressed.

"Well, get this, girl," Carl replied. "Jimmy figured that Monica's advice saved him and his clients over five million dollars in the short run. And the new clients he's picked up since then, and the new accounts from the old ones? We're talking huge, huge numbers here. He's just taking some of the cream off the sides of the bottle for this gift."

Robin blinked. Somehow, she had never given much thought to how much money Jimmy handled. And although in her old life she knew many people who would consider such amounts the mark of a small business (hell, she'd been at auctions where minimum bids started in the millions), she was still impressed.

That night, she tried to estimate how much money her owners had invested in their slaves. Even though she still had no idea how much money she had gone for, she knew that she was due a specific amount when her new contract ended…should she decide not to continue.

Adding percentages onto that amount to figure out the value of Raul and estimating that Muscledog was worth more because of his build, she started coming up with big numbers. And granted that Carl was purchased six years ago, his experience added to his value. Now, add room and board and medical care, and the fact that only two of the slaves really replaced people who would be paid a full time salary, given the amount of work really needed to run the house and take care of the two men.

It was definitely not the picture that Chris had painted for her, of a family slave whose work was necessary to keep a business running. But it was sure nice to belong to rich people, she reflected. It just adds to the security. I have a good life. I do.

The next day, Jimmy told her to cancel the search for the gift. "She says she doesn't want anything that'll sit in her house and catch dust while she's away," he said to Robin, who was not used to getting explanations. "Can you imagine? I decided to send ten thousand dollars to this little AIDS clinic in Washington and tell 'em it's in her name. What do you think? She'll like it?"

Robin blinked, thought fast, and said, "Sir, would you consider a different type of donation?"

"More money? Do they need it that badly? Or does it sound cheap?"

"Well, no sir, it's very generous. But Ms. Monica once told me that, um, her mother died of breast cancer, sir. And that she was thinking of endowing a new research chair in her name, but she hadn't raised all the money yet."

"How the hell do you know that?" Jimmy grinned. "Pillow talk?"

Robin blushed, but nodded.

Jimmy nodded. "Good thinking, Robin. I'll take care of it."

And Robin basked in the warm feelings that ran through her. Monica might be a little annoyed at the presumption, but she would have to be pleased when Jimmy and Eric's donation came through.

Eric scoffed a little, although not seriously. "Now, wait a minute, doesn't this seem a little unnatural to you? Fags raising money to fight breast cancer! I mean, what's next? Lesbians doing their thing for prostate cancer?"

"Well, they sure working their butts off for AIDS," Jimmy countered. "Let's set a trend for a change. Look — you even get to wear a pink ribbon."

Eric naturally didn't fight for long, and Monica was overwhelmed by the surprise donation to her fund. She thanked them with flowers and kisses over the phone, but told them that she couldn't make it back to California for several weeks; she was busy in DC.

And when she did make it, they gave her a real hero's welcome, with Raul outdoing himself in the kitchen and a houseful of friends who didn't quite know the whole story but were glad of another opportunity to party and listen to all the insider news of the nation's capital.

And Robin found herself soundly spanked and thoroughly ravished that night, as though Monica was trying to make up for the last aborted evening they should have had.

With her bottom still sore, and her thighs still wet, she lay cuddled in Monica's arms, breathing together with her, until the sweat began to dry from their bodies. Then, she pulled away, went to the bathroom, and came back with a warm, damp washcloth and wiped Monica's body down until she purred. It had become a regular event, this after sex wipe-down, and they both enjoyed it.

When she came back, she knelt on the floor and laid her cheek against the mattress so that Monica could easily touch her. Monica instantly did, running one manicured hand over Robin's head and stroking her hair.

"You told them about the research thing," she said quietly. "That was very sweet of you."

Robin blushed. "They wanted to give you a meaningful gift," she answered. "I had very little to do with it."

"You know, they still want to give me stuff," Monica stretched out and relaxed. "They want me to tell them what 'thing' I want tomorrow, before I leave. What do you think I should ask for? Half the kingdom? The prince's hand in marriage?"

Robin giggled. "The BMW coach-and-four? Freedom for your people?"

"Hm, good ones. But there's no place in DC I can park a damn coach, and my people seem to be quite capable of getting their own damn selves free without any help from me." She sighed and turned over onto her side. "Actually, I figured out what to ask for when Eric swore that I could have anything I wanted except for that piece of graffiti and that illuminated butt fucking you found him."

Both women giggled. Robin slid down onto her pallet. Monica turning onto her side was a prelude to sleep. She thought of asking what Monica was going to ask for, but shrugged it off and settled comfortably against the bed.

I'll find out tomorrow, she thought.

Chapter Twenty-Four

Monica was brief and to the point. "I want Robin."

Eric's mouth dropped open. Jimmy grinned.

"That's what you get for being vague," he drawled. "Tell her to ask for anything, and she takes you seriously. I knew we should have qualified that offer."

Robin, who was helping Muscledog clear away the breakfast dishes, almost dropped her handful. Luckily, he was there to steady her. She did gasp, though, and colored deeply when it was clear that everyone heard her. Burning with curiosity, humiliation and excitement, she had to be pulled into the kitchen. She could still hear the incredulous reactions of her owners, dimly now, as Raul stepped in to tap her on the top of the head and stare down into her eyes.

"It doesn't concern you," he lectured firmly. He took the dishes from her, and directed Muscledog to keep working.

"But it does!" she answered in a whisper.

"No it doesn't," he cautioned her. "When it does, you'll be informed. Now get your ass upstairs and stay in your workroom until you're sent for. And don't try to stall!" He gave her a rough push, and she scurried. Passing through the dining room and heading towards the hall and the stairs, she felt the eyes of the two men and one woman upon her, silent for every step she took through the room. As soon as she mounted the stairs, she could hear them resume.

"I assume you would want us to fulfill the contract, too? I mean, she only signed up, what...a month ago? Come on, Monica, have a heart. You got us in a vulnerable moment, and you're taking advantage of it." That was still Jimmy.

251

Robin's throat tightened. She moved slowly, carefully placing her foot lightly on each step, fully aware of her disobedience.

"Listen, if it's that much of an imposition, I withdraw the request," Monica said lightly. Robin felt an awful weight settle in her chest, and without warning, tears gathered in the corners of her eyes. She forced her legs to move, even though she could hear Eric saying something else, something about how valuable she was. By the time she reached the room she called her office and sank down into her chair, she was crying hot and terrible tears.

I didn't realize how unhappy I was, she thought, laying her head down on her folded arms. *Until now. Until I thought that I could go with Monica. Oh, God, how did I get into this? Am I in love with her? Do I hate it here that much?*

I don't care how valuable I am, she cursed, sniffing and trying to control the sobs that were shaking their way through her body. *I don't care how much I cost or how long my contract is for! I don't care about honor or service or anything! I just want to be with someone who loves me!*

And that one clear thought hurt more than any of the others. With a curse, she stood up and threw herself out the door and down the hall to the small bathroom that the slaves shared. There, with the door shut and cold water running from the tap into the sink, she slammed her fists down against the tiles and rocked back and forth, a torrent of tears flowing through strangled cries and choked coughs.

How pathetic, she railed at herself. Spend your whole fucking life wanting something spectacular and special, give up everything every normal person wants and gets, and then come down to the simple answer that all you want is someone to love. *What a fucking mess!* She pulled a white towel from the rack and thrust it under the cold water and applied it to her face and her pounding forehead.

All this time, all this energy…and I could have stayed with Maria. Moved in with her, and had a lover and a girlfriend who tied me up and played SM games with me whenever I wanted. And I wouldn't have to sleep with people I didn't know, or wonder if she was going to get pissed and beat the shit out of me, and I could work and keep my own money and buy whatever I wanted and wear what I liked…and…and…

"I'm such a whiner," Robin said out loud. She looked up into the mirror, at her flushed face and reddened eyes, and lowered her head quickly. I didn't get here by settling for less. I knew that I wasn't going to end up in a perfect situation. I need to get a grip on things here. I'm an adult.

Tears still gathered and spilled down her nose. Desperately, she dug into the medicine cabinet and swallowed three aspirins, and drank down some more cold water. Deep breathing, and more chilling touches with her wet towel, and slowly they came under control. She combed her hair out and arranged it properly, and hung the towel to dry, moving carefully and concentrating on what she was doing.

I have to be patient, she reminded herself. I'm not even thirty yet. This is only my first owner. Next time, I won't re-up, and Chris will find me a new owner. Or I'll take my money and give it all up. But this is what I have now. I'm not going to be the one who fucks it up.

Back in her office, she turned her computer on, and sorted through her faxes. There was work to be done. And she got lost in it for about an hour, and then the intercom beeped on her phone.

"Yes, sir?" she answered.

"Pick up on line two, Robin." It was Jimmy's voice. She obediently switched lines. It was probably one of his parents; they always asked to speak to her when they called.

"Hello?"

"Robin." Chris' voice hit her right in the sternum, and she could feel the carefully corralled torrent of emotions swell against her new barrier.

Ohmigod, she thought. A wave of dizziness passed, and she clamped one hand onto the edge of her desk. "Chris?"

"Your owners would like me to negotiate a contract change with you," he said. She could hear something in his voice that sounded vaguely like amusement. She could see his smile, tight and ironic. "They would like to transfer your accommodations, but retain your services."

"Wha-what?"

"It's not entirely unheard of, but an interesting situation. In effect, you would be physically present in someone else's home, but your professional services, in this case, your art brokering skills, would still be available for them. As your trainer, I must caution you that your workload will, in effect, double." He paused. "But I get the impression that you might not mind this."

Robin scratched the surface of her desk. She was staring ahead of her, and her heart was pounding so hard that it seemed to echo in the telephone receiver.

"Why…" she swallowed and cleared her throat. "Why do you have to ask me? Don't they have the right to, um…give me away?"

"Your contract establishes them as responsible for your living expenses and requires them to maintain a proper environment for you, in part exchange for your services. Now, they are requesting that someone else be responsible for boarding and keeping you, while you still serve their purposes. They are not signing over your contract intact, but requesting a substantial alteration. Do you need time to consider this?"

Robin closed her eyes. "No. No, sir, I don't. I accept whatever changes are necessary."

"What a surprise. Well, enjoy Washington, my dear. I will speak to you next year, on your anniversary."

"Chris!" Robin clutched the phone. Words long unsaid wound themselves up, and she almost cried again. "Thank you."

"You are welcome, Robin. It has always been interesting dealing with you. Now pass me on back to your various owners and we'll get you settled."

She hit the intercom button and connected him back with Jimmy's line, and sat still, feeling shivers run their way through her. Her head still pounded, and her eyes were tight and aching. Shivers turned into full tremors of her flesh, and she hugged herself and stared at the wall for several long minutes, unable to either break or bear the silence. It all seemed unreal. Too fast. Too impossible to believe.

But when Monica turned up in the doorway, dangling a ring that held one key on her index finger, her mouth turned up into a wry and satisfied grin, Robin couldn't help but throw herself across the room, collapsing at the woman's feet and clasping her around her knees. Monica laughed, and pulled Robin's head into her, cradling it and stroking it, and finally pulling Robin up to kiss her.

"I guess you're coming home with me, kiddo," Monica said, pulling Robin's head back. They were both breathing a little hard, and Monica was barely controlling a broad grin. "And I guess you don't mind."

Chapter Twenty-Five

"Just a warning," Monica had said, as preparations were made for the transfer of Eric and Jimmy's only female slave. "It's not going to be like you're used to!"

It was true. From an airy and sunny southwestern style house with a pool and a jacuzzi, where the slaves had a room with a bath and Robin had her own office to work in, she was now moving into a narrow and shaded townhouse not far from Dupont Circle. It did boast three bedrooms, and Monica turned the small guest bedroom over to Robin both for living quarters and a working space. Her computer, fax and files were shipped from California, and a phone line hooked up, just so that she could continue being her masters' broker.

It had been the best solution they could come up with. After Monica had so casually given up, Jimmy and Eric exchanged guilty looks and tried to talk her into some "thing" else...surely she could take some other gift from them? But the friendlier she was and the more she objected to disturbing them, the more guilty they felt.

"Listen," she confided to Robin, "From the trouble I saved them, they could buy a twin for Muscledog and have enough left for a year's supply of Alpo."

It was Eric who suggested that the main reason why they couldn't easily part with Robin was that they had truly counted on her work for the next two years. And when he and Jimmy met eyes and looked back at Monica, she could see their brains churning away at an honorable compromise. It might be hell on the person in question, but then...

"What are slaves for, anyway?" Jimmy had asked. "Let's call that sonuvabitch trainer of hers and get him to agree to the changes."

And it was done. And in two days, Robin bid tearful farewells to her fellow slaves, and went back home with Monica. *Home.*

To narrow, tree-lined streets that curved and circled, to Ethiopian restaurants and tiny bookstores and life inside a major city again. The first thing that Monica did was establish quick ground rules.

"Don't call me ma'am any more." She grimaced and then grinned. "It makes me feel old. Just plain Monica will do, or Mo, if you like that."

Robin grinned back, fingering the new chain and lock around her throat. "If I like it?"

"Well, look. I'm one of those poor kinds of masters that can't afford formal behavior. Hell, I can't even afford you. In fact, I think that I'm so poor that I might have to bring you to bed just to keep warm in the winter. This is not sunny LaLaLand anymore…it's the cold, harsh world of politics and big business." Monica's dark eyes flashed when she teased, and they were dancing when she said these things. "In fact, I think you'll be spending a lot of time in my bedroom. It's been a neglected part of my life." When Robin blushed and dropped her eyes, Monica laughed out loud and hugged her. "That's what I love about you, darlin'. You're so damn easy to embarrass!"

Other rules — basically, Monica traveled. A lot. And her house (and two cats) would now be Robin's responsibility. Robin would also assist the young man who handled most of Monica's paperwork and correspondence. She would be doing a lot of domestic chores, a great deal of packing and unpacking, and do things like make the house warm and welcoming for Monica when she came back from her trips.

"That's what I really wanted you for," Monica admitted. "I just kept thinking how nice it would be to come home to someone like you after doing three states in three days. Eat real food instead of take-out, let someone else handle all the stuff I had to do all alone, and then slip into bed with someone who was happy to see me. It was either you, or a nanny and a big dog."

There would be no special outfits to wear at home; in fact, Robin had to buy some new jeans and shirts to wear. After all, most of Monica's associates had no idea that anything like the Marketplace existed.

"You're back in the closet about your slavery," she joked. "Don't hold your breath waiting for your liberation movement."

It was like being back in college, and moving in with a new roommate. Except that Monica directed, and Robin acted. Even though it might have been years since Monica had owned a slave, she sure wasn't awkward about it. There were no gaffes, no moments of indecision. And although Monica offered Robin choices from time to time, she rarely stopped to ask for an opinion, or to see if something was all right.

Which suited Robin just fine.

For a few days, they were concerned with moving in, and Robin learned the layout of the house and where everything was. Then she set up her new office and spent a day re-establishing ties and contacts and arranging her files. She slept in the double bed in the room that was now going to be hers, feeling vaguely disoriented by the expanse of the mattress and the excess pillows. But for the first week, Monica did not invite her to bed or use any form of pleasure or discipline other than a soft kiss or two and some gentle, encouraging pats.

On her seventh evening in her new home, Robin received the summons she had been waiting for. As she hung up from one of her west coast contacts and began to shut her "office" down for the night, she turned to see Monica leaning into the doorway.

"I figure it's about the right time to welcome you aboard, kiddo," she said. Robin took a quick breath and smiled; her heart had already started to dance in reaction to the sultry tone in her mistress' voice. "So strip down and get your butt over to my room. I think it's been too long since you got it warmed."

"Yes, ma'am," Robin answered automatically, her fingers already starting to undo the buttons on her blouse.

""Tsk, tsk," Monica shook her head. "Forgetful, huh? That's one punishment I have to deal with first."

Robin blushed, but kept undressing furiously. "Yes, Monica," she agreed.

There were no special punishment places in Monica's house. Robin hurried to the largest bedroom, and gasped with delight, because Monica had lit candles on her shelves and window sills and in her corners, casting wavering, subtle lights and shadows over the room. The bedcovers had been pulled off, and piled to one side, and leather cuffs were already on the bed, along with a riding crop and two whips. Robin put the cuffs on when Monica pointed to them, and eagerly got into position on her belly, spreading her arms and legs wide for Monica to fasten them down.

"First the punishment," Monica whispered, trailing a soft bundle of leather tresses over Robin's back, "and then the welcome."

Quickly, she switched the whip for the crop and delivered twenty-four fast and stinging blows to Robin's ass. Robin squirmed just a little, feeling the tapping blows like little splatters of annoying pain, covering her rounded cheeks in a pattern that followed the outer curves of the flesh and made it grow hot and tender. And when it was over, she sighed, and said, "Thank you, Monica." Instantly, Monica's cool hand was brushing over the hot points.

"So well behaved," the older woman replied lightly. "So good. Let's do something nice now." And the first fall of the soft whip caught Robin right at the underside of her butt, thumping lightly between her legs. So did the second and third. Each fall made Robin moan with pleasure and more gratitude, and as Monica stepped up the impact of each blow, it only served to make Robin begin to breathe heavily and tense and relax in her bonds.

But every time Robin began to whimper in pleasure, Monica would switch off, either changing her aim to cover Robin's shoulders or thighs or upper back, or she would change her tempo and strength, brushing her lightly with the entire whip, or stinging her quickly with just the tips.

Soon, Robin's body began to warm, with pink areas springing up wherever the whip kissed her. And still Monica continued sensuously, until it seemed that Robin began to pant with every third blow. Then, Monica switched to the longer and more punishing whip, and began to lay into her new slave, making pink spots red, and painting broad lines of color and long lines of heat, working steadily up and down Robin's body.

Robin hadn't been beaten like this in months; her owners never used lover's techniques like this, and few of the guests bothered to put so much time into making her feel things. And as Monica began to pause and stroke her between sets of particularly hard strokes, Robin couldn't help but groan and push her heated flesh back against Monica's hands and fingertips. That only made Monica laugh and back away, and begin to strike her again.

Turning her over was quickly done, and Monica used the crop to tease her, trailing it over her breasts and tapping it against her nipples, and then passing it along her body to tap it harder over her pubic mound. After a few minutes of that, which left Robin stretching and arching and making little mewing sounds, Monica picked up the softer of the two whips and began again, bring color and sensation first to Robin's breasts, and then across her belly, and then over the fronts and insides of her thighs.

Robin fell into a vortex of sensations; every minute, a new pleasure was added, every shift of her body caused new and wonderful spasms of warmth and minor pain. She cried out like she hadn't in ages, and licked her lips and bit at them in a pointless effort to remain still and quiet. But unlike Eric and Jimmy, Monica delighted in every new whine and whimper and rewarded them with harder shots and more searching touches. Before long, Robin felt like she was one long mass of awakened nerves, ready to pull against her bonds at the slightest touch, her flesh red with impact marks and the flush of her own excitement.

When Monica laid the whip down and drew one finger along the edges of Robin's cunt lips, Robin came without warning.

It was so lightning fast that Robin couldn't even draw a deep enough breath to sustain it, let alone warn Monica or ask her for permission. Robin's hips rose up, and thrust against Monica's hand, and that one pressing finger, and Monica laughed and drew away.

"Bad girl," she said softly, picking up the riding crop again. "I wanted that one."

"I'm sorry, Monica," Robin managed to say, her throat catching on every word.

"Too bad...now you're going to have to wait longer before the surprise."

Robin didn't bother to ask what the surprise was; besides, she was distracted by the stinging smack of the crop's flapper against the sensitive flesh that had just throbbed with such delightful intensity. Robin moaned and then yelped as Monica delivered a rain of slaps all over her cunt, and then down the insides of her thighs. The puffy flesh of Robin's cunt lips grew red and angry quickly, until Monica's fingers could wrest a strangled whimper out of Robin with just a light sliding touch.

And then Monica left her there for a few minutes, staring at the ceiling and feeling the waves of pounding heat from the beating. Robin's back felt wonderful, warm and aching and good against the softness of the bed. And her pussy, spread wide and dripping wet, also ached, in so many different ways that it was hard to tell which was the most insistent.

When Monica came back, she pulled a box from under the bed. Robin couldn't see what it was, but could hear the scraping of it against the floor and the snapping of latches being opened. Then, Monica re-appeared, rising to fix a pair of screw-type nipple clamps on Robin's very erect nipples.

"I can't wait for the surprise," Monica said, tightening the clamps until Robin winced. "So consider these the rest of your punishment for coming without permission."

"Yes, Monica," Robin whispered back. She winced as the clamps bit into her flesh, but watched Monica eagerly for evidence of the surprise. Monica stepped back and picked something up from the floor. It looked like a flat pad, attached to a long slender chain. In Robin's inquisitive stare, she carefully pushed it down the front of her jeans, leaving a trail of silvery chain coming out at her waistband. Then, Monica leaned down and turned something on. It sounded like a light hum.

"I got this little toy thinking about you," Monica said, sitting on the edge of the bed. "I can't wait to see how you like it."

And slowly, making sure that no other part of her body touched Robin's, she extended one hand and touched Robin on the lips.

And Robin jerked at the touch of an electrical shock! It wasn't painful, and her eyes widened as Monica laughed. Robin pursed her lips, and Monica obliged by passing her fingertips over then. This time, they stayed longer, and the buzzing was hot and tingly and made all of Robin's body shiver. Monica trailed her fingers down Robin's body, and everywhere they touched, a little static electricity followed, dancing and jumping along Robin's skin.

She played like that for a while, testing Robin's tolerance and reactions, holding her hands closer and then farther away, curling her fingers at the base of Robin's breasts and then across her stomach. "Isn't that nice?" she asked teasingly. "The minute I felt this, I knew I had to use it on you. It's as much fun as I thought it would be." She giggled and tapped her fingers lightly on the tops of Robin's thighs. .

Robin didn't know whether to jump around, tense, moan or giggle. The sensations changed rapidly from buzzing to a stabbing, needling annoyance. And when Monica touched her clamped nipple tips, Robin couldn't help but yelp, loud, and then moan as Monica trailed the sore tips with her tongue. For one second, Robin thought that she was feeling the after-shocks of the electrical toy, but then she realized that Monica's tongue was acting as a transmitter as well. It was almost overwhelming. And when Monica got up onto the bed and positioned her face over Robin's spread legs, Robin began to whimper.

The touch of that electrified tongue on her swollen lips was incredible! Using just the tip, Monica worked a series of light shocks all along Robin's soft wetness, pushing the flesh and gently poking at it, spreading her wider and opening her to more pinching and stabbing darts of static electricity. When she raised her head and looked at Robin's flushed face and tense body, she laughed.

"You can come if you want to," she said before getting back to her amusement. And at the third or fourth strong touch of Monica's tongue on her engorged clit, Robin did, and her own convulsions of pleasure lasted so long that she could barely tell when Monica turned off the machine and touched her with hands and lips that held only the heat of their owner.

Robin did know that when Monica shucked her jeans and turned around on the bed, lowering her own wetness to Robin's mouth, that she was delirious with pleasure. It was hard to remember that she was bound to the bed; all she wanted to do was clasp Monica's thighs to her, pull on her ass cheeks and press her face up into that fragrant delta, drowning herself in the feminine moisture that was proof of Monica's arousal. But she was stretched out, held immobile, and Monica teased her for a good long time before letting Robin's searching, hungry mouth settle and work.

And when Monica had her fill of that, she turned around again, and settled down on her side, next to Robin's body. They were both panting, both flushed, and both smiling between deep breaths.

"And you know I'm not finished with you," Monica said, unhooking Robin's legs. "Bring them up, open yourself wide. I want to see what you can take."

Robin eagerly brought her knees up, and leaned back against her shoulders as Monica began to work her fingers into Robin's cleft. Robin was so wet she was almost dripping, and Monica slid four fingers in comfortably. In fact, Robin arched her back and spread herself wider, feeling that incredible fullness, and the delightful pressure that made her want to shake and moan and swallow Monica's hand. This time, there was no sharp pain. This time, she felt like she was a warm nest, engulfing Monica like a living thing, taking all she had to offer. Monica had a bottle of lubricant over by the side of the bed, but with one answering thrust up and then forward, Robin took Monica's thumb into her body and Monica's hand formed gently into a fist.

"Oh, yeah, that's my baby," Monica crooned. "That's my sweetie. That's it, eat me up, sugar. You're all mine now."

Robin trembled with passion and tension, and moaned at the sensation. It felt so good, and so terrible, and so amazing! She could look down her body and see Monica's arm making small, tight movements that all became heavy, shifting pressures inside her body. Every shift of position was as powerful as any thrust, and even the slight turning of Monica's hand was a wave of pressure that made Robin's entire body shiver.

"I do," she moaned, keeping her legs wide. "Oh, yes, I do belong to you…"

And Monica rolled gently and placed a kiss on the top of Robin's spread mound, licking lightly at the exposed clit. And Robin came again, no wild thrusting this time, but a steady pulsing that flexed and pulled at Monica's hand until Monica swore and laughed, and by the time Monica eased her hand out, they were both sweaty, red with passion, and exhausted.

Later, with all the toys put away and Monica and Robin both cooled and snuggling under the covers, Monica turned Robin so that Robin had her back to her. Spoon fashion, they cuddled, and Robin could feel the heat of Monica's softer body against her back. It was comforting beyond belief. Outside, it was raining, hard, and the splattering sound of the drops against the windows was a wave of white noise that was as soothing as the softness of the bed and the heat of the two bodies in it.

Monica caressed Robin's body with long sweeping movements, settling her down into a position that she found comfortable. With one hand wrapped around Robin's waist, Monica whispered, "I'm going to have you pierced. Right up behind your clit. It's the latest thing, and it looks so pretty."

"Thank you," Robin murmured back. *That sounds nice*, she thought. And she contained the giggle that threatened to follow; had it been so long ago that she trembled at the thought of a piercing? And one behind my clit, at that! But if Monica liked it…

And they listened to the rain together, until Monica's steady breathing indicated that she was asleep.

But Robin stayed awake, luxuriating in the wealth of emotions and sensations that had collided in her. The weight of Monica's arm, and the scent of the room, the heat from her back and cheeks, and the delicious feeling of warmth between her legs. Even the tingling of her sore nipples was nice. And it was so good, to sleep with a woman in her own bed, to feel her body, the softness of her breasts, the roundness of her belly! To fill herself in the scent of a woman's passion, to taste the sweet saltiness of her excitement, was so right, so fulfilling.

So nice, Robin thought, snuggling deeper down. This is what I've always wanted. I'm still a slave, I'm still completely owned, but the person who owns me…loves me. And I love her. This is the best of all possible worlds. For once, I can be sure that it just doesn't get any better then this.

Probably.

And outside, the sounds of the rain began to grow faint as the nation's capital got the first snowfall of the season

262

A Familiar Ring

A bonus story for this edition of The Slave

A Familiar Ring

Robin lay supine, looking up at the ceiling, and thought that it could really use a coat of paint. As she added that task to her eternal list of projects, she felt a twinge of sharp pressure alongside her clitoris, and winced.

"OK, that's not right," murmured the woman whose gloved hands were rummaging through Robin's genitalia. "How about here?"

The sharpness eased into the firm, but not-painful grip that the thumb and forefinger had just a moment before, and Robin sighed and nodded before remembering that with her knees up and the woman's head down, it might be hard to see.

"That — doesn't hurt," she said cautiously. "But it feels — pinchy."

The young woman prodded a little more, moving her fingers up. "How does it compare to here?"

Robin ground her teeth before she snapped out, "The same as it felt a minute before!" Instead, she counted to a brief three, and said, "It feels better lower."

"OK, OK, let's see. You're a borderline case, I think. Your clit is huge, though. Must be nice!"

It is, Robin thought, when it's not being poked and pinched by a teenager.

Which was not exactly true. Although her current tormentor had the ink black dyed hair of the teen goth crowd and the sweet face of a middle–class former Catholic school girl, she was solidly in her twenties, just a few years behind Robin herself. Surely, it just *seemed* that they were from different generations.

"Well, can you do it?" Monica asked, impatiently. Robin's owner had taken a keen interest in the proceedings until about fifteen minutes ago, when watching had probably become as boring for her as feeling it all had become tedious for Robin. She had taken a break and come back, expecting to see the clamp in place, and her voice was just slightly testy.

"Sure, sure!" The young piercer pulled her hands away and nodded. "It'll be a little tight, that's all. Close to the nerve bundle. But I've done them like this before. I'm gonna change gloves and start unwrapping the tools." As she snapped her latex gloves off and pitched them into the trash, Robin sighed. It was a relief to get away from the tight, probing fingertips.

And yet, perversely, it had also been erotic, to a point. Even though she was on her back on the kitchen table, staring up at the lazily turning ceiling fan and thinking that just maybe her mistress should have considered a shop, instead of bringing a piercer home.

But it had been so exciting, the night Monica came home from a party and announced that she had found the woman to do the long–awaited triangle piercing that she had wanted to adorn Robin's clit. Monica didn't always take Robin out with her when she went to parties, whether they were very vanilla fund raisers, pretty staid lesbian–only gatherings, or even the Marketplace and non–Marketplace SM play parties. Sometimes, it depended on whether Monica had another date, and sometimes on what role she needed or wanted Robin in for a night. But it was not a hardship to skip any of them, especially the non–Marketplace leather events. Robin had had quite enough of those in her life, and didn't miss them. Plus, the lack of direction from Monica about exactly what protocol to follow when at one of those events was problematic. There were times when Monica just didn't understand how much a Marketplace slave stuck out.

But that night, she had gone with some mutual friends, leaving Robin home to welcome her back with hot tea and a warmed bed. And when she had settled comfortably, she looked at her slave with a sparkle in her eye and said, "I think it's time to get you ringed, slave!"

Robin had gasped, even as she felt a tingle spread down between her legs. "Did you find a piercer, Monica?"

"Yep! Cute little thing, too, if you like goth chicks with tattoos and eyebrow piercings. She turned this other girl into a work of art at the party – you should have seen it! Needles everywhere, in patterns. Her name, if you can believe it, is Arcadia. She works at some funky store called Radiance, and she says she can do triangles, no problem, right here; we don't have to go to some parlor somewhere. She's sending me a catalog of jewelry, said it'll take about three weeks to order something special." Monica's eyes brightened at the sight of Robin's deepening blush and the slight look of fear in her eyes.

"Yes, that's right," she crooned, snapping her fingers to call Robin to her side. "Three weeks, give or take a few days, and at last I'll have that handy–dandy little attachment point right down where it counts."

Her fingers stroked between Robin's legs, to the shaved and already swollen and damp pubic mound. Her fingers slipped up, and up, to the protective fold of flesh over her slave's clitoris, and gave the whole area a tweak. Robin gasped and flushed as her owner toyed with her, imagining a delicate gold ring tucked up there, a tiny ball resting over the exposed portion of her clit.

"Oh," she said out loud, helpless in her thoughts. "Oh, yes, Monica, please, mark me! Put your ring in me!"

"Oh, I will," Monica assured her. "And if I like that one, maybe we'll get your nipples done, too. Now it's time to show me how grateful you are, slavegirl. Get some of those plastic clamps – they're going all around your pussy while you go down on me. And they don't come off until I get off, understood?"

Robin understood very well. She worked hard to please, as she always did, and thrilled to Monica's easy arousal and quick orgasm.

No matter how scary getting pierced was, anything that turned her owner on this much had to be worth doing.

Of course, when you are on your back on the kitchen table, watching a woman with her hair dyed almost matte black tear open a plastic bag with a large and scary looking clamp in it while moving her head up and down to some sort of music that was playing only in her head, the aspect of what turned an owner on seemed to fade.

Arcadia had brought scented candles with her, samples from the store she worked at, but they had done nothing but make Robin sneeze, much to her embarrassment.

"All right!" the young woman said, as she positioned herself and her new tools between Robin's legs. "I'm going to mark off the points for the needle and set the clamp. Now, it might tickle a little, and the clamp is a lot of pressure, OK? Let's see…"

She leaned forward again, and Monica moved in closer, taking Robin's left hand in both of hers. Robin felt grateful for the touch, especially as she felt those blunt fingers prodding her again, pinching the area behind the long bundle of nerves that formed her clitoris.

"Really close," Arcadia murmured, more to herself. "Looks like here…and here…" Robin felt something scratchy and soft for a second, and then again, and she could see Arcadia's head bobbing as she moved it from side to side to examine her marks. Then, she saw a glint of something shiny.

"Here's the part people hate the most," Arcadia said, as something cool grazed Robin's sensitive, bare flesh. "But don't get too stressed, there's not much more to go."

"Owww," Robin said, as the clamp tightened. "Oh – lower, lower, please!"

"Oh! Well — OK — just a sec…" The clamp loosened, and the tightness in Robin's stomach released along with the pain around her clit. She saw little balls of light dancing in her peripheral vision, and blinked to clear her eyes. To her humiliation, she felt them dampen with tears.

"Heh–heh, just a little off, I guess. Here we go, this should do it."

The second time was much better, even though it was still very harsh. She dimly heard a minute clicking sound, breaking through the agony that was flooding her brain. No clamp on her labia ever felt as scary as this one, pressing upward against her clit, forcing the tip out of the hood, making her feel exposed to danger. And it hurt, really hurt! Like some sort of tiny vicious animal grinding down on her between the legs, capable of ripping out her flesh in a single mouthful. Robin gasped for breath, and then panted it out, struggling to slow it down the way she had been taught.

"That's it!" Arcadia cried. "Hey, you're good at this!"

"Such a good girl," Monica whispered into Robin's ear, and Robin sniffed and sighed, and the pounding in her ears lessened. She *was* a good girl. Her mistress was proud of her. This was nothing, nothing! Just a little pain, and then it would be all over…

"OK, here comes the needle — take a deep breath…hold it…let it out…now!" Arcadia had to move the clamp slightly and that tiny jar made Robin freeze as red and orange sparks seemed to shoot from behind her eyelids. Then, Robin's eyes flew open as a brand new sharp pain hit, and by the time she moaned, Arcadia was already laughing. "It's in! The worst is done, now. Monica, you wanna come and see, before I get the ring in?"

"Oh, yeah!" Monica exclaimed. She dropped Robin's hand and moved down between her legs, and whistled. "Oh, that is so hot!"

"Isn't it? I love seeing the needle poking through there, it looks like it's actually going through the clit."

Robin shook slightly, and gripped the edges of the sheet-covered table. It was so very hard not to tell her to just hurry up! The removal of the clamp made her bite her lip sharply to keep from screaming out something profane. But there was still more poking near her crotch, and then a cool sensation that tickled slightly, and then she heard Monica gasp.

"Oh, my God, that is beautiful! Oh, Robin! It's perfect!"

Robin smiled weakly as she felt something tap her clit and realized that the ring was in at last and that would be the gold ball that was supposed to be positioned over it at all times from now on. The sound of Monica's genuine glee helped her recover from the shocking intensity of the needle passing through her flesh, and already, she could feel her muscles relaxing again, barely aware at how tense she had been.

"Good deal," Arcadia said, snapping her gloves off again. "I already gave you the talk about how to take care of it; are you still clear on everything?"

"Yes, thank you," Robin said shakily.

"Excellent! Don't be hanging weights from it or anything until it's fully healed, OK?" She chattered on for about a minute or two as Robin tried to stay focused, but her words seemed to run into each other.

Pierced, Robin thought. I'm really pierced. If I put my hands down there right now, there will be metal going through my body. But she couldn't make her hands move. She did finally shift her heels over the edge of the table so she could let her legs dangle, and the pressure eased from her knees and upper thighs. But even as she thought about sitting up, she had a slight panic reaction — would she crush the thing? Would it hurt?

"You probably want to see it," Arcadia said with a laugh. "Oh, shit, I left my mirror home. Monica, do you have a hand–held mirror I can borrow?"

Robin pushed herself up on her elbows. There was a mirror upstairs — but it would be improper to send her owner to fetch it! But even as she moved, Monica was already on her way out of the kitchen, and Robin bit her lip again in frustration.

This just didn't feel right, she thought, as Arcadia threw her tools into a plastic container and snapped it closed. As if to support that thought, the new piercing seemed to suddenly throb.

A week later, it was still tender and red around the edges, as she saw every day when she examined it in the mirror she placed on the floor between her legs. She dutifully washed the site and avoided doing anything that might irritate the area. It continued to throb from time to time, especially at night for some reason, when she was trying to sleep.

After the second week, she found a hard little spot right next to one of the holes, and although it didn't hurt, it bothered her. Arcadia was not very helpful when she called her at work – she suggested putting ice on it. When Robin insisted that it wasn't swelling, but something hard and finite that she could feel under her fingertips, Arcadia made some vague comments about seeing a doctor and said she had to go, because a customer was there.

Robin decided to wait before calling a doctor, and by the end of a month, it seemed all right. The little lump didn't go away, and it still felt uncomfortable. But it didn't hurt. Not much, at any rate. And the piercing itself wasn't infected; she was keeping an eye out for that, too.

But neither did it heal the way that Monica had seen and heard about on other women. It remained tender to the touch. The very motion of walking was often enough to make the area sore, and when her clit was sore, Robin was not very amenable to intense play, although she tried very hard to mask it.

Robin felt crushed. Here was her owner's big fantasy, and her body wasn't living up to it. Before her new hardware was installed, the worst case scenario had been that the ring's placement would make her horny all the time. Instead, it made her either ache, or become too sensitive to touch. It didn't seem fair.

At six weeks, Monica gave the ring an experimental tug, and Robin winced in a bad way.

At two months, it seemed to be much the same.

"Funny," Monica said one night, running a gentle finger along the side of the ring. "I wouldn't have guessed you'd be this sensitive. Your clit can take a hell of a lot of stuff. I guess we should give it a little more time."

Maybe we should take it out, Robin thought, grinding her teeth at the echo of the twinge of pain. It frustrated her, this contradictory desire to both have it and get rid of the damn thing. Every morning as she examined it, she was starting to wish it *would* become infected. Then, she could honestly say that something was wrong and it was damaging her, and safely remove it.

But it wasn't that bad! Yes, it was uncomfortable, and sometimes painful, but no more than a bruised toe or a loose tooth. And it did indeed look beautiful. Even before she had gotten over the strange feeling of nausea that would strike her every time she realized that a needle had passed a metal ring this close to the nerves that made having sex so much fun, she had to admit that it was a decoration beyond compare.

But when she tried to jerk off for Monica's voyeuristic entertainment, her fingers had to be really gentle, and stay away from putting any pressure downward on her clit. If she pressed down and in at all, the underside of the ring seemed to stab into her, and it just disrupted her search for pleasure as well as a splash of cold water would. Plus, when she did get close to orgasm, it felt like a very slender little noose, sometimes almost pleasurable in its discomfort, but usually just a distraction.

A little hand-held vibrator made her explode in orgasm in seconds, but left her feeling sore as the pleasure faded and her swollen clit pressed against the edge of the ring.

Hanging weights from it was out of the question. Tweaking it, even flipping it up and down was just an annoyance, and not a shortcut to arousal.

But it wasn't bad enough to call for its removal!

Monica was as disappointed as her slave, but never suggested that they take the damned thing out. She insisted that in another month or so, it would get better, and that in the meantime, Robin would simply have to deal with the inconvenience.

Of course, Monica's love life wasn't going to be impaired by a little discomfort that her treasured slave was experiencing, and Robin was grateful for every opportunity to please her owner. It became rather one sided very fast, and if she had to admit it, Robin was less displeased with that situation than she ever would have thought herself to be.

After all, it just seemed natural! In fact, without Monica's insistence upon getting Robin off as many times as possible before exhaustion set in, Robin was free to explore how many times her owner could take pleasure. And there had been many times when Robin had collapsed into sleep feeling a little odd at having been the center of erotic attention on a night when Monica hadn't seemed very interested in the same herself. It smacked of being catered to, in a way that reminded her sadly of some of her older relationships.

But with her clit off limits (or brought into use specifically for genitorture), Monica seemed perfectly comfortable taking her own pleasure and then sending Robin off to her own room or keeping her for the night. And *that* was wonderful. It was one thing to be useful in terms of housekeeping and business. It was another thing entirely to be a living sex toy.

One evening, Monica handed Robin a sheaf of papers about a conference on the west coast. "I'm going to go to this," she said. "Register me, and book me a nice room, a suite, I'm going to throw a party or two. I'll be staying in town afterwards, though, for about a week, so book me a return flight the following Friday— no, make it Monday. Might as well have an extra weekend for fun and games."

"Yes, Monica," Robin replied automatically. "Staying at the same hotel?"

"At their rack rate? No way! I'll be moving out on Sunday and staying with, um, a friend. I'll get you the address so you can get me the rides I need." Monica turned away abruptly and Robin cursed herself for asking — even though she needed to know.

Monica had a lot of "um, friends" in her past, present, and likely, her future as well. This was not a problem for Robin. After all, Robin thought, if she tricked with me when I belonged to Eric and Jimmy, why the hell wouldn't she have other girls, too? A slave was never in the position of dictating how their owner should arrange their sex life, period, and Robin had known that way before she even entered the Marketplace.

But there were times when Monica acted as though her various tricks and girlfriends and lovers were something to be avoided in discussion with her slave. Which was awkward, especially when Monica wanted to arrange three-somes and little sex parties with her various partners and friends, some of whom knew Robin was a slave, and some of whom thought she was a girl-friend and some of whom thought — well, who knew what they thought?

The important thing was what Monica wanted; didn't she see that? Monica had owned at least one other slave, she had a lot of business associates among Marketplace owners. She should know that there was no need to hide or feel ashamed about her relationships for the sake of her property.

Repeatedly, Robin searched herself, her mind and soul, for jealousy. She found none. Her throat bore a collar. A contract guaranteed her place. She knew that no matter how many other women Monica enjoyed, whether for a night or as part of a long–term fuck buddy circle, Robin was the one who cooked for her, who kept her life together, who could be counted on to be calm, cheerful, and quietly accepting. Robin belonged to her in a way no one else really could.

If I were the type of person who couldn't stand non-monogamy, Robin thought, then I wouldn't be a slave. I'd be someone's lover. But I can do this. Better yet, I can do this and be happy about it. How do I make sure that Monica understands that?

The only really annoying part of Monica's almost two week long trip was that it would be two weeks of being alone. Robin kept the house well. There were no long–standing projects that awaited which would be best done in the absence of her owner. Well — she could paint the kitchen ceiling.

Her personal spending money, her allowance, as Monica jokingly called it, was plentiful for someone who had very few expenses. She thought of taking in some movies, going to some local restaurants, maybe investigating some museums. But a mere week before she was ready to go, Monica came home one night and took Robin by the hair and pulled her up against her body, making Robin shiver in delight.

"Sensitive little kitten," Monica laughed, pulling Robin's head back. "I've got a surprise for you!"

Robin giggled and writhed comfortably against her owner. "What is it, Monica?" she asked softly.

"Found you some babysitters," Monica purred. Her mouth was right next to Robin's ear. "I didn't want my baby to be lonely and bored while I'm away. So, when you pack my bags, better make one up for yourself, too. After you drop me off at the airport, you're going to go somewhere else!"

Robin's eyes, which had closed in delicious pleasure, opened sharply, and she was grateful she was not facing Monica at that moment. "Somewhere else? But — where?"

Monica let her go and walked into her little living room and flopped down on the couch. "Oh, it's not far," she said, taking the question literally. "I'll have directions for you." Then, she relented and grinned. "Don't worry — these ladies will know what to do with you! It's Judy and Khim. They said they'd love to keep an eye on you while I'm away. And I figured you wouldn't mind."

Robin's eyes widened even as she went into the kitchen to get Monica a drink. Judy and Khim!

No, no, she didn't mind at all, although at first she didn't know why. Neither Judy nor Khim were exactly her type, except in the fact that they were older than she was, and she always appreciated older lovers. They were a couple, naturally, and Monica had known them before Robin had come to live with her. They were both into SM — in fact, the only times Robin had seen them had been at the non–Marketplace play parties Monica had taken her to.

Khim was definitely a top. She was taller than Robin, and substantially curvy, with bright, jade eyes and a deep, wicked laugh. The last time Robin had seen her, she had been wearing a magnificent British made corset with gold Chinese dragons scampering around her body, her breasts compressed and held up for attention. She had been busy attending to her partner, Judy, whose petite body had been twisted almost double and secured in full suspension, a feat made even more astonishing by the occasional giggle that escaped from the totally immobile form. Robin remembered wondering how the smaller woman could even draw a breath, let alone snicker and giggle with delight as ropes tightened and moved and she went spinning or gently rising and falling to Khim's expert manipulation.

Later on, there had been jokes made about Khim's style, and the fact that only the extremely flexible Judy could be so twisted into pretzel shapes and hoisted up like so much laundry. But the two women laughed, both at themselves and the picture they presented, full of confidence and erotic energy.

That wasn't all Robin remembered. The more she thought about it, she began to realize why she was interested in finding out more about them, and felt safe about being loaned to them. It was Judy and Khim, out of all of Monica's non–Marketplace friends, who never asked uncomfortable questions or got flustered in front of her formal manners and made a fuss. In these play party settings, Monica often introduced Robin as her slave, and Robin's collar, of course, never came off. Robin did not go into all of the behaviors of a Marketplace client, but she did remain silent until spoken to, and she stayed at Monica's side except when sent away, and she was generally quieter and more well behaved than any of the other slaves there. (If indeed there were any slaves present. She certainly never noticed any.)

This sometimes upset people, and sometimes confused them. More than once, Monica got elaborate praise for "training" Robin, something that drew the attention of every other person in the room, exactly the kind of thing no Marketplace owner would do.

But Judy and Khim just nodded to Robin when she was introduced to them and continued their conversation with Monica. And unlike a few other people who did at least that much, they never asked Robin for any sort of service themselves, or referred to her in any demeaning ways.

In other words, they had good manners.

Well! Good manners, experienced players — they were already far ahead of many of Monica's SM pals, no matter how sad that was to admit. What could possibly go wrong? Either she would move in like a temporary kinky roommate, or maybe they might go as far as have her do some cleaning and cooking and think of it all as a little vacation for themselves. Either way, it wasn't something her relationship with Monica depended on, and it just might give Monica great face among these soft world people she cared for so much.

Robin delivered a drink with a smile and sank down to her knees next to her owner's leg. "You are so good to me, Monica," she said, laying her head against Monica's knee.

"You betcha," Monica said, leaning back with a sigh.

The directions to Bethesda were easy to follow, and by the time Robin got to the correct address, old doubts had seated themselves firmly into her psyche. It wasn't just the memory of Troy, although that was certainly there. How could she avoid comparisons? Troy had loaned her to a friend who, although safe, was hardly an experienced or demanding master, let alone Troy's equal. Now, Monica was loaning her to amateurs — nice, safe ones, sure, but not Marketplace owners. How could this be anything but disappointing?

Plus, there was no way Robin could be comfortable trying to pretend that she could use a safeword or tell these nice women that she wasn't in the mood or anything that felt like the regular way of doing thsi sort of thing among equals. That would be betraying her beloved owner, who deserved to have an obedient slave who reflected well upon her. Not to mention it would just feel — odd — after all these years to negotiate with a top, to set limits. But would not being willing to pretend that she was free seem even odder than being a good girl?

And, there was also a sense of anxiety over how to behave. Sure, they knew enough to not touch or chat with her at an SM party, but Robin knew that she craved the discipline of her daily existence. It was what had been missing in her years before she took the collar — a feeling that she had a place, with responsibilities and duties which mattered, a place that was recognized and at the same time taken as the right of her owner. She had only seen glimpses of that potential when she had been free, a person here and there, perhaps one relationship among hundreds of relationships which mocked her in its balance, until she found it herself.

Oh, well. She pulled in front of the house and put the car in park with a sigh. She had not packed much, as per Monica's instructions, so with her bag over her shoulder, she prepared herself to be invited in for coffee and some genial lesbian SM play.

There was a note on the door, with her name on it. For a moment, as she detached it, she felt annoyed — did they go out, leaving her to wait by the curb? She opened it and read, "Enter, strip, and wait on your knees by the coffee table in the living room."

She felt a shiver of excitement run through her. How delightful! How risky! She grinned at the thought of a nosy neighbor picking up this little piece of paper, and folded it carefully before stuffing it into her pocket. OK, she thought. Maybe Judy and Khim will be a lot more fun than I imagined.

Robin turned the door handle and let herself into a dark front hallway. To her left was a dining area, the table piled high with newspapers and bills and other household flotsam. The living room was to the right, she could see a tall bookcase filled to overflowing, and a long, sturdy coffee table. She put her bag down and started to strip immediately, with the order taught to her by Chris, top down, layer by layer, even though there seemed to be no one watching. She folded her clothing and laid it all on top of the bag, and then took what she imagined to be a good position near the end of the table.

Surprisingly, it felt good! It felt like one of Monica's tricks, the little games she played to keep Robin on her toes. Maybe Monica was more hands–on about this little two week stay than she had suggested. She had only said, "I told them they can do anything they wanted as long as I get you back in one piece," Monica had leered just before vanishing into the terminal at the airport. "So, I'd be nice to them!"

You got me, Robin thought, with a slight smile. Tricky woman.

She was too well practiced to start fidgeting within minutes, but she was aware of the time passing. From time to time, she heard a sound in the house — the ticking of a clock, and then its chime, a creak, something that might have been a voice. But no one came near the hallway that led into the room she knelt in. She didn't move, other than to make sure her legs didn't fall asleep, and from her position found that her temporary mistresses read science fiction and fantasy and books on geography, politics, human resources, mysteries…they read a lot. At least one of them did crossword puzzles. Books and magazines were everywhere, some shelved, some stacked, some turned to open pages. They didn't use coasters as often as they should, and Robin itched to find the wood cleaning supplies and get the top of this nice old table clean again.

But when the clock informed her she had been waiting for nearly 20 minutes, she finally heard a door opening somewhere inside the house and human voices. She sighed and composed herself, wiggling her toes for one last time.

"Good girl!" came Judy's voice from the doorway. "Isn't she a good girl?"

"I know 'em when I see 'em," Khim said with a satisfied laugh.

Robin was already facing the door, and she kept her eyes down, and back straight. It was tempting to do a full presentation bow, bring her head down to the floor, a formal way of offering yourself to a master or mistress for the first time, but she dismissed the thought. It was too Marketplace.

And if by magic, Judy asked, leaning down a little, "But shouldn't you be bowing?"

Robin gasped at this intersection of thought and words, and then swept down into the presenting bow, her cheeks turning pink. It's a coincidence, she thought furiously. Remember not to show too much of our way!

"That's better," Judy said, bringing herself back up. She was even shorter than Robin, with somewhat larger breasts. Where Robin was almost elfin in features, Judy was softer, sweeter — but with a devilish edge to her. "You wouldn't want to disappoint us on the first day, would you, slave?"

"No, ma'am," Robin said softly. "Please forgive me, ma'am."

"I might be persuaded to be merciful," Judy said with a grin.

"Yeah, I wouldn't worry about her," Khim said, tapping one foot. "I'm the one you should worry about."

Indeed, she was, Robin thought. Because Khim, along with enjoying bondage and knives and needles and whips also used canes — and no one had caned her since that time in California. Monica never did.

Did Monica tell them what I think about canes? Robin suddenly thought in a panic. Oh, no, what if she didn't? For a second, she wanted to ask for permission to speak, to ask about this, but that was wrong, wrong, *wrong*. She must not give out her desires or fears like that, certainly not when she hadn't even been asked!

"Well, great, now you went and scared her," Judy said with a laugh.

"Good!" Khim said. Today, she had not gotten dressed up in one of her exquisite corsets, but looked nonetheless impressive in black leggings and a silky top that did nothing to hide her figure. "But I admit that scaring you was not exactly what we came in to do, Robin. We just need to establish some ground rules. Look up at me."

Robin did, and was once again struck by how sharp Khim's deep green eyes were.

"Pretty basic stuff. You're the slave, we're in charge. Ma'am is fine, so is mistress, don't go overboard with repetition. Follow orders, and if you don't know, ask. You will not get punished for asking, only if you don't ask."

Robin could barely keep from nodding. Instead, she held herself still and said, with some relief, "Yes, ma'am."

"Monica told us what you can do and what you can take and what you're used to with her. We might do things a little differently, but I don't think it'll be too hard to adapt. We're in this for fun — and to get a little long overdue work done around here." She sighed and looked around at the disarrayed room. "I don't think you'll be bored," she added. "But anyway, one last thing to get out of the way. Are you in any way not willing to do this? Tell us now, and you can go home. We'll tell Monica it was our choice, because we got too busy, had to visit a sick aunt, something like that. I swear we won't say it was your decision."

Robin blinked in astonishment. That was one thing she hadn't counted on hearing.

And — she was a little nervous and doubtful. Wouldn't it be a lot easier to say "yes" and go home, paint the kitchen and get some alone time?

She glanced quickly up at the two of them and their suddenly earnest faces — they weren't joking around. She felt, deep inside, that they would do as they said, and let her go, telling Monica some silly story. And somehow, that made it easier.

"I am here of my own free will," Robin said clearly. "Thank you, ma'am, for asking. But I am yours to command."

Judy beamed. "I like her."

"Good! Then let's have the welcome party before we get to work." Khim reached down and threw a narrow leather strap around Robin's neck. "I know your real collar doesn't come off, but we don't take service around here without a collar of our own, so here's something new for you, Robin!" She buckled it on; it fit smoothly and comfortably, the inside surprisingly soft.

"Thank you, ma'am," Robin said, unable to keep the tears from forming in the corners of her eyes. It was such a nice gesture, so reminiscent of good times and bad. And it was sweet of them to once again acknowledge her collar, and to call it real.

How little you know, she thought, even as she saw Khim make a hand gesture. She was on her feet, feeling the tingles along her ankles and knees as she rose, before she realized what happened.

That slight upward motion, the hand held at eye level to someone on their knees — that was almost certainly a Marketplace gesture!

There were no universal protocols in the Marketplace. There couldn't be, since once the slaves left the hands of their trainers, their behaviors were determined by owners. But it had been explained to her, both by Ken Mandarin and Chris Parker, that there were guidelines covering the most basic commands, with postures to be taken and responses made which would be easily adaptable once the personal taste of an owner were known.

"But why teach me only one set of movements if there are dozens?" Robin had moaned once during her training. "What if I have to do it all some other way once I'm sold?"

"You are being conditioned to obey," Chris had said, looking into her eyes. "Your *obedience* is what is being trained, not the positions. When you have new ways to behave, it will hopefully be your obedience which will enable you to learn and please your owner." And he had run her through the motions over and over, until she did obey instantly, learning to watch his hands, the slightest shift in his body, or even his eyes, when she was allowed to look up. His litany of "Again. Again," whether softly uttered or sharply snapped became as agonizing as his strap. But in the end, she obeyed. Instantly.

It had come in handy in California, where indeed, her Masters had a different set of positions they liked — they spread legs wider, and they liked hands down the sides rather than across the back. But once she knew the proper ways to respond, she took direction as quickly — as she just had.

But Monica knew better than to give Marketplace training guidelines to people outside! Didn't she?

"Get a move on, slavegirl, let's not make your first visit to the basement a punishment for tardiness!"

"No, ma'am, right away, ma'am!" Robin hastily moved, horrified that she had frozen in place and still reeling from the possibilities.

Once she got downstairs, after her temporary mistresses, she gasped and then had to struggle to keep from grinning. The last time she had seen Judy and Khim had been at an expensive private dungeon owned by one of D.C.'s better professional dominatrices. But it was now clear they never had to go far for a quality playroom.

The low ceiling probably inhibited playing with long whips, but added measurably to creating an atmosphere something like a grotto designed by a sensual hedonist. Apart from a curtained off area, the entire space was given over to a long, waist high table, a wide armed St. Andrews cross with interesting holes cut into the arms, and a sturdy looking frame that supported a sling. The floor was covered with overlapping rugs, and the walls had one long rack of whips and cuffs, and an assortment of drawings and paintings of women in bondage — and not a few men, as well.

But Robin's eyes went back to the sling. Had it been that long since she felt Monica's hand sliding up inside of her? The last time had been long before the ring went in, that was for sure. Despite a warning twinge between her legs, she wanted nothing more than to feel that full again, to feel the firm pressure of a hand expanding her from the inside, something so unique and so perfectly wonderful that she had never discovered another sex act like it. Ken had taught her to take a fist — but Monica had taught her how to love it.

I don't care if I don't have an orgasm, she thought, thinking of how wonderful it would feel to lie back and spread her legs like that again. I rarely come when I'm fisted anyway. Oh, Judy's got nice, small hands — I wonder if she likes to fist?

But Judy had opened a cabinet and withdrawn a big bundle of blue rope, a wicked gleam in her eyes.

Well, Robin thought, getting tied up is nice, too.

Judy unraveled her rope, and made a simple knotted loop and tossed it over Robin's shoulders. Working quickly, she wrapped the ends around her body, crossing them over Robin's collarbone, and then under her breasts. It seemed all too fast at first — there was a line going down Robin's spine, and every once in a while, Judy would move her around and pull the strands of rope past one point or another. Before long, the blue lines seemed to divide Robin's body up into little diamonds. Rope passed between her legs, and Judy grinned for a second as Robin tensed, but then Robin felt her slender fingers pulling the rope apart so that it ran along the insides of her thighs, around her sex instead of up and through it. She sighed even as Judy chuckled.

Slowly, Robin was being dressed in rope — like a form–fitting garment that drew her body up tight. But no part of her was actually bound to something else — it was more like being wrapped up somehow. Khim lit some candles and watched in appreciation while Judy worked — wasn't it interesting that they both did rope work so well, Robin thought.

But — this was not something Marketplace owners were known for, she remembered, thinking of the mysterious way they seemed to know how she was trained. In fact, owners were less likely to get extravagant unless they had a particular fetish — she had been warned about that and had ample opportunity to witness it as well. Being freed from having to cater to the fetish desires of the slaves — other than that overwhelming need to serve in an ordered and safe way — owners didn't have to set up elaborate scenes if they didn't feel like it. Decorative bondage had not been of interest to any of her owners, although Monica did like to tie Robin to the bed from time to time.

In a way, Robin thought, as Judy wound rope in more intricate patterns down her arms, this is sort of like serving Monica at my old place in California!

How strange.

"Very pretty," Khim said. She was now sitting on the table, her legs swinging.

Robin looked down at herself — she was covered in criss–crossing rope, all blue, marking her pale skin into patterns. She shivered in appreciation and said, "Thank you, ma'am! It's beautiful!"

"I need to see it better," Khim said. She pointed to the clear space at the base of the table. "Go there and show yourself."

Robin froze once more. There it was again! Yes, it could have been just a coincidental phrasing — but "show yourself" was a standard instruction for Marketplace slaves!

So, were they owners or not? Robin shook slightly, afraid of either possibility. If they were, then she was being hesitant, or downright disobedient. If they were not, she dared not show them the formal series of poses taught to her as ways to display her body before a potential buyer.

"I — I don't understand what you mean, ma'am," she finally managed to say. "I beg your forgiveness, but please explain…"

Judy laughed suddenly, and Khim grinned too. "Never mind that," the taller woman said in a commanding voice. "You know what we mean. Do as I said."

Robin couldn't help it. Her body moved, despite the warning bells going off in her mind. They must be owners, she thought desperately, even as she crossed her wrists behind her head, showing off her tightly bound body. They have to be. Oh, please, let them be. The barest of nods, and she turned, the hardest part, bending over like that…she could feel the ropes tightening around her hips, loosening around her waist, stretching up her calves and thighs. As her asscheeks parted slightly, her bare pubis seemed tightly framed by the ropes alongside of it, the ring hanging free of her for an instant.

Then, slowly, she rose and then turned once more, dropping gently to her knees and feeling the rope harness tighten in new places. Gracefully, she brought her hands down, and then crossed her wrists behind her back, feeling the layers of rope keeping her from tucking them up next to her the way she should have.

"Oh, that was nice!" Judy exclaimed.

"Yeah," Khim agreed. "Come over here, Robin, let's get to know you better."

Robin rose and followed her instructions, and soon found herself on the table, on her back, her arms and legs tied down with red ropes, all along the sides. Judy ran the ropes up and down and in and out while Khim moved a basket of something to the table and brought candles closer. Before Judy had even finished, Khim was pulling long, colorful clamps out of the basket.

Each clamp had a tight, narrow grip, and Khim put one into every diamond shape the ropes left on Robin's body. She worked fast, with a cheerful assurance, seemingly ignoring Robin's gasps and hisses as each one went on. Some were nice — she liked the grip on the inside of her arms. Others were erotic — her nipples were already hard before Khim got to them, and the clamps made them ache delightfully. But some just hurt. The ones over her collarbone seemed agonizing, and if she twitched just slightly in her bondage, their shaking made her gasp.

Judy finished tying off the last few inches of Robin's body and grabbed a handful of clamps herself and also went to work. Before long, Robin was covered in these clamps, many more than Monica liked to put on her (more than Monica owned, in fact!) and in places she had never been clamped before. She shivered again, and set them all dancing, which made her two tormentors laugh.

"We'll warm you up," Khim said, picking up a candle. "Don't you worry!"

Very carefully, wax covered just the tips of the clamps. From two sides of the table, the women worked on her, and every time the sensations shifted, Robin struggled, unable to keep still. But of course, there was nowhere to go! The body harness was tied down tight, and every time she stretched or curled, it tightened all over her, giving her wonderful freedom to squirm and pay the consequences.

Each dribble of wax from the candles awakened the nerves pressed at the base of each clamp, and then spread out. The little glowing points were like bites — tiny, hot bites, everywhere from her shoulders down to the balls of her feet. Different colored candles made little splashes of color in between the ropes, covering her small breasts. The line of clamps in between and on top of her thighs were repeated targets because the skin there seemed extra sensitive and made her twitch and shudder.

She felt her arousal grow, that steady progression that started high and spiraled up from there. It was so wonderful to bottom to two women! Oh, what a dream of hers this had been, and how wonderful the reality was! It was one thing to bottom to Monica and her friend of the moment, always fun and sometimes surprising. But two women who knew each other so well — two women who had planned this, not one women who was leading while another watched or followed…oh, it was heaven!

How could she have doubted Monica? How could she have worried about this?

"I think she hates this," Judy said suddenly. Robin's eyes flew open in panic, and she heard the two women laugh. She blushed, deeply. How could she have been so sloppy?

"Oh, no, no, please, I am so sorry, ma'am, I love it, thank you, thank you so much!" Robin said. Oh, how Chris would have laid into her for that! Had she gotten lazy all of a sudden?

"That's better," Khim said, judiciously adding a dollop of wax on top of one nipple. Robin hissed. "Wouldn't want to think that you were just enduring this for our pleasure now."

"Oh, speak for yourself," Judy said. She tipped a bit of wax from a black candle onto an area of uncovered skin on Robin's thigh. "I like it when they're doing it for me."

"OK," Khim said easily. "Suffer for her then, and enjoy it for me. Are the instructions clear?"

Robin couldn't help but giggle. "Yes, ma'am, thank you, ma'am!"

"Good…good girl."

Robin flushed again, this time in pleasure. She couldn't help it — being praised always made her like this. And now that she knew that they enjoyed her reactions as much as Monica did, she let go a little more, fighting back the years she had spent with two masters who wanted her to keep as still and silent as possible whenever she was in pain.

When they were either bored or finished with the wax, they played with the clamps — shaking or twisting them, and then finally starting to pry them off. As most of them came off, there was only a sharp stab of the reawakened nerve, but a few actually made her yelp. Bits of wax cracked and sometimes peeled off, and in between the ropes, Robin's body felt warm and glowing, with star–like points of pain that made her purr.

Judy ended up touching the ring first, and Robin couldn't help it, she jumped, her body held down in the ropes, but obviously in greater discomfort than either the clamps or the wax had caused. Judy smoothed her cool hand down on Robin's belly, making soothing sounds. "Don't worry," she said. "We know it's still healing. It'll be OK. I won't touch it again."

And without warning, Robin's eyes started to tear again. It had all been so perfect! She had been having such a good time, and these women had turned out to be so wonderful! Her fears about inappropriate behavior, about not getting along, about unrealistic expectations, had all vanished under their expert hands, and now this damn ring had to make her react like a novice! And to hear the genuine concern and the patient reassurance that she would be taken care of was just too much.

282

"What's wrong?" Khim asked, leaning over.

Robin didn't want to answer — she just wanted the entire moment to vanish away like it never happened. She struggled to keep herself still, to fight back the tears, but the same bondage that made her feel so eroticised also kept her from wiping them away, and they trickled down the sides of her face. "I'm — I'm sorry, ma'am," she said, trying to keep her voice level. "Please, there's nothing wrong. It's just a little tender — nothing really! Please don't stop, please!"

"Well — I hear that," Khim said with satisfaction. "We were about to move on anyway. Pass me something sexy, Judy!"

Robin saw a silvery glint above her, and then Khim showed her the curved, wicked little knife. "You want to keep very still," she said softly. "You don't want me to slip."

"No, ma'am," Robin whispered. She even smiled — it had been years since someone played with knives around her. She had liked them then — she liked this even better.

The last time she had been menaced with a knife in SM play, it had been one of her aborted attempts at dating. A male top had suggested that they try a roleplayed rape scene, and she had been very eager. It was something she could not have done with her previous top, Maria, who didn't like any scene that suggested real force. But one of Robin's biggest secret turn ons was being ravished, preferably by more than one man, and she definitely had fantasies of being pressed down and violated. So, this friendly, slightly overweight man set up the scenario and "raped" her at knifepoint in his apartment, after dinner. The set up was fine, and the start was as much of a turn on as she always anticipated it could be. But it turned out that among other things, he wanted her to suddenly switch gears from fighting him, screaming and begging for it to end, to then enjoying it and asking for more.

The first "Beg me for it, bitch," was hot.

The second one was just — silly. He had dropped the knife and was busy trying to get the right angle to fuck her. He was so engaged that if she was still pretending to struggle, she could have quite accidentally kicked him right in the balls. She decided that such a level of verisimilitude wasn't on his agenda. Sadly though, she felt no sense of danger, not even pretend danger, so when he growled the command for her to beg for his big dick, it was almost tempting to ask "why?" Instead, she did her best to enjoy the fuck and then lost his phone number.

But there was no implicit threat of force here — she was already quite helpless. No, this was the eroticism of the blade, the sensuous thrill of the steel touching her skin and pressing, feeling it glide underneath the edges of the layers of wax, a bizarre skinning effect that made her relax back instead of tense up.

The tears stopped almost at once, and she breathed gently as Khim worked. How nice it was to say that she was all right and be taken at her word! How nice to just go along, keep going...for their pleasure as well as hers. She sighed luxuriously and when Khim was shaking the wax off her fingers, she stretched, just a little, to feel the continued constriction of the bondage.

"Yes, that's it," Khim crooned. "Isn't that nice?"

It took longer to get the wax off than it did to put it on, but some of the minutes were spent with the sharp edge of the knife against the smooth skin under Robin's knee, or around her heels, or on the inside of her arm. She held herself still as possible, breathing in sighs of relief as strip after strip was taken from her body.

"Don't think we do this every night," Judy cautioned at one point, finding a neglected clamp and removing it. Robin gasped at the sudden pain. "This is just to say hello!"

"Yes, ma'am," Robin whimpered. "Thank you, ma'am! It's wonderful!"

They did not try to play with her clit or her cunt, staying away from the area almost so perfectly that she felt both relief and shame. She could feel the wetness between her spread thighs — there was no question that from the moment she knelt by the coffee table, she had gotten aroused. Oh, she could use an orgasm, and a big one! Or several in a row, for that matter. She groaned as Khim applied her knife edge to her wax covered breasts, and resigned herself to an orgy of frustration. Maybe, if the two women were interested in hearing what she wanted, she could beg them to fist her.

Finally, she felt the slide of loosening ropes, and realized that Khim had stopped scraping the wax away. She could still feel bits of it here and there, clinging to her skin in places the knife couldn't reach or where Khim didn't care to go. She felt a little dizzy, off-center. It had been so wonderful to have to lay there and accept all that attention — yet if Monica had done it, she would have felt bad! She couldn't clear her mind to puzzle over that contradiction and still manage to get up, as the hands on her body were nudging her to do. She rolled over and sat up, her legs over the side, feeling the bending and twisting of the rope harness as it pulled more wax from her skin with every movement. It was maddeningly hot.

"Thank us," Khim said, coming around the table to stand in front of her. Without thinking, Robin dropped to her knees and kissed the flat of the knife blade that was offered to her, and then the hand holding it, and then went down to kiss the tops of Khim's shoes. For a second, she almost froze again — but then she thought, how many other things could she have meant? This is pretty standard in porn, isn't it?

284

She repeated the motion for Judy, and then rose to her knees, her head bowed. "Thank you, ma'am," she said softly. "Thank you, ma'am! That was so wonderful!"

"Of course it was," Judy giggled. "I bet you haven't had a lot of Owners who got that fancy with you, huh?"

Robin's head jerked up. She caught a certain inflection in Judy's voice — something she hadn't heard in some time! She blinked in the flickering light of the many candles still perched around the room, as Khim laughed.

"Uh–oh! Something gave us away," Khim said, even as she put the knife down.

"Upps!" Judy said, looking around. "What did I say?"

"Owners. Everyone says 'doms' now," Khim said. "I keep telling you that. You keep using Marketplace words."

"Shit," Judy muttered. "I hate that 'dom–sub' crap."

"And it gives you away every time," Khim laughed. "Especially when you say it like that. Hell, it turns *me* on when you say it like that. *Owners,*" she echoed with perfect mimicry. "So, don't leave the poor slave down there shivering, let's get her upstairs and get the rest of the wax off!"

Robin had hit the floor again, her head all the way down in the posture taught to her as correct for a slave who has realized they had made a grave error. From between her bent arms, she said, "Please, ma'am, this slave begs forgiveness; please, this slave was not aware you were Marketplace owners! This slave will never fail to display proper protocol again; please allow this slave to make amends or take any punishment you desire..."

"Shh, shh," Judy said, leaning down and tapping Robin on the shoulder. Robin shook — and then peeked up. Judy was smiling, her bright smile cutting through the dim light on the floor. "It's OK, we're not owners," she said. "We're slaves."

Retired slaves to be precise. After Robin shut her mouth and blinked, the two women hauled her up by her still-macramé'd arms and helped her up the stairs. They used hot water and the hand–held massager to help her get the rest of the wax off, talking to her while chips of wax scattered everywhere.

It was easy to believe that Judy had been a slave. Robin kicked herself for not noticing things like the way she held herself and the way she listened intently, and of course, for the way that she almost always seemed to be ready for the lead that Khim took, whether it was in movement or play. Looking into her large gray–blue eyes, it was easy to see that she had once taken a collar. There was a depth there that Robin had seen a few times in her experience. In Greta, the physician slave, and sometimes in Raul's dark eyes, on the nights when he was quietly reflective and talked about his experience. And of course, in Chris Parker's eyes, that sense of having belonged — of longing and the knowledge of a mystery the rest of the world had no concept of.

In fact, it was easy to imagine Judy her in her younger guise, lithe and laughing, eager for play or sex, delightfully fun to touch. Helpful and cheerful. She must have been so damn *cute* up on the block, with her big, firm breasts and her wide smile.

But Khim? Tall, impressive Khim?

"What, you think only little frail girls like you get to be slaves?" Khim had laughed, seeing that slight look of doubt in Robin's eyes. "Big girls can be very popular, you know." Robin must have looked shocked that Khim could read her that easily, because Khim shrugged. "It takes lots of folks to make it all work, you know. Besides, I can't be insulted if after all these years people don't spot me as a slave. I'm not one any more. Haven't been since before I left my last contract." She sighed. "I hope that never happens to you, Robin. I hope you're always content to be owned while you are owned. Because it sure sucks to be waiting out your time, knowing that it just doesn't feel right anymore."

"I think it's worse to be out and thinking you made a big mistake," Judy said. By that time, they were all seated in the master bedroom, Judy in a big chair, coiling the used ropes, Robin on the floor and in her bathrobe, Khim sprawled comfortably on the bed. "At least when you got tired of it, you knew it was only a matter of time before you got your walking papers and a check and you could say adios. For me, I spent way too much time thinking I'd made the biggest mistake of my life and wondering what the hell to do with myself."

"But — why did you leave?" Robin asked cautiously. She had been given permission to act under a very lenient verbal protocol for their discussion.

Judy shrugged. "Wasn't my choice. Circumstances, that's all. When my last contract didn't get renewed, I thought about going back to the block and I just couldn't take it any more. I thought maybe it was time to try the real world again. But I missed it so much, I signed up for the first Reunion I heard about!" She laughed and tossed one of her coiled ropes to Robin and then a tangled mess after it. "See if you can make it like that, OK?"

Robin obediently picked up the tangled rope and started to unravel the knots in it. "I've never gone to a Reunion," she said, referring to the private vacations for slaves which the Marketplace arranged and partially subsidized. "Are they nice?"

"Nice if you're looking to hook up," laughed Khim. "We met at one!"

"But — forgive me, but I thought you didn't miss the Marketplace," Robin said. "Why did you go to a Reunion?"

286

Khim sighed. "You know, it's one thing to not miss being a slave. But I missed being around Marketplace people! There was no one to tell my stories to. No one I could bitch with. Sometimes, I'd go to the parties, you know, the soft world things, and I'd just feel…weird! Like I was from another planet or something. I'd be having a good time, playing or talking or whatever — and then suddenly I'd think, 'What do these people have in common with me?' — and I'd go home. Not much fun."

Robin nodded. "I used to feel like that even before I got into the Marketplace. Meeting you two was different. Oh, I am so stupid for not realizing why!"

"Well, don't be," Judy said with a grin. "Not everyone notices, you know. If I could only bring myself to talk like everyone else…"

"But I felt you were different before," Robin insisted. She explained why to the two women, who looked thoughtful and then pleased with what she had to say. Then, Judy shook her head anyway.

"Well, thanks," she said. "But when I said not everyone notices, I meant someone a little closer to home, too. Monica doesn't know, and we'd prefer to keep it that way, as long as keeping the secret doesn't make you disobey a direct order."

Robin gasped, but covered it up quickly as Khim yawned and stretched. "Wow, what an afternoon. I think I'm going to take a little walk and stretch out. Judy, would you introduce our temp slave to the kitchen and see if she wants to show off the cooking Monica always brags about?"

"As you wish," Judy said with a wink, and Robin had to get up and move right away. But that didn't stop her from thinking all the way downstairs.

"If Monica didn't tell you I was Marketplace, how did you know?" she finally asked Judy, after she had slipped the foil wrapped fish into the oven. Judy was showing her where the china and silver were kept.

"Oh, I guess the same way you spotted us," Judy said, pulling out a pair of candlesticks. "Here, put these out, it's an occasion. But don't put them out every night, OK?"

"Yes, ma'am," Robin said. She settled two tapers into place and continued to set the table. She had been given only two settings, and she felt that usual sense of shame and pleasure when she realized that she would be eating in the kitchen or on the floor.

"I mean, when I saw Monica bring you in that first night, my first thought was something like, who did she borrow you from? Monica's got great taste, but she never showed up with someone who — I don't know — who really knew how to act, I guess. Mo is not the pickiest of people when it comes to playmates, even bottoms. So when she showed up with you, I thought either you were slumming, or she had finally lucked out and gotten someone who could be worth something."

At first, Robin didn't know what to say. It seemed slightly disrespectful — but no matter how she examined it, what Judy said was a little harsh, but true. Monica didn't demand that her bottoms show signs of high level protocol, and she really wasn't interested in training. She did know how to treat a Marketplace slave, and thank goodness. But there was apparently no desire in her to repeat that sort of behavior with someone of the soft world.

Which, Robin reflected, only makes sense! Why apply one standard to people who shouldn't be held to it, and why ruin a Marketplace relationship by not observing the boundaries there?

"But when Khim said there was something about you, too, that's when I knew. Khim doesn't — well, look for the same things I do. So when we compared notes, we decided that you were either a former slave or a current one. Either way, we had to touch base and say hi! Not too many of us around here, you know. There's a couple of guys over in D.C., and we keep in touch with some of the people we knew when we were in service. But not too many do, you know." She sighed. "I guess it's like anything else — you leave behind a whole lifestyle, for better or worse, and you want to get on with other things. But thank God for Reunions, or I'd go crazy. You should go to one; they're fun."

Robin smiled but didn't comment. She had been notified of the potential to go to these slave–only gatherings, but it seemed pointless to her. Her small amount of free time during her contracts was the only thing that didn't belong to the Marketplace. Why not spend it lying on a beach, or skiing, or something totally different? But there was no need to mention a disagreement with Judy.

Robin served the dinner the way Chris and Raul had both drilled her, dressed in the simple black dress she brought with her. Judy and Khim did not seem interested in keeping her naked all the time, which was a relief. She did in fact eat her dinner in the kitchen, perched on a stool by the counter while listening for the sounds of crystal clinking and silver rattling, and judging when it was time to go out and remove the plates and refresh drinks. To her pleasure, Khim and Judy discussed their household business, gossiped, and talked to each other and only complimented her on the food, and not on her service.

This is going to be easy, she thought with delight. What a nice way to keep busy when Monica is away! And a fine way to make sure her service skills hadn't been forgotten in Monica's slightly free–and–easy lifestyle.

She felt a slight twinge at the thought of having to keep their past from her owner — and curiosity about why she should. But it was very doubtful that Monica would ask a direct question that would force the information out, and there was certainly no harm in not mentioning it. Robin cleaned up that night and happily went to sleep in the guest room by herself, setting her travel alarm for bright and early the next day so she could start on the housekeeping. Judy and Khim might very well be former slaves, but they sure didn't bring with them a sense of the anal–retentive call for order that was hammered into Robin during her training.

But she didn't even mind that. It was always nice to be needed. Especially by people who knew the effort it took to serve!

Days passed so quickly and easily that Robin could barely believe it. Judy and Khim were perfect owners for a pair of former slaves — they stayed out of her way when she was working, took control of her for their own purposes cleanly and without apologies, and played with her somehow almost every day, even if only for a few minutes before they turned to each other, stumbled into bed and waved her from the room with laughs.

She tried very hard not to disappoint, and they were more than pleased at the amount of trash she managed to remove from the house, and the gradual shine that came up on shelves, table tops, and fixtures. She aired out their bed every morning and dusted everything she could find, and soon clutter gave way to order. She even found their neglected pile of mending and the things she couldn't do herself she quietly snuck out to a local dry cleaner, leaving the receipt with the other bills to be paid.

As the weekend rolled around again and they had time at home, they prepared to make more erotic use of her in elaborate ways again, like the day she was welcomed. This time, it was Khim who summoned her downstairs, and when she got there, she was surprised to see Judy, her hands tied behind her back, blindfolded, kneeling in the open space by the table. She was naked except for a soft leather strap much like the one around Robin's throat, and Robin felt a sort of ghostly thrill at seeing it. There didn't seem to be two free women and a slave in the room any more, but two slaves, older and younger, sisters in some mystical otherworld. Judy's breathing was slow and deep, lifting her breasts softly. She was not the sprite Robin had imagined any more, her body softened in age, but her skin was tender and white, her posture beautiful. She displayed neither impatience nor boredom, only an alert sort of expectation, her head slightly cocked to catch stray sounds.

Robin could only wish that she looked as charming when she was in a similar position.

Khim was in one of her beautiful corsets again, this time a scarlet one that made her figure goddesslike in its strength and beauty. But instead of a skirt or panties, there was a harness around her hips, and between her thighs was a formidable dildo, with black and red swirls in the stylish silicone.

Robin thought that if there was ever truly a divine androgyne, s/he would look like that.

Khim laid a finger across her lips and Robin didn't make a sound. At a hand gesture, though, she stripped, quietly, and put her clothing aside. She began to feel nervous as Khim reached over to a rack and pulled something down — it was another harness. Instead of being stiff, shiny red leather like Khim's, it was an old, soft canvas. The dildo it came with was less ornate as well, but still respectable in size. Robin glanced up, and Khim nodded, and for the first time, Robin slipped the straps of a dildo harness around her body and settled it between her legs.

It felt awkward at first. The cock hung between her thighs and felt like it would surely slide off in a moment. Khim reached around her and tugged and pushed, and positioned the harness better. Before she tightened the straps, she took a scrap of soft cloth, folded it over several times and put it over Robin's clitoral area, and then pulled the straps of the harness tighter. Robin felt the compression around her already swollen and slightly tender clit, but it wasn't sharp, and the cloth would hopefully be a sort of buffer for any — pounding movements.

But I never did this, she fretted, as she gazed down at her new toy. I know, it seems weird that it's one thing I haven't done in a fairly perverted life — but no one ever wanted me to!

She remembered Chris talking to her one day about being asked to top. "It's unlikely that you will be," he had said, while she knelt at his feet, taking her eternal mental notes. "You are young and inexperienced. You will probably not be called upon to manage a staff, and owners who like to be topped generally look for slaves who are specifically trained to do so. But you never know if you will be acquired by an owner who wants to create a top from nothing — or that your owner's tastes might change, or that they may want you to work with them on another slave, upon a guest, or on some free lover of theirs. When that time comes, you must pay as much attention to those tasks as anything else, and above all, strive to please. Never show the slightest discomfort at being asked to do any form of topping. It might make your owner embarrassed, and that is unacceptable. That look in your eyes right now is wrong — you think you will never be able to top, even if commanded. Don't even try to contradict me, I can see it. Rid yourself of both the look and this stubborn belief that you will be able to choose what your new owner wishes of you. If you do not know how to physically do something, and attempting might be dangerous, then of course you must say so. But otherwise, you must deliver your obedience and your service with the proper attitude and be grateful for the chance to give pleasure when it is done."

Sure, it was easy for him to say! He liked being on top; he had been a frightening sadist for all of his cool distance. She couldn't imagine him staring at a sex toy in confusion and wondering what to do with it.

For one second, she remembered a wonderful evening with one of her former masters and one of her fellow slaves, when she had been fucked by the slave who was being fucked by the master. Oh, if only that was what Khim had in mind!

But Khim was holding something else out to her — a short, fat whip, the strands almost velvety in her fingers. If she had any hope of backing out of this for fear of being dangerous because of her lack of experience, this toy killed that possibility. The only way she could hurt someone with it was to force it down their throat.

"Time to party, sweetheart," Khim suddenly said, and Robin jerked. So did Judy, whose head shot up. She had been perfectly silent in her patience, and Robin absurdly felt proud for her. How many years had she been out of the collar, and yet she fell into the old behaviors so easily and beautifully!

Khim reached down and took hold of one of Judy's upper arms, and nodded to Robin to do the same. Together, they hauled her up to her feet, and Khim pressed her against the table. Robin couldn't help but notice that Judy had flinched when Robin touched her — maybe Judy didn't even know that Robin had been called down!

"You need this," Khim was whispering into Judy's ear. "So I don't want to hear any complaints…"

She stepped back and with one easy backward swing, brought her own whip down on Judy's ass. Judy bent forward at the waist, her body braced against the table, her wrists still tightly joined behind her. Robin's arms ached in sympathy — she didn't much like being bent over like that without her arms to brace her. But as Khim mimed, she drew her own arm back and with the middle of the tress bundle, hit Judy's ass directly across the center. The impact thudded back up her arm, and Robin gasped as Khim laughed. Judy gasped too, and then giggled, kicking one foot slightly back.

"That's right," Khim said, delivering another hard smack to her lover. "You're going to get 'em twice as fast tonight."

Robin hit again, this time aiming a little lower, and found that she hit the sweet spot right under the curve of Judy's sweet heart shaped ass. Judy moaned and hissed "Yess!" and Khim laughed again.

"Oh, I think we should hear a lot of that tonight," she said, smacking again. "I like that. Don't hold back. Show our little guest what a good slave you were. What a good slave you still are."

Robin fell into the rhythm easily, and gradually lost the fear of missing her target. The whip was heavy enough to weary her after a while, but the tresses delivered their soft thumps with no complaints at all from their target, and if Judy's moans were any indication, she wasn't doing a bad job at all. In fact, it had a lot in common with giving a massage — she moved, and Judy responded, the flesh warmed, and so did the room. Khim was magnificent to watch, her eyes flashing like green amber in the playroom light, her arm unerringly accurate. From time to time, she aimed at Judy's legs or her back, but kept Robin hitting Judy's ass over and over again, until it first turned pink, and then red, and then was actually hot to the touch.

By then, Judy's moans and "yes's" had faded to a constant stream of sighs and minor whimpers. Robin understood that state very well! Monica could take her there when she got fancy, taking out her deerskin whips and lined cuffs and really working her over. How nice to know she could help do this for someone else! Why — it didn't feel like topping at all, just another form of…service.

Oh, Chris, you were right again, she thought. I wish you could see me now, whipping the hell out of this woman's butt! She grinned suddenly and realized, to her surprise, that her nipples were hard and she was kind of damp where the straps held that cock between her legs.

Khim sighed and raised a hand, and Robin stopped. Khim ran fingers down Judy's ass and Judy moaned and shivered, and rose up on her toes. "Oh, isn't that nice?" Khim asked, scratching her nails across the tender skin. "And in half the usual time. We might have to get help in more often. I think you'll *really* like act two."

Khim pointed to the side and Robin hung both whips up on the rack and looked at the top of the cabinet. There were two condoms and a tube of lubricant. She swallowed hard and picked them up.

Khim had Robin cover her dick — and didn't insist that she do it with her mouth, something that Robin certainly had done, on real cocks and fake ones, but not terribly lately. She coated Khim's red and black cock with lube, too, and realized why when Khim didn't slide it up into Judy's lightly fuzzy pussy, but into her tight little asshole instead. Robin gulped and felt another surge of moisture between her legs. It had been far too long since she had been fucked in the ass! It was not one of Monica's favorite activities. But it was apparently one of Judy's, because she hissed and groaned, and arched herself backward to take that cock easily.

"Oh, yeah, that's my sweetheart, that's my girl," Khim crooned. "That's right, take that big cock. And you know what? It's not over!"

She reached forward and pulled her lover to her, and then, with her cock still seated firmly in Judy's ass, turned her around, so that Khim was bracing her ass against the table and Judy was facing Robin.

Robin knew what she had to do. With Khim's nod, she covered and lubed up her own cock, and felt the twinge as her own fist put pressure on the padding that covered her ring. Well, to hell with you, she thought furiously. It's been more than two months! I don't care how much it hurts. I'm going to do this right.

She had to bend her knees to angle the cock against Judy's cunt, and was thrilled at her first touch of the short hair and soft skin as she found the swollen and wet opening with her fingers. Judy gasped along with her, and her hips moved, just so, and Robin knew that the head of her dildo was in. She straightened her legs slowly, and felt the pressure build at the base of the dildo as more and more of the shaft slid inside of the tiny woman who was sandwiched so firmly between Robin and Khim.

"Oh, yes!" Judy cried out, her head falling back onto Khim's shoulder. "Oh, yes, oh, give it to me, now!"

Khim laughed, and Robin felt the startling shift in pressure that told her that Khim's cock was moving — and then a second later, Judy started to move too, her body humping slightly forward.

"That's my sweetie," Khim chuckled. "Taking it all. Here's a little more — just the way you like it!"

Slowly, Robin moved her own hips. The steady ache of the ring became intermittent stabs of pain, but she ignored it. Judy was having a wonderful time! Her body arched and rocked as the two cocks plundered into her, rhythms establishing, in and out, back and forth. From time to time, Khim pulled her lover back, stretching her body, impaling it from behind in a sharp thrust while Robin sped up, or rocked from side to side. She cupped her hands around Judy's breasts, lifted and pushed them together, and Robin needed no command to lean in and take each of Judy's nipples in her mouth, one at a time, sucking and flicking at them with her tongue.

It was that combination of penetration and nippleplay that made Judy gasp sharply and thrust back and forth between the two cocks inside of hr. Her wild thrashings almost dislodged Robin several times, and the sharp pains around her clit ring intensified enough to bring tears to her eyes. But it was so good, so hot to do this, to be melded together with these women in a sexual fury! She held on and ground in tighter and deeper, working her fingers down to the base of the dildo and letting the back of her hand bump and grind against Judy's clit until the woman came, screaming into Robin's ear.

293

They disentangled themselves, and let Judy slip to the floor. Khim pointed, and Robin collapsed behind Judy and untied her wrists.

"Oh — oh, that was hot," Judy sighed, with a short giggle following. "Let's keep her." She wiggled her fingers and swept her blindfold off.

Robin blushed in pleasure and pride. "Thank you, ma'am," she whispered.

"I have a better idea," Khim said, stretching out. "Let's show her a good time now. How about we test the cling?"

Robin's blush deepened, and then the hot stabbing of the pain between her legs made her drop her eyes. Yes, absolutely, she wanted to get fucked herself, until she, too, was sitting stupidly on the floor with a happy smile on her face. But — there was no way she was going to be able to relax enough to take a hand with this steady pain!

"What's the matter?" Khim asked, as she stripped the condom off her cock. "Is it the ring?"

Robin nodded helplessly. "Yes, ma'am. I am so sorry."

"You know — I think it's time we took a look at this up close," Khim said. "Up on the table and let's have that harness off."

"Well — it isn't infected," Khim said.

Robin sighed. Once again on her back with her knees up, but at least there wasn't a kitchen light fixture in her eyes. In fact, the gooseneck lamp had been turned onto her crotch, a little embarrassing, but sort of interesting in a kinky way. She just wished it was for some weird interrogation scene rather than yet another examination of her stupid body modification.

"But look," Khim said, and Robin could feel her finger gently touching one side of the area under her clit. "Isn't that awfully close to the skin here? Robin, I'm going to touch it a little. Call out if it's too much."

A very gentle, slow touch, and Robin winced. "It — that hurts," she said between her teeth. "It really hurts."

"The top of your clit looks sore," Khim noted. "In fact, there's almost a callus here! My God, how have you lived with that?"

"It's — not that bad," Robin said weakly. "Sometimes, it's kind of good…"

"You know, there's a difference between suffering in silence for the erotic amusement of mistress and becoming a martyr," Judy noted with a sigh. "I wish I could tell you where the line was. I think we should call Nicky. This one is out of my league. Why on earth they want to pierce so close to the clit, I don't know. But I don't think it should be this tender for so long, and I don't like the way it looks like there's a scar at the piercing site."

"I think you're right," Khim said. "Don't worry, Robin, we'll get this sorted out."

They took her to a professional piercing place called The Lance, which had a charming purple sign hanging over the door. It was decorated in pseudo—medieval style, but had gleaming cabinets full of beautiful jewelry and giant posters of different types of piercings adorning the walls. Nicky turned out to be a woman perhaps only a few years older than Arcadia. In one of the three private rooms at the piercing parlor, she had Robin sit on a sparkling gynecologist's table and gently prodded the area around her piercing.

"Well," she said, after her examination, as she pulled her gloves off, "you are definitely borderline for a triangle piercing. In fact, I wouldn't have done this one myself. That ring is right up alongside your clitoral bundle, and it's a little crooked, too, higher on one side than the other. If you are really experiencing this level of discomfort, I'd suggest taking it out. You can keep it in for another two weeks, maybe a month, and see if it gets any better. Sometimes it will. Not everyone heals within the standard range, you know? But it shouldn't be getting in the way of your sex life. I think these things should help you get it on, not get in the way." She laughed, and flashed her tongue stud.

Robin struggled to keep panic back. She couldn't ask to have it taken out without Monica there! She bit her lower lip, agonized, and Nicky patted her on the arm. "I'm going to go outside for a smoke. Why don't you talk to Khim and Judy for a few minutes. Take your time. It's not going anywhere."

Khim didn't hesitate for one moment. "Well, let's take it out!" she said.

"Oh, come on, we can't," Judy argued. "You know that!"

"The hell we can't," Khim insisted. "If she had a cold, we could give her medicine. If she broke her toe, we could take her to the hospital. Her owner gave her to us, made her our responsibility. We are obliged to take care of her."

"But — forgive me, Khim — those are Marketplace rules," Robin said gently. She could barely hide the disappointment in her voice — she was so close to getting rid of the damned thing! "And if you don't want Monica to know that you were — you know–"

Khim pursed her lips thoughtfully. "Well — I don't know. Maybe that's just a logical thing to assume for any grown–up, don't you think? I mean, the SM thing is still there, she did loan you to us as a slave. I think it's reasonable for us to assume that if you needed a medical thing taken care of, that we should just — do it."

"But it's not an emergency," Judy said. "I'm sorry, Robin, I know, it would be better out — but you can last another week with it. And the decision isn't ours to make, it's Monica's."

Robin nodded, accepting it, and then Khim shook her head. "No. Let's ask Nicky if anything can be done to lessen the pain. If not, I think we should take it out."

Nicky was consulted again, and she obligingly took another look. "Well, the problem," she said, with Khim and Judy peering over her shoulder, "is that there's nowhere else for the ring to go. First of all, this is as slender a ring as I'd put here. In fact, I don't like to use 14 gauge for these piercings, much less a 7/16. But even changing the size will do nothing for the fact that the bottom passes right up against her clit. Clit gets swollen — presses on the ring. Get hot — get hurt. Your body has already tried to adjust already — I can see where the ring has been migrating a little, that's the scarring you mentioned, Judy. Who did this, anyway?"

She didn't recognize Arcadia's name, and when Robin forced herself to remember the name of the shop that Monica had mentioned, the three woman gazing at her pubics turned to stare at her face in shock.

"That's not a piercing place," Khim said. "That's one of those new age bell–book–and–candle shops. You know, dream catcher in the window, tarot cards? Since when did they start piercing?"

"Since never," said Nicky. "Looks like someone worked a scam on you, Robin, I'm so sorry. But if they said that was where they got their training — I don't know. That's a pretty shitty thing to do."

Robin closed her mouth, and thought back. Had Arcadia ever mentioned that she *pierced* at this place of business? Well — no, not specifically.

"That settles it," Khim said. "Some chick we don't know puts a ring in your pussy on the kitchen table and the piercer we know says it probably shouldn't have been done? Forget about it. Take it out."

"But—" Robin started to object and then shut her mouth again, not wanting to discuss ownership issues in front of Nicky. She looked at Judy, who met her eyes and smiled, just a little.

"It'll be OK," Judy said firmly. "Trust us on this."

And it was out in two seconds and put in a little plastic bag for her to take home. The pressure was gone, although the feeling of soreness didn't fade right away. When Khim stepped out to talk to Nicky, Robin turned to Judy and sighed.

"Oh, I wish it didn't happen like this!" she said mournfully. "I wanted to get rid of it, but not like this!"

"I know," Judy said sympathetically. "But Khim and I will smooth it over with Monica, you'll see. It was just getting in the way. She'll understand."

296

"Do you think so?' Robin asked. "She wanted it so much!"

"Look — if it was infected, you wouldn't think twice, right?"

Robin nodded.

"Well, this was disturbing your ability to serve properly. We wanted to fuck you — the ring was in the way." She took Robin's hand and squeezed it. "It'll heal up fast, and Monica will love to have you back, ready for action."

"I feel so weird about it, though," Robin said. She sighed and let her head fall back. "It was only one more week. Maybe I should have kept it."

"Don't start with maybes," Judy insisted. "A slave can't live on 'maybe,' a slave has to live in the now, and in the immediate future. Look, if we have to, we'll tell Monica why we felt we had the authority to do this. It won't kill us."

"Judy?" Robin said hesitantly. "May I ask a question?" When Judy nodded, Robin asked, "Why don't you want to tell Monica that you were slaves? Why is it different to tell her than it is to tell me? She won't treat you any different!"

Judy looked a little uncomfortable, and then took a breath, thinking. "It's not that simple," she said carefully. "We can come out to you because you're a slave, you're one of us. But owners — they *are* different. And it's not the dominant/submissive thing, either, or dom–sub, whatever." She giggled, and then turned serious again. "It's that — well — in our experience, owners just do behave differently when they know you were a slave. Even if you were one years ago, way before they ever met you. I like Monica! And it's clear she really adores you and is good to you. But if she knew we were former slaves — well — I just think she'd see us differently, and I wouldn't like to be uncomfortable around her."

Robin nodded and was about to promise that she would do her best not to betray their identity when the door opened again, and Khim came back in. She looked at Robin, still nude from the waist down, and grinned.

"I think it looks better already," she said. "So, get up, get dressed, and let's go home."

Judy already had Robin's panties in one hand, and she passed them over. Robin decided that this time, she would say nothing, just play the cards she had been dealt. But, as she slipped back into her skirt, she did promise herself that nothing short of a direct question would get the history of her temporary tops out of her. Even if she felt that Judy's opinion of Monica in particular was wrong.

Nicky sent them home with a pre–printed sheet on piercings and how to take care of them, and the very next morning, Robin woke up feeling a bit

297

odd. It took her a few minutes to realize that the constant sensation of sharp pressure was gone, and the relief from that little fact almost made her cry. The area was still tender and sore, but there were no jarring moments of biting pain when she moved, none of the lightning fast twinges that struck her when the old ring had twisted or moved the wrong way. Surely, she thought, as she made omelets for brunch, Monica would forgive this action.

That afternoon and evening, she did indeed get her turn bottoming in the little basement playroom, a delightfully heavy flogging followed by a rather rough — and completely satisfying — anal sex romp. Khim's cock felt as wonderful in her ass as she suspected it might, and on her back in the sling, with no pressure on her clit at all, she screamed out in laughter and pleasure.

Two days after that, as she washed the area around her clit, she could that she could still feel tenderness around the holes, and that tiny hard lump was still there, but everything seemed to be healing just fine. She ground up an aspirin tablet and mashed it with water and spread the paste over the little lump, another suggestion from Nicky. She wondered if they had gone to Nicky first, would the piercing have been better? But the pleasure in having it out was astonishing. How had she lived with that constant irritation every day?

She was given permission to have an orgasm — or as many as she wished — the night before they returned her to Monica's house. (She would be getting there a day before her owner, to get things ready.) When they asked her what might facilitate her pleasure, she struggled with an automatic "whatever would please you" response and instead, glanced back at the sling and then at Judy's exquisitely small hands. Khim grinned in appreciation and got the lubricant and gloves.

They bound her, her legs spread wide apart, her ankles held high in leather loops. Once again, a spotlight centered on her crotch, and this time, she allowed herself the full pleasure of imagining a very kinky sort of medical examination. At first, she tensed, waiting for the feeling of the narrow little ring pressing against her clit — but instead, she felt the full range of arousal once more, with no tiny stabs of distracting pain, and she came even before Judy worked into her past the thumb.

Judy's hand was small and narrow, but her fingers were elegantly knobby, like a piano player's. As she turned and flexed and wiggled, Robin gasped and moaned and felt every tiny shift. The thickest part of the hand spread her so wide that she felt about ready to burst, and then slid in so neatly, the convulsive waves of orgasm just drew Judy's hand in past the wrist. Khim hooted in appreciation as she pinched Robin's nipple, watching from over her shoulder.

"I'm next," she whispered to Robin, pinching harder and twisting. "I gotta get some of that for me." And between the two of them, Robin felt like she had been gang banged — deliciously, deliriously gang banged, until she couldn't tell who was in her for how long and when she had stopped or started to come.

It was a glorious evening. She slept, for the only time during her trip, in their room. Properly on the floor, but comfortably on a little sleeping pad, with a fluffy comforter to wrap herself in.

The following morning, Robin packed her things and was ready to go right after she cleaned up after breakfast.

"We have a little errand to do before you can go home," Khim announced, as they were heading to the door. "I hope you don't mind, but we will need your help."

"Of course I don't mind!" Robin exclaimed. "Please, let me help with anything you need."

"Good! Follow us in your car. We'll take our collar back when we're done."

Robin threw her bag in the trunk and did as they asked, following them into the D.C. area again. As they passed through familiar landmarks, she began to get suspicious, but when Khim signaled to park, she realized that they were once again at The Lance, Nicky's piercing shop.

Oh, no! she thought. They don't want to put it back, do they? It just healed! But she found a parking space and went into the shop to meet them there, in the main showroom. The three of them were almost alone — the only other person there was a slender, black haired man studying a tattoo magazine by the counter.

Khim was holding a clipboard and a pen.

"This is a test of your obedience," she said seriously. But her eyes were dancing. "Sign this."

Robin took the clipboard and looked down at it. There was some type of form on it, she could see the space for her signature at the bottom. But the top part was covered with one of the colorful brochures that showed the styles of jewelry available, and she couldn't read what she was agreeing to.

She took the pen Khim was offering her and tried not to show her panic. What could she be signing? An agreement to get pierced again? Permission to have the ring removed? She didn't do this last time she was here! Could she — should she! — even sign anything without her owner present? If she were not truly owned, this would be the time when she called her safeword. Or, just said, "No way!" and refused.

But they knew who and what she was.

I was trained to obey, she reminded herself. I trust them.

She signed carefully and dated the sheet.

"Thank you," Khim said taking it back and unclipping the brochure. "Nicky said to use examining room one."

Robin went to the room in silence and sat at the edge of the table. Just a few days again, she would have scooted up there gingerly, careful of the pressure over her clit. Now, she could just sit down, like a normal person. It made her dizzy to think that she might have to be stuck with the same discomfort again!

But — maybe it would be nipple piercings, she thought suddenly. Monica said that she might like those, too! That would be nice! A good surprise!

She looked up as the door opened, and Nicky walked in, with a little bag in her hand. She grinned and said, "You didn't have to wait for me! Take the pants off again, and if you want to give yourself a quick wipe, use the bathroom through that door."

Robin swallowed hard and stripped her sneakers and jeans off. She prayed that it wouldn't hurt quite as much this time, even as she suspected that it would hurt even more.

There was a knock on the door, and Nicky called out, "Come on in!" and Khim and Judy came into the room, also grinning. They were holding hands. Nicky pointed out space near Robin's head. "Just stay out of my light and way," she cautioned. "And we'll be done in no time."

To Robin's dazed expression, she held up a little plastic bag that had inside of it two bright steel rings. They were thicker than the one that had been her triangle.

"This is what you wanted, right" she asked idly. Robin glanced to one side, to a wickedly grinning Khim and found her voice. "Oh, yes," Robin said. "That's it."

Judy giggled hysterically and bent her head into her lover's shoulder.

"OK, then. Thanks for shaving, that always makes the job so easier for me! Let's see where you like them." Gently, Nicky ran her fingers down Robin's outer labia and pinched the sides. "Here? Higher?"

Robin looked to the side again, and this time Khim's expression was perfectly clear. From this moment, it was up to Robin.

"Lower a little?" she said.

Nicky slid her fingers down, and when she reached the spot Robin thought felt wonderful, she said so. And from then on, the actions seemed to blur into one another — cleaning the area with a chilling wipedown of antiseptic, marking, clamping…and all accompanied by gloves being changed and chucked away. Nicky apologized for the harshness of the clamp, but when it went on and she secured it with a rubber band, Robin almost sighed. Yes, it hurt — but it wasn't that stomach tightening scary hurt that the clamp under her clit made. There wasn't even that frightening clicking sound.

And the needle going through her this time was less of a shock — and much less painful! Her eyes closed in reaction to the split second of almost hot pain. But it was very fast, and when it was done, she couldn't feel anything really very different!

"Wow, the steel looks great against your skin," Nicky said in appreciation. "I'm putting its sister a little lower, since you like the sensation lower. That way, they won't hit each other too much."

Robin nodded, and endured the entire little operation again, and then Nicky finished by closing the rings around the little balls. She tossed off one last set of gloves and dug a mirror out of the drawer at the base of the table and held it up. Robin had barely noticed that Judy and Khim had come closer, their bodies next to her on both sides. She looked down the end of the table, into the mirror and saw her shaved crotch once again decorated. Through her outer labia were those two beautiful steel rings, laying on the pale skin. They were breathtaking — perhaps not as pretty as the ring with the delicate little ball over her clit — but astoundingly attractive themselves.

"Thank you," Robin said, barely able to breathe. "Oh, yes, they are wonderful, thank you!"

"My pleasure. And I think these will heal up much faster then your triangle. You know, I asked around, and no one who works here as a professional has heard of the girl you told me about. It's a shame — I mean no one wants the government poking their heads into our business and all, but piercing is serious shit. You shouldn't do it at home with a stranger, you know? Take my card. In a couple months, couple years, you want to try a different one, maybe a clit hood piercing, call me." Nicky gathered her tools and left the room with a wave.

Khim and Judy looked at the rings from the other side of the table and nodded. "Yeah, I think Monica will forgive you," Khim said.

"And us," Judy added. "These look much better than the triangle! And they're much more useful!"

"I — I can't thank you enough," Robin said. "But — do you really think Monica will be OK with this?

"Don't you worry about it," Khim said. "We'll take care of everything. Hey — we're Marketplace. We take care of our own."

Monica loved them.

"Oh my fucking God, they're gorgeous! One on each side?" Apparently, Khim and Judy had explained something that Robin's owner accepted, and although she did a little teasing about punishing her, it was all in fun, and if

Monica was really disappointed by the lack of a triangle to play with, she didn't say so.

The new rings seemed to be as little trouble as the triangle had been great trouble. They turned easily in their holes when Robin cleaned them with Provon, a cleanser Nicky had supplied her with, and stopped aching before two weeks were up. The first time that Monica gently tugged at them, Robin's eyes almost went to the back of her head, it felt so good! And they were just as fun to play with on her own, too — their gentle, thick weight a different feeling under her fingers when she showered or played with herself. The weird feeling of having metal rings attached to her never completely vanished.

But that was fun, too.

Robin never knew exactly what Khim and Judy had said to Monica, other than admitting what they had done. But much later on, she was lying in Monica's arms one night, and Monica said, suddenly, "I saw Khim and Judy at that party I went to last night."

"Oh, how are they?" Robin asked.

"Great, just great! They have some new chick hanging with them. Well behaved kid, too, reminds me of you. Except that she's a tough little butch number." Monica chuckled. "I think they might be considering taking on a housegirl. You know, I almost wanted to take them aside and tell them about the Marketplace. From what you told me about how they treated you, I think they'd be good owners, if they could afford it."

"What — what an extraordinary thought," Robin said, grateful that she was turned away from her owner. "Yes, I think they'd be good owners, too."

"Well, if this new thing doesn't work out, maybe I will." Monica yawned. "OK, scoot. Back to your room, I'll see you in the morning."

Robin rolled off the edge and turned back to kiss her owner a gentle good night. As she closed the door behind her, she let out the breath she had been holding and broke out in a grin. Oh, wouldn't that be a funny conversation to listen in on! But as she walked down the hall to her own room, she wondered about the new girl in the hands of Khim and Judy. The well behaved one.

Have fun, she thought, a wish sent out into the night. All of you. As much fun as I do.

Before she fell asleep, she touched the rings one more time. I'm really pierced, she thought. A pierced, owned slave.

Perfection.

About the Author

Laura Antoniou's work has become well-known in the erotically alternative community as the creator of the Marketplace series (The Marketplace, The Slave, The Trainer, and The Academy), originally written under the name Sara Adamson. One Marketplace character also appears in her first book, The Catalyst, but she leaves the reader to figure that out. The only independently written Marketplace short story, "Brian on the Farm," appears in Lawrence Schimel and Carol Queen's ground-breaking anthology, Switch Hitters: Lesbians Write Gay Male Erotica, and Gay Men Write Lesbian Erotica (Cleis), which has been published in English and in German.

Antoniou has also had great success as an editor, creating the Leatherwomen anthologies which highlight new erotic work; By Her Subdued, a collection of stories about dominant women; and No Other Tribute, which features submissive women. Her nonfiction anthologies include Some Women, and an homage to author John Preston entitled Looking for Mr. Preston. Antoniou's books have been published in the United States, Germany, Japan, and Korea, to international acclaim.

Antoniou's short stories also appear in other anthologies, most recently in SM Classics, edited by Susan Wright; Things Invisible To See: Gay and Lesbian Tales of Magic Realism, edited by Lawrence Schimel; The Second Coming, edited by Pat Califia and Robin Sweeney; Once Upon a Time: Erotic Fairy Tales for Women, edited by Mike Ford; Ritual Sex, edited by Tristan Taormino and David Aaron Clark; and Best Lesbian Erotica 1997, edited by Tristan Taormino. Antoniou was also a columnist for Girlfriends magazine from 1995-1997, the submissions editor for Badboy and Bi-Curious magazines from 1995-96, and is a regular contributor to The SandM Utopia Guardian.

Antoniou is currently finishing the fifth book in the Marketplace series, entitled The Reunion, which is expected out sometime in 2000, and beginning the sixth book, entitled The Inheritor. She is also currently working on a collection of her short stories, and a new book titled Serious Player.

Web page: www.iron-rose.com/marketplace

The Marketplace Series   by Laura Antoniou

Mystic Rose Books follows the publication of the fourth book in the series, The Academy, with the reprinting of the first three novels and publication of a new book, The Reunion. The Marketplace, The Slave, and The Trainer return enhanced with the addition of new material. The series chronicles the adventures of those who inhabit an enticing alternative reality built around a slave based hierarchy. Following is the publication schedules for the series.

THE MARKETPLACE
"Compelling, charged with electricity . . ."   - Kitty Tsui

The first volume in the landmark Marketplace trilogy, the series that set the standard for contemporary SM erotica. After Sharon, Brian, Claudia, and Robert are accepted for training by Marketplace representatives, they struggle to overcome their shortcomings: pride, selfishness, immaturity and perfectionism.

Who among them will survive the training meted out by the rigorous and unrelenting Chris Parker? And who will uncover the truth of his or her own sexual need to submit?

THE SLAVE
"There's a new voice in S/M fiction these days, and none too soon . . . Thank goodness Sara Adamson has exploded onto the scene!"
- Kate Bornstein

The second volume in the Marketplace Series, The Slave describes the experiences of Robin, an exceptionally sensitive submissive who longs to join the ranks of those who have proven themselves worthy of entry into the sexual training ground of the Marketplace. Follow Robin as she is educated in the arts of submission and service by the meticulously ethical Chris Parker, the person in whom she will confide her deepest sexual secrets.

THE TRAINER   2001

"This is domination and submission at its best - a very well-written work that holds from page to page . . ."
- Shiny International

In the third book of Sara Adamson's Marketplace Series, would-be trainer and spotter for the Marketplace, Michael LaGuardia, learns there is more to the art of commanding respect than meets the eye. Moreover, iconoclastic master trainer Chris Parker doesn't seem to appreciate Michael's potential. What can he do to get his attention? What does Michael really want from Chris? And when will Chris finally divulge his long-hidden secrets?

THE ACADEMY, TALES OF THE MARKETPLACE

The long awaited fourth book in the Marketplace series! Taking up where The Trainer left off, as Chris Parker and dozens of other Trainers journey to Okinawa. This book explores both the strict, hidden order behind the men and women who train the exquisite Marketplace slaves and the mysteries behind Mr. Parker himself. The Academy is a full length novel incorporating independent short stories written by Guest Authors. Karen Taylor, Cecilia Tan, Michael Hernandez, david stein and M. Christian delve into the world of the Marketplace and turn up tales of power, sex, and surrender, the kinds of stories Trainers tell each other to inspire, teach. . .or warn.

THE REUNION   2001

More from the characters we have come to love as book five of the Marketplace Series reunites Chris Parker, Robin, and others in a castle in Ireland. Once again Antoniou brings us a compelling novel bursting with raw sexuality, set within the hidden world where slavery is absolute and personal honor is valued above all.

Other Titles from Mystic Rose Books

DHAMPIR: CHILD OF THE BLOOD
by V.M. Johnson

Vampyres walk amongst us. Here, for perhaps the first time in this century, a vampyre of the Clan of Lilith invites us into her life through letters to her newly made "cub" and to those she calls her "food." In Dhampir, Child of the Blood, the myths come alive, but they are not as one expects from the myriad fictional accounts. Courageously, Johnson uses her real name, discusses real people and events and passes on to us the history, legends and wisdom of The Clan of Lilith handed down by her sire when he made her. Frank, explicit letters from a mother to a daughter about life and survival as one of the newest members of the vampyre Clan of Lilith.

TO LOVE, TO OBEY, TO SERVE
by V.M Johnson

Within these pages are the real life experiences of an extraordinary woman as recorded in her journal. Vi Johnson is one of the most loved and respected women in the leather community. She entered the Leather s/m scene in the 1970's, as a slave. A slave's duty was to Love, Honor, Please, and OBEY, sometimes blindly, often at great personal cost. To own or live the life of a full time slave is, and has been, the stuff of s/m fantasies and erotic stories. The life recorded here reveals those realities, which are quite different from the fantasies. Most of all this is the journey of a woman following her dream.

SCREW THE ROSES, SEND ME THE THORNS
The Romance and Sexual Sorcery of Sadomasochism
by Philip Miller and Molly Devon

"Screw the Roses, Send Me the Thorns is about enhancement of the human sexual experience through the use of restraints and disciplined applications of tactile sensations. It is a gentle and experienced guide taking the reader from the introduction of the principles of S/M to step-by-step instructions on how to apply and receive 'discipline'... Dominants and Submissives practicing within the guidelines... in this book can find a safe and rewarding way to make reality of their fantasies." Dr. Wm. Granzig, President, The American Board of Sexology

A thorough guide to sadomasochism by two experienced players. This popular book strips away myth, shame, and fear revealing the truth about an intense form of eroticism too long misunderstood and condemned. It is fully indexed and includes over 225 photos and illustrations, a 250-plus word glossary, appendices with contacts for SM resources.

Order by mail at:

Mystic Rose Books
P.O. Box 1036/SMS
Fairfield, CT 06430

Or online at WWW.mysticrose.com

___Dhampir: Child of the Blood
        by V. M. Johnson $8.95

___To Love, To Obey, To Serve
        by V. M. Johnson $17.95

___Screw the Roses, Send Me the Thorns
        by Philip Miller & Molly Devon $24.95

___The Academy, Tales of the Marketplace
        by Laura Antoniou $13.95

___The Marketplace
        by Laura Antoniou $13.95

___The Slave
        by Laura Antoniou $13.95

___The Trainer
        by Laura Antoniou $13.95

___The Reunion
        by Laura Antoniou $17.95

___Shipping   (add $3.75 per book shipping)

___Total (check enclosed)